Praise for Mary Anne Kelly's previous novel, *Park Lane South, Queens*

"This delightful debut introduces a modern yet traditional New York City family—Stan and Mary Breslinsky and their three daughters: acclaimed photographer Claire, police officer Zinnie, and fashion columnist Carmela, plus Zinnie's four-year-old son Michaelaen.... Kelly escalates the suspense while demonstrating an unerring sense for the nuances of family and other relationships."

—*Publishers Weekly*

"Kelly...makes all of this seem so real—so dense with details is it—that it's hard to relinquish the warmth and vitality of the Breslinsky household when it's over."

—*Washington Post Book World*

"Set in the Richmond Hill neighborhood of Queens, New York, this outstanding first novel revolves around photographer Claire Breslinsky, who has returned to her childhood home after ten years abroad.... Kelly's unusually compelling and sensitively written novel boasts a well-crafted plot and excellent characterizations."

—*Booklist*

"In recreating the Richmond Hill neighborhood where she lives, first-time novelist Mary Anne Kelly has brought together a sharply drawn ensemble of characters, each with a distinctive voice.... Kelly's name can rightly be added to the growing list of women writers who have added depth to the mystery genre."

—*San Antonio Express-News*

Beneath her on the stairs something in a man's urgent voice stopped Claire dead. "Yeah, sure, that's right," Andrew hissed. "Keep it up." He sounded mean. Claire could see the back of his handsome fair head.

"Come off it." The blonde woman's face was green and twisted in the awful light. She tripped back down the stairs.

Claire waited for Andrew to move on. His hands were knotted into lifted fists. She was frightened by his stillness and the dark, unyielding rage that held his purple neck.

That was when she began to suspect Tree hadn't died the way they'd said she had. She had been murdered. And Claire knew then and there who had done it....

FOXGLOVE

MARY ANNE KELLY

ST. MARTIN'S PAPERBACKS

FOXGLOVE

Copyright © 1992 by Mary Anne Kelly.

Cover design: Robert E. Santora. Cover illustration by Nancy Stahl.

Library of Congress Catalog Card Number: 92-25323

ISBN: 0-312-95202-3

Printed in the United States of America

St. Martin's Press hardcover edition/December 1992
St. Martin's Paperbacks edition/March 1994

10 9 8 7 6 5 4 3 2 1

For my mother, Helen, and my father, Bill, the indomitable Kellys

PROLOGUE

The day after all that rain the sun was really bright. They were outside, in front of the house. She walked over to where her son Anthony stood, bent and still. What on earth was he watching, so intently? He'd been quiet for so long. She drew the heavy branches of the bushes back, the branches all dark then light, and saw into the eyes of the bird the cat was eating. They weren't startled, the eyes, they were languid, disturbed the way a lover's would be, interrupted making love. Claire froze in horror. She had intruded upon this submission, this act of dying. The fluffed-up, opened bird looked at her with glazed-over eyes, no longer trying, no longer fearing. It was committed now to being eaten. Participating, even, with passive devotion. Exalted devotion. Ashes from the phoenix. Anthony, absorbed, said, "Oh." The obscenity was Claire's alone, still watching, for she alone was never longer innocent.

CHAPTER 1

It was Mary who'd found the ad in the Tablet. *"Unusual house for sale by* owner," it read. "Holy Child Parish north."

"Hmm," said Claire.

"Take a quick drive up," Mary told her over the phone. "What have you got to lose?"

"By the time I get Anthony away from the TV and dressed and into the car—"

"From the phone number it's up around here. Anything four-four-one is north of Myrtle."

"Ma. Anything that far north would cost too much. You know Johnny. He won't even look at anything—"

"I know time waits for no man. You're the one always spoutin' about how you've got to take a chance. Claire. Do yourself a favor. Call the nice lady up and inquire."

Claire lifted the white kitchen curtain and looked at the brick of the wall just an alley away. She could hear her small three-year-old Anthony rewind the videotape once again to the excellent fight scene. There were no little boys on the block here for him to go outside and play with; there were only the ones big enough to ignore his alluring new toys on display on the driveway. Away they would ride on their dazzling two-wheelers while Anthony, ears very red, watched them go every time with renewed, puzzled sadness.

"And what makes you think it's a nice lady who's doing the selling?"

"Oh, 'tis. It always is. And you could take his cousin, Michael-aen, along with you. Anthony's always good when he's along."

3

"Not that good. I do like the bit about 'unusual' house, though. Only a nut would write that."

"And a nut's just what you need."

"You can say that again."

"Yes. It's just foolish of me to get you all worked up about it when Johnny will turn around and hate the whole idea."

"I never said that he'd hate it. Johnny would like that it's in Holy Child. He'd love Anthony to go to the grammar school. It isn't his fault he can't live in the same precinct where he works."

"I know, I know. It's just a shame, is all. He *would* have to work in the same precinct where you grew up."

"I wouldn't have met him if he hadn't."

"Of course you're right," Mary said.

"Give me that number there, Ma. If I can't get away for a while, let me anyway dream a new life."

And call up she had. Only it hadn't been a nice lady as Mary had so picturesquely predicted, but a man. Quite an old man in fact, from what Claire could make out over the phone. Measured and deliberate. Reserved. Not pushy at all. Take your time, he'd told her about coming to look at the house. If not today, some other time.

She tried to forget about it right away, while they spoke. The house was, after all, smack in the middle of Johnny's precinct and even if she did like the place, she'd never get the chance to have it. She hung up the phone with the dim sense that nothing would ever come of it. Nothing seemed to come of anything these days. No, no, she mustn't feel that way, she was a lucky woman, a happy woman. One didn't leave one's husband because he refused to move to the neighborhood of one's childhood. Although, she supposed, one could. In circles she had lived in up till recently, one certainly did. Splendid people. Divorcing for reasons as simple as sexual boredom.

Unfortunately, Claire had discovered the most amazing thing about herself the moment she'd become a mother. Ethics. Bourgeois ethics, true, but ethics nonetheless. She could never leave the father of her child. Nor separate the father from the child. Not for something as complicated as the wrong neighborhood. Only something far more simple could separate them: the end of love.

No, Claire felt the very way Mary Kate had done in that John Wayne film, *The Quiet Man*. Not able to settle in until she had her own things about her.

Or, in this case, her own place about her. Not some gaudy, treeless racetrack trap she'd had no hand in choosing. This was his place, not theirs. Out back the trucks and Caterpillars from Aqueduct converged upon her rusty yard in an ongoing, fruitless attempt to beautify the garish periphery of Rockaway Boulevard.

Out the front door of this house, Johnny's house, Claire could just see long brash lines of dressed-up women ramble up the path of Johnny's past. They strode in determined succession past mummified fig trees and clairvoyant grapevines. To be fair, the women in Johnny's past didn't bother her so much; the line was not that long (and if it was, there was safety in numbers), but she thought of these neighborly women as one excellent point for her argument to move. Not that her parents' neighborhood, where she wanted to move, was a whole hell of a lot better in the eyes of, say, the world. There wasn't much of Queens that was desirable anymore. But that didn't matter to Claire. She loved the lost grandeur of the Queen Annes and Victorians in Richmond Hill. If she had to be lower middle class (and she did), she thought she might as well do it on the more genteel lawns of the past and Richmond Hill, not on pied-and-quartered perfections of swept and displayed concrete of South Ozone Park, where they lived now.

Claire had always thought that love would be enough. But it wasn't. It wasn't the point. Honor. And place. Hadn't Johnny seduced her with the lure of a house in Richmond Hill up on Eighty-fourth Avenue? A house with a kitchen from the forties and a fireplace and a lot of work to be done, but by golly for her he would do it? He had. And then balked at the mortgage. Claire, four months pregnant, bleeding, and persuaded by the obstetrician to put her feet up, was in no position to argue.

She did not want to be sullen. She was thankful, after all, for what he *had* given her; stability, order, a healthy son. Although—a niggling inner voice pursued the issue—she'd given him these very things as well. Oh, it was useless thinking about it. Johnny simply wasn't allowed to live in his precinct and he refused point blank to transfer. Why should he, he argued, and of course he was right.

When they'd met it had been almost sure that he was to be transferred. Then out of the blue and the obscure world of politics, he hadn't been.

"So just change precincts on your own," Claire had said.

"I worked too hard for this," he'd say. "Too many years to just dump it."

"Not dump it," Claire replied, and she'd tried not to look as if she was gnashing her teeth. "Just move it over. Like I've done these last five years."

Still and all, he would say, look at all the long years he'd spent building up contacts, his position, not to mention the respect of his peers and so on and so forth, and only a fool would expect him to give all that up so a wife could move back to a silly old neighborhood where she hadn't lived for years anyway; a place, by her own admission, she'd been relieved to get away from in the first place, where the streets were superior, she now said, because they were shady and on a slant.

"On a slant." Johnny would look at her beneath hooded, Italian eyes. He would think about her thoughts. At first he'd done this indulgently, deriving enormous pleasure from her unfamiliar motivations. He'd never known anyone like Claire. So pretty and good. And still she'd made him hot. Before her he had always gone for sluts. Now here he was in bed with some Buddhist nun or something. And on top, she was a Catholic. At least educated as a Catholic. Claire had spent so many years in the Far East researching Buddhism and Hinduism that her knowledge and tolerance of heathen ideas were impressive. Fortunately, her moronic superstitions kept him from taking her too seriously.

Claire drifted off for a moment. It was true that she had spent all that time in those places, but it hadn't been for research, really. She'd only stopped at the ashram to have her tire fixed. Dear Swamiji had offered her a place to stay for far less than she would have had to pay in town. He'd needed the money—all the poor swami had was one follower and that fellow didn't look like much: young, lanky, good-looking, mad for rock music. One day, as Swamiji said, he'd turn into something, but right now—well, right now it was all you could do to get him to go clean the loo. Swamiji

6

would shrug and they would both watch young Narayan snap his fingers from the room.

There had been so much to do at the ashram: clean up after the parrot, the monkey, and the lizards (well, not really the lizards; they cleaned up after themselves). The creatures' presence was just to ensure the perception that Swamiji's little ashram was filled with life, despite the fact that he had no followers. Swamiji grew healing herbs and dried them. He rolled many of the sediments into pills and sold them to the nearby Tibetan Buddhist seminary, where they were packaged and sent off to Delhi. They would eventually wind up, Swamiji informed Claire proudly, in the far-off land of Berkeley.

After a very short while, Claire made herself useful; living in Germany had honed her cleaning skills, and before you knew it Swamiji couldn't do without her. As he couldn't pay, he'd made her president and secretary of the ashram all at once. He'd called her Maharani Claire because she'd take no guff from Narayan, even had him eating from her palm with stories of photo jobs in Paris and Milano. There she would be, bending over her camera in the clean morning light, just set to photograph the dried haws of hawthorn (Latin name Crataegus oxyacantha L.) placed above the herb's calligraphed label describing "History, Habitat, Medicinal Action and Uses." (The purists from the far-off land of Berkeley seemed to like the calligraphed labels. They should only know they were penned by an unholy Irish Polack girl from Queens.) And there would be Narayan, pungent with orris root and anise, asking, Please, was he tall enough to model? Would an agency, a good agency, ever accept him? These were the starry truths young Narayan pondered day and night as he penciled long, sincere requests for funds from concerned private parties in Switzerland on behalf of Swamiji.

Sometimes Johnny did wonder if Claire didn't really have the odd screw or two loose. It didn't bother him so much that she talked to plants, or even dishes ("No, you're not the one I want, you daggle cup, get back up there on that old shelf and let me have the blue one, your cousin."). Cousin? He would sit there still and pretend to continue reading the sports page, but he would be wondering what would come next. And this was the woman

7

raising his son? He sighed. What was really odd was that he felt completely safe and at ease with her doing it. There was no one wiser or kinder than Claire. She might be crazy but she wasn't nuts. Not diabolically. He'd seen enough half-tanks out there on the job to know she wasn't one of them. She wasn't cruel. On the contrary. Her light blue eyes would fill up twice a day at breakfast, listening to the news. She would brush her long brown hair angrily from her crumpled face, and he would express his obligatory, disgusted "Tch" at her oversensitivity, but their eyes would meet above the empty glasses of orange juice and they would both think, Dear, dear Lord, never please let anything like that ever touch our Anthony.

If anyone ever tried to hurt Claire, Johnny would happily shoot said party's eyes right out. And if she ever tried to leave him, he'd shoot her, too, no questions asked.

Now, at breakfast, Claire tilted her hand-held head and looked up at her husband. Johnny poked around at a cavity with a bright red party toothpick. He had to get to a dentist, he thought, then promptly forgot as she stirred her bowl of hot, light coffee round and round. He eyed her tits in that goddam yellow slippery robe.

In Claire's experience (and Lord knew she'd had plenty of that) there were two kinds of men. The first found himself a little plot of life and worked it, farmed it. The other never figured out what it was he was looking for but on and on he looked, unbroken, untamed, and internally ill by forty-seven. Johnny encompassed both these types of males. At least in her eyes he did. She found herself hating Johnny Benedetto and most things about him often. Nevertheless, all he had to do was graze her with his breath and she would consciously go warmer. He kept her erect. On her toes. She didn't know how he did this, but she was aware that it was done. Even though Johnny was irrefutably the least intellectual man Claire had ever been with, he was also the smartest. And he had a sixth sense about things, things and people, that Claire had forgotten could exist in men. He'd told her, "You know, even though I believe you've got to go by the book, it's still the days I just follow my instinct that I'm the best cop. You lose touch with your instincts and only go by the book, and you lose something, you're out of touch. You're walking on theories."

Claire understood this man. She liked what he meant. She felt him looking and her breathing quickened. Now if only their Anthony would put the Peter Pan tape back in, they'd manage five minutes alone while Hook plotted Tinkerbell's dark, very deadly demise. Intimacy was a reprieve from their dread of each other. An island they both knew how to meet on.

The telephone rang and put the pain back in Johnny's bad tooth. He got up to go without saying a word.

It was Carmela, Claire's slightly older and, yes, much more beautiful sister. Carmela called every time at the wrong time. She had, in fact, a consistently unerring sense of bad timing, did Carmela, and she would not be hurried. "Hello, darling," she said. "You sound out of breath."

"I just ran up the st—"

"The reason I called, dear heart, is to ask you to come over next Friday. I'm having a couple of the old crowd—"

"Johnny's working Friday night." Carmela knew very well Johnny was working. That was, no doubt, why she'd make the engagement for then. Those two could do without each other. For her part, Carmela considered Johnny a major galoop. Dangerous, yes. But unable, in the end, to read a simple menu out loud without making some third-grade mistake. Worse than that (and this was, Claire supposed, the really indigestible part), he could obviously care less about her superb and slender thighs. Johnny was one of the few men not bowled over by Carmela's tart movie-star charms. "Too many years workin' Vice," Johnny explained away his indifference with a shrug.

"Oh," Carmela said. "Pity. Well, we'll have to carry on without him. I'm sure I can recruit one of the men to drop you off home if it runs late."

"Ah. And where shall I dump my son now that we've got rid of my husband?"

Any sarcasm was lost on Carmela. "Hmm," she said. "Mommy would be best. She's never busy on Fridays. Unless there's a novena. Have you got a religious calendar? We must know before we ask her or she'll lie and pretend it's some obscure saint we've never heard of, just to get out of it."

9

"So why don't you tell me what's so important about having me at your party."

"Can't I ask my sister to come to my home without being suspected of treachery?"

"No."

"Well, if you must know, it's Jupiter Dodd, that old queen from *She She* magazine. He rather fancies you, or your work, if we're allowed to separate one from the other at this point in your career. Are we? Anyway," she continued without waiting for a reply, "he'll be here and this is a command performance."

"That old queen," as Carmela so flightily dismissed him, was a highly respected critic and probably the main reason Claire had found good work at all in New York. And, if Claire remembered correctly, it had been she who'd introduced him to Carmela, not the other way around. But it didn't matter. Claire was so deep in this supermarket slash playground slash shopping-mall world that she was no longer sure she'd ever been out of it. The glossier, gossamer plane of photography-as-life was more like a dream. Her interactions with Jupiter Dodd had, after all, taken place a good four years ago. He'd put one of the more prestigious galleries on to her work and then the most remarkable thing had happened: out of the blue she'd gotten outstanding reviews. When she'd meant to follow her purist inclinations, to please herself, she'd wound up pleasing just the right people. It was almost embarrassing, the critics were so kind. Unfortunately, their coverage of her portrayals was so condescending to the very subjects she had meant to present in a standing position—plain, honest, working-class people shot in the garish light of their gaudy excesses—that she suffered for them every time she reread those reviews. The good thing was that the people themselves didn't mind you looking at them with warped vision—as long, it seemed, as you looked at them.

She hadn't made a pot of money. Johnny was dreadfully impressed with his own wife's name staring at him from the newspapers, but after the subtle brouhaha of his colleagues' "hey hey, how 'bout thats," he thought some great wad of moolah was bound to arrive. It stood to figure, he figured. Why else would anyone work so hard for so long if not for money? Why indeed?

she asked herself. Of course she did make some. But after you deducted for film, lab fees, studio fees, and that whole gap in time when she hadn't worked, it really wasn't much of a living. If her medical and dental insurance hadn't been paid for by Johnny's excellent on-the-job coverage, she certainly wouldn't have been able to survive from her "Art."

"Carmela, I'm sure he's forgotten all about me by now."

"Listen, he won't come if you don't."

"Oh." She could hear what it cost Carmela for having admitted this, and rewarded her by pretending not to notice. "I'll see what I can do," she said.

"That's not good enough."

"I'll come."

"Lovely." Now that she had what she wanted, Carmela could afford to be magnanimous. "And how is my beautiful, brilliant nephew?"

"Fine. Would you like to say hello? He's right here."

"Um. Not just now."

"How's Stefan?"

"He's fine. Why?"

"What do you mean, 'Why?' You asked how Anthony is and I'm asking how's Stefan?" Of course she shouldn't have bothered. Any reference to Stefan by Claire only meant one thing to Carmela, some shady innuendo to their past relationship, when Stefan had "courted" Claire. She ought to know better than to mention him, because it never failed to set Carmela off. Still, it wasn't Claire's fault Carmela had settled down with someone she'd rejected. Claire was getting to the point where she was starting to resent being resented. "Look, I only asked how he was to let you off the hook about talking to Anthony. I know it can be boring listening to some three-year-old drawl on and on about nothing he, you, or I can make out. And if you want to make an issue out of this now, you have all my attention."

"Of course not, my love," Carmela choraled prettily, happily. Once she'd irked you she felt a whole lot better. "I'm glad to have you on the phone at all, my little prize fighter. You're always so busy. We never get to talk anymore. And apropos Stefan, you're

11

probably right, I am edgy about him. Do you think it's easy being married to a bona fide Polack?"

Claire most certainly did not. She leaned over to shut off the little black-and-white TV she kept on the counter. She only kept it on to catch the first ten minutes of the Regis and Kathie Lee show on weekdays, when they talked about what they'd been up to the night before, what restaurants they'd been to, and who they'd run into. After that she lost interest. The guests didn't intrigue her at all, just what went on each night in the city without her.

Carmela continued. Did Claire know what it was like attending cocktail party after cocktail party, not with interesting types as one had foreseen, but with deliberately tedious colonists—or at least that's what they thought they were. They drank on and on and did not get drunk. They leered on and on but were too polite (or paranoid) to touch . . . and Stefan! (here Claire settled down for a long winter's nap) Stefan was without an iota of a doubt the very worst of the lot, insisting they continue to live on and on in this drafty mausoleum of a house in this long-ago outmoded neighborhood and now, now did she know what he wanted her to do? Did she? She did not. He wanted her to give up wearing the diamonds he'd given her when they'd married, that she'd come to cherish, that were hers to do with as she chose, that were now, he'd decided, too ostentatious, those days are over. I ask you, what days? Here he is jogging through the streets of Queens wearing his great-grandfather's family ring worth three yearly family incomes, and he has the audacity, ah! And you know what else? This is the latest. He's got me on high-estrogen-content birth-control pills so my breasts will be big. I mean, this is an irresponsible attitude towards women in general, isn't it? Towards health? Towards life the natural way?

Claire, who baptized each suspicious menstrual clot, agreed.

"Do you know," Carmela asked, "what he has for breakfast? Wheaties."

"Oh dear. Oh yes. I see what you mean . . ."

She went on and on, did Carmela, enjoying herself, analyzing, portraying Stefan wittily at his worst, telling all—and then finally finishing him off with tight-lipped satisfaction. Claire couldn't help feeling sorry for her. She knew when the tale ended, so would Carmela's happy rage and yes, even now she could almost see Carmela's crestfallen eyes gaze startled, puzzled, at her scarlet toenails. Claire remembered those toes from when they'd both been very little girls and Carmela had been so proud of hers, beautifully shaped and long as little fingers. She'd known even then that she was the stunner. Claire remembered those toes gripped and planted to the diving board so long ago and herself, her blue fingers chewed up and happy, just almost touching the cool, perfect tootsy from underneath the diving board. "Jump!" she'd cried out. "Just jump!" And Carmela had instead turned around, thrust her chin into the air, and carried herself hurriedly, importantly away. Away from Claire, away from the dumb kids, away from the fun.

Now, Claire always tried not to see the beginnings of yellowy calluses beneath Carmela's unsuspecting feet. She didn't mind her own body rotting away so much. When she'd happened to see the total, irrevocable devastation of her elbows in a two-way department store mirror once, it had been more of a shocking awakening than the end of the world. So the days of succulent, presentable flesh were at last at an end, she'd thought, and was surprised that she could moan good-naturedly about it instead of hiccup in hysterical distress. She knew, at least, she'd used this body fully. Had enjoyed it as much as it had been enjoyed by others. But Carmela. Carmela had always waited, in some strange way—even though she'd seemed to have had it all. She'd always held something back in the guise of irony. Claire knew she was afraid. Had always been. And she had to protect her.

"Oh," Carmela's contralto came back into focus, "just in case nobody told you, they're bringing that badly behaved dog of Freddy's to the pound."

"Excuse me?"

"The little one. The runt. You know. Nobody wants her."

"What do you mean, nobody wants her? Freddy took her. He wanted her. She's his." (Freddy was Carmela and Claire's mutual brother-in-law. He was divorced from their other sister, Zinnie, but somehow, through habit and the fact that he was Zinnie's boy Michaelaen's father, they'd all remained involved.)

"Well, she's not his anymore. He's taking her out to the North Shore shelter or something. She peed all over his antique Dhera Gaz for the third and last time. You know Freddy, three strikes, you're out."

"I can't believe this. You can't take an animal and then just decide you don't want it."

"Sure you can. People do it all the time. That's why all the pounds are full."

"Why don't you take her?"

"Me? Are you kidding? The only dog Stefan would have would be a whippet. Or a Russian wolfhound."

"Jesus."

"Yeah."

"What about Mommy?"

"She's got the two puppies, Claire."

"You've got two, you might as well have three."

"I wouldn't want to be the one to tell her that."

"Mmm," they said together in characteristic, synchronized, well-modulated sibling-phonics.

"Get that thought right out of your head!" Claire said.

"What? I didn't say boo."

"You know what you're thinking!"

"Claire, I would never suggest that you take that skeevy, ugly, uriney mutt."

"I will not have another dog in my life," Claire vowed out loud.

"Hey, listen. I know what you went through when the Mayor died."

"Yeah. And the Mayor was this skeevy, ugly, uriney mutt's grandfather, don't forget."

"What I cannot forget is the vile smut trollop that was her grandmother."

"Carmela. She was a French poodle."

"Exactly."

"You don't mean that."

"I most certainly do. If she had left the Mayor alone, he might still be alive today."

"Oh, come on. At least be fair. The Mayor used to gallivant as far as Queens Boulevard looking for a little action. What about Zinnie? Michaelaen would love a little dog."

"That's all she needs. A dog. Suppose she has a collar? An arrest? Sometimes she doesn't get home for eighteen hours. As it is Michaelaen is more at Mommy's than he is at her place. I can't imagine why she ever wanted to be a cop. Can you? Uh oh. Here comes Stefan. If you're coming up to Mommy's later, do you think you could drop off that lovely dress of yours from Peshawar? The one with all the threads and things? I'd love to wear it. It always reminds me of that Dylan Thomas poem, how did it go? 'Here were fond climates and sweet singers suddenly.' Don't ask me why. Ciao, then." She hung up the phone.

Claire stood very still in her kitchen. She opened the window up all the way, then wet the wooden table down for it to dry in the air. One of those little feather whites, the ones you wish upon and fling into the sky, came in and passed directly in front of her face, easy bait. She went for it. Whoops! She went for it again. And again and again until it eluded her up and away outside across the alleyway, gone for good. She rested on the sill and looked out. The mailman passed and went. Anthony leaned on her shoulder from behind. "He's going to the Bat Cave," he confided.

"Ah," she said.

Then the telephone rang. "What now?" she said. "Hello?"

"Claire? It's me."

"Johnny, what's all that noise?"

"All hell is breaking loose over here."

"Wait. Wait, Anthony. Let me talk to Daddy first. Where? Where are you?"

"I'm here. At the one-oh-two. Guess what?"

"Honey, what?"

"I've been transferred."

It was the afternoon. She was sitting there in her car, outside the house that was for sale. Anthony was asleep on the back seat, mouth open, done waging war off in Never Land and now at last he was kaput. For the while. Claire had dropped the dress for Carmela off at her mother's, but that had just been an excuse. She'd really come out here to have a look. The house, wrapped

15

in a porch, sat there stout and calm and trusting; looking right at her, it was waiting for her to find a way to take charge.

It was of a cream color. Faded yellow, roofed and trimmed in darkest green. There was a small lawn in front, a peach tree on it, and a wide lawn on the side. It looked as if there was a nice square back yard, but you couldn't tell, as the house was hedged high with juniper, hollyhock, foxglove, and lupin. It was old, all right. The roof didn't look too good. What struck Claire most of all was that this was exactly the perfect house. With all the others she'd looked at (and she'd looked at what felt like three thousand), each one had had one thing in common with the one before it and the one after it. They were each of them next door to the one Claire would have liked. It had been, with uncanny regularity, so.

There had to be some catch here. And if there wasn't, Johnny would certainly hate the house. Something. Life, with the exception of the existence of her son, couldn't possibly be that perfect. Why, just to look at the place. A screened-in porch. A tear of overwhelming hope and hopelessness rolled down her cheek. Desire, she had learned all those years ago in India, was the source of all unhappiness. Of heartache. Fortunately, though, it was also prerequisite to all progress. If you didn't mind thinking of Western benefits as progress. Claire, having experienced the incomparable bliss of an epidural during labor, did.

Claire sat on in the car, a wonderful car; one thing about Johnny, when you were with him you might not be rich but you drove a great car. The only thing was, he would take it away from you the minute he got it totally restored, and he'd sell it. Well, he wasn't going to get his hands on this one. It might have more than a hundred thousand miles on it, but it was a Mercedes, midnight blue, its cracked butterscotch leather smelling luxurious to Claire every time she climbed into it. It wafted its delicious, masculine scent even now, the comfy seats heating up with sunshine. This was her car. And her house.

"Psst. Hey, toots."

Claire jumped in place. It was a girl. A woman. Was she blocking her driveway? What did she want? She had no idea—uh oh. It couldn't be. It was. No, it couldn't be.

"Cat got your tongue?"

"Tree!"

Oh, it was her all right. It was Tree. Wicked, wonderful Tree, who'd enlightened and taunted her all through grammar school. Of course it should not have been so unusual to come across a friend, an old girlfriend, when here was where she'd grown up, but it was. Anyone their own age not dead or on drugs had moved away. To the city. Or at least to Manhasset. But here she was.

"Are you visiting your mom?" Claire asked her when they finally stopped hugging through the car's moon roof.

"Hell, no. I live across the street."

Claire covered her mouth with her hand. "Oh, Jesus, this is too good to be true. I'm looking at this house here."

"This one? Kinkaid's? What for?"

"To live in. I mean if Johnny, that's my husband, if Johnny would go for it."

"Claire. That would be so great. I knew you were married. I see your sister Carmela all the time. Didn't she tell you? You mean she never told you? No wonder you never called me, then." She spotted Anthony in the back seat. "Oh, God. Is he yours? Is that your boy? So big?"

"Yes, he's three. Have you got one?"

"A girl." Tree's eyes shone. "I can't believe Carmela never told you. She's seven. Oh, you'll love her. He'll love her."

They looked each other up and down again. Tree's purple sundress shimmered with red and plum embroidery. She shook her head. "Can you come in? Have a cup of coffee?"

"I can't. I have to go get Johnny. This Mr. Kinkaid said we could look at the house at five. But we could stop over later?"

"Theresa!" a man's voice called loudly, angrily from across the street.

Tree's bright eyes darkened. "Oh. Shit. I'd better get going, too. Have to pick up the kid. You'll come back another time?"

Had she flinched? Claire kept on smiling. "Of course. What do you think? I'm going to let you go after all the times you made me break up when I had to recite in school? Hah?"

Tree laughed. She looked over her shoulder. The man was coming across the street. He smiled. Nicest guy in the world. Handsome.

"Come over in the daytime," Tree said quickly, softly. Harriedly.

"My pleasure." This handsome man stuck out a firm hand and shook hers good-naturedly.

Tree introduced them. Her husband, Andrew Dover. He gave Claire an appreciative grin. He didn't look at Tree. "Theresa," he said, "your daughter."

"Yikes," Tree agreed. She took off. He strolled back across the street with his hands in his pockets, no sweat.

Claire was so excited about the house that she hardly thought of Tree until she was doing the dishes after supper. She mopped the plates thoughtfully, remembering how she had admired her back in school. If she admitted the truth, she'd wanted to be just like Tree. Courageous, she thought, smiling. She couldn't wait to meet her child. For Anthony to meet her. Perhaps she would be more like the Tree she remembered. It wasn't that Tree had changed exactly. Oh, well, wait, yes, she had done exactly that, changed. But of course, so had she herself. Tree was probably thinking the very same thoughts about her at this minute. Except that there was something else. Something almost dissipated about Tree.

Tree had been, all those years ago, Claire's idol. Tree would flaunt her brazen attitude at any authority: the nuns, one's own mother. Getting into trouble wasn't the end of the world for her, it was where she seemed to feel she belonged. At least for all the time she put in in the cloakroom, it would seem so. She would hang her head and she would blush, but those eyes would twinkle. Tree would maintain her *U* in conduct all through school.

Claire had been afraid of her. Tree dared to be bad. Claire might have been bad herself, but she was too dishonest to admit it before authority, or even to get caught. Claire found it more acceptable to present herself as well behaved, well motivated. Secretly, she'd admired Tree's success with rebellion, her comfort within her own skin. Her world did not collapse with punishment, scolding. On the contrary. She not only didn't get away with it, because she was almost always caught and punished, but what upset Claire was that Tree was admired, not only by herself, but by the nuns as well. Claire could see that they got a kick out of

Tree's escapades, and every time she saw it she was eaten away with jealousy. Tree's notoriety reminded Claire how dishonest she was with herself, with her family, her life. She would have loved to have been as bad as Tree if she'd had the nerve. So not only was she dishonest, she was a *Feigling*, a coward. And she knew it best when she was with Tree. Tree, small and pearly, eyes mocking, forehead high, defiant. Deeply clefted chin. She would knit her imperceptible brows together, turn her face away from you, and watch you sideways, mocking, with a too-much-vinegar expression and her corkscrew curls recoiling.

Claire had learned to be more free from having known Tree. She was revealed to herself through the jealousy. It had been the hard way and it had hurt, but Claire had learned. She'd had to make a choice. You learned and grew or you stayed where you were. In Claire's case that meant staring endlessly, eyes lowered, into the gummy, dried-up etchings of initials in her wooden, well-behaved school desk—or letting go, flying freely in her mind where no good nun could find her. She hugged herself with anticipation. To have Tree across the street like that would be just too good. Too good to be true.

Time continued, dreamlike and warm, without Claire, who was busy. One fleeting moment did pass while Claire was on her knees in the bathtub, with water streaming from the faucet, drain unplugged, just a hurried wet wash to go, her hair up in a knot on the top of her head, busy with the foamy Dove, when from somewhere she heard her luck shift. Like a favorite song starting up after one you can't stand. Like a breeze. A sudden breeze. Maybe that was my luck shifting, she said to herself. She shrugged. Or maybe—she scooped water over her face—I just ovulated.

When time resumed, Claire had to go to Liberty Avenue and see the real estate agent who was selling her house. She had to stop at the bank about that other, hopelessly confusing, mortgage. She had to pick up Anthony from her mother's. Arriving there, she came in, dropped her sample fabrics from the upholsterer on the table, and sank into a chair. Zinnie was there, too, so she pried her shoes off and dug in to stay for a while. Mary was talking up a storm, as usual when she had adult company over, preferably one or more of her daughters. The mini-house was having a sale. (All the ladies from the parish sent their second-hand things there.) The block association was going to have a meeting to discuss the graffiti on the railroad arches out back on Bessemer and Babbage. She went on and on, did Mary. Claire was gazing at Mary's flourishing tuberous begonias. How ever did she get them that big?

"I said, did you hear what I said, Claire?"

"Sorry. What?"

"Didn't you know the Medicino girl? The singer in Carmela's play? Theresa Medicino? Wasn't she in your Brownie troop or something? You know, the one who married that Andy Dover fellow, the one does so much for the P.T.A.?"

"Ma. What are you talking about?"

"Well, that's what I'm trying to tell you, dear. That she died. Up and died just like that. Be laid out at Mahegganey's tonight. You knew her, didn't you? I'm sure you did. You used to call her, what was it, something funny . . . Treeza, no. Tree. Remember, Claire? Gee, she was young. That's why you've got to live your life now while you've got it, for who knows—Claire? Are you all right, Claire?"

Claire was looking straight ahead at Tree. She was watching her, and Tree was smiling, her sharp little teeth very white in her face. She was standing in front of the house Claire so wanted. Dead in front. Her dun, fairy bells of brown hair would be framed now forever in sunlight and ravishing foxglove.

CHAPTER 2

Maheggaeny's Roman Catholic Funeral Parlour on Myrtle was all white, polished, grim and Colonial, run by, of all things, a Protestant. The place, like some dreaded relation caught sight of years later, was in no sense a stranger to Claire. Her own twin brother Michael had lain there a young man, a boy, crisp in his New York policeman's fine uniform, not worn long enough to be shiny from ironing. A waste. A dead waste. Claire sat in the car a while longer and looked at the place. She could still see her mother and father, arms clasped around each other, holding each other up there in the vestibule, sodden with grief, bewildered by the fanfare of Police Department tribute.

The show of support had been fantastic. There'd been no end to the steady stream of young men and women coming and going in uniform. It had even, Claire smiled through her great rush of sadness, been beautiful. Well. That was then and this was now. She'd never recovered; she'd run away for ten years, that was true enough, but she'd come back. And now she had a life. A good life she refused to feel guilty for. With trembling fingers, Claire reached for a cigarette, then realized she'd given it up more than four years ago, when she'd become pregnant with Anthony.

The parking lot of this place was rarely as full as it was today. Even the streets. Up and down, the cars were wedged one up against the other. Another florist's truck arrived, double-parked, and dropped off one more extravagant arrangement. The smell of flowers reached right out to the street and it all came back to her, right down to the mahogany casket that had housed her silent brother.

She did not hesitate going in. These were her things, her memories, no one else's. She wasn't going to let anyone find her outside looking at this place, remembering. If she saw somebody, anybody, watching her with an oh-look-at-the-poor-thing look on their face, she would lose it. She couldn't afford that. Falling backwards after all these years. Michael was dead and that was that. She was fine. Just fine. She took the steps at a brisk gallop. The very cement beneath her feet came back to her, with cracks just the way they were back then, those steps she'd memorized and thought she'd forgotten. Ah, well. Just do what you have to and be gone, she reminded herself. No one's looking at you, and even if they are and feeling sorry, is it the worst that could happen? Don't they have their own dead to remember? Is there anyone who doesn't have their own sorry dead to remember?

She walked forward carefully. She wouldn't want anyone to come up to her and actually show her sympathy, take her arm, believing her not to be able to handle it. . . . She wouldn't have it. Then a surge of not caring lifted her, freed her from the desire not to be pitied. If they pitied her, then that was all they could see, because that would be all that there was. She felt the strength she had earned from her grief. She wasn't going to deny it now so that they wouldn't feel a certain way. Claire did feel the cold sweat underneath her arms and on her lip and the ringing in her ears. She sat down slowly in the back of the room when someone got up. She would just sit here. Not move, not try to get up. She wouldn't fall down if she just sat here.

The crowd was backed out to the street. Well, of course it was a well-attended wake. Such a young woman. One whose husband is as active and well liked in the community as Tree Dover's. There she was. Oh my God, there she was. Claire would look at the flowers and not at the wax-white profile of Tree. In that box. She couldn't bear the thought of looking at her old friend turned to wax the way her brother had. She couldn't bear it. Claire tasted the back of her hand, brown and salty, alive. She stood, tripped over someone's feet, struck through arms and legs and people's still summer clothes, and made her way through the crowd and down the hall, out to the hazy porch filled with smokers. She found an empty folding chair at the back.

"Doesn't she make a magnificent corpse?" the woman behind her said.

Claire looked at her blankly.

"Oh, sorry. I'm Mrs. Rieve."

Claire, always polite, always, even on the brink of nervous collapse, extended her cold hand to the sinewy, outstretched one offered her.

"This is the best spot," the woman continued loudly. "You can still see the body but you can talk if you like. Know what I mean?"

Claire closed her eyes.

"You ask me," Mrs. Rieve whispered suddenly, "it was that wild life-style killed her. They don't lay you out in your red dress for nuthin', you know. And I don't buy that coroner's bit. About a stroke."

"What?"

"Where there's smoke there's fire, I always say."

"Mrs. Rieve, I'm afraid I don't know what you're talking about," she said, but it was a creepy feeling that gusted through her insides and raised up the hairs on her neck. People did, after all, kill people. It happened every day, according to the papers.

"Why, surely she must have confided in you—aren't you the one who wrote the play?"

"Mrs. Rieve, I only just moved back to Richmond Hill."

"Oh?" Mrs. Rieve regarded Claire with one wary eyebrow up.

Claire caught sight of the husband, Andrew, who was shaking hands up near the casket. Tree was indeed dressed up in scarlet, Claire was shocked to see.

"Looks more like he's runnin' for office than grievin' for his dead wife, don't he?"

Claire silently agreed. How could he have put her in red? There was a very pretty woman standing near him, also shaking people's hands. Claire wondered who she was. She seemed to have the situation well in hand, whoever she was. Kindly pointing out available seating to flabbergasted old ladies, directing women with children to the rear. You couldn't fault the woman. She seemed tremendously wholesome. Her high color came from Nordic eons of oatmeal and salt seas, not makeup, and her natural blond hair, very thick and dark and rich, was restrained for the moment in a severe, if bursting, bun.

"Who's she?" Claire couldn't help asking Mrs. Rieve.

Mrs. Rieve snorted. "You mean Goody Goldilocks? That's Portia McTavish. You don't know her? Oh. I guess you'd be older, wouldn't you?"

Stung, Claire heard this woman's radiant name with a stab of instant jealousy. Now she could never name a daughter that. Here was a name she'd kept in her hat all these years and now *tzak*, just like that, along comes this one. And not bad to look at, either. She is, Claire was suddenly more interested to see, downright pink in the cheek whenever anywhere near the handsome, bereaved Mr. Andrew Dover.

One couldn't blame her for that, surely. Andrew Dover seemed well liked by just about everyone. Claire wondered where the little daughter was. Who would be with her, the poor kid? Tears welled up at the thought of her own Anthony facing life without her if she were to die. Who would love him the way she did? Oh, it didn't matter about the name Portia. She was lucky she had her one child. At least somebody out there had that lovely name to live up to.

And then, Carmela came in. Trust Carmela to stop the show in a navy-blue suede Italian design with black trim and matching lamb's wool beret. Still ridiculously warm for that sort of thing, mulled Claire, anyway glad to see her. Carmela walked right past her, though, after paying her respects. Blowing in one door and out the other, without a glance at the common folk all sitting there; she just kissed Andrew's cheeks, then Portia's, deposited a waft of Cartier in the already heavy air, then was gone. Probably ready to drop dead from the heat herself if she didn't get out of there. Claire was glad she hadn't informed Mrs. Rieve that that was her sister. Even Mrs. Rieve was rendered mute at the sight of big-time Carmela, wife of a diplomat, a woman who knew how to carry herself. She'd probably come in the limo and had the chauffeur at the door. Made sure everybody got a gander. She wore, Claire almost laughed, gloves. There was a pack of Marlboros on one of the standing ashtrays. It looked mighty inviting. What the hell. She hadn't had a cigarette since she'd gotten pregnant. She was only waiting for a good reason to pick them up again. And when there was a good reason there was never a pack around. This was certainly as good a time as any. She opened the cellophane. Already her head swam in nicotonic expectation. She held the bugger up. Ah, sophistication. She put it between two ready lips. And then she saw the little girl outside the open door, sitting on the concrete steps. It was just the back of her head, but it had to be her. Those ringlet curls. Just the way her mother's used to look. Claire put the cigarette down and walked outside. In the driveway an elderly woman sat upright, open-mouthed and sound asleep at the steering wheel of a seen-better-days Coup de Ville.

Claire knew better than to say hello. She searched her purse for something to intrigue a child. Nothing. Of all days. Here was a woman who couldn't pull out a charge card without a Ninja Turtle sticker attached to it, who carried yo-yos in her makeup bag—and here she comes up empty. Claire dropped to her knees. "Oh, my God," she said, so the kid looked up, "I've lost my contact lens. Do you think you could help me?"

She was already certain no one could do enough for this child, and so of course no one could reach her. Claire remembered her own grief and how she couldn't get out of it until Swamiji had needed her help. So Claire was going to need this kid's help. "My son, Anthony," she started right in talking as she groped the ground, "he's almost four. Well. We just moved. Right across the street from you, as a matter of fact and Anthony, he's depressed because he's got no one to play with. Well. You're an only child, too. You must know how it is. I'm just thinking. Seeing as how we live so close by and . . ." She rambled on that let's face it, he was becoming a problem and, gee, this was really good her running into her like this because she didn't know where to turn. Claire asked, did she think she could ask her father if they could work something out? Like maybe help her a little bit with Anthony? And what was her name?

The child, looking not in her eyes but at the open back door of Mahegganey's white-and-green funeral parlor, shivered. "My name," she said to her, "is Dharma."

* * *

Now that Claire had secured the child's father's offhand permission to take her away, what was she going to do with her? Anthony would still be on his excursion to Toys "R" Us with his grandparents. Claire drove up Freedom Drive through the only road still open through the park (the rest was permanently reserved for joggers), then thought better of it. The woods would undoubtedly remind Dharma of happier times with her mother. What child grew up near Forest Park not learning happiness from good times playing Big Ball with her mommy under the pines, ice skating on her ankles around the carefully choppy pond, waving every time around to Mommy, tasting summer water on her face from the cement sprinkler?

No. She cleared her throat, deciding she'd drive her somewhere else. A different way, where Dharma had never been. Where she herself had never been, for that matter. As long as she had Dharma with her she would not break down, wouldn't sin. It would fit in nicely. One more day of abstinence. Tomorrow she would smoke. Claire drove up Park Lane South, made a left on Metropolitan, and then a right onto the Northern State Parkway. "So. Where shall we go?" She looked optimistically into the rearview mirror. There was Dharma. Huddled as one can be by a window, looking out, her top teeth over her unsteady bottom lip tight as a vice, her mother just dead. Her father willing to let her ride off with a neighbor he'd only just met.

"I have a terrific idea," Claire barked, her voice beany cheesy on a ledge. "There's this dog. Some dog. My brother-in-law, Freddy, he's married to my sister, Zinnie, the detective, she's an undercover policeman is my sister Zinnie, and . . . I'm sorry, what? Did you say something?"

Came a wee voice: "I said I know Zinnie. She's Mrs. Stefanovitch's sister. The lady who came to the wake in the limousine. Her sister. There's a rich one and there's a poor one."

It took Claire a good moment to digest this news. "That's right," said Claire. "And the funny thing is, Mrs. Stefanovitch is my sister, too. The brunette, the blond, and then me in the middle. Red. Sort of. Did you know that?"

"No," she said, the voice a bit more there.

"And who do you like the best?"

"I like Zinnie very much," said Dharma, more certain than before.

"Yes, I suspected that you would." How like Zinnie to go by her first name, even with a child. And how very like Carmela to be "Mrs. Stefanovitch." Especially with a child.

"Well," Claire continued, not caring if she rambled, just to get the child's attention, keep it off her own reality, talk to her as though she were an adult. Don't patronize the poor thing, she hissed inwardly, it won't work. Claire had heard her newly-aroused grandmother do it at the funeral parlor and she'd watched Dharma patronize her right back. She'd not do that to her. If she's lost her mother, holy God, didn't she deserve to be talked to on at least an able-to-deal-with-it level, so eventually, she would be? "My sister Zinnie's ex-husband gave away a puppy because the puppy peed all over his very expensive carpet, you see. He gave the dog to the North Shore animal shelter. I thought we might take a ride out there and visit it, see how it's doing, sort of. Would you mind if we did that?"

"No," Dharma said, not wild about the idea from the tone of her voice, but not against it, either.

"Thrown away, the dog?" she asked.

"Mmm," answered Claire, uninterested as she could sound.

"We don't have to meet the man who threw the dog away?"

"Him? No, just the dog."

"Oh, I'd like to meet that dog." Dharma smirked sarcastically, one eyebrow raised up in stunning replica of Tree's in childhood. "Sounds like a helluvan animal."

They drove north in companionable if stressful silence.

They drove south with the dog in Dharma's lap.

"What we'll do is this," Claire chattered brightly, "we'll keep the dog overnight and tomorrow we'll bring him over to school and ask who wants a puppy. Surely there are plenty of families who'd love to have a puppy. Kids only have to look at a puppy and they fall in love."

"You might as well face it," Dharma said, very matter-of-fact, "no one's going to fall in love with this little runt just from looking at her. You're going to have to think of some hard-luck story to sell her with."

Claire noticed Dharma's good funeral parlor dress was wet all around the mangy dog. That meant her leather seat was also wet. Claire sighed. Dharma sighed. The dog, wounded, car sick and baffled once again, sighed too.

"And I said," Johnny shouted from behind the bolted door, "you're not getting in this effing house with that effing, filthy dog!"

"Johnny, please. Be reasonable. It's just for the night."

"Ha! That old one. Forget it!"

"Johnny—"

"I said no!"

"Johnny—"

"Claire, go away and come back without that mutt and I'll open the door."

"I can't believe this is happening." She was just about to add that he might let her in just to get some rags and Murphy's Oil Soap to mop the back car seat when she realized this would do little to help her case. And what if Andrew Dover were across the street watching her husband bar her and Dharma from their house? Who was this barbaric entity to whom she'd bound her very life? Why had she married this man? She remembered very well why. She hadn't wanted to be one of those perfumed frowzy women in everyone's family who has no family of her own and so comes dressed up and laden with cream cakes, sitting on the outskirts, but always taking up the comfy chair on each and every holiday.

She had wanted her own life. Her own clan. Her own children. And yes, her own man to fight with. And when they'd found that she was pregnant, that week when every coffee she drank tasted fishy, he had been more than adamant. She'd kept herself single up until the fourth month, just in case they lost the baby (in which case there would be no reason to marry) but she hadn't lost it, she'd grown and blossomed and continued to bloom, seventy-five pounds she'd put on, in fact, and the whole time Johnny would walk her anywhere she wanted to waddle. And he would always walk a little bit ahead and to the side like a football tight end, one hand extended and ready to knock over anyone coming too near. God, how they loved each other, these two disbelieving, cynical misfits, suddenly believing, suddenly fitting. Their eyes would meet with liquid love across any miserable moment or place, and the whole room could feel it. Well, maybe not. People said later they couldn't believe how fat Claire had become. "I'd like to see them give up two compulsive packs a day like I did, cold turkey," she'd think complacently, smugly, schlurping her black cherries over vanilla Carvel.

"Darling," said Claire in a lower key, taking a newer tack. "I'm here with Dharma Dover. You haven't met Dharma yet, have you? No, I think you were on duty that day." (If the orphan part didn't get him, the reference to his responsibility and authority surely would.)

Johnny opened the door all the way. From the look on his face, Claire knew it was the orphan part that got him. Johnny's mother had died when he was eleven. He'd come home from school one day and all his neighbors had been in the kitchen. Sometimes, late at night, Claire would be awakened by flailing arms and legs. Johnny would be trying to fight off those neighbors and get into the bedroom to hold onto his pretty mother. ("She's already cold," Nicky Antonelli's mother kept shrieking in his nightmare. "Don't let him get to her!")

Claire would leave the bed (she'd learned to after three or four times of getting bopped in the eye) and would come back with a glass of cool water to hold to his lips when he'd wake up and find himself crying. When it first started happening, he used to tell her it was from Nam, something that happened to him in Nam. He thought it wouldn't be manly to tell her the truth, a grown man crying like a baby over the death of his mother. But once he had told her. And she'd done the right thing, she hadn't followed form reactions, which were to hold him in her arms and comfort him. Something told her this wouldn't work. She'd turned her back on him and gone into the bathroom, coming back a good two minutes later with the water.

"Dharma Dover, eh?" Johnny crossed his arms suspiciously and looked the small girl up and down. "If you have any idea of bringing that mutt in here you'd better head straight up to the bathroom with it and give it a bath."

From the expression on her face, Claire thought Dharma was

going to bolt or burst into tears. Instead, she said, "Tch," and went off to look for the bathroom. Anthony, all eyes and open mouth, flew from his hiding spot and led girl and dog up the stairs. Claire looked at Johnny, and he narrowed his eyes at her. "And you," he said, "don't be thinking I'll go suddenly softhearted on you and fall in love with that ugly scrap of dog meat. Jeez, that's an ugly dog! I hate dogs. You should never have brought it here. And what do you think you're doing with the kid?"

"Johnny." Claire shook her head distractedly while she pulled a pan from under the cabinet, lit the stove, and started to pull chicken and vegetables from the refrigerator. "If you could have seen how that kid was being taken care of! The grandmother was supposed to watch her and you know where I found her? Drunk and out cold in a car by the waiting room with a run up her stocking and her daughter-in-law inside dead. It was a sin. The kid was playing out in the parking lot! Well, not playing. Sitting there on the back steps of the funeral parlor, Johnny, with her mother in the casket hardly cold.

"And I even went up and talked to Andrew Dover. You know, sort of to notify him of the state of his mother out there drunk when she should have been looking after the child, and I asked if I could be of assistance and said I would be happy to look after the girl for the afternoon. I didn't even get to the part about giving him our number yet and he says, 'Sure.' Just like that. No asking me for my number or anything. I mean, I gave it to him, but I'm sure he lost it. Can you believe it? I mean, I know he must be crazed, but you have to think of the child. That would be your only reason to hold it together, wouldn't it? I mean, it would be for me. Or you. I hope. I think. I mean, God forbid." She raved on. She hardly knew Johnny was there after a while, she just kept talking, angry, trembling, brutally scrubbing the chicken with coarse kosher salt. They could hear the two children up the stairs laughing at the ugly dog. Johnny came up behind her and put his big head down on her shoulder from behind. Claire stood there with a knife and a carrot in her hand and Johnny pressing on her, and she realized she hadn't heard her son laugh like that in a while.

The front doorbell rang. It had a rich, refined, grand-piano-in-the-drawing-room ring to it that Claire never got tired of hearing, but just now she could have done without it. She handed the knife and carrot to Johnny and went to answer it. It was Portia McTavish, pretty as a picture. Her eyebrows were up in polite interest, her nice hair arranged in a more stylish twist now, her eyes, slightly mocking, held back and above Claire.

"Oh, hello," Claire said, surprised, wiping her chin with the back of her hand, hoping it wouldn't be coated in chicken fat.

Portia smiled. When she smiled, she lit up like a Lutheran. "Hi," she cooed in a three-syllable, we-understand-each-other conspiratorial song, "I'm Portia McTavish. I just found out you got stuck looking after Dharma and I just wanted to rush right by and take her off your hands."

"But she's no trouble," Claire frowned, annoyed that Portia would assume that the child would be a nuisance to her. "I've enjoyed having her, really. She kept me company, to tell you the truth. Drove all the way out to Port Washington with me."

Portia's pretty, beady eyes took in the foyer and all that was—or wasn't—in it. They hadn't gotten to the foyer yet, and Claire felt it already falling short of this establishment-oriented person's expectations. She knew Portia was establishment-oriented because of her shoes. Claire had photographed too many fashion layouts not to immediately recognize the good stuff. The life she'd once led gave her an immediate feel for what was good, what was pretending to be good, and what was just plain cheap. You can always tell how someone appears to herself by her shoes. Who she is that moment is portrayed in the shoes she's got on. Portia's opinion of herself was very good indeed. The leather was subtle, low to the ground, and cashew-colored, hemstitched along the rim with an intricate Indian princess Morocco stitch. Expensive shoes. Understated. Claire tried not to look down at her own vagabond unwashed Keds.

One of the hardest things, for Claire, about not being wealthy, was the inability to buy good shoes. She loved her Keds, savored a life that was conducive to wearing them all the time, but she really did miss sticking her big long feet into sinfully gingerbread shoes. Why did this woman remind her of this? Claire didn't need to be wealthy, felt sorry for people stuck in the appearances and the roles that it cast you into; she was all right where she was, wasn't she? Her dream, her family in this house, had come true for her. She was standing in her own doorway in her own dream; kindly tell her why was she feeling so darned uncomfortable. Because, she knew, some people simply had that effect on you. They looked at at you under their own myopic magnifying glass, giving nothing, offering nothing, instinctively knowing you'll fill in the slack with your kindness. They stood there, like Portia, with their minuscule waistlines accentuated sharply with a slender belt, and made you ask yourself how long it had been since you'd had one on yourself? How long had it been since you'd worn any item so fitted it required a belt?

Johnny, who came out to have a look at who was there, had himself what seemed to Claire like a very long look. Claire found this annoying, but she didn't like to show it. Not for Narrow-hips here. No nine-pound child had ever passed through *that* pelvis. And perhaps never would. She might be daintily built, but she wasn't the youngest, noted Claire with satisfaction. It registered in her heart that this was an unworthy thought. It did. But she was still annoyed that this woman had been alive and flushed and happy (she couldn't hide the fact that she *was* happy, for all her displays of deep sighs preceding tch-tch-tchs) at the funeral parlor, talking to Andrew Dover, and Tree, Claire's only just rediscovered Tree, was dead.

"Well, come in while I get her," said Claire, understanding at once that this woman was not going to disappear until she had gotten that for which she'd come. She left Portia and Johnny talking in concerned tones. If Claire ever had any doubt that she was in love with Johnny, all she had to do was to leave him alone with a woman like Portia McTavish for fifteen minutes. Then the passion ran rampant in her own imagination, and she could feel her pulse clicking briskly in and out of her emerald-green heart. Never mind. A little while and she'd be gone.

Claire found the kids in Anthony's room, the dog in a towel on the floor between them, and Claire was struck once again by Dharma's strong resemblance to her mother. That determined, cleft chin. She had certainly charmed their Anthony. He seemed to be as captivated with Dharma as he was with the dog. They were building the dog a house of blocks. They would get her settled and in there and then she'd whack her way out of it, having figured out quickly enough that this was what was getting the big laugh. She might be ugly, but she wasn't stupid.

"Damn straight," thought the dog, already world-weary and adept at telepathy.

Claire cleared her throat. "Portia McTavish is here to pick you up, Dharma."

"Well, I'm not going with her," Dharma answered without turning her eyes to Claire. She didn't sound petulant, merely firm. Claire couldn't help the shoot of joy that leapt through her at Dharma's decision. It meant that she would rather be here with Claire's family than with Portia McTavish. Claire knew it didn't mean she didn't want to be with her own father. A parent in grief is not a true parent for the moment, needing understanding himself the way he so understandably does, but the idea of the child rejecting Portia in her favor was undeniably agreeable.

"She's not going, Mom," Anthony repeated patiently, as though his mother were an out-island Greek or intensely hard of hearing.

Claire hesitated. Did Dharma want to be forced, the way children so often did when they were unsure? The dog crossed eyes with Claire. She didn't look any better for having had a bath. Bedraggled little wreck, she shook like a vibrating toy installed with fresh batteries.

"Maa-aa," Anthony whined familiarly, "go away!"

"Tell you what," Claire decided. "I'll suggest we keep things the way they are. I'll set up your sleeping bag for Dharma—"

"No, *I* want the sleeping bag!" Anthony cried.

"Okay, so you sleep in the sleeping bag, that's more polite anyway, and I'll make up your bed for Dharma."

That decided, the children forgot her and went back to their serious and gentle investigation into the canine world. Mentally noting that she would need to do an urgent hand wash of a couple of sheets and pillowcases, spin dry them twice and then throw them into the dryer, she came down the stairs to find Portia alone. Good, she thought, then saw Johnny returning to the living room with a drink. It threw Claire off for a moment to see Johnny coming in like that, drink in hand, shit-ass grin on his face.

Claire smiled brightly. Portia gave a characteristic shake of her wrist, her gold bangle making no sound against itself, and Claire lowered herself opposite her. Her easy chairs might not be new, but the covers were, old-fashioned muted yellow chintz. Claire had hunted through hundreds of tacky neighborhood fabric shops to come up with something like the expensive ones in the magazines, and she knew she had done well here; you couldn't do better than these. This, and the fact that the cushions were indeed good goose down, gave her the courage to say what she did. She was, after all, the lady of the house. "Dharma will be spending the night here," she said with more authority than she felt. "It is late and the children seem to have settled in."

She need not have bothered to continue. Portia seemed quite happy with the decision without even an explanation. She took a deep breath, exonerated, and let it out contentedly. She stretched her toes, settling in, and fluttered her mascaraed lashes. "John," she said, "what were you saying?"

"John?" Claire sucked in her cheeks. She had to sit very still while Johnny continued his story about the child murderer of Richmond Hill. He had played a role in the murderer's capture, and Claire concentrated on her own battered fingernails while "John" embellished his part for his captive audience. This, then, was the true test of marriage. Not adultery, not the strains of time, but listening to the same, same, same story fall from your husband's vain lips onto unmarried, unattached, feminine wide-eyed violet ears.

She would let it go. She would let it pass. She would wrap it in an imaginary ball and breathe it out and blow it up to the sky and send it far, far away. It was up the chimney, over Forest Park, it was speeding north over Queens Boulevard on its way to the city. She would puncture the bugger on top of the Chrysler Building. It would fragment in pieces all over nonchalant Murray Hill. She smiled. She must be gracious. A good sport. She ought to be flattered. Her husband was, after all, an attractive, desirable man and she ought to have the good sense to appreciate his worth and enjoy feminine covetousness.

She ought to, but she didn't. Not with this woman. This, bitch. All right. Calm down. Don't lose control. At least wait until she leaves before you do. Claire grabbed hold of the chair arm and kneaded it till her thumb grew numb. How would they get rid of her? Or, how would *she* get rid of her, as Johnny didn't seem to be in any rush. Uh oh! Claire stood and ran into the kitchen, remembering her chicken, then realizing she'd better just throw some of those carrots in the soup before she went back in or they'd never have supper. Then, while she was doing it, and so as not to hear the two of them enjoying each other, she snapped on the radio. Who should it be but Mozart? I'd rather be in here with him than in there with them anyway, she snarled to herself.

How funny life was. Years ago, she would have raced back inside to supervise Johnny's apparent interest, torture herself if she had to, but be witness to it all she must be; and now here she was, in her own happy kitchen, the evening light just the way she'd always hoped it would shine for her, right on the still life of a table there. How many people had an eat-in kitchen this big? She congratulated herself. If people wouldn't be the way you wanted them to be, at least the things about you could comply with your dreams and moods and wishes. Claire snapped a leaf of tarragon from the overflowing window box. The next thing she'd do was go find that big tick-tock alarm clock she'd seen in the attic. The puppy would think it was her own mother's heartbeat and sleep through the night. Maybe.

Good old Mozart, she marvelled as the room opened about her, and how right she had been to leave that long-legged, antique stove dark blue. She'd had Johnny mortar in a blue-and-white handpainted tile she'd shlepped from Mykonos on the splashback. It was a scene of the three windmills over the village hill. The hell with them, she thought. Soon enough propriety would drive Portia away, and if it didn't she'd make Johnny's life such a living hell that he'd think twice about neglecting her for a woman she couldn't stand.

This was very simple to do when you spoiled a man rotten the way she had done, and still did Johnny. Just let him have a couple of days of no freshly ironed shirts, no coffee continental on a tray with Lorna Doones and a flower on his napkin beside the *News*.

No bubble bath waiting for him when he walked in the door, no hot supper on the table. She didn't do these things for him because they were expected of her. She did them because he treated her a certain way, as though he was in love with her, and she reciprocated in kind. If he thought she was going to let little googoo-eyes in there ruin her fantasy—always a woman's reality—he was momentarily to be rudely awakened. She scraped a shard of nutmeg over the soup and sat back down with some nice baby white potatoes. Anthony couldn't bear them, but if she kept them whole and out of his bowl he'd never notice. Would Dharma eat? If she wouldn't, she'd keep it to the side for her. When her brother Michael had died she hadn't been able to eat for days, and then would suddenly wake up ravenous in the middle of the night.

A sharp rattling behind her turned her head. It was Carmela, making faces at her through the pane. Sophisticated women, whenever they got together they were dimwits once again. Always enemies, at least Carmela was an old, familiar enemy—and one she loved.

"Why didn't you knock on the door like a normal person?"

"I was enjoying watching you thinking with your lips moving."

"Did I really?"

"Just like Daddy."

"Why on earth did you come to the back? Great lady of the manor. What will people say? What's that?"

"Oh. Your dress. The one you loaned me."

"Feels like a year ago." Claire sat back down. "So much has happened. I've got Tree Dover's kid Dharma upstairs with Anthony and a dog—Freddy's 'frigging dog—up there with them."

"When did this happen?"

"Today. Everything today. What's today's date? I ought to write this one down. And I went to the funeral parlor—"

Feminine laughter from inside brought their gazes together.

"It's what's-her-face. Portia McTavish."

"Oh. Her."

"Yes. She's come for Dharma. For Andrew Dover. You know."

"Sure." She took a snapping bite of a carrot. "A little hot for chicken soup."

"Yuh. It might cool down. It's never too hot in here, anyway."

Claire wasn't going to say "If I didn't make the chicken I'd have had to throw it away." Nothing turned everybody off dinner as much as the thought it wasn't bought, intended, and designed for that day.

Carmela's eyes swept the room. However much money was spent, she could never seem to capture Claire's wizardry with color, with things, making a room come to life. Claire had old paintings even in the kitchen. Bright children's paintings, odd things she'd collected round the world full of water and blue skies. The only prints she allowed herself were some obscure Renoirs. You couldn't fault her for those. Claire's style was clutter and clean empty spaces. You felt as though you were in some granny's house, left of the ashram. Once you sat down in the easy chair it was hard to get up. Carmela knicked in the direction of the living room. "Is she staying?"

"Over my dead body."

"Good. Then I shall."

"Good. Hand me that celery. Where's Stefan?"

"Some meeting or other. You want this dill?"

"Yes. Now. What else?"

"How about this bread? It's hard as a rock."

"Give it here. I'll do *some*thing with it."

"You're a rip," said Carmela. "May I have a soda?"

"Just don't take Johnny's last Coca Cola Classic. He thinks it's the Chateau Pumpernickel of sodas. On second thought, help yourself."

"Ooolala. Trouble in paradise?"

"Don't be so pleased, if you don't mind." Her fingers, she noticed, were trembling. "I'll fry up some croutons."

" 'I'll fry up some croutons!' If my husband were in the living room with Portia McTavish I'd be more likely to be making martinis."

"Yeah. Well, that's the difference between me and you."

"Honey?" Johnny stood at the door. "Oh, hello, Carmela."

"Don't get so excited," Carmela snorted, "I'm leaving after supper."

Johnny smiled, preoccupied. "I was just thinking. Should we ask Portia to stay? Considering everything?"

"Considering what?" Claire glared at him.

"Well. She was Theresa Dover's best friend."

"I hardly think that, Johnny." Claire made a face like bad fish. "I hardly think Tree Dover's best friend would be laughing it up in my living room while Tree was still open in her coffin."

"Laughing it up?"

"One thing I love about men," cut in Carmela, "is their abject innocence when it comes to vile women."

"Oh good heavens!" Portia stood behind Johnny. "What an absolute treasure of a kitchen!"

Claire said nothing. If this was going to be Johnny's friend, let him bother.

He jumped aside, elevating his great thick arms about himself in presentation. She must have heard Carmela. She couldn't possibly not have.

Portia smiled innocently at all of them. Was she really dense? Or did she simply not give a damn?

"Portia dear," said Carmela, tipping her cheek in a benevolent Auntie Mame, "how delightful to see you again. And in such glowing good health!" She did not get up. Portia had to bend down.

"Ah, Carmela! Imagine running into you here."

"Imagine what?" Carmela said to no one. "She is my sister, after all."

"What is that lovely aroma?" Portia sniffed the air.

"That," Johnny said out of the side of his mouth, "is my wife's great cooking."

Claire did not look up. She continued grating Emmentaler cheese into sour cream. But she could feel her shoulders loosen. She could feel herself relax enough to remember to take the pie crust out of the freezer and throw it into the oven to defrost. One thing she would not do was to chatter politely with them and make everyone feel all right, the way she usually would have done. She had Tree Dover's little girl upstairs, motherless. That gave her some severity, some dark truth that she wouldn't give up. She would hold onto her feelings of hurt for as long as she bloody well felt like it. And they could all go jump in a lake. As it always is, when you feel your most indisposed to being kind, the balance turns; people sense your disregard and turn solicitous.

"Need any help, honey?" Johnny came over to her and put his arm around her waist.

"I need a slice of ham for my quiche. Can you go down to the pantry and get it for me?" For one wacky moment, Claire wondered if Portia were about to follow him down the stairs. She did watch him go with what Claire considered a rude open mouth, then seemed to flounder, no longer to know who she was or what she was doing there. Was she really one of those people who took their power from the admiration of men? No one was ever just one thing, of course; the moment you categorize someone they turn around and prove you wrong, and Portia might just be a buff, a harmless idolizer of detectives, hanging on their every word as though there would be some answer there, or safety, some reflected shine from their golden badges, some sexy lick from the hidden burly gun beneath a dark pant leg.

Claire had grown up close to those very feelings herself. Her own twin brother Michael used to drag her down to the 102 when they were kids, he loved the idea of cops so much. They used to sneak into the horse stables and chitchat with the grooms. The cops themselves would come in and out like movie stars, in boots and badges. There were two of them, Charlie and Andy, who used to sit underneath the trestle in their squad cars and have lunch from Jahn's. They used to talk to them, to Michael really, while Claire kicked stones and climbed the logs old Mr. Lours had five feet high for his fireplace.

Michael would come away from those talks very private and boy-like. He was lost to her then. And he was lost to her now. The only great decision in Michael's life had been whether or not to go to college first. He decided not to. He should have gone. Zinnie had. Anyway, before you knew it the whole family was attending his graduation from the police academy. They'd been so proud of him. It wasn't just that he'd become a cop, but that he'd achieved his dream. There had never been a doubt in anyone's mind as to what Michael Breslinsky wanted out of life. He was a natural hurry-the-crowd-along kid, even in grammar school, when the nuns had given him a badge and had him directing schoolyard traffic, supervising kiddie-brawl breakups and lavishing authority on the needy-of-stern-father crew. He would have made a wonderful father, Claire thought.

All he was was twenty-one when he'd taken a knife in the heart and died on the spot in a stairwell on Decatur Avenue. He was so used to taking knives and guns away from little kids, so used to being trusted and loved, that Claire didn't believe it had ever dawned on him that any paranoid junkie would do him bodily harm. It must have been such a shock to him to die.

And here she was. Married to a cop. There were moments she couldn't believe that either, but here she was. She regarded the knife in her hand.

"How's Andrew?" Carmela asked Portia.

Portia made a sorry face and shook her head. "A basket case, I'm afraid. I believe he hasn't sat down since she died." She turned to Claire. "That's why it really is so nice of you to take Dharma for the night. I can't imagine her getting any sleep over there with him pacing back and forth and all the lights on." She shivered.

"You were Tree's friend?" Claire asked bluntly.

"Tree?"

"Theresa. Sorry. I always called her Tree when I knew her."

"Oh, yes. We all were." She looked to Carmela for confirmation. Claire wondered fleetingly, jealously, why Tree hadn't bothered to get in touch with her when she seemed to know Carmela so well. When Carmela didn't look up, Portia continued. "And Andrew's friend. He sort of had a hand in everything over at church. You know, all the secular events. Sports. And Theresa had such a beautiful voice. Well, Carmela can tell you that. She was her Snow White. The lead in her play."

"Really?"

"I suppose that's all cancelled now."

"I don't see why," Carmela said.

Portia's face drained of all its color. "You can't possibly mean to go on with the play."

"It's my play." Carmela lit the cigarette between her lips. "Not Tree's." She raised her eyes coolly to their shocked faces. She shrugged. "All due respect," she added.

Portia McTavish's piggy-widdle blue eyes filled up with tears.

She blinked them back, missionary of the braveries, and smiled at Carmela. "I suppose now that you'll be looking for a new Snow White, then," Portia said. A bit too casually, Claire thought. She couldn't possibly want the role for herself? Could she? Well, why not? What better platform upon which to seduce the entire male population of Richmond Hill? And Carmela would import all and any city stuff she could. She certainly had a vast source, what with Stefan's contacts with the U.N.—they'd all arrive in navy blue, they and Carmela's own artsy, magaziney crew. They'd probably get off on the idea of a slumming jaunt to Queens, just the thing to make them all feel like big shots. No wonder Carmela wanted her to juice up her relationship with Jupiter Dodd. She wouldn't mention it now, in front of Portia, but Claire wondered if Carmela still planned to have her party on Friday.

"You never told me, Carmela." Claire turned to her sister. "What your play was about. Or anything about it, for that matter."

"You never asked," said Carmela.

Was Carmela as put out about this as her tone indicated, or was she pretending to be to store up good will for some near future advantage? Knowing Carmela, it was probably both. "So what's the story?" She sat down.

Carmela primped her hair with a bent ring finger. "The Snow White thing," she said, "turned around. I've painted the wicked queen a tempestuous Bette Davis. The way the older woman was in *All About Eve*. You remember."

"How could I forget? You made me watch it every time it was on. And it was always on till two in the morning. On a school night."

"So naturally, Snow White is very much the upstart Eve Harrington, a calculating bit of a bitch."

"Oh no!" Portia cried. "You can't paint Snow White in a harsh light. Why, she's a girlhood hero!"

"Passive? Dumb as dirt? Malleable?" Claire said. "Hooking up with the first rich guy who comes along? She's not my hero."

"Come to think of it," Carmela turned her not-unqueenly eyes to Portia, "you'd make a pretty good Snow White, yourself."

"Me?" Portia, quivering between injury and flattery, decided to choose what would suit her best. "I should love to play Snow White," she said demurely, eyes chastely down.

"I'll bet you would," Carmela sneered, and looked at Claire. Carmela would often kill and then dissect for Claire's enjoyment. In this case, with Tree dead, Claire found it all just sad. Pathetic and sad. And what was worse, Claire worried that Carmela had married herself to a Polish Addison De Witt.

Carmela leaned in closer. "Do you remember Daddy once when we were little, drunk?"

"No."

"And he," she snorted, "he'd been painting the house, so he put up all these—like, fences, so we couldn't climb out with him, don't you remember?"

Carmela was just trying to alienate Portia all the more. She was doing a good job. Confused, Portia fidgeted in her purse. Carmela laughed so hard tears came to her eyes. ". . . And he was calling, 'Mary! Come get me! I'm out on the birch tree behind the blockade!' "

"So what's the point of the story?" Portia finally said.

"There is no point," Claire snapped.

"Anyway," Carmela said, pulling herself together, "this is of course the musical Snow White, a modern-day adaptation. Young girl from broken home comes to New York and falls in with a weird rock group—"

"How weird?"

"Oh, you know, garden-variety, everyday weird, all skulls and drugs on the outside, money-mad and corny lyrics on the inside— Doc's pre med, Sneezy's got a coke habit, Bashful's in therapy, Grumpy is, well, to be frank, me."

"You?" Claire, taken off guard by this uncharacteristic observation of self, laughed out loud.

Carmela's eyes, rewarded buttons pushed by Claire's sob of sudden laughter, glittered. She continued, "You might think Holy Child an unlikely stage to present the play. I suppose it even is."

"Well, it's charity," Portia supplied, "for the battered-women's shelter."

She really is stupid, thought Claire, pleased by the news.

"And free talent," said Carmela.

"Yes," said Claire.

"Ma." Anthony came in quickly and stood directly in front of Claire. "Mom," he said accusingly. "What have you done with my bottles?"

Claire went red. "Oh," she said. "I've put them away. I told you I did."

"Yes, but where are they? Hah?"

"They're in the broom closet, in a plastic bag."

"Show me!"

"Anthony, as you see that I am very busy, why don't you find them yourself. And don't sound so accusing. I told you I wouldn't throw them away without your permission and I won't. Go and see for yourself."

"Ma," Anthony gestured patiently. "I wouldn't sound that way if you didn't look so guilty."

"Oh, Anthony, I'm not guilty, I'm losing patience."

Appeased by the ring of truth, he broke his ninja stance and neared. He leaned against her arm. "Maybe I'll just have a Juicy Juice, then."

"That's a good idea. That won't rub against your two front teeth the way those bottles were beginning to do. And you know you can always go back to the bottle if you must. Just let's try and get through today without it, shall we? You and I? I have the feeling if we stick together we can do it."

"Yes," Anthony agreed. "One day at a time."

Carmela dropped her lighter and had to go under the table to fetch it.

"Now watch this," said Anthony, "watch very carefully." He held his yo-yo on a string and swung it as a pendulum. "You are getting sleepy. Very sleepy. So sleepy that—now watch—'Hocus pocus,' " he softly said, and he meant it.

Claire yawned obligingly and let her head hit the table away from the knives and the vegetables.

"Well—" Portia stood, out of reasons to stay and bored by the sudden intrusion of yet another demanding child. She let herself out without much of a fuss. Claire watched her snail-paced retreat with an increasing sense of relief.

"Claire," Johnny said, at the door with a big hunk of nice provolone, "there's no ham down here."

At least, Claire noted, his eyes did not dart about the room looking for his new friend.

"Yes there is, of course there is." Claire remained with her head on the table and looked at him heavily. The idea of finishing making dinner was suddenly very tiresome. Portia McTavish's departure had drained her, just as her presence had pumped her with nervous, livid energy. Portia might have bothered her, but she'd reminded her of another dimension as well: the leafy green and nowhere land of edge, beautiful women, of complicated men who were no good, no good at all as they sat there grinning through hashish fumes, of conversations where you didn't know where it was going, what would come of it, a land of danger. Ah, danger.

How long had it been? Sitting idly all day long in bustling white linen cafés and long weekends riding in horse carts under boulevards of orange trees in Marrakesh. She was back in Queens, in Queens! She had failed. It didn't matter now where she had been, what she had done, when all of it had led to now, to this. They weren't in some cultivated Connecticut dale, a right haven to come home to, with galleries and bookshops past the pleasant church yard. Here were out-and-out drug dealers and deliberate shopping malls and marathon, sound-elevated television commercials and polyester overcoats in summer as the ladies walked like white-haired zombies through air conditioned aisles of chain-store syndicates. Now now, calm down. She was tired. Drained from all the goings on. Here were also people who counted on her to stop them from drinking Coca Cola and eating breakfast cereals composed of pure sugar, who wanted her, whether they knew it or not, to scrape them carrots and cut them into little daggers of health. She was needed here. She was no longer a vagabond adventuress. Her life had meaning, if not *pfff*. And anyway, she smiled to herself, what else could one ask of life if not the first half rowdy pleasure and the other contemplative effort? She had done well, if you put it into perspective. If she wasn't rich and well situated, wasn't it because she'd chosen the other way—and not because it had chosen her? Look at all the rich men she'd rejected. Some of them so rich it would make your head twirl—or at least Carmela's. Just look at Stefan. She'd dumped him, hadn't she? She didn't spout about it either, did she, although even admitting it to oneself was enough right there to make you ill. Anyway, she had gone for the love instead of the money. They would build their kingdom together, she and Johnny would, and when she got into bed at night and the sheets smelled of him, she wouldn't have to gag and think of other things—she'd get downright hot and grope for his hairy bear arms, and they'd lie in the watermelon light of the Chinatown lantern he'd bought her on Mott Street. So what was so bad?

"I'll show you where the ham is, Daddy." Anthony brought her back from her reverie. "Come with me!" Anthony jumped in place, thrilled to be the expert.

"Anthony, what's Dharma doing?"

"She's upstairs, Ma. Daddy, come on, I'll show you."

"Is she all right?" She watched identical dark heads, one big one, one small, dart down the stairs.

"Sure." Anthony's voice trailed up. "She's crying on my bed."

The women traded looks. "I'll go," said Claire.

She heard Dharma before she saw her, muffled little-girl cries underneath the covers. All alone in a big foreign house with total strangers and no more mommy. Claire's heart went out to her. She looked at the palms of her own hands. How was she going to help this little girl? What could she possibly say to make things right? Claire thought of her own mother and what she would do. "Nothin' ya can do." Mary's lilting voice seemed to speak to her. "Just be there. Be there and lick the wounds."

Claire cleared her throat, walked over and sat down on the edge of the bed. She let her cry it out. Eventually, the sobs subsided and turned to sniffles. The tousled head emerged reluctantly and the eiderdown fell back, revealing the fluffy damp dog as well. The dog and Dharma looked at Claire, their lives a mess, their destinies entwined.

"Private ladies' meeting, or may I join in?"

"We were just looking for contacts," deadpanned Dharma. She smoothed the dog across her lap. Dharma wore three rings, the way her mother always had. Claire, whose mother did not ap-

45

prove of jewelry for children, and who could never have afforded such frivolity if she did, seemed to remember these very rings glinting provocatively across the classroom long ago. Eighteen-karat gold Italian jewelry. Miniature jewelry presented by godparents at every occasion.

"Those were your mother's rings, when she was small, weren't they?"

"Yes, they were."

"I remember them."

"Yeah?"

"Yes. Your mother used to have the best reading voice, you know. I used to get very upset because Sister would always choose her to read for story time, instead of me, you see, but once she'd begun—" Claire closed her eyes, remembering. "I used to put my head down on the wooden desk and just take off—"

"Mommy!" Dharma cried, suddenly remembering all the times she'd read to her. Her shocked, poor face dissolved into renewed wracking sobs at the realization that this would never be again.

"Oh. Oh, gee," Claire said standing up, then falling helplessly back down into the rocker. This wasn't the kind of trouble you could cure with sentimental stories or cuddles with puppies or a sleep-over in someone else's bed for the night. What a jerk she was for having thought she could have interfered and made a positive difference. "Oh, God, Dharma. I'm so sorry. That was so insensitive of me. Let me call your father, please. Let him come and pick you up. Or I'll bring you home."

Her arms hesitated, reached out, hesitated. Before she could even pull them back, Dharma was in them. She wasn't much bigger than Anthony, so frail and all narrow elbows; all that hair gave you the impression that there was some sturdiness there, but there wasn't. Poor thing. Poor thing. They rocked and rocked.

"Do you want me to call your father, now?"

"No."

"Well, I'll wait. We'll wait till after supper, all right?"

"No. I don't want to go home. Please." Her voice rose up in a forlorn plea.

"Dharma, I love having you in my home. You must believe that. I just didn't want to intrude upon your need to be with your father, now, when you must need him. I didn't want my selfish needs to interfere with your right to grieve privately. That's why I suggested you go home. It's such a comfort to have you with me, you can't imagine." Claire felt her eyes fill with tears at the truth of what she said.

"Mommy!" There was Anthony at the door then, his face not yet past the shock and onto the recriminations part—how dare she hold another child inside her arms! They were his arms! His! She could see the blood bubble behind those black Sicilian hot spots. He was not a little animal, her Anthony; she saw his wild face soften at the sight of Dharma's haggard, teary face lifting to look. Soften and care. He took two steps forward in pure compassion, then remembered his machismo and went back to his post in the doorway.

"Aunt Zinnie's here, Ma," he said with some reserve.

"Zinnie? Michaelaen come with her?"

"Yeah. I better go help him set the table."

"Oh. Are they all staying for supper, then?"

"They sure are!" Anthony whooped and cantered down the hallway.

"Glad somebody told me," Claire thought blandly as she went back to rocking. It was grand to rock. She hadn't sat in this chair in months. Anthony was growing so quickly. She could put it by the window and face it towards the fireplace—or what would be the fireplace once Johnny knocked that plaster out. The dog hopped down from Dharma's lap and raced downstairs. She'd got hold of Michaelaen's scent, probably—or recognized his name. The dog knew Michaelaen no doubt from Freddy (her former master), before he'd given her away to North Shore. Freddy was Michaelaen's dad, and although he and Zinnie were divorced, they remained great friends. Freddy had a few years ago decided to accept himself as he was, homosexual (bisexual, insisted Zinnie). He had separated from Zinnie and Michaelaen, given up his job as an insurance salesman, taken Zinnie's and his savings, and risked it all opening a restaurant in Forest Hills. It turned out to be just the thing. Not only did he love doing it, the area seemed to crave an artsy, clean-tableclothed place just then. After one false start up on Queens Boulevard with an incompetent lover in charge and a place that was better suited to beef burgers and ribs for lawyers and frantic prisoners-to-be (it was, after all, just across from the courthouse), he'd been smart enough to get two beat-up stores together on a pretty street, gutted them, put roof windows in, placed tables on the sidewalk, attached an awning—even hung twinkle lights in the back yard on the trees and set tables out there, too. Then he'd made a deal with a Soho gallery and hung great big showy pictures all over the place. He was very good with the music, too, mixing Mozart with light jazz with Billie Holiday with quick shots of carefree rock and roll and then back to Telemann. Everyone wanted to eat, meet, or get drunk up at Freddy's. You can't mix blue collar, gay, and yuppie—you had to cater to one or the other—but Freddy did. And he did it very well indeed. He used too much garlic on everything, everyone said—you could always tell if someone had been at Freddy's the night before—but that didn't stop them from coming and having a damn swell time while they were there. He could be perfectly unpleasant, Freddy could. Scathing, in fact, if you crossed him (every week there was another story about some waiter reduced to tears) yet everybody was drawn to Freddy. You couldn't help it. Which goes to show you how enigmatic a thing charm is.

Even Stan Breslinsky, stodgily conventional father of Claire, Carmela, and Zinnie, bowling champ and opera lover, kept a pile of "free coffee with dessert after lunch during the week" coupons in his hardware store behind the cash register, and when decent-looking customers came in he'd dole them stingily out like prizes at a congratulatory dinner. Freddy may have deserted his daughter, but he was, after all, the father of his grandson and entitled, therefore, to his support.

And Zinnie was not the type to abandon one of her own, leastwise the husband who'd abandoned her. She would shrug, would Zinnie, implying you didn't know the half of it, then get on with whatever it was that had to be done. Lord knew Zinnie had plenty to do.

She'd gone through the police academy quietly—everyone said it was a tribute to her dead brother Michael; she'd idolized him after all—but hero worship wasn't what made her a good cop. Surely it had started her on her way, Claire pointed out. Yeah,

Johnny would say, but the men on the job didn't respect steady, just-do-your-job from a woman. You really had to excel with that bunch of Brooklyn honchos. Zinnie was a hell of a cop.

Whenever Claire started going off the deep end about anything or anyone, all she had to do was think of Zinnie and her big-hearted, matter-of-fact view of life and she felt better. She just had to imitate her in attitude and her spirit followed.

She wasn't a saint, Zinnie. She had a temper like an August squall and a vocabulary like a rollicking vacationing longshore-man, and she was as quick to criticize as to forgive, but every time Claire thought of her she was glad, and that is saying quite a bit about any human being, in the end, where we all get on each other's nerves and we all get disgusted and fed up.

Claire rocked and sighed and thought what had to still be done before dinner could be served. She hated when everything was catch as catch can. Dinner parties ought to be planned and set with flowers on the table. All hers were haphazard, with her silver set missing a fork at least and the napkins nowhere to be found and the minute you all sat down the nice music that had been carrying everything along stopped abruptly with the scraping of the chairs and dinner invariably commenced with a long, loud commercial for Radio Shack. Ah, well, life was more important than an organized living room, hubbub preferable to a clean kitchen floor. Wasn't it? Something crashed below. Certainly it was. The doorbell rang. "I'll get it!" shouted Anthony and she could hear him and Michaelaen tearing through the house. She hoped it wasn't Portia, come back again, and so it wasn't. "There's a man down here," Carmela hissed from the bottom of the stairs. "A Mr. Kinkaid."

"Oh. Him," Claire said, relieved. "We bought the house from him." Mr. Kinkaid was temporarily living in a half-finished base-ment apartment up the block. This arrangement was provided by a long-time neighbor until Mr. Kinkaid's condominium on the golf course in Florida became available. Mr. Kinkaid was becom-ing something of a likable old pest. He excitedly rubbed his palms together in diabolical expectation of cold weather and Johnny's skyrocketing fuel bills. He didn't understand how a healthy girl like that Dover woman could just up and die. He wouldn't like to point no finger, see, but there've been things going on in that there house make your hair stand up on end.

"Oh, Mr. Kinkaid, do be real," Claire would say. She had had it with violent crime, vicious neighbors and, finally, Mr. Kinkaid himself, who likes his tea sweet and he'll take it in his old recliner under that there winder. Thanks.

"Is he all right for the moment, do you think?" Claire called down. "I'd like to try to convince Dharma to eat with us."

"All right would be putting it mildly, I think." Carmela twirled one fancy earring between manicured fingernails. "He's helped himself to the easy chair in the living room. Got his feet up, too. On your new hassock."

"Be right down," Claire said, and she was, Dharma in tow, all cried out for the moment, curious as well to see what was going on.

Zinnie had efficiently wound up the quiche, adding sour cream and fresh spinach, Claire noticed from the mess on the table, and had had the good sense to stick the thing into the oven, so they were that much further along. She'd emptied the entire bottle of Yugoslavian wine into the soup, too, while she was about it. Claire rallied between annoyance—now they would have to drink beer or juice—and the wish that she'd thought of it herself. It smelled absolutely good. Inside, there was Mr. Kinkaid, poor gnarly thing, looking out his old window at his—or what had been his—front yard. How devastated he must be, Claire sympathized, not having it to enjoy to himself anymore. Johnny sat politely in respectful, if bored, deference to age and fellow—if former—property owner.

"Yes, sir," Mr. Kinkaid sighed as she came in, "nothing pleases me more than the thought I'll never have to mow that goddam lawn no more." He let out a gleeful cackle.

Johnny's eyes scanned his moderately long sweep of lawn protectively. He couldn't wait for the lot to grow so he could get out there with the electric lawnmower that had come with the house.

Zinnie was out on the grass with Michaelaen, doing something, digging and sticking wires into the earth from the look of it, and after saying hello to Mr. Kinkaid and begging him to stay (really just so she wouldn't have to face talking to him at the moment),

Claire went out the front door and stood looking at them from the porch. Her porch.

"So what do you think of my asylum, eh?"

"I want to ask you something," Zinnie said without looking up.

"Shoot."

"Could Michaelaen and I move in with you guys for a week?"

Claire gulped. "Of course you may," she said, looking for all the world as though it would be the most delightful experience.

"It's just that Freddy's having our apartment painted and Michaelaen's allergic to paint and if we move in with Mommy, she'll never let us go. Please, Claire? This place is as big as a boarding house. You'll hardly know we're here."

"Okay, okay. You're on the top floor. Choose a room."

"And will you be happy, Charlotte?" Zinnie put two little sticks in her mouth as if to light them.

"Oh, Jerry. Don't let's ask for the moon." Claire half covered her eyes with her lids. "We have the stars."

Zinnie let her breath out more easily. This is what Claire had always wanted, after all. A home full of love and people and all that. She always said she did. "You're gonna love it even more after I get done doing what I'm doing."

Claire's heart leapt in fright. Johnny had developed what might well be diagnosed as lawn neurosis. She sympathized. She supposed she was just pleased to be where she was. She was finally in the climate she cherished, happily strolling down long-out-of-vogue streets like some aborigine who walked apparently useless invisible song lines.

Later, Claire would look back and remember the very moment, out there on the porch, thinking all was well. Because that was the last time for a long time it would be so absolutely so.

She stood there, equal parts Chanel and holy water, surveying her domain. The dog scuttled out on her miniature legs, halting decisively between Claire's well-worn sneakers. Down went the fluffy skull kerplunk on Claire's big toe.

She looked down at the mutt. "I see you've figured out upon which side your bread is buttered."

"Most floozies do," Carmela muttered from behind the screen.

"Floozie's good." Claire enjoyed puncturing Carmela's blast of disapproval. "It fits. What do you say, old girl? How's that for a moniker?"

"Hullo," the dog seemed to say, Floozie's injured eyes looking into hers. "About time you got to me."

"Yes. She says she likes it."

"She does, does she?" Carmela's tightening lips and skeptical tone indicated that Claire had, as usual, gone too far. Claire felt a sudden clear and sympathetic understanding for herself and why she'd stayed away ten years. There really was no stress to dealing only with people who didn't matter. It was the ones you loved and who loved you who would kill you. However calm you might be, however advantageously, emotionally, your menstrual cycle was placed, there were those who wore you out and drained you just being near.

And, she thought happily, realizing suddenly that it was croquet hoops Zinnie was assembling, there were those who charged you up and filled you with energy as well.

"Floozie," rather sweet in her newly shampooed ginger coat, trotted across the porch, put one paw out and patted the naked universe, then closed both eyes and dropped into the azaleas.

"Tch," said Carmela.

Floozie picked herself up, sniffed about and took a discreet constitutional behind the basil bush.

"Uh!" Carmela said.

"Good girl!" Claire cried.

"Remind me never to eat pesto at your house again."

"Oh, Carmela, you're such a fuddy duddy." Claire swept the puppy onto her breast and smothered her with approval and kisses. Michaelaen distributed mallets to Anthony and Dharma. The first heady game of croquet was under way.

"Uh oh!" Zinnie looked up from her spot on the lawn. "Claire! I thought you never wanted a dog again! Just look at you. Slobberin' all over it. Jesus! That is not the dog to get involved with. Didn't Freddy tell you how she destroyed his apartment?"

"I haven't spoken to Freddy in weeks. He hasn't even seen the house." She wondered if she ought to give him a call. Freddy liked a mob.

"Well, ask him. Just ask him. That dog is trouble."

"What rubbish." Claire pressed her nose against the clean puppy tummy. "Freddy probably left her all alone all day long in that apartment. How can a wee doggy like this be trouble?"

Zinnie and Carmela locked world-weary eyes but said not a word.

A translucent moon but escaped them in the pale cool sky. Across the street, blue music came from Tree Dover's house and the sun went down behind it.

CHAPTER 3

Mary came over in the morning. It was fair, with the still mist of early. She rubbed her big elbows, but that was as far as she'd go to acknowledge the cool. Mary would wear her thin housedresses straight through to the end of the year, relinquishing them only then to the sturdier armor of Orlon and white pearly buttons. Over the back yards she strode, cutting her way through the September flowers and larks in the rectory garden, across front lawns and back, her great donnering breasts and strong thighs apump, worried lines her starched uniform over the grace and the hard-earned clean lunacy of serene goodly woman, crestfallen acceptance the only haphazard of time. Mary's neat braids were wrapped, sunlit, around her head. Without the pins they would sit there just as well, kinetically bound. She'd cut them once, in a desperate urge to assuage what was to come, but she'd felt like a faker, someone she'd never be: a woman in a corporate office, someone who would wear those jackets, who had her nails done by the week, not by the wedding or the christening. And so, back they'd grown and here she was, herself, better off and the good Lord knew with enough to do.

"Hullo." She clopped on the screen with big knuckles. "It's me."

Claire's face lit up when she saw her out there. "Hey," she said.

Mary didn't love Claire any more than she loved any of them, but with Claire there was a special bond of pain; she'd lost a son and Claire a twin, and for the two of them there would be no comfort, only the ever-widening lightening of time, then the sudden horrifying grasp of remembrance. It didn't make it better, but they shared it and kept it, the same festering pain that between them was faced, like the thought that can't bear thinking, when done is just lost.

"I've brought you some puppy porridge."

"Oh, good. She loved the hard bagel Johnny gave her, but all she did was tear it up into a million crumbs."

"Thus the vacuum cleaner."

"Yes."

They looked together at the monster machine that took up so much of the kitchen. It was one of those ugly old-fashioned ones that no one wants to store but when you really needed a vacuum, you couldn't beat it, so no one had ever gotten rid of it, just passed it on to the next likely victim. Every time Claire used it she couldn't help marveling what an utterly magnificent machine it was, whooshing up all and anything in its way. (Putting it away was another story altogether.)

Mary watched her old vacuum cleaner, puzzled. She remembered how Stan had named it Lips Lummox, back in the days when it had been theirs. Long enough ago it had been when she'd first lain eyes on that snout. Funny how it had survived when so many others hadn't. She and Stan had only just married when one of his horrid, silent relations descended upon them, some aunt or uncle or other toting babka and sausage and outrage that their talented piano-playing impresario Stanley would marry an Irish immigrant with not only no grand education, but who couldn't, if her very life depended upon it, carry a tune. Their Stanley, you could just read their minds by looking at the cloud of disappointment and disgust across their wrinkled brows, their chins up suspiciously, like something here smelled off. Their Stanley: doomed.

Which one had presented them with this vacuum cleaner? It didn't matter much now, they'd be long dead. Still. Some things you looked at brought back the hurt of years ago as if it were yesterday. There was no birthright baby grand for Stanley, as he'd expected. Not even an upright. It was, instead, a vacuum cleaner. Oh, yes, she remembered now. It was the aunt with the three chins. She'd brought her own music stand with her violin when she'd come to stay. Mary still remembered the look of bewildered hurt on Stan's face when he'd unwrapped the vacuum cleaner.

She would love him all his life for the hurried phony flash of delight he'd bestowed upon her then, so she wouldn't see his shame for her sake.

Claire sighed and Mary sighed about their different things.

"What's with the little girl? The Medicino girl?" Mary asked finally, suddenly.

"Dharma? Her father came for her very late last night. I almost hated letting her go. It's funny. She's more like the Tree I remember than Tree was."

"Time marches on, me darlin'."

Claire squinted into her bowl of milk coffee. "Mmm, I mean something else. Only I don't know what. You want breakfast?"

"I'll take my breakfast with my grandson, if you don't mind."

Mary looked down at the nutty old wood of the table. Her old table from when she and Stan had started out. It wasn't pretty, but it was sturdy and Johnny had sanded it down to Claire's "country French" specifications. Carmela had had it first, but she'd given it back. Or, rather, Stan had retrieved it before Carmela's first husband Arnold had sold it at his yard sale. His horrifying, vindictive, divorce yard sale. It had never been grand enough for Carmela anyway, Mary thought with the mixture of pride and shame she so often felt when it came to Carmela.

"So, what about this play Carmela's got going?" Claire asked pleasantly, instantly reading Mary's mind with troubled, albeit recovered, familial telepathy.

Mary shrugged, pretending not to care too much. She knew that Carmela suffered every time she saw her old rejected table so successfully renovated. Claire had always taken Carmela's rejects and turned them around and made them beautiful. This infuriated Carmela, but then, so many things infuriated Carmela. One couldn't keep up. Had Carmela married Stefan because Claire had toyed with the idea herself? It was hard to know who or what Stefan Stefanovitch really was. So wrapped up he was in himself and others in his image: sophisticated connoisseur of wines and women, cars and countries, ideas as commodities.

Carmela had the mansion on the hill, all right. And all the atrocities that went along with it.

"Ma!" Anthony cried from just outside, "the dog threw up!"

Claire landed in the real world with a thud.

"Is she all right?"

"Well, now she's trying to eat my flip-flop."

"So we'll interpret that as she's all right, okay?"

A laugh hooted through the screen.

"Get the hose and wash it away, oh, the heck, I'll be right out." Claire stood reluctantly.

"Let him be," said Mary. "Now that he thinks you want to do it, he'll be all insistence to do it himself. Sit down now and tell me what you think of Carmela's play."

"I don't think anything at all. The first I heard of it was yesterday. I think. Nobody tells me anything."

"Ooo. I hope that's not the verge of recrimination in your voice. For it's you who's in your own little world, isn't it?"

"I am?" Claire was delighted to hear anything at all about what people thought of her, that was how often it ran directly opposite to what she expected them to think. "And here I was thinking of me as a regular busybody."

"Huh! I'm sure I don't know which is worse."

"Neither do I," said Claire with sincerity.

"Well. It's a play about people at least. Not your angels and symbols."

"I can't imagine Carmela writing about the supernatural."

Mary gave her a funny look.

"I mean, Carmela's so down to earth. So you're pretty safe there."

"Don't be too sure. Just when you think you know someone, they'll turn around and be somebody else, won't they?"

"They will?"

"Sure. Just look at the play she *wanted* to put on!"

"Which play?"

"Oh glory be, now don't go back and tell her I told you or she'll say I'm tellin' tales out of school, like. She wouldn't want me to tell you about what didn't work out. Carmela is so—"

"—touchy," Claire supplied.

"Well, see, it was to be a story about the Virgin Mary falling in love with a visitor from outer space."

"Ha! She did, sort of."

"Carmela had her secretly meeting him for mint tea over in Nazareth, against her parents' wishes and all. Then before you know it, they were having it off in the desert." Here Mary's face went red. "There was no question of marriage," she continued, tight-lipped, the scandal an appalling concern to her now. "He had to go back to wherever it was that he had come from. In the end, the family found a nice fella from the town, the carpenter's son, a simple, good fellow, and they married them off."

"The mint tea is good."

"Oh! Don't go telling her that! She'll think she ought to go back to it!"

"Mom. Carmela would certainly never take up something because *I* thought it was good. On the contrary."

"Still and all—the worst of it was, it was a musical. I mean, a musical!"

"Yes, well, she is her father's daughter. Oh, don't worry. I'll never even mention it, all right?" Mary lived in a world of don't mention this's and don't mention that's.

"Aunt Claire?"

"Ah, it's Michaelaen, is it?!" Mary sprang from her chair and gave the big eight-year-old boy a bear hug. He let himself be smothered, wiped his mouth with one arm, and grabbed a doughnut from the counter with the other. A powdered sugar doughnut it was, still soft and squishy with freshness. Michaelaen, Zinnie's son, was always dropping over; even when Claire and Johnny had the house in South Ozone Park, he would come over sometimes after school. He would take the bus, all by himself, arriving blasé and carrying big-boy geography books and looseleaf binders. He sported his shirt purposely out of his uniform trousers, his skateboard an integral part of his being. Zinnie was often stuck in court and Claire felt better if he came to her for supper. Johnny could always drop him off at home later, when he was working nights, and when he wasn't, Zinnie would pick him up sometime, today or tomorrow, it didn't matter to Claire. Claire loved that kid. And Anthony was as good as he could be when his big cousin was around, following him all over the place. "Race ya," he'd say, hopefully, as they leapt from room to room. And Michaelaen, good natured as Zinnie, so often complied.

He stood there now, self-important, self-assured. Not shy before his aunt and grandmother, Claire noticed, congratulating herself and her mother. Not all children could be themselves with adults, but Michaelaen was. They had both contributed a lot of time to making this so. A lot of hours reading this kid stories and playing Mr. Potato Head went into making this fellow look into your eyes without guile or mistrust. This, Claire knew, was a success to be counted, shared by them all, especially her mom and dad, while Zinnie had had to work. Her dad had walked him through the woods with stories and silences and plain old being there—there had been a time when Michaelaen hadn't been so trusting—the divorce, of course, and other things. Horrible things. The important thing was that now he was. He was opening, he announced, a detective agency. Five dollars a case. Only twenty-five cents, he rushed to assure them, deposit. Five bucks if he solved the case. Mary made a great show of looking for a quarter.

Really it was only Carmela who wasn't that close with Michaelaen. She wasn't that into kids, really. Not yet, anyway. One day, Claire hoped, she would get pregnant and that all would change. It would soften her, loosen those brittle bones, she wouldn't look at herself so much as a failure. It didn't matter that to the world Carmela looked like the undefeated champ; Claire understood her better. True, she had the house at the top of the hill, mansion really, but Claire understood from having known Stefan first what price Carmela must be having to pay to live there. It would always be Stefan's deal. Cool, flaxen-haired, fast-driving Stefan, who, every time you crooked your little finger to pick up his fragile champagne crystal, watched you with sardonic, superior eyes. He enjoyed making you feel the fool. Expecting, waiting, even, for you to break that glass. And Carmela, knowing, deeply, herself to *be* the fool, fit snugly in.

Carmela didn't have to work as a fashion columnist anymore (it wouldn't become the wife of a diplomat like Stefan) and so she was a playwright. Not successful as yet, but then most playwrights were unsuccessful so that didn't matter. What mattered was that Carmela's title be pronounceable at cocktail parties. "My wife,

Carmela Stefanovitch, the playwright." The way he had of saying things would make the listener feel inferior and out of touch for not knowing who she was. Oh, well. That all didn't matter.

Johnny staggered into the kitchen and lurched into the bathroom.

"What was that?" Mary's voice rose shrilly.

"It's all right, Mom, it's just Johnny."

"Why doesn't he use the bathroom up the stairs?"

"Beats me. He says it's too small and if he closes the door he feels all boxed in. This is an awfully big bathroom."

Mary looked doubtful.

"I think he likes to see what's going on," Claire whispered. "You know. Johnny Dick." She walked over to the big kitchen window and poked her head out.

There was Tree Dover's house across the street. A moaning in the glaring sunshine, right now, empty of a woman rushing up stairs and down to the dryer, silent and quiet in her kitchen with her coffee cup, nervous and balanced by the moon, the months, the years. Claire blinked at the closed kitchen windows, no friend inside them now, the way there might have been, to catch sight of, run out and go gossip with. Floozie looked up through the screen at her with perky, smart little eyes that summed you up. Funny how she seemed to zoom in on Claire's thoughts. Always looking up at her quickly and shrewdly when she felt anything palpable. There was, of course, no single reason for Claire to think this, it was just a feeling, odd and true.

Claire did a double take.

"What's the matter now?" said Mary. "You look as though you've seen a ghost."

"No. It's just that I—it's Dharma Dover in the yard."

"Well, that's good. Do her good to play with the boys."

"Oh, I don't mean that. I'm glad to see her. I just can't figure her father letting her come and go as she pleases just now." She turned to look at Mary sitting there. "Wouldn't you think he'd want her with him all the time? Every minute?"

Mary made a wry face and shrugged heavily. "Everyone carries grief in a different way, Claire. He might not be able to bear the sight of the child just now. Not be able to handle her grief as well as his own."

"Yeah. You're right. Ma. How does he—I mean, what does he do? What kind of job—always home?"

"He's in real estate, Claire. He makes his own hours." She stopped and looked at her daughter. "You must have heard of 'Dover Estates'?"

" 'Estates,' is it? Thinks well of himself, eh?"

"Well of the neighborhood. And the only one who does," she sniffed. "Those big real estate conglomerates don't give a hoot or a holler who they sell to. Andrew Dover sees to it the neighborhood doesn't go to—" She looked at Claire's Greenpeace-liberal shoulders at the window. "Gypsies."

"Hey!" Claire shouted out at the kids. "Anyone want orange juice ice pops?"

"Ma," Anthony waved her away, annoyed. Any chance he could get with children was gold for him. He didn't want her intruding upon that.

"Right," she said and shut the window. She stood there, then opened it again. "Dharma," she said, "would you come over here for a moment?"

Dharma came. She held the dog. They looked up at Claire with bold, unshrinking eyes, the two of them, little orphans. Not any more, thought Claire, in a surge of effusive emotion. Not any more. I'll take these two on as my own. She sucked a great gust of air up through her nostrils in ferocious promise. It would be a karmic debt paid off.

In high school, some principal or other had had the bright idea of rounding up the sophomore class and leading them on four trains into Brooklyn to some orphanage. These private-school girls—and that's all they were was girls, skirts rolled up above their knees in case Prince Charming rode the A train too—went down to Brooklyn and everyone was assigned a kid. Claire's kid was Anthony. She thought. Yes, now that she thought about it, his name had been Anthony as well, remembered Claire, and he had looked at her with big Diana Ross eyes and had said, "You gonna come see me?"

"Yes," Claire had said firmly, hoping she meant it.

She guessed she had, at the time.

"Really?" asked the little boy, not believing her.

"Yes, really," she'd said, and smiled her charming smile, her eyes misting over at the goodness innate of her.

That smile had fooled a lot of people, had made an awful lot of false promises in its time, had done a lot of damage, hadn't it? It wasn't the teary-eyed promises that meant anything, that got anywhere, that anyone lived up to; it was the ones people kept, annoyed, maybe, but kept.

"I just wanted to say," Claire started to say then stopped as she thought of that little boy on line in the schoolyard, watching while the other girls came and no one came for him until it was clearer and clearer as the time went on, that nobody would come for him; nobody ever did. They must have assigned him another girl. And still, Claire saw him every morning in the papers, every evening on the news, a gangly kid, arrested, then a bigger guy, a man, been up in prison and released, coming uptown to see his parole officer. On the F train when she went to the city she saw him all the time, sitting there half-looking at her with mistrustful reproach in his eyes. She'd never come. The glitzy immediacy of debate club and hitch-hiking down to Greenwich Village to hang out with musicians had knocked that great goodness right out of her. He had been lonesome and she could have made a difference. It was not arrogance this time. She really had let that soul completely down. She knew it then, she knew it now.

"Dharma," Claire said easily, "would you help me with Anthony this year? It's just that I'm having such a hard time with him and if I had someone young, someone who could get through to him, like . . ."

And Dharma, slowly becoming aware that she was again being called upon for help and it wasn't some pitying grown-up funeral-parlor soppy stuff here where Claire would fall into her arms sobbing, decided, for now, she might give it a go.

Floozie looked up and caught Claire with suddenly impressed bright eyes.

"I hear you're running Cascade now," they seemed to say. This family was always using some old Bette Davis film as their point of reference.

"Yes, Doctor Jackowitz," Claire agreed, kneeling down to tousle the dog's fluffy, nifty head. "I'm running Cascade now."

Claire returned to the funeral parlor in the afternoon. Not having found the courage to walk up to the body at the wake, she knew she'd have to go back or regret it. She returned before hours, when no one was around. Mahegganey's was a family funeral parlor. They all used Mahegganey's.

Claire walked in without hesitation. Tree was all alone. She knelt down on the padded velvet stool and said her Our Father out loud. The hearing is the last to go in the dead, she knew. "Oh, Tree," she said, tears already running down her cheeks, "I'd forgotten I knew you so well. I'd forgotten how much you mean to me. You meant to me. How much you've influenced my life. I wish I'd told you before. Before this—"

When Claire did finally finish, she stood up and saw Andrew Dover pass in the hallway. Embarrassed, she dried her eyes, then wondered why the hell she should feel embarrassed. Outside, she heard Andrew talking in hushed important tones on the office phone. He had, she supposed, the makings of a bigshot. Claire wondered just how big? And how far was he prepared to go to get there? Murder? She held her purse in both her hands and went quietly back home.

In the playground on the Overlook, the highest spot atop the neighborhood, above the cloying magnificence of everybody's fabric softener, where Forest Park ends, or begins, birds from everywhere stop, leave, and stop again, stunned into circling confusion by furious global warming, overcrowding the woods, bunking into each other, sending birdwatchers berserk with good fortune.

From her spot on a bench by the sprinkler, Claire watched Dharma douse her angry Anthony with one more round of a blue pailful of water. Floozie the dog sat majestically on Claire's soft lap. The leaves were in the trees, on the ground, in the air.

All at once, it was fall. After the nerve-wracking white light of summer, it was the most wonderful thing to sit still in the round rusty yellow of it. Tomorrow was Carmela's grand party. Claire pulled her legs up underneath herself on the park bench and savored her position. She had settled on what she would wear. It wasn't a dress, really, but a ready-made, one of those Punjabi dresses over pants that you could suddenly find in shops all over Jamaica Avenue. It was apricot with threads of green and vague cream-colored stencils, trimmed and dotted in tiny almost indiscernible gold stars. The whole effect was shimmering and light and when she had put it up against her face in the store the proprietress's face had burst with happiness. There was no question, she had had to buy it. Such solicitous, forthright approval must be respected. And it had come with a silk peach scarf so deliriously soft it resembled the underbelly of a leaf to the touch.

Zinnie was off tonight and was to stay home with Michaelaen and Anthony. And Dharma, too, of course. This arrangement was working out quite well. Dharma was allowed to stay the night. This and any other night. Claire rocked back and forth, disturbed. Both Anthony and Michaelaen were better behaved with Dharma in the house. Each child was awed and if not silenced, certainly quieter, from Dharma's enormous loss. If nothing else, it was a great learning experience, reverence for life and all that, but Claire was growing increasingly unnerved by Andrew Dover's behavior towards Dharma. If it was none of her business then she wouldn't feel so involved, now would she? She was just waiting to say something to him, to Andrew, about it, and she was just waiting for him to say to her it was none of her business. "I lived too many years in Germany to feel like that, to let that kind of an attitude just go by," she would say to him. She had her arguments ready, like packages in her arms to drop into his, just in case he ever dismissed his formal, grieving, polite attitude and showed his proper self. Big phony. Claire was furious at him. The gall of him, to be alive and happy while Tree was dead. She knew he was happy. She wasn't fooled by that morose puss he would put on for the outside world when he walked out the door and down to the church. Claire, home all day with the children, out beating a rug in the rain, had heard him whistling, heard him clear as a bell when he'd thought no one could hear him. What was it he'd been whistling? It didn't matter. You don't whistle when you're in grief. You don't want to do anything but think about, talk about, and cry about the one who's gone.

Claire looked at Dharma. They were all in a cluster. Someone had brought their new Play-Doh up to the playground and they were all around it, greedy to be in on its lovely smell, its untouched newness. Only Dharma looked off into space. Inconsolable. Claire made another silent prayer that her Anthony wouldn't lose her until she was old enough to want to be lost. It wasn't right. So just let Andrew say one word to her about whose business it was. Just let him try. "Long Way to Tipperary." That was it. That's what he'd whistled. Twit.

So Mary was coming over for the first part of the evening, while Zinnie wrote up her bills, and she would keep them occupied with making jelly tarts. Mary was very good at all that. All three daughters had fond memories of jelly tarts in times of crisis. It wouldn't be bad. Playing with the dog would keep the kids occupied for a while. She'd let them take Floozie on a good long walk with Aunt Zinnie. You never had to worry about them when Zinnie was with them, she would protect them and hold their interest. And if she didn't, they'd get the old one-two right into the grubby corner—so they knew just like magic, she would shrug, what was expected.

"Kids!" she shouted, gathering the scattered entrails of her bag about her. They came, slowly at first, then became revved up by the novelty of their spontaneous idea of racing down the great hill all together. Excitedly they left the park, the thought of a race gaining momentum. Unfortunately, fatigue won out, and before they even reached Metropolitan Avenue screams of ownership over some staff-like stick one of them had picked up ("It's mine!" "No mine!") were obliterated by "I saw it first," and "No, I did! Gimme back!"

Claire noticed that her son was the crankiest in the bunch. This was nothing new. He always was. You'd think she'd beat him when he was an infant, the way he carried on. Dharma had lost her mother, Michaelaen had been through a divorce and a terrible trauma known only to himself, and who behaved atrociously? Her tyranical, whiney son. So what was she supposed to do? Smack him silly? Yes. She was going to have to start to whack him if he didn't shape up. A good bop on the butt, that's what he needed. Maybe it was the move. Maybe not.

Yesterday, she could have killed him. They'd been up here at the Overlook; she'd specifically taken them up here to be out of the vicinity because Andrew didn't think Dharma should be at the funeral and had asked Claire to keep her. Claire had been only too happy to oblige, agreeing that putting one's mother into the earth was hard enough at middle age, and probably insufferably traumatic at seven. So she'd taken them up here and they had been getting along fine, playing kickball, when Anthony had spotted the hearse and funeral party winding up Park Lane South. Claire had signalled to him with her eyes not to say a word, but he had. "Look," he'd shouted, and Dharma had looked, along with everyone else in the playground. Claire could have died for her, that little girl, standing there by the sandbox in her chartreuse dress, her fingernails still chipped pink in polish her mother had let her put on. Claire hadn't known what to do. She had sat there, frozen, and Dharma had stood very still and not bothered with Anthony or any of the others. There she'd stood and looked down the great hill and held on to the tall, chain-link fence.

That had been yesterday. Well, there was nothing to be done.

Dharma came running back to her. Claire noticed her clothes were all wet. Normally, she wouldn't take notice, but the weather was changing and you couldn't leave her like that for too long.

"We'll stop off at your house and you can run in and get some dry clothes. All right?"

Dharma looked down at herself. "Good Lord," she said, the way a woman would. She must have spent most of her time with her mother, Claire thought, her adult behavior was so pronounced.

"Dharma, is there anyone from school, some little girl in your class, someone you'd like to invite over? I wouldn't mind. One more or less."

Dharma shook her head.

"Then you don't mind hanging out with us? Helping me with Anthony? At least for a while?"

"No, Mrs. Benedetto. I told you already three times I wouldn't. Really."

"That's fine. Look, Dharma, I'm all for form and proper behavior, but if you'd like to call me something else—I don't

know. Mrs. Benedetto seems too formal for the way I feel towards you. I don't suppose you'd like to call me 'Aunt Claire' or
something like that . . ."

"No."

"Oh. Well, no, of course not. So. Fine."

Claire watched her run off, back to the children. They had
grabbed sticks and were using them as staffs, great herders they
were, now. Dharma had to run to catch up. The hill was steep and
it warmed up. Claire blew on her upper lip. To the right were the
woods and they followed the path that rimmed it. To the left was
Park Lane South and across that Stefan's house. Carmela's house.
Claire still thought of it as Stefan's. Actually, she didn't think of
it as either of theirs. Years ago, when she'd gone to high school on
the bus, she would pull the buzzer here to notify the driver to let
her off at this stop. So everyone, those all-important other passengers, would think she lived specifically in this villa. She was quite
sure they would know it would be that particular villa, to which
she belonged, no other. She fit so well to it, with her sweater
nestled onto her shoulders just so well bred, with the pearls, the
single strand, and her so-well-scrubbed fingernails buffed, not
polished. They were not just passengers on a bus, these passengers, they were her public, the audience hushed in a Lincoln
Center theater. They were savvy. They watched, on other nights,
Fritz Lang in black-and-white. They certainly were not simply
people on their way home. They were her audience. When, years
later, as if by magic, she had literally run into Stefan jogging
through the woods and he had invited her home, home being the
very villa of her adolescent dreams, she had taken it as a sign. The
fact that Stefan was handsome and interested in her had not been
as meaningful as the mystical incredibility of what was going on.

Yes. So long ago. Even what had happened later had been so
long ago. Four years. The fact that she had met Johnny at the
same time had been rich with meaning as well. It had allowed her
free will over destiny. Or so it had seemed at the time.

Claire felt the opulence jiggle in the rear of her thighs as she
marched down the hill. She let it jiggle, jiggling it more for the
good it would do them. She looked, no doubt, like a wooden
soldier, but what she looked like now had not the same signifi-

cance it had once had. I've changed, Claire told herself, astonished, relieved, appreciative. I'm another person looking back on someone else.

She caught up with the children at the crossing, as the cars whizzed by on Park Lane South. You had to be careful here. After that it was as if you descended into the tops of the trees. The villas changed here to stately rundown elderly Queen Anne Victorians and Colonials. The neighborhood wasn't as fancy, but it also wasn't irritated by the interjection of rude apartment houses. Here it was quiet, you could park anywhere you liked. As a matter of fact, in this part of town, the homeowners considered the street in front of their own homes their private domain, and if you parked once too often in front of someone else's house you'd find your tires flat. "And rightly so," you'd hear them say.

Claire's heart still leapt at first sight of her house. She felt herself hurry toward it, so much still to do to make it really perfect.

Johnny had already started pulling down the walls around the chimney. It was an awful job, and every room was littered on the first floor, but when it was done, when the fireplace flues were open and the stones and tiles restored to their original grandeur, Johnny said a fireplace like this would really heat the house, not rob from it, the way the modern ones did. To have four open fireplaces in one house was a wonderful thing for the both of them. It meant so much. Especially to him, who'd only known fireplaces in films. They would whisper about it in their bed when Anthony was asleep, how wonderful it would be when it was finished. They would invite Red Torneo, Johnny's old friend from Brooklyn, and sit him in front of the fire and make him drink hot toddies. "He'd go for that," Johnny would say, and she could tell, by the unconscious wiggle of his bare toes against hers, how the idea genuinely delighted him. His eyes would be wide open in the darkness and he would be dreaming out loud. "And then," he would say, drawing it out for her so she could savor it too, "then, we'll invite your friends from overseas and they'll take up the whole top floor." Johnny liked to be fair.

Claire smiled. She wondered who on earth he thought she would invite. There was no one there who was interested in her life any more.

Johnny would hold her softly in his warm protective arms. She was important here, she knew. Her life meant more now than it ever had. She would hear his breathing change and feel his grip go slack and peaceful. She was important here. Still, she stayed awake and overheard the mindless chatter of the world she'd left behind. It glittered and disdained and chirped until it turned into the odd, occasional late-night squirrel on the roof, hurrying before the raccoon came down at last from the oozy wood.

Dharma stood and looked across the street.

"Michaelaen," Claire said, "would you take Anthony on in and turn on the Disney Channel and let him have a Snickers from the tin drum? One Snickers, remember. Just one. I'll take Dharma over and help her get some dry clothes. And give Floozie fresh water, if you think of it."

"I can go by myself," Dharma said.

"Never mind," Claire dismissed her. She was very good at this when she meant it. She would narrow her eyes and look a certain way, the way she'd seen Sister Saint Stephen do so many years ago. Sister Saint Stephen had done a fine job of terrifying the entire class of sixty-four children. "You'll not go anywhere alone while I've got charge of you. Got that?"

Dharma pursed her lips but waited for Claire while she opened the door to let the boys in. They walked across the road together, and Claire remembered the time she'd first come to this place and sat there in the car with Anthony asleep and Tree had come upon her. How astonished they'd both been. And Claire remembered still the way Tree looked forward to her meeting her daughter.

Claire didn't want to go canonizing Tree in her mind, now. She remembered, even then, a light but deliberate sense of reserve, not wanting Tree to enter entirely into her world, not inviting her directly to her house. She'd known, even in that short meeting, a feeling of caution, of not surrendering everything at once. She hadn't given Tree her number straight away. One holds on to painful memories, even broken ones that seem so pointed. When they were children, Claire had lured Tree into her garage with the promise of a ride on the silver painted scooter bike. It was an unusual bike; it had no chain, just a smooth rubber loop thing. It was great fun. Claire, though she only measuredly liked the thing, recognized it immediately for what it could bring her, and that was a chance at the notorious Tree Medicino's friendship. And it had done.

And then, one day, Michael, Claire's brother, had hot-rodded the thing down to Jamaica Avenue and the rubber loop had slipped off and broken. Claire still remembered the moment when she'd told Tree she couldn't have the bike today, it was broken, sorry. She remembered still the unhesitating look turn from impatient waiting joy to raging fury. Not disappointment, fury. She had not even waited to play out the day but had gone, just like that, and had not come back. Not that day nor any other that winter.

When Mary had unconsciously bullied her with an unthinking "Where's that friend of yours, the one you just can't live without," Claire had answered with an unconcerned, "Oh, her. She's boring." "Like a lightswitch, that Claire," Mary had dismissed her, had shaken her head and gone on smearing apple butter onto toast.

And Claire could remember arranging her face to appear nonchalant, involved all at once in the setup, the pretense, the job of convincing the viewer she was fine and dandy, busy, like all of us, pretending not to feel, until, who knows, maybe we don't. Or at least we don't know that we don't.

"I have to go in the back way," Dharma said.

"You haven't got your key?" Claire asked. They crunched uneasily along the white pebbles in the drive with their feet, neither looking forward to this.

"My father said I didn't need it today. Because I would be at your house and all."

"Oh, yes, of course. The back door's open?"

"No. I climb inside the bathroom window."

"Do you really?"

Before anything else, Dharma had hoisted herself up onto the sturdy Rubbermaid garbage pail. In the small window she went. She appeared, some moments later, at the back door, not smiling.

Claire hesitated. She had overstepped so many bounds already, today. "Shall I come with you?"

"Yes," Dharma said quickly.

Claire went in. A morbid thrill of curious expectation went right through her. The kitchen was brown, all brown. There was a brown shiny refrigerator as well. Orange and yellow silk flowers were on the round Formica table. It was not Claire's style, but it was cozy. There were plenty of cabinets. Dharma waited while she took in the room. "So come on," she said.

They walked along a corridor that reminded Claire of her Polish great-aunt's place over in Ridgewood. It was a narrow house, full of beams, wallpaper trim and excessive dollies and runners. It was dark, the shades were drawn, and if that wasn't dark enough the furniture was mahogany. The only touch of something else was Tree's great collection of hats. They lined the walls on pegs. It gave the gloomy Victorian interior a touch of the theatric, backstage at the Valencia vaudeville theater. There were big hats, little hats, plumed hats, pill boxes, and bonnets. Claire loved Victorian exteriors, but she wasn't too crazy about these heavy interiors. Now that she was in, she couldn't wait to get out. "What's that smell?" She sniffed the air.

"It's myrrh. Mommy always burned it in the egg. The brass egg."

"Ah. Which room is yours?"

"In the front." She touched Claire's arm. "I'll be right out."

Claire didn't like to intrude upon a little girl's messy room and rumpled bed. She remembered her own hurricane of chaos as a child. Dharma's ringlets hardly bounced as she made her way down the hallway. The walls were also dotted with Tree's extravagant and picturesque hats. Claire followed her with a craned long neck and was astonished to see a spotless room, a made-up canopy bed and a dainty white shag rug. It was the room of a television child, hardly anyone Claire would know. Dharma walked directly to her low white dresser and opened a pink and golden jewelry box. A ballerina pirouetted around an oval mirror. "Somewhere, My Love," the music box warbled. Dharma relieved her fingers of her rings and shut the box. She opened a drawer of folded little-girl tops, pulled one out, opened the drawer beneath it, inspected the row of folded little-girl bottoms, chose the corresponding pair of pedal pushers and shut that drawer as well. She turned to see if Claire was watching, but Claire had apprehended this and turned her back on Dharma so she'd have some privacy without shutting her door. She sensed that Dharma was too polite to shut it in her face. She hummed the little ballerina's song so Dharma would know she was fine, not a care in the world, and she was out here, planted firmly, not leaving, not coming a bit closer. "La-la-la," she sang, then saw them and almost missed a beat, but didn't: a pair of butter-soft beige moccasins in hurried discard atop the landing on the stairs.

Claire kept on humming, singing, singing, humming. Jesus, let's get out of here, she whispered silently to herself, and turned back to see if Dharma was almost ready. Come on, come on. She couldn't bear the thought of the two of them coming down the stairs and Dharma seeing them together. Portia and Andrew. It wasn't possible. But it also wasn't possible that Tree would have had the same shoes she'd so admired, and that they would be lying about. It was too much to imagine. Claire was petrified, afraid to speak and at the same time afraid not to. She held her right hand with her left, her shoulders squinched up with indecision. "La-la-la-la-la," she continued her piece. She held her elbows now; she was quite cold.

Dharma stood before her and they turned in silence and left the house. The light swallowed them up totally like darkness and hid them from each other. Dharma trotted hurriedly along, relieved in her sly way that Claire hadn't noticed who it was in the house. Claire walked briskly alongside her, ashamed for the both of them. She didn't like it. And then again, suppose this Portia person had been up the stairs on her own, furrowing through bureau drawers—or even worse, alone on Tree's dark, tumbled, anguished bed?

CHAPTER 4

Claire closed the good green door. She padded the chamomile-riddled path down to the sidewalk with mounting excitement on soft Pakistani slippers. She used to wear them all the time, and so they were as comfortable as fancy shoes could be. Only recently, as more and more people would stop her to ask where she'd bought them, had it occurred to her to conserve them. She would never find their like again, that was for sure. How often did one get to the Khyber Pass, after all?

It would do her good to be out and about. Johnny and she had fought before, during, and after supper. A hurling of words and recriminations, then again some just-thought-of slight seeing its opportunity now and grabbing it. It had all started when Claire noticed the pile of bills, stamped and completed, still sitting in their pile in the hallway.

"Yeah, so?" he had said.

"And what does that mean, 'yeah, so'? It's the nineteenth and you still haven't sent out the bills!"

"I haven't got any money to cover them." He'd shrugged.

"Honey, all the money's in the account. All you have to do is send—Johnny, you don't mean to tell me you spent—how on earth could you have spent all—"

With that, Johnny had flung his great self onto the sofa and shut his eyes.

"Don't you pretend to be going to sleep, you big fake!" she'd shouted.

Anthony stood, legs planted far apart, in the nearby room only halfway lit up by the dusk. He'd been through plenty of brawls, had Anthony, was even now gauging how bad it would be from the decibel level. Just when everyone thought, Oh good Lord, that was it and surely one of them would be out the door with a suitcase, they would instead heave and collapse, spent, on opposite easy chairs and Daddy would say, stupidly, "Okay, enough's enough. Friends again?" And what would Mommy do? She would laugh!

Anthony shivered and went off in search of Michaelaen, who would be one of two places: under the porch or upstairs in the closet. He wasn't one for the fights. On second thought, he would leave him alone. Michaelaen had called him a pest. Dharma was back in her house. Anthony was glad, because he didn't really want to listen to her cry anymore. And all the time she was here she would hog Floozie. When she was gone home he got a chance to look over her jewels. He knew where she kept them, har-har-har, inside her little sewing basket. Dharma put a lot of stock in her jewels. She would close the door—what a dope, there was always the keyhole—and then she would touch them and look at them like Daddy would look when he held Mommy's hair in his hands. Anthony schmoozled his face down into the dog's fluffy fur. He had his old soft green baby blanket, the one grandma had knit him, cozy around her. He fussed and clucked and tucked her in and whispered secrets to her till both of them were flaccid with love and asleep.

Claire stood at the end of her walk and wondered briefly if she should take the keys with her. Why bother, she decided against it, retracing her steps and putting the lot into the pot of still bright-red geranium. She looked left and right but no one had seen her. There wasn't a soul on the block but old Mr. Kinkaid coming down from Park Lane South with his mean bag of groceries. She hastened her step so as to be able to greet him. Her motives, unclear to herself, moved quickly, and she realized as she sorted them with her steps that she was only doing this to get him out of her way. If she dealt with him now, she told herself, he would have no excuse to show up tomorrow. But even as he neared, she knew her reasoning to be ridiculously reasonable—and Mr. Kinkaid was not. He was like some cloying twenty-four-hour virus, oozing toward you with a psychic antenna, his power being your politeness, his inevitable stay up to his own languishing whim. Claire strode purposefully up to him, distributing her white light around herself comfortably, then put on a happy face.

"Got yourself all rigged up for somethin', eh?" he said accusingly. "What's doin'? Boss ain't home?" he cackled unpleasantly.

He reminded her of her disparaging Polish great-aunts. Her mother always said they weren't happy unless they were miserable. She and Claire would lock sparkling, collusive eyes across the room. And that reminded Claire. If Johnny had spent all the money this month already, how would they ever put the required thirty bucks into their piano fund? She better speak to him about that. That was one thing she had to have. A grand piano. There would be no getting around that. Anthony would play, even if she had to go to work in the five-and-ten to pay for his lessons. He would play if for no other reason than to show up those Polish aunts now making life miserable for the dead souls over in hell, for that was no doubt where they were.

Mr. Kinkaid hadn't shaved for a couple of days, Claire noticed. How men hated to shave! Once they did it, they felt so happy, but they always needed a reason, or a wife, to get in there and make them do it. ". . . And," Kinkaid sucked an incisor for emphasis, "didn't I tell you to watch out for those Murdochs?"

"Murdochs?"

"Those Murdochs in the yellow house down the block there. Down there."

"Oh . . . What about them?"

"Well, you can see for yourself. They put that 'For Sale' sign out there for the whole world to see. Not nice and confidential like I did. Putting it in the *Tablet* for my own kind. These type of people, they'll just sell to anyone, anyone walks in off the street. Blacks. Injuns. Sheeks. They don't give a damn." He noticed Claire made no rejoinder. She was remembering earlier on in the week when indeed she'd seen a family of Punjabis streaming from the Murdoch house. If only there hadn't been so many of them, perhaps the residents up and down the block wouldn't have been so frightened. But they were frightened. You could tell, the way they came out with red little eyes and arms folded across their chests, scowling frantically at the likes of the strangers. They didn't

75

see the graceful beauty of the ladies' saris floating in the end-of-summer wind; they smelled the threat of curry and a town that was no longer Mayberry. You couldn't console them with the news that most of these people moving in around here were socially upscale of them, teachers and doctors and lawyers in their own countries, because this would surely complicate their rage. "That, that," they would sputter, ". . . is because our hard-earned tax dollars get sent over there and they got nothin' better to do than go to them lousy schools we paid for."

"What the hell," Mr. Kinkaid said, "it's not my problem anymore. You're the ones got to deal with them good-for-nothin's. You mark my words, you won't recognize this street one year from today. This whole block will be in shreds."

"Surely not in shreds, Mr. Kinkaid." Claire smiled.

"Graffiti all over your fresh-painted garage there. You'll see what I mean. You'll lose that holier-than-thou attitude real quick when it starts costin' you in your pretty little pocketbook."

"Good thing you'll be leaving town soon, then."

"What's that?"

"Just kidding. A touch of levity."

Kinkaid ignored her. "And you heard what they did now? They discontinued the Q-ten!"

"What's that, the Q-ten?"

"The bus line that goes up and down Lefferts Boulevard to Union Turnpike."

"Really?"

"Yeah, they're getting rid of the buses and putting on a couple of elephants instead."

"Good night, Mr. Kinkaid."

"Just a joke. You remember jokes?"

Claire made a face not unlike Kali, the Indian goddess whose tongue sticks out all of the way and reaches right down to her horrible chin. She boggled her eyes and rattled them round in their sockets. She was quite good at this.

Mr. Kinkaid ducked appreciatively away, shielding his rear end with one plastic bag of white bread and a Budweiser beer.

Claire breathed in the cool, now familiar, Richmond Hill night air and continued on her way. She passed Iris von Lillienfeld's, a gracious lady in a gracious old house. She must go visit her this week. They had been through quite a bit together some years ago, when Claire had first returned to America. Iris had known her when she was a wee girl, one of a pair of rambunctious, then-redheaded twins. She even still called Claire "Red." She was, Claire fingered her long dark hair reminiscently, the only one who did. Claire couldn't help remembering four years ago, give or take a month, when she'd been up this same hill with both sisters, Carmela and Zinnie dressed up and in tow, only it was she who had had her eye on Stefan—and her sisters were along for the ride. Interesting the way things turn out when you stick around long enough to find out, Claire mulled. Stefan and Carmela's house stood finally, majestically, there, with its parapets and what-nots, its roof of slates and its oval-topped windows all set for Rapunzel. A calliope of Bavarian blue-and-white awning tents were on the lawns, gazebos of charm (and just in case of rain) for the evening. A stately if not homey place.

Zinnie, the youngest, the undercover, the spunky blond, had met a guy here last time, a handsome doctor at that, but it hadn't worked out. Zinnie wasn't one to stay home and play do-as-you're-told. "He wanted," you would often overhear Zinnie say, "a floor monitor, not a partner." For someone as independent and "in charge" as Zinnie was, this was not the right man. She was so used to calling the shots that once, when Zinnie had heard him say, "Hon, would you take off work this Thursday? That's the only day they can deliver my couch," she had looked at him for a moment with her mouth open, decided not to take offense, and had nicely explained to him that she would probably have a collar on Wednesday and have to be in court all day Thursday.

"Yes, but I still don't see why you can't take off Thursday," he'd persisted.

"But I just explained to you—" Zinnie started to say, until he interrupted her.

"Zin, sweetheart, the court system in New York is so backed up as it is, one day more or less isn't going to make a hell of a whole lot of difference."

"It's not, heh?" Zinnie shot back. "What about the perp sittin' in the can waiting to go up? I mean, he or she might not be a person to you, but to her kids holding up day after day in a foster center, or his wife—or the other arresting officers' families who have better things to do, it is their time—what I mean is, a whole lot of people are involved in any bust. You don't just put their lives on hold because some department store finds it more convenient to deliver from nine to five, Monday to Friday."

"But I want this couch!" he'd almost shouted. "Stop being such an idiot!" People at the surrounding tables stopped talking and looked at each other with eyebrows up.

"Hey." Zinnie remained deliberately calm, the way she always would do with psychos and irate personalities. "All I'm asking you to do is rethink your request. There is no reason I can see for getting insulting. Maybe you could take off, yourself."

"That's a little ridiculous, don't you think?"

"What is?"

"I mean, I'm a professional."

"Yeah? So what, nonprofessionals don't have rights? And by the way," she'd added. "I consider myself a professional."

He'd burst out laughing.

"That's it." Zinnie put down the fork she'd been twirling round and round her pink spaghetti. She stood up slowly, her eyes always on his, watching them change from annoyance that she was off to the ladies' room when she still hadn't committed to Thursday, to bewilderment when she laid out a trio of tens on the table, to real shock when she turned and left them looking at her back and the beautiful head of flotsam, thick blond curls he'd never get his effing fingers through again. For Zinnie it was that simple. She might spend weeks sitting around her apartment wrapped up in a horse blanket, snivelling into aloe-laden tissues, but he'd never know. And it's better than spending the rest of your life apologizing to yourself for giving up your dignity for a permanent toss in the hay and a hand to hold onto, she would later say, detoxed of this guy. Cured. "So I guess I really didn't love him, anyway. Just the idea that he was the perfect catch. So I'm no better than he is, right? Go figure."

Claire huffed and puffed up the hill. She made sure she walked across the road from the woods, not just in it. There were so many loose dogs around lately. Big fellas too. They gave you the creeps.

78

What were people doing—sending their dogs out on their own because they didn't want to be bothered carrying around pooper-scooper bags? Here she was at the private hedge border of the other happy couple, Carmela and Stefan. At least they'd stuck it out, got to know each other and still they stayed together. So something worked.

Now what the heck? Someone was checking her out from across the street? Don't be silly, she scoffed. Some weirdo jumping back behind a tree was as normal as apple pie in this park. Probably just another yanker. Most of them were harmless, she knew, but shivered all the same. Ominous feelings were not foreign to her, and she'd learned they were, some of them, false. She was glad she hadn't brought the car. The guy could well be a car thief. This was grandstand auto-thief country here. That is, if you could find a parking spot anywhere. With all Stefan's money, he'd never be able to buy spaces up here. Even his enormous driveway out back would be filled by now. No, Claire's good old car was snug in its own handy spot right in front of the house. The sound of tinkling piano drifted across the lawn. French doors opened and Nick and Nora Charles flitted across the patio.

I am dressed, she instantly knew, completely wrong. She had half a mind to turn around and hightail home, but just then Carmela spotted her, looked her condescendingly up and down, then rushed with open arms to enfold (cover?) her.

"Carmela. I just saw you this afternoon."

"Ah-ha-ha-ha." Carmela's was a belly laugh. "Everyone!" she called out. "Everyone! This is my dear little sister, Claire. Come! Come and meet Claire. Richard! Oliver! Darlings! Come meet my famous-photographer, world-traveler, guru-groupie, deluded and now retired-and-living-as-a-recluse in Richmond Hill North, sister, Claire Breslinsky."

"Benedetto," Claire corrected, sore. She used her maiden name herself but she didn't like anyone else to do it for her. From Carmela especially, it smacked of disrespect to Johnny.

"Why so frosty?" Carmela smiled into her ear.

"Guru-groupie?" muttered Claire.

"Now, now," Carmela laughed at the room, then snarled into

Claire's ear, "This is your coming-out party, doll. Let's not be unappreciative."

"Remember who you are," Claire heard dear Swamiji's caring words caress her through the moment. So she wasn't good at parties. So what? She could leave whenever she chose. What was that, French-aproned help? And each carrying glittering round trays of what was surely white and costly Californian. One thing about these two, they knew their wine.

She saw, across the towering room among well-dressed minor players, the short but perilous Jupiter Dodd, bon vivant, cause of all the commotion and, as usual, enjoying it. Their eyes crossed but did not meet. They would get to each other later, after they'd sorted out what else was going on. They would be each other's just desserts. Claire snatched a glass of wine from a costumed lizard gliding by. She only took three sips, but that heady glow registered with an almost audible click. Ay-ay-ay-ay, thought Claire, settling into its loveliness. What was that they had on? Some sultry samba thing. Shades of Rio de Janeiro. There was a disc jockey, Claire noticed. He wore the required one earring, one pony tail, one silk T-shirt, and a Mano suit. Last time Stefan had hired a tuxedoed quartet, but this was nice. She perched on something that would in someone else's home have been a radiator. It was an encasement wrapped around the entire room, latticed and painted white. The whole floor was of varying shades of white. That would change quickly enough if they ever decided to have kids, she thought wryly. It was all certainly opulent. Somber, though. Taking itself pretty seriously, with lilies from Holland in great cut-glass vases. There was, somewhere up there in the sky, a chandelier to warm any Mediterranean's heart.

Standing elegantly tall alongside the burled-walnut Biedermeier highboy was Freddy, Zinnie's ex and Michaelaen's father. Claire didn't know why she was so surprised to see him here. This was his territory now, wasn't it? There was no reason for her to dislike Freddy. He was sharp, entertaining, good to his own, talented, and reliable. Still, there was something stilted in their communication. He always made her feel as though she had no sense of humor. You could put him anywhere, sit him down or stand him up or turn him upside down, and you'd still have your full frontal for the men's fashion section of the Sunday *Times*. Nothing matched, but everything blended together in muted years-ago Abercrombie and Fitch.

"Hello," he said, and shook her hand while he kissed her cheek. "I've been trying to get hold of you."

"Really?" She was the least hard-to-reach person she knew.

"I had three of my waiters drop a rug off at your house."

"Not the famous Dhera Gaz?"

He looked taken aback. "What are you, a witch?"

Oh, how tempting it was to let him think just that. She smiled something inscrutable and said nothing. And, on second thought, even a well-intended admission would let him know she knew how the dog had ruined it for his fastidious specifications and the gift was somehow left-handed, something less than perfect.

"I didn't want you to feel unrecompensed for housing Zinnie and Michaelaen," he said.

"Hey. Quit it. They're my family, too."

"Dear Claire. You are so good."

She eyed him suspiciously. "Well, so are you."

"Michaelaen asleep?"

"In Zinnie's closet."

"That's good. Then he's asleep by now. So. That means you and Johnny are fighting."

"That's true," Claire admitted. No use denying it. Everyone knew Michaelaen hid from the first barks of hollering. No one knew it better than Fred. And she and Zinnie never fought. Whereas she and Johnny were becoming quite famous.

"Too bad," Freddy flopped onto the handsome settee. "I was just about to offer my congratulations."

"Ah," said Claire, "you've got to come over and see it."

"I hear she's a beaut."

Claire warmed. "Oh, Freddy, and just wait till we get the fireplaces opened!"

Freddy looked at her strangely. "Oh. The house. Yes. Yes, I will come. Michaelaen loves it."

They watched the party, both rocking convivially to the now Trinidadian music.

"You didn't mean the house, did you?" Claire said finally.

Freddy laughed. "No, I meant the horse. Johnny's horse. Your horse, for that matter."

"I'm sorry?"

"Oops."

"Whose horse?"

"The horse Johnny bought that is now sitting in a stable at Aqueduct. At the track. Claire. The racehorse."

Claire held the glass till it was upside down, and still she kept it like a hat on her nose. She watched the chandelier through it, dazzled by the kaleidoscope of shimmering crystal and knowing if she ever put the glass down she would have to think about what Freddy had just said. She did.

He said, "I hope I haven't gone and ruined a perfectly good surprise."

She smiled at him with her mouth closed. He covered his eyes with his hands and peeked at her through carefully buffed pink fingers.

"Uh oh. Promise me you won't accuse him till I get there."

"Nonsense, Freddy." She followed the lead he'd unknowingly provided. "I wouldn't breathe a word. I wouldn't want to ruin his surprise. Not for the world. I think it's sweet." There. She'd be damned if Freddy would watch her squirm.

The bastard. The filthy, lying bastard. She would kill him. At very least, she would divorce him. She felt her stomach unclench. Yes, divorce. Anthony looked at her with puzzled, frightened eyes. All right, not divorce. She would kill him. She would take his revolver out and shoot the bloody, slimy, stinking lowlife. She searched the table in front of them for a pack of cigarettes.

Visions of herself haunting one Salvation Army after St. Vincent de Paul after another and back, on the Saturday before the antique and jumble shop owners got there, flew through her mind. She plucked a glass of white wine from one more endearing serf, capsized it neatly, and went on to the next. She hadn't minded ferreting through other people's garbage to find stuff renovatable enough for her family. And how many dumpy upholstery shops had she waded through till she came up with the cheapest and the best?

Lord knew, her flag went up and her heart would start pumping at the very hint of a yard sale; any heap of junk on someone's front lawn would plunge her foot down on the brake. Some of her happiest memories were when she was pregnant and driving around Richmond Hill on a Saturday. As the older residents packed up to move to Florida, frightened by the daunting certainty of other-cultured neighbors moving (oh my God!) right down the block, they grew panicky and careless, letting go of all sorts of unbelievable treasures for a song. Fruitwood chairs hidden under studded patent leather, held sturdy for generations by four-inch European dowels and now sitting under someone's indifferent Japanese maple with a skeptical sign asking fifty dollars Scotch-taped haphazardly on it. What would they do, take them with them? To the land of chrome and wicker? To whom would they leave them? Sons and daughters crunched into studio apartments in the city? Pay storage?

"You mean fifty dollars for each one or fifty for the set?" Claire had pointedly taken her car keys out.

"Kit and caboodle," the fellow had said, eyeing her knees.

"I'll take them," she'd said, noticing somebody else parking his car and getting out with that money-in-his-pocket jaunt.

Johnny had yelled for three days over those chairs. But she'd stuck to her guns. She knew what was good. And the best part of it was the minute she'd had them at the upholsterer's and they'd stripped off the patent leather, some woman had come in, taken one look at the first chair, and offered two-sixty for it. "So you can imagine," she'd chirped triumphantly to Johnny, "what they would go for in the city. And what they'd be worth when I'm finished with them."

Johnny wouldn't let on that they were a success. Oh, God forbid. But whenever any of his friends came over they never failed to mention the chairs. "Whoa!" They'd back up appreciatively. "Must be those antique chairs Johnny found!"

Claire would let them go on thinking Johnny had found them. What did she care? It only meant Johnny would love her that much more. What a gal! he must think. She had thought. But you see, now, he hadn't. All he thought was that she'd keep on saving him money and he could go on happy, lucky to spend it. She could feel her blood boil. A racehorse! She wondered, suddenly, if she couldn't drop dead right there from a quick cerebral hemorrhage? No, there was Anthony. She couldn't. There was Anthony. There was no piano. And there was Freddy, still beside her, pleased to watch her expression harden like loose sand from mud to cement. And he was enjoying this, wasn't he? All at once, it came to her. He disliked her, she realized, surprised. It weighed her down and she was transported right back to sobriety. Across the room, Portia McTavish danced. She was very pretty, Claire admitted to herself grudgingly, what with her high color and enthusiastic graceful-ness. Claire watched her stupidly, entranced with the vivacious energy Portia poured out of her dress and into the room. She was quite glad that Johnny had not come. She might hate him, but at moments like these it was clear to her just how much she loved him.

Suddenly, near the wall alongside Portia McTavish's gyrations, Claire recognized Andrew Dover. It couldn't be. How could he be here with his wife just dead? But he was here, drowning himself in a glass of Stefan's good Glenfiddich from the look of him. She was not shocked, she was stunned. How could a man lose his wife, the mother of his only child, and act like this? And where was Dharma? She'd practically pushed the kid home so she'd spend some time with her father, and now he was here. Claire put her glass down on the white thing, the whatever-it-was. The paint, she noticed absently, was beginning to peel. She crossed the crowded room.

"Andrew." She had to raise her voice to be heard. "Are you all right?"

"I am," he enunciated carefully, "getting there."

She tried to laugh.

He leered at the dancing form of Portia McTavish.

"How's Dharma?" Claire said to him.

Andrew's head shook up and down wildly. "Much better," he finally shouted back at her.

"Who's with her?" she wanted to know.

"She's fine," he said.

"Andrew. Excuse me, Andrew!" she had to tug on his sleeve. "Does that mean she's alone?"

"Mrs. Rieve next door keeps looking in on her." He closed his eyes. "Dharma won't let her stay. Says Mrs. Rieve's a witch."

"Look, Andrew. I'm going to call my sister, who is staying at my house. I could ask her to run over and take a look at how Dharma's doing if she has a chance."

"No, thanks." He grinned. "Can't dance."

Claire thought he was overdoing the drunken slur bit.

She was angry at him for not showing more compassion toward his daughter, and angry at herself for not showing enough compassion toward a man who'd just lost his wife. She turned her back on him and left the room for the relative calm of the cool, dark hallway. There was no telephone. She climbed the impressive staircase and imagined what happy compensation it must be each morning for Carmela as she regally descended it. Compensation for what, Claire was not exactly sure. The master bedroom was the first door on the left. Claire couldn't help remembering the time she had considered spending half her life there herself. She knocked and went cautiously in. Wow. Nice. Like the digs in an English castle. Or at least a Hollywood version of an English castle. The phone was on the nightstand and Claire perched herself carefully on the bed's maroon silk coverlet. She dialed with the careful deliberation of someone who had one too many under her belt. It rang a couple of times. Claire could imagine Zinnie, frowning, turning down the volume on her earphones, tripping lightly to the kitchen phone. At last she answered. Her mouth was full.

"Hi, it's me, Claire."

"What's wrong?"

"Nothing. Everything all right home?"

"Fine. All asleep. Right after you left. Oh. And Freddy's thugs dropped off a rug. It's rolled up in the foyer. The dog ate the whole box of Chips Ahoy, though."

"Uh oh."

"Yeah."

"Keep her in the kitchen, then."

"She's sleeping on Anthony's head."

"Tch."

"I put them both on Anthony's bed."

"Look. There's something else. Dharma's father, this Andrew Dover fellow, they live across the street in the house with the brown porch—"

"I know Andrew."

"You do?"

"Of course."

"Oh. Well, he's here, can you believe it? And he's drunk."

"Poor guy."

"Poor guy?! He could get drunk at home, couldn't he? I think he left Dharma all alone. And he's drooling all over Portia McTavish."

"What else is new?"

"Really? Since when?"

"Claire, they all go for Portia. She's prime rib. Or hadn't you noticed."

"I think she's a skunk. But yes, I had noticed."

"And?"

"And I thought maybe you could cross over and peek in on her. Like, don't scare her or anything, just ring the bell and drag her out by the hair and make her stay at my place for the night. And leave a note indicating where she is."

"Suppose she won't come?"

Claire chewed her jagged thumbnail. "Then let her be, I guess. I don't know what to do. Call child welfare? What?"

"Gee, I don't know about that, Claire. I mean, the kid's mother just died. You really think it's a good idea to get her involved with a whole new set of strangers? Some of these foster-care places can be pretty scary to a kid. At least here, she's familiar with the place. She's got you across the street if she needs someone."

"Go over and get her, would you, Zinnie? I'm so worried about her. I'll call you back in half an hour."

"How's the party?"

"Oh, very grand, you know. Spectacular booze. I'll call you back."

She hung up the phone, used Carmela's pretty bathroom and noticed, on her way past the inlaid rosewood rubbish bin, a heap of Q-Tips, stained black. Poor Carmela, she thought, standing there at the mirror, touching up her jet-black hair at the roots. She bet that parted-down-the-middle hairstyle would have to go. And soon. She went back in and dunked her face into a cold handful of water. Really, she didn't look too bad, she admired. Nothing perked you up more than a well-lit reflection of yourself, and Carmela's mirror was so generous. It would be, though, wouldn't it? Everything was, in the end, how you looked at it, and reassurances like this might be fleeting, but they did do you good.

Already she felt more gently inclined toward Johnny. After all. He couldn't very well have discussed the idea with her. He'd have known her reply would be no. Was it really so terrible? It wasn't as though he'd taken a mistress. After all, the money he must have spent was the money he'd earned restoring cars. Everything he made on the job went straight into the mortgage and insurances and food and clothing accounts. Or it usually did. She knew what was up. He'd gambled with his car money, gambled big, and won. There was probably somebody else in on it. There always was. Probably Pokey Ryan, his old partner. No, it wouldn't be Pokey. Pokey wasn't quick-witted enough to make any money gambling. Unless Johnny had talked him into investing his savings. She hoped it hadn't been Pokey. She doubted it was Red Torneo, Johnny's dinosaur, the cop who'd practically raised Johnny after his mother had died. He was the gnarly old fellow who'd gotten Johnny into fixing stationhouse cars when it looked like the kid was hooking up with the wrong crowd. So Johnny had wound up fixing them instead of stealing them. Johnny had kept his hoodlum friends, but he'd turned his life around and ended up emulating Red Torneo and joining the department.

Not the coldhearted in-laws who'd fed him their leftovers and sent him off to school in hand-me-downs from their well-suited kids, things Johnny's mother's inheritance helped to buy. If Johnny considered anyone family, it was Red. She must call Red. They hadn't seen him all summer anyway, what with the move and all the goings-on. They were due. Red used to have a floating café down in Sheepshead Bay. Johnny had taken her there when they'd met. A nice little place he'd retired to over there by the boats, but the zoning laws had been changed or whatever it was and Red had been forced to sell out to the city. All a crock of horseshit, Red said. Anyway, he'd found himself a new little place over in Brighton, on the boardwalk there, on the Russian Riviera. Brooklyn had changed, said Johnny. But Brooklyn had always changed, said Red. That was the point of it.

They must get over there and have a look. And soon. She switched off the light, edged herself out onto the balcony, and stood gently with her cheek against the cool, rich woodwork. The music was more to her taste way up here, where she could hear it, not reverberate in it. The hallway in darkness was cast in blue shadows. It was nice. This suited her. Johnny suited her too, she realized, missing him. She'd done the right thing marrying him. It would be all right. Claire had been through too many unhappy relationships not to appreciate the good in this one. And she was no quitter. Not when she had something real to hang onto.

The sound of rustling interrupted her thoughts. It wouldn't do to be found lurking about in the dark. So unseemly. Nosy in your sister's boudoir. She moved forward into the light so that whoever it was would notice her and not be startled. But just as she hesitated, the drape loosened and fell across her shadow and something in a man's urgent voice beneath her on the stairs stopped her dead. "Yeah, sure, that's right," he hissed, "keep it up."

"Keep what up?" Portia McTavish yanked her arm from Andrew's grip and faced him, laughing.

"You know what," he said. He didn't sound very drunk now. He sounded mean. Claire could see the back of his handsome fair head.

"Come off it." Portia's face was green and twisted in the awful light.

She pushed him soundly and tripped back down the stairs. Claire grasped her chest. She dared not move now. Andrew was clearly humiliated by this girl. Claire stood quite still and waited for him to move on. Instead, he stayed there, looking after Portia. His hands were knotted into lifted fists. When would he move? Claire was frightened by his stillness and the dark, unyielding rage that held his purple neck. He said something she couldn't hear for all the music, then followed Portia back into the glittering havoc.

That was when she began to suspect Tree Dover hadn't died the way they'd said she had. She had been murdered. And Claire knew then and there who had done it. She felt it as sure as she was standing there. A chill went up her spine. Maybe he'd had help. Maybe he'd done it on his own. But he sure as hell believed he'd gotten away with it. He was on to the next episode in his life. Well, Claire would be gol-darned. The green-and-purple drapes hung heavily and shimmered. She felt, like the moonlit passage just before her, wet and self-occupied, atonement for her grief.

Dharma, so little, sat looking in her mother's three-way mirror. She was wearing her pretty pajamas and her hair was brushed one hundred strokes into all those ringlets. Dharma hummed, in soft angelic tones, the song her mother was to have sung in Mrs. Stefanovitch's play. "Que Chelita Manina," she hummed.

She took the bright-red lipstick from her mother's golden tube. She held it, her eyes lighting up with an eeric new glow. She put the lipstick on, rolled it on, top and bottom, round and round she went, her eyes holding onto her eyes in the mirror, one small bedraggled phoenix here, taking off within the iris of its own relentless festering. She let the lipstick go at last outside its own prim borders.

Claire stepped, after a while, carefully back into the party herself, feeling as though she'd do well to test the temperature with her toe, which of course she dared not do and so she stayed there on the sidelines of this shimmery pool of mainstreamers, hoping to spot her friendly old drink. It had been duly removed. "Sheesh," Daddy would say, "Coney Island waiters!" She deliberated whether or not to leave. If she went home now she might be able to run over and assist Zinnie in getting Dharma. Carmela wouldn't like it if she left, though. She would consider it to be a great breach of contract, that subtle, unspeakable contract between sisters whose terms read according to what each knows the other can and will do. Carmela was not likely to give her an Indian burn or a tickle torture, means once used with great success, but she still knew just how to get you going. She would bide her time and wait for her chance, and nothing would stop her from going through with whatever she'd decided would work. She would accuse Claire of showing off, of playing the prima donna, coming and going like that. Putting in a quick appearance and then rushing off. "So affected," she would confess to their mother, tattling yet again. And Claire would have to watch their mother's disappointed, cheerful face drop and wonder why Claire could not give that extra inch; it was little enough to ask after Carmela had gone to such lengths to invite all her friends for Claire's sake.

She sighed. She gave up. She sank down into the opulent white silk sofa and resigned herself to having to remind herself, on and off, to breathe.

"Hi ya." Jupiter Dodd tipped at the waist, took hold of her hand, and touched it with a small kiss.

Claire stood happily. "How nice of you to come and say hello!"

"If Mohammed won't come to the mountain . . ."

"Oh dear. Am I that perverse?"

"Was Mohammed perverse?"

"Are you that mountainous?"

They looked together at his trim little body. Jupiter Dodd had a nimbus about him. Claire wasn't sure just what it was. He certainly frightened most people. There was an air of nothing-to-lose about him that scared most people half to death, but also made them worship him—from afar. He wasn't just honest, but often cruel and at anyone's expense. So you took your life in your hands.

"You are surrounded, I see," she said, "by your usual herbaceous aura."

"Now what do you mean by that?" He put his nose right up to hers.

"Oh, I don't know. That's just what comes to mind. Herb as in tart and herbaceous as in perennial. You know, woodsy. Tied to the earth. Both at once. And here we go again."

He snapped his fingers. "There! I knew I adored you! You always say exactly what you mean, whether people will understand you or not. And, by the way, they most often don't, you know."

"But you always do."

"Ha. I always have to ask."

"And you always say what will cut to the quick."

"Why is that, do you suppose?"

"Because that's what people expect of you. I think you feel that you'd be letting them down if you didn't draw blood at least once in every conversation."

He grinned wickedly. He lit his entrancing Pall Mall. "You don't seem intimidated."

"Because I'm busy being jealous of you, lighting up your cigarette."

He didn't, as anyone else would, offer her one and he did it, or didn't do it, to be cruel. Fortunately, this turned out to be the kindest thing, because the moment passed, the alarm stopped ringing, and by the time he was on to his third puff, the appeal wore off. It was always the chumminess, the camaraderie of the incineration that got her going. After one or two puffs it became apparent that the smoker's teeth were indeed due for a scraping, his breath dependent upon the equally stale breath of the conversant, and the cigarette itself a shackle rather than an adornment. Claire manifested the freedom she experienced by giving her spine a good, sturdy stretch. Jupiter inspected her from behind his undulating blue veil of smoke. "So the life of housewife suits you," he said.

"Thank you."

"A bit thicker around the middle, I see. You're not, um——"

"No, you worthless bag of bones, I am not."

"Ah. Good. Because motherhood, though blessed, does tend to use up one's creative energies, don't you think?"

"Yes, I do. That's the point."

"Oh, please don't take offense. You are the most splendid woman here, if you want my opinion. I don't go for the scrawny type."

"Jupiter, you don't go for any type in the female category."

"True, but you don't have to jump off the bridge to know you'll be dead. And as Irwin Shaw said, after a woman passes thirty, she is forced to make the choice between face and fanny. And present company, he was glad to see, had successfully vied for the face."

"I think it was Somerset Maugham said it first."

"There. You see? You just can't keep a good line down. I might add that you are the best-dressed woman here. Oh, you know, they've all clearly *been* to Paris, but you, my dear, have obviously lived there."

"Thank you." Claire smoothed her starry lap with pleasure. "Only why do I get the feeling I'm being fattened for the kill?"

"Because you must be that way yourself. If you want something, you no doubt first pave your way with compliments. It truly does take one to know one, you know."

Justly mollified, Claire admitted to herself the succession of elaborate meals she'd concocted for Johnny before making any sizable request. "Touché," she said and laughed.

"That's better. Shall we sit down?"

"Thank you."

"It's for me. I've just been through a bout with phlebitis and I can't stand for very long."

"Uh oh."

"No, I'm fine. I can walk all day long. As a matter of fact it's the best thing for me. I just can't stand."

They settled into the comfy sofa and looked about, like any old couple getting ready to watch the tube at night. Both held captive by the visual, they made a happy pair, dishing all present, making each other laugh.

"So what's all this about a play?" he asked.

"Haven't you spoken with Carmela?"

"Carmela. She knows the best way to get my interest up is to remain tight-lipped. She pretends it's all top secret."

"It's worked, hasn't it? You're here."

"I'm here because of you. As you well know."

Claire started to cry. She did not sob, but great, glycerine-like globes fell down her cheeks in a rush. It was his being nice that did it. She was doing fine, on her guard to his barbs, and she just wasn't prepared for kindness.

"If you don't stop this instant," Jupiter said, squashing his cigarette out in the stately crystal *aschenbecker,* "I shall get up and walk out and I shall never bother with you again. I promise."

Claire laughed. She blew her nose with the white linen handkerchief he offered with a backward hand. It trembled, his hand. So opposed he was to any form of intrusive intimacy, despite all this tough talk.

"I'll be good," she said finally, meekly.

"Oh, look. Jumbo shrimp. I wonder who Stefan is trying to impress? It can't be me. He knows me. Just throw a little lumpfish caviar into a jelly dish and I'm his. It must be that appalling huddle of Boise, Idahoan, businessmen."

Claire closed her eyes. Little Dharma. Andrew. Portia. A race-horse. Her own fat stomach. It was all too much.

"Claire. Perhaps you ought to go back to work."

"I thought I was working. I've never worked so hard in all my life, really. The laundry is the part I can't quite figure out. The more you do, the more there is. You ought to see my laundry room. I always thought if I would have a laundry room it would be all blue and white and with towels neatly folded on a papered shelf and the smell of clean lavender would waft from hanging ribboned bunches. Like the rooms I used to shoot. My laundry room has towels dragging around the cement floor in damp trails, and the basket overflows and has never been empty, so I bought an enormous one to hold it all and now that's overflowing as well. There is a scum in my fabric-softener compartment and the whole place reeks of moist, soiled sock of man."

"Tomorrow you shall regret having told me all this."

"May I tell you something else? I think my neighbor might have killed his wife and gotten away with it."

Jupiter snatched a shrimp from a passing tray and popped it into his mouth. "Needs horseradish," he said.

"Did you hear what I said?"

"Well, yes. I'm just waiting for you to tell me how."

"I don't know how."

"If you don't know how, you can't do anything about it and if you can't do anything about it, you might as well shut up and not talk about it. Slander, you know."

"You're a fine one to mention slander as an encumbrance to revelation."

"Encumbrance to revelation! Honestly, Claire. People just don't talk that way anymore. If," he muttered, "they ever did."

"So swell. So I should forget about it. That's what you're saying?"

"What I'm saying is this. There are toxic dumps appearing all over Queens, all over the city, all over the state, and they will lead to the deaths of many more people inevitably than one cozy little unprovable murder. You might put your energies into catching those hooligans, the people responsible for that stuff. It would certainly do more good."

"And I'm telling you that a man might have gotten away with killing his wife. It happens. Autopsy experts have a lot to do, too, you know. They can slip up. Well, they can. What? You don't think real evil exists? That there are people out there planning devious atrocities, I mean knowingly being evil? And getting away with it?"

"I think there are some really sick people out there, sure."

"Yes, but I mean evil."

"I think you spent too many years in Catholic schools. And I am advising you not to talk about it to anyone else. For now. Are you with me?"

"I'm always with you, you old fox."

"Then why don't you come work in my office? *She She* needs a good staff photographer."

For several terrific moments, Claire imagined herself arriving in the city each morning, dressed however she pleased, drinking Jamaican Blue Mountain coffee out of endless paper cups, shooting fashion layouts at the Cloisters and Broadway stars for the columns up at the Carlyle at night, chatting over after-midnight suppers at Elaine's with lonely-for-their-therapists, bright TV people in from the coast for three days at a clip. She saw herself standing at the pay phone by the door, stuffing quarters into it, trying to reach her son. "Mommy?" he would say, rubbing sleepy eyes. "Mommy who?"

"I'll have to give it a few more years, Jupiter Dodd. But thanks for the offer. You are so very good to me."

"What is it exactly that you want to do? Shoot weddings on weekends? Because that is what it will come to. Police families are notoriously poor. They all buy houses in washed-up neighborhoods because those are the only mortgages they can afford. And even those drive them slowly to the poorhouse. Oh, I've seen these police families at Christmas fundraiser parties at the precinct. All the children dressed carefully in brand-new polyester outfits. The women done up in last year's clearance from Penney's and the men, oh, the men, the cops themselves, waiting stolidly for Santa in their prerequisite walrus moustaches. So depressing."

"Why, you lowlife piece of shit! Those are the families of the guys that risk and give their lives for the sake of good. But I suppose you are too fancy a person to care about real stuff like that. Like plain old on-sale, bargain-basement, polyester decency. Your sphere is style, not content, isn't it? There's no black and white revolving around your system, is there? It's all an up-to-the-minute, hundred-percent-cotton shade of bloody gray."

"Ouch."

"Ouch this!" she said, thrusting an obscene arm into the air the way Johnny would do. She tingled with emotion. This was the end of Jupiter Dodd, but she didn't care. She just didn't care anymore. She was sick to death of an entire phony-liberal population who supported the rights of the slimiest criminal and allowed their law enforcers to be scorned and spat upon. It stank. Her breath went in and out, in and out. Slowly she came back to where she was, heard the music, saw the people at the party around her, felt Jupiter Dodd still sitting there.

"Well, why don't you leave?"

"Because if I get up, I've got to find someone else to talk to and I shall get bored. Also, my feet hurt and I am quite comfortable. I only wonder what could have happened to your formerly per- fectly good sense of humor."

"Still perfectly good. Just more highly evolved than resorting to taking easy digs at the good guys."

Jupiter didn't say anything. Someone had put on an Aaron Neville tape while the deejay had his break. Claire was tired. She was tired of being defensive. She relaxed. They accepted bright new glasses of wine and sipped them appreciatively. The party had changed gears and was now at a carnal peak. "What would you shoot," Jupiter finally asked, "if you had all the money in the world?"

"I'd shoot the grand old houses of Richmond Hill," Claire replied without hesitation, surprising herself.

"So good. So shoot them. If that's what you want to do, that's what you'll do best. I'll pay you. We'll run them in *She She*. Before

95

you know it, we'll have the gay community buying up the local real estate. Can't you just see it? They'd be holding open-air concerts on Sunday at the bandshell." Jupiter threw back his head and howled with laughter at the idea, his idea. The power, really, was what tickled his funny bone. Oh, it did him good to come to Queens.

"Johnny bought a racehorse," Claire said then.

"Johnny, as in your husband Johnny?"

"Yes."

"Didn't I just get finished sitting through a fervent speech for the oppressed, honest cop?"

"I'm sure he didn't use his salary."

"Ha. Certainly not."

"There wouldn't be enough of it for that. That goes for the bills. He's got this fancy-car renovating thing going on the side."

"And when does he sleep?"

"On the job, probably. He's hardly ever home."

"He's having an affair."

"No. No, I don't think so. I mean, one never knows. But I think we're all right in that department. It's the only department we do do well in."

"Hmm. Yes. You can tell you like each other."

"I think he won big at the track and went in on it with someone else."

"Yes, but still. How could—"

"I think he bought it up at Saratoga. He went up last week with some of his shady friends. They have this race, the first race, where first-time owners can buy horses. A claiming race. Someone probably ran one, snuck one in, just to see how she would do, and Johnny picked her up."

"Why, that's wonderful!"

"What's wonderful? He didn't pay the bills off yet this month. He's never done that before."

"Well, that's to his credit. Claire. You know how it is with race horses. There's always some new expense. Shoes. Bridles. Vets. Trainers."

"Jesus."

"Yes indeed. Look, Claire. If you're that upset, why don't you put your foot down?"

"I don't want to. I don't want to take away his dream and have him tell me for the rest of our lives what he might have had if I'd let him see it through. I want it to come from him."

"He'll probably lose the first time out, and that will be the end of it."

"Yes."

"What's the horse's name?"

Claire noticed Jupiter's bright-eyed interest. There really was something about a racehorse. Perhaps she ought to loosen up, enjoy the fun that was to be had here. Johnny wasn't stupid. "I don't know. Johnny hasn't even told me about it. He's kept it from me. Which is why I'm upset, if you want to know the truth."

"Ah."

"And that bit about putting my foot down. That foot hasn't got a leg to stand on. I mean, what am I going to do, leave him? I've just moved into my dream house. He knows I'm not going anywhere. He knows I'd never break up the family over a . . . a pet."

"Well, let me know, when you find out." He adjusted his tie. "I have been known to place a bet. Now and then. On a good hot tip."

"Jupiter Dodd?"

"Yes, Claire Breslinsky?"

"I'll start shooting houses in the morning."

"There's a good girl. Uh oh. Looks like Stefan and Carmela are headed our way."

Claire looked over Jupiter's shoulder and indeed beheld the strangely amiable approaching duo. They were linked arm in arm, for one thing, and they both wore charming, pleasant smiles, things they did not normally bother with for someone as uninfluential as Claire.

"Hello," they said, the hostess and the host full steam, one handsome couple. They gushed over Jupiter for a good long while. Freddy poked his head in for a moment and Claire noticed Jupiter sucking in the proverbial gut, standing just that much straighter. Freddy wanted to know, "Look here, what have they done with the Pernod," and off he went then without so much as a nod or a how-do-you-do. Jupiter returned to his more characteristic slouch, and Carmela began to praise Claire to Jupiter—unnecessarily, thought Claire, since it was she who had found Jupiter first, at an art exhibition Stefan had brought her to, and it was Jupiter who had found work for Claire shooting a series of women's sculptures when she'd first returned to New York, then handled a critically successful show of her work in Soho. But facts had never stopped Carmela; most of the time people forgot the correct order of events anyway, if you let them, if you went about it right.

Stefan made sure they both had lots to eat. He could be very solicitous when he felt like it, and he felt like it now, arranging elaborate platesful before them, salmon bits and crab and even herring in cream on posh crackers and then they were gone, job done, the perfect dignified and vanished couple.

"I was at the filming of one of those talk shows, the other day," Jupiter said. "Remember Paul Winchell and Jerry Mahoney?"

"Sure."

"Well, they were on and boy were they funny. Still. After all these years. They were telling a lot of Polish jokes. You know. The way they will, and all of a sudden, out of the audience, stands this very irate gentleman. 'I am the Polish ambassador,' he announces, 'and I take great offense at what is being said here today.' Well. You could have heard a pin drop. Paul Winchell stood up and he apologized. You could tell he felt awful. He must have apologized ten times. The ambassador stood there listening to him and then he said, 'It's not you who offended me. It's the little fellow there beside you.' "

Claire and Jupiter laughed like a couple of Irish longshoremen, then wheezed, in fine spirits, to reflection. Really, it was hard not to poke fun at Stefan, there was something so stuffy about him.

"Wonder what they want?" said Jupiter.

"Whatever it is, it must have to come from both of us. My sister apparently thinks you'll do anything I ask you. I really feel, for the first time, as though I've got her over a barrel. Not a pleasant thought, although I'm sure she suspects I've spent my entire life trying to put her there."

"Freud would have a party."

"Yes."

"Shall we dance?"

"What, me?"

"Why not?"

"All right."

Up they stood, he bowed, she curtsied, and off they went, happy as pie in each other's light arms. It was not an everyday thing to discover someone with whom you could dance well. Even one's husband or lover does not often match terpsichoreally. You remember high school dances and the unlikely partner with whom you found yourself agitating successfully. In a normal circumstance, one wouldn't be caught dead with that person. But there one was, one song after the happy next, unable to stop being Ginger to his Fred, Tina to his Ike, Margot to his Rudolf, childishly delighted and unaccustomedly light upon one's feet. So it was with Claire Breslinsky and Jupiter Dodd. They dipped. They swayed. They did not break at the end of each song, but stood together bright-eyed, shoulders straight, alert for the disc jockey's next selection. He was, they were quite sure, now playing just for them. They switched, at one point, to drinking Absolut and fresh limes, entitling them to quite a bit of ambitious hootchy-kootchy 'midst the malagueña. No one was paying them any attention, or so they believed, and so they persisted cheerfully into the long bright night.

When it was over, Jupiter Dodd drove her home. Her mother slept peacefully on the sofa. Pretty drunk, Claire went upstairs and found Dharma in bed, safe and warm, between Anthony and Floozie. She staggered down the stairs and flung open the refrigerator. There was an awful lot going on in there. Too much, she knew. These days, she found herself preparing meals for her family that she would hitherto not even have sat down to. Pork chops. Nathan's vacuum-packaged hot dogs. Anthony loved them. She did, too. She, great former staunch vegetarian. She tried to remember if she'd bought any of those nice Martin's potato rolls? The whiter the bread, the sooner you're dead, her inner voice told her while her less-evolved libido licked its lips.

The telephone rang. She picked it up before the first ring left off. Her mother slept on, snoring reassuringly inside on the sofa. She was sure it would be Carmela, wanting to dish her guests.

It was Swamiji, just arrived from Delhi, here now at Kennedy, wasn't it exciting? "I am on my way to the land of Berkeley at last, at last. Oh yes." Claire could just see his head wobbling elastically. "I am veddy veddy weary indeed."

"My God!" she shouted, then whispered, "I can't believe it! Where are you now? Just stay right there! Don't move from that spot! I'm coming to pick you up. No, you don't go anywhere, you don't check in, you just stay there exactly where you're standing and I'll be there in twenty minutes. Ten minutes."

"Oh, no, I must protest," came a not-very-convincingly disputing voice, a voice veddy weary indeed.

"This is me, Swamiji," she informed him, using the sassy Brooklyn out-and-out intimidating tone that Johnny used so successfully on her. "Just hold onto your hat."

Claire lurched across the room. Good thing her keys were in her hand already or she never would have found them. It was a little bit like going to pick up Gandhi himself. Swamiji even looked like the old boy, wiry and swaddled in homespun. She turned the radio on as she careened along the Van Wyck, then the freshly paved new airport road, empty at this off hour. Claire made for the international arrivals building, drove right up alongside the privileged cavalcade of taxis, put the gear in park and scanned the near deserted walkways. Her heart filled up and choked when she spotted him. She abandoned her treasured, illegally parked car to the gods and leapt screwily over the hood. Claire covered Swamiji's nut-brown chilly arms with a tarpaulin of imaginary warmth. He was just as she had left him. Her guardianship.

What she was not prepared for was the sight of Narayan as well, literally looming over frail Swamiji, although why she was surprised she couldn't imagine—the idea of Swamiji traveling alone was incomprehensible, he would give his ticket to the first down-and-out who hit on him—so there then was Narayan, the hope of modern India cast in basic bronze, only this Narayan seemed a different fellow altogether. Gone was the shallow, hopeful, extroverted expression of solicitousness he'd worn when she'd known him, the whimsical, silk-shirted, guitar-strumming, well-born, gangly boy whose despairing family had had no other choice than to send him to Swamiji to try and find the sense in him. (It had been that or let him marry that horrifying Vaisya merchant's daughter.)

He was a foot taller, for one thing, and broad. That was her first thought. Her second was, where would she find the sheets? Then she remembered. She could put them on the rug. Freddy's old Dhera Gaz. Floozie wouldn't mind. And there were plenty of old quilts.

She could tell Swamiji was overwhelmed at the sight of her.

"By golly," he said, acting big, "there's a nip to the air."

"Hop in." She threw open the door. "Mr. Kinkaid's gonna really love you."

When they got back to the house, Zinnie was up, searching the front and back lawns with a flashlight for some sign of Claire's body. "Oh, hi," Claire called. "Wait till you see who I've brought."

"Just like that," Zinnie glared. "You know what time it is? It's three-a-fucking clock in the morning!"

Claire didn't know whether to laugh or cry at the sight of Zinnie's snarling, pale white face. What she didn't see was the way Narayan set mesmerized eyes upon Zinnie. And what would have surprised her even more were the bold, unflinching eyes that Zinnie set right back on him.

Zinnie, without waiting to be introduced, stalked haughtily off.

"Gee," said Claire in the doorway, waiting for the two of them to take it all in. On the table, there was a letter addressed to her between the stack of bills. She picked it up. It was, she already knew, from Tree.

CHAPTER 5

Carmela walked into Claire's Sunday-morning kitchen. The smells of garlic and oregano and fresh basil held up her head and made her have to sniff in. "I've got to hand it to you," she said, "marrying an Italian is going to insure us all full stomachs on weekends." And, she thought, bad breath on Monday.

"Isn't it marvelous! Could you hand me that ginger there? I've got to make bean curd for Swamiji, and I don't want to have to save that till later."

"Swamiji?" Had Claire gone and invited those horrid neighbors? Was there no end to her ridiculous communal guilt?

Claire beamed above her bowl of masala and dahl. "I have company. Special visitors from India."

"Oh good." Carmela frowned.

"Try not to sound so thrilled, please."

"All right." She sat down, away from the hubbub of cutlery and chopping blocks. One wouldn't want to be mistakenly recruited.

"I see you shined up those copper pots and molds I gave you."

Claire clicked her tongue. "You wouldn't believe how long it took me to polish them up. I almost hate them. Really. I hope they stay polished for a good long while because I wouldn't want to go through that again in a hurry."

I should have kept them, thought Carmela. I could have had one of Stefan's Polish lackeys do them. They sat and did nothing but drink vodka, they might as well sit and drink vodka and be useful. His Polish mafia. More like his Polish welfare system. No wonder they couldn't afford to have the first floor repainted.

"What's that?" Claire nudged her chin in the direction of Carmela's package.

102

"What, this? Oh, nothing. Just a copy of the play."

"The play?! What do you mean, nothing? Can't I have a look?"

"I sort of thought we could run through it."

Claire wiped her hands on a red-and-white checkered dish-towel and sat down across from Carmela. There was no question of continuing stand-up preparation for the meal. She must give her entire attention to Carmela, or one day it would all be her fault should this play fail. But she really was interested. She couldn't deny that. There would always be the thrill of privilege when the grand big sister deigned to take the younger sibling seriously. She knew Carmela didn't really want to discuss her play, she just needed someone to talk out loud to, someone unimportant who wouldn't say much. One thing she could do now, though, was roll up her ground meat with ice slivers and Locatelli cheese, some breadcrumbs, and an egg.

"What are the little bits of ice for?" Carmela demanded, curious despite herself.

"Keeps the meatball moist while it fries," she said, throwing chopped garlic and basil into the enormous flat bowl.

While Carmela read, Claire rolled. She made little tiny meatballs. Johnny loved them that way and could never get enough. Big fellow that he was, he enjoyed small portions. Lots of small portions. When he discovered two Indians sleeping their transatlantic flights off on the dining room floor, well, here was where she was going to let go and let God. Anyway, hadn't he always said she should invite her friends from overseas to stay? What would he do, leave her? He was certainly going to make a lot of noise. These meatballs would plug him up, and then she could bring up the horse. Although she had considered holding onto this until she absolutely could use it to her advantage, not just as justification for what was her prerogative by right. After all.

"Mom?"

"Yes, Anthony?"

"There are men in the dining room. Dead."

"No, dear, they're sleeping. They're friends of Mommy's."

"I don't think so, Mommy."

"Yes, dear. They are. That's Swamiji, I've always told you about."

"Swamiji?" Anthony turned and went back inside to have another look. What a terrible disappointment! Mommy had always told him about the Indians! Indians wore paint and feathers and carried tomahawks. These fellows here smelled very curious and they looked like every new storeowner along Jamaica Avenue. These could not be the Indians she'd been talking about! Floozie left his arms and walked carefully over to the two of them. He hoped she would bite them. Instead, she sniffed the narrow, older one and cuddled into the crook of his arm and went back to sleep. Uh! Disgusted, Anthony went back up the stairs to wake up Michaelaen. He had seen Dharma in his sleeping bag as he'd gotten out of bed, but he didn't want to wake her up. He sighed. Even he didn't have the answers to what was going on with Dharma.

Anthony, proprietor, elbows out, trudged sturdily along the bannistered hallway, went up the narrow third-floor stairs and was stopped by the sound of Aunt Zinnie singing to Michaelaen in their big room. The both of them were holed up in the closet and the door was shut. Michaelaen sometimes spent the whole night long in there. Anthony sat down on the window seat and waited and listened. Aunt Zinnie was singing "You Don't Know Me." When she sang the words "I never knew the art of making love, though my heart burned with love for you," her voice did not crack or falter, but it reached so sad a sound that Anthony put his fists in both his eyes, disenchanted but still listening, for another little while, and he stayed still.

Downstairs, Claire and Carmela had stopped talking as well. Zinnie's voice, even when she held onto it, traveled far and wide and went into the very you of you. Claire held her mortar and pestle, cut gentle roses on her listening hands, and Carmela turned her head so Claire wouldn't see the depth of her renowned to be forgotten, but still very human emotion.

Swamiji stood, little fellow, stock-still at the tall pantry door. Claire was delighted to see him. She restrained herself from jumping up and throwing her arms around him. She pressed her fingertips against themselves and put her face behind them. He did, too. Then he came, smiling, into the room. "Jesus!" Carmela shouted, jumping out of her chair in fright. Claire put one hand on her shoulder in a calming, threatening gesture. "Carmela, this is my dear friend, Swami Brahmananda. Swamiji, my sister, Carmela Stefanovitch."

Unperturbed by Carmela's reaction, Swamiji calmly greeted them, then passed them, covered his body with his dark cashmere shawl which, when opened, turned into a cozy burnoose. He went into the back yard and took up the lotus position in a shaft of warm sunlight on a table underneath the grapevine.

His eyeballs went up into his head and he stared at the women with the whites of his eyes. Carmela, still grasping her chest, shuddered. "You're not going to let him stay there like that!" she whispered shrilly.

"Are you kidding? I wish he would stay here forever. He's filling our home with good karma."

"Does Mommy know?"

Claire stood and busied herself with sudsing a board in the sink. "What does that mean, 'Does Mommy know'? As if we were going to get in trouble like little kids or something. For bringing something forbidden into the house. This is my home, after all. And Mommy would welcome any of my guests as I would hers."

"Oh, I doubt that," said Carmela. "Has she seen his royal nakedness, there?"

"Carmela! He's not naked. He wears his little loin cloth thing."

They both laughed.

"Actually," Claire said, sitting back down, "I think she missed him. She runs out of here like a bat out of hell when she wakes up. On go the slippers and her trench coat and she flies home to get breakfast ready for Daddy. If she had seen him, she would have come to wake me up. Or at least called the police."

"And who, pray tell," Carmela did her Our Miss Brooks impression, "is this?"

"Ah, Narayan," Claire said, "come in, come in. Meet Carmela." Narayan, educated in the ways of the world, auspiciously kissed Carmela's hand. Carmela wore a Girard Perregaux watch, which didn't escape Narayan. He might have changed a lot, but Claire remembered still the skinny boy who plied her for information, any information at all, if you please, concerning the who's-who and what-fors of the West. Claire looked down at her own big-faced old Croton. It was a man's watch, from the thirties, sensible and plain, with a brown pigskin band. She held it fondly to her ear. You could pay your great fortune for your watch, as Carmela's husband had undoubtedly done, but there was no sound on Earth quite as fine as the intricate, rich hurry-hurry of an old wind-up Swiss. She smiled at Narayan. "Swamiji is 'sitting' out in the yard. Will you join him or have breakfast first?"

Only the great dignity of his class and the long suffering rigidity of Swamiji's training kept Narayan from flinging himself across the table first and scarfing everything edible in sight. She saw those hungry eyes. She remembered how, as a boy, he had literally wept at the loss of a pistachio ice cream cone in the dirt. She had loved him for that, she remembered. There was nothing more responsive in Claire than to a man's great battle with roaring appetite. To this she could relate, having a roaring one herself.

Narayan bowed his head to this strange new matriarch, this former maharani—once stick-thin, her only real possession her precious bag of cameras—with whom he'd joked and sallied. She was quite different now. She must be very rich as well. The size of this house! Narayan opened the back door and saw the great yard bright with yellow sunshine. There were mums in all colors, and fire flowers lined the ivy covered garage. Small trees of roses grew from a bed of Carribbean colored portulaca. A fan of water sprinkled to and fro from a yellow plastic fountain apparatus attached to the hose. Geraniums in red and purple rimmed the long, broad beds of grass. It was the season of marigolds and they were everywhere, small and tall, saffron-bright orange and shimmering in the fresh, clean, start-again light of morning.

The sound of Zinnie's voice floated over and filled up the yard on the breeze. ". . . Afraid and shy, I let my chance go by, a chance that you might love me, too." This, then, was Narayan's first glimpse of America. He breathed the air. He walked gingerly across the grass to the redwood picnic table upon which Swamiji sat cross-legged under the ceiling of grapes. He joined him there and joined him far away, right there where he truly was.

Carmela watched him through the blinds. "Not bad. Just let them know from the first that you'll be needing their room vacant by Wednesday. Say you've got guests coming from Germany or something. Otherwise, they'll just stay forever. They're probably out of money already. Next thing you know they'll be asking you to sponsor them for green cards."

"Carmela, it's not like that. Swamiji is on his way to Berkeley. He's been invited to speak at some seminar about the value of herbs in medicine today. Narayan is accompanying him. Narayan might appear to be nothing but hunk at first glance, but after his years with Swamiji he went on to university at Oxford, my dea-ah, just like your Stefan. Only I believe he left, unlike Stefan, with a First, returning to India on a fellowship to assist Swamiji."

"Good God. Not really?"

"Yes, really."

"I wonder if he's brought a tux?" She peeked back out through the blinds.

"I don't think so. At least not from the look of their packs. They've come as traditional Indians, it seems."

"I'll bet I could get them to speak at Stefan's ladies' luncheon next month."

"That's quite a change from 'scoot them out as soon as you can,' " said Claire.

Carmela snorted. "Who knew?"

"Hello, Dharma." Claire looked up. She stopped herself from taking the child in her arms. She was covered in her rumply curls and Claire couldn't help knowing how her mother must have loved to hold her and smell her and keep her cozy on her lap, the way she did her Anthony. Dharma stood there in her pink nightgown, bewildered.

"Something woke me up," she accused Claire.

"Yes, well, we're well into the morning now and people are out and about. Toast? Eggo? Cheerios? Frosted Flakes?"

"Frosted Flakes, please," Dharma chose, and she sat down at the table.

"Well, I can see we'll never get to my play," said Carmela rudely.

"Don't be silly," Claire said, shutting the fridge with her toe. "Orange juice or apple juice?"

"Orange."

"Now. Where were we?"

"Snow White."

"Yes, and why Snow White again?"

"It's a myth," Carmela said. "It didn't start with Walt Disney, you know."

"No, I know. 'Schneewittchen' has been terrifying German children for ages." She scratched her head. "And what part are we up to, now?"

"We hadn't started."

"Right. Okay . . . So. What's the opening scene?"

"The curtain opens on the queen, not a kid, brushing her hair before her Depression-furniture mirror. She's an aging rock singer."

"Oh, that's good. You could use that great old set Mommy's got in your old room."

"That's what I thought. Anyway, she reads a resumé from a new backup singer, some young girl who's applying for the job."

Claire touched her apron pocket where Tree's letter was.

"What?" Carmela said.

"No, nothing."

"Yes, something. You went all white. What don't you like?"

"Nothing," Claire lied. "I just wish Zinnie could get in on this. She would be some great Snow White."

Carmela smacked the table. Dharma jumped.

"Exactly!" cried Carmela. "If you would talk to her, she would."

"Please. Zinnie does as she pleases. Always has. What makes you think anything I would say would make a dif—"

"You know, I really hate you two." Zinnie came in shaking her head. "I really do. Plotting and conniving behind people's backs. Why don't you just come out and ask a body?"

"Hah," said Carmela. "As if you would."

Zinnie said, "How about, 'Zinnie, I would really like it if you would be in my play.'"

Carmela swallowed. "Why, Zinnie, I really would love it if you would be my Snow White."

"Well, I won't."

"You see!" Carmela shouted at Claire. "You see how she is!

108

She won't be in it but she wants the chance to turn me down. You're happy now, you little bitch?"

Claire and Zinnie both looked at Dharma but Dharma, seemingly unmoved, continued to eat her Frosted Flakes.

Zinnie, calm, said, "I said I wouldn't play Snow White. I never said I wouldn't be in your play."

"What?" Carmela and Claire said in harmony. Zinnie's abhorrence of public attention was well known to them. The idea that she would participate in any way was something entirely new. Their father loved Zinnie's singing voice so much that he would burst into tears when she went into any refrain. This so embarrassed her that she had simply given up singing around any of them. And so it had been for some years. If ever you wanted to catch her, you had to do it from another floor.

"I would, however," Zinnie said as she sat down with them, "consider the part of the wicked queen."

"Would you, really?" Carmela smiled, her eyes twinkling. She gazed off into space and raised up her hands as if she saw some vision. "I can just see it. Yes. We could give all the good songs to you. And give the little ingenue ditties to someone really young and hateful."

"Portia McTavish," said Dharma.

They looked at her, as if for the first time.

"Of course," agreed Carmela.

They all had a good laugh.

"What's this?" Their mother, Mary, stood in the doorway behind an assortment of boxes and bags from Gebhard's bakery. "Conviviality?"

"Hi, Mommy." Up they all jumped and unloaded her of her things. The buttery smells of special crumb cakes escaped through their white paper baggage.

"Let's get this baby into effect," said Zinnie and scooped one out and slid it onto the table.

"Mind you only eat the one." Mary lifted off her hat and patted her hair in the pantry mirror. "The cookies in the box are for the children. The crullers in the big bag there are for Johnny and no one else, and the other special crumb is for your company,

Claire." She knicked her head to the side as though there were water in one ear, indicating the men outside in the garden.

"So you've met my guests," Claire said.

"No, but I nearly tripped over them on my way to wash up in the wee hours." Mary sat down and faced them, her three long-haired daughters, not one of them in a hurry for once. It seemed to Mary the last time she'd lain eyes on the three of them not running out the door it was last Christmas morning, each one of them busy at opening her gifts. She took them all in like a breath of air.

Claire put a mug of hot tea down in front of her mother.

"Kind of you to think of them, like that, Ma."

"Where's Dad?" asked Carmela.

"Where else would he be?" That meant he was at the store, his hardware store. Even though he'd sold out to a family of Korean people, he still spent most of his time there. The customers probably still thought he ran the place, but he didn't, he had no business there, not even for a small salary. But that was where he would go, every day, climbing the ladder for squirrel screws nobody else would know where to find, chatting with this one and that.

"He'll be along when it's time to eat," Mary said. "Mr. Healy from Jacksonville is stopping in the store, Stan figures. His sister's on her last legs in Mary Immaculate and they flew up to see her. Helloo, Dharma! There's a good girl, eating your Frosties. Where are my grandsons?"

"Michaelaen's having his shower," Zinnie said. "And Anthony went out with Floozie. I'd better go get Michaelaen out of there before he uses all the hot water."

"What, in the front or the back?" Mary asked Claire.

"In the front."

"Do you think that's wise, dear?"

"I'll go check on him," Claire said, then she really had to fry those meatballs. "Anthony!" she shouted out the front door. She saw him leaning on the johnny pump up the block, expressing his views on the-good-Lord-knew-what to busy Floozie, sniffing the information-laden earth.

"Bring her back up here," called Claire.

"She has to take a dump," Anthony informed the neighborhood.

Floozie, yearning for oblivion, went round and round in a circle.

"I'm coming," Claire said between a whisper and a sentence to no one, grabbing a ready penny-candy paper bag and going out to join them.

"Hi, there!"

Claire turned, caught unawares, and was face to face with Andrew Dover. He was a handsome bugger, was Andrew, even at this awkward time of day, but then so many men were like that, she'd noticed, not like women, who had their good hours and their bad. She herself was having a crummy one right now, she knew, sweaty from standing over the stove and all the rest. She stood with the open brown bag in her gritty, eager hand and the letter from his dead wife in her peach-colored apron pocket.

"I'm glad I didn't have to ring your bell," he said in confidential tones. "I know you've got guests."

"Just family," she defended them, forgetting for a moment that Swamiji and Narayan were hardly family in this fellow's opinion, his daughter inside. He'd caught her, as usual, off guard.

Andrew rubbed his hands together. "So," he said, indicating Carmela's silver car, "could you move your guest's car from the front of my house? I need the space free for a delivery."

"Oh. Sure. Of course." Why so formal? He knew it was Carmela's car. He must. How many brand-new silver British Sterlings with DPL plates were there in Richmond Hill, after all?

He smiled and turned. Was that it?

"Andrew," she began. She didn't care now if her tone was harsh. "Don't you think you'd better go in and say good morning to your daughter?"

Not offended, not at all, Andrew gave a breezy tut-tut-tut and kept on going. Then he stopped. He'd thought of something. He turned and gave Claire his most charming smile. "As long as she's doing so well with you—" he said. "I mean, if it ain't broke, don't fix it. Agreed?"

"No, Andrew, I don't agree. You're her father and right now I—"

"Mom!" Anthony interrupted her, "Mom, c'mere with that bag!"

Claire abandoned her disapproval and took care of what needed be, then followed Anthony back into the house. Dharma was leaning up against the table, her mouth full with big buttery crumbs, and across the street you could hear Andrew hammering. Claire felt like screaming. "Carmela," she said, "Andrew Dover asked if you would move your car."

"Why?" she looked up, annoyed.

"He's having something delivered and he would like the front of his house free."

"Who makes deliveries on Sunday?" she asked. She would have refused, but Dharma stood there still, watching, and she thought twice. She went out, finding the keys in her black Coach bag. Claire had Carmela's old brown one, which she cherished. Carmela had literally thrown it at her one day, insisting she didn't want it anymore. It looked too battered, she'd said, which was exactly why Claire adored it straightaway—it reminded her of an old saddlebag—butterscotch-colored and soft with use. She'd slathered it in lanolin hand cream and buffed it dry with a Turkish towel rag.

Zinnie, inside, smacked Michaelaen on his rear end.

They all looked up. Michaelaen would not cry in front of them, but he wouldn't come in either. Claire pretended not to have heard. That was Zinnie's business and she wouldn't interfere. She wasn't going to trade horrified looks with her mother across the table, either. If Mary had chosen never to hit her children, that was Mary. Personally, Claire tended to agree with Zinnie, lately. The things her son said to her! Any day now she was going to smack Anthony as well. The only time she'd really done it until now was that time when he was two and he'd raced, regardless, into the street. She'd whacked him good that time. Scared the pants off him, too. Well. At least he'd never gone into the street after that. Not even a little bit. Maybe he was going to be psychologically deranged whenever he crossed the street as an adult, but at least he would be there to cross that street. Claire sighed. Who knew anything?

A long time ago, very pregnant with Anthony, Claire had

strolled imperiously, benevolently, down Liberty Avenue. A mother crouched on the ground over her tear-stained three-year-old. She was shrieking, no holds barred, at the stubborn little boy who, even now, refused to have his shoe returned to his foot. The woman's eye caught Claire's appalled gape. Never, but never, would Claire subject her precious child to this humiliation and disgrace, and her expression said very plainly so.

The woman glowered at Claire. She looked Claire up and down. Slowly her nostrils flared. "Just you wait," she rasped.

And so it was. Claire saw that woman's face each time she yelled at Anthony, by God. Every single time.

"Oh, yeah?" Michaelaen's whining voice brought her back to the present. "Then I'm not going with him at all."

"Fine with me," Zinnie's voice shot back. "That just means no TV all weekend. No skin off my teeth."

She came into the kitchen with her lips pressed tight against each other and two bright patches of red on her cheeks. Her dark-blond hair had been pulled from its knot in her rage and she looked, Claire could not help but think, like Jupiter's symbol itself.

Narayan, disarmed, stood up. Zinnie flushed. Annoyed at herself for standing so still at the sight of this stunning hulk of a man, she threw her strong shoulders back and ripped right past him without so much as a how-do-you-do.

Now most people, when they came in contact with Swamiji, acted differently than they normally would. They pretended to be calm, first off, and made a great show of arranging their auras into decency. So it was a great treat for Swamiji to witness manifest emotion. He smiled, and his little head went back and forth and round and round the way an Indian's will.

Pleased, Claire presented her sister. "Swamiji," she said, "this is my sister Zinnie."

"Delighted." He bowed. "The tempest from the night."

"North American wildcat," Narayan said, his well-bred voice mocking, but his eyes unconditionally sincere. "Very rare."

"Don't anybody get up," Zinnie cracked as she sat down hard on her empty shoulder holster.

When Carmela came back inside, Stefan was with her. He'd been jogging through Forest Park; he did this every day. They all hated him for it. Stefan was fit, something they would all very much love to be. Not enough to do too much about it, but enough, at least, to hate him. The thing was, Stefan was so rich, lived on such another planet, *came* from such another planet, that it was difficult to know on which level one should hate him. Ah, well. Claire looked around her. This was hardly poverty. And all the money in Stefan's world hadn't made her sister happy.

Stefan retired to the kitchen bathroom for a little while, helping himself to a thorough sink bath. He was meticulous, was Stefan. He wouldn't want to offend. Affectionately, Claire went to fetch her brother-in-law a nice fluffy towel. One of those big bath sheets Johnny had come home from Atlantic City with would be good. She knocked on the door and passed it in.

"Thanks, darling," Stefan said, and she stood there as he closed the door, washed his hands, and straightened the towels. It wasn't the darling bit that got her; Stefan called everyone "darling." No, that wasn't what froze her momentarily to the spot, it was the alcohol-tinged wind that contained it. Claire walked busiedly over to the kitchen sink and washed the arugula leaves.

There had been a time, quite a long, exasperating time, when Johnny's and her married life hadn't been muddled simply by financial woes and everyday arguments. What had started off as Johnny's occasional beer had become Johnny's guzzling beer had become Claire spending an awful lot of her pregnant afternoons returning empties. That became gee, this is getting a little ridiculous, which became not only no one to talk to when Johnny was gone, but no one to talk to when Johnny was home.

It was her mother who'd caught on. Mary's father had been an alcoholic, had abused her whole family verbally, had wound up beating them, she would never forget, and she knew the signs better than anyone. She knew it in her own daughter's forced cheerfulness, her lapses into dark, narrow facial passages when she thought she went unobserved. Mary had had to shake her to get it out of her, but then out it had come, the lot of it, the whole sorry story. And Mary, instead of giving Claire sympathy, as Claire had expected, had blamed her, had actually shouted at her, as though she were standing there sound asleep. She'd shouted at her that she was enabling him to go on living like that every time she cleaned up his vomit, so he would not be faced with it the next day. Claire shuddered. She remembered it all, all too well.

Claire felt Mary's watchful eyes even now. "I don't know why they can't get the sand out of the arugula before they sell it to you," she laughed.

"You'd think they would," Mary agreed. "The prices they charge."

Claire hoped Mary wouldn't go quoting those prices just now. She could just imagine Swamiji's shock if she did. Oh, well. That didn't matter. It did one good, anyway, to be reminded how ridiculous one's priorities were. She smiled at Swamiji and he giggled back at her. She had to go over and give him a great hug, which her mother didn't like at all, but Swamiji squirmed with such happy delight that even she laughed. And Dharma laughed as well, Claire noticed, while the dog dug herself a cozy little spot in the lump of an old couch pillow Anthony had lugged down from the attic.

The front doorbell rang. It was Freddy and Stan, and Floozie went a bit wild in her enthusiastic defense. Any two fellows would have been big enough to start her off, but the fact that Freddy was one of them—Freddy, her betrayer, Freddy, her first great love who had not only left her, but had abandoned her to prison and probable death—well, hell hath no fury.

It took Michaelaen in the end to come downstairs and calm the dog down. Michaelaen didn't want to come downstairs, and only this mission of mercy would bring him. He'd brought her soothing tick-tock clock and smoothed her fur with gentle words. Floozie finally relented and sighed, point made, family alerted. Claire couldn't help chuckling to herself. They'd all been so adamant in their insistence to let sleeping dogs lie, as it were.

"Scrappy little bit," Stan admitted as he moved onto the bench.

"Hi, Dad." Carmela leaned over and gave her father a peck on the cheek.

"Who's that?" Stan pretended not to recognize her. He shook Swamiji's hand. "I know my daughter all these years, and I've never seen her in the same thing twice."

Freddy, more rattled than he let on by the ferocity of this horrendous dog—this, this mongrel—placed himself in between

Stan and Zinnie. God. He should have had her put to sleep when he'd had the chance. He'd only taken her to keep in the restaurant overnight, anyway.

"So." Stan picked up the first of a row of ironed napkins lined up for the dinner table and dropped it to his lap. "They actually talked you into taking that pup, eh? Zinnie said they would. 'Just you leave it to me, Dad,' she said. And she was right. A bit of a risk, I thought, driving it all the way out to that there animal shelter. But Zinnie said, 'Relax, I know my man. Once a sucker, always a sucker.' "

Claire, who had not really been listening, poured the fat into a cut-off milk container and jolted the hot pan under a steaming sear of water from the faucet. "A sucker?" She looked at Zinnie, who was trying not to laugh.

"Bigmouth," Carmela mouthed.

"Dad," Zinnie said as she served him one of Johnny's designated crullers and poured him a cup of coffee, "Stefan's here. He's just primping in the bathroom."

"Ah." Stan rubbed both hands together. He approved of this son-in-law. Good Polish stock. "This calls for a celebration. Any vodka in the larder, Claire?"

"Uh. In honor of his holiness, here, I thought we'd wait till dinner." She didn't like to mention she'd polished that bottle off before they'd even moved in.

"What about that Wild Turkey?" Zinnie suggested.

"Hmm," said Claire. That one was gone, too. It wasn't that she minded having admitted drinking her own liquor. She just would rather not, she explained to herself. And she couldn't well blame it on anyone else. They all knew Johnny didn't touch it anymore.

The conversation had moved along to other things. They were talking about cars, now. Stan was explaining to Narayan how you had to have a lot of air and a little gas to be efficient. "A balance, so you completely burn the gas, see. The mixture I had going was just too rich for my old Betsy."

"Betsy," Carmela yawned, "is my father's favorite child. His Chevy."

"Chevrolet," Freddy clarified.

"Well, she was blowing black smoke. It was raw gas."

Stan said, "I had to adjust the choke. The choke controls the mixture of air and gas.

"When the choke closes, it increases the gas intake. The more closed it is, the more gas it sucks. You see, the pistons going up and down cause a vacuum pulling whatever is in the choke area down to the manifold." The minute he said "manifold," Narayan knew he was lost. He continued to look into Stan's busy mind through his eyes, but he kept seeing nothing but Zinnie.

Everyone else watched Stan with dazed, uncomprehending, polite expressions.

"Hey," he said. "Here I was getting four miles to the gallon and now I'm getting eight. Eight!"

"Hmm!" Narayan smiled at him.

Anthony leaned on Swamiji's naked knee and peered into his face. "You have a elephant?"

"Not many left of those, eh, Swamiji?" Stefan leaned towards him.

"No, not many. One friend of mine does. Jagir Singh. He has a lovely—"

"There was a famous bow hunter," Stefan said, "can't think of his name, he felt he could kill an elephant with an arrow. Well, no one could do that, the arrow would just bounce off his hide—but he'd insisted that he could. Everyone laughed at him. And then he did it." Stefan grinned. "Does anyone know how?"

Carmela drummed the table with wifely impatience. "No, of course we don't know. Just tell us."

"He shot the elephant in the ear."

"Yuch," said Claire.

"What he did," Stefan said, "was draw a line back from where the eye is, back to the ear, and he shot the bugger, thwack, into the brain and killed him dead."

Swamiji looked out the window, now.

"Through the flap, of course," Stefan said. "This was in Africa, though. I think."

"Oh!" Mary said. "That reminds me. Mr. Kratzer was up in the woods Tuesday and he let his Scottie, you know his cute little black Scottie, the one ran around like a bossy little sheriff—"

"Yeah, yeah, yeah. So?" Zinnie said.

"Well he let him have a run around on his own and he lost sight of him for one moment. Off chasing a squirrel he went just for one moment and those wild dogs took off chasing after him. They got him, too!"

"What?" they all said.

"Yes."

"Is he dead?"

"No, but he might as well be. Those bloody dogs tore him up nice and proper."

"Gee, whiz," Zinnie said.

"They come tear up my pails," Freddy said, "I'm putting poison out."

"Well, that's what everyone is saying," Mary said. "But you can't poison animals."

"I wouldn't hesitate," Stefan sniffed, remembering how he'd had to kick a couple of them off last week, while jogging through the woods. Unnerving, it had been.

"And what about the rest of the animals? Or some innocent dog on a leash, sniffing by. You can't," Mary insisted.

"One could put out black pepper," Swamiji suggested.

"And rose branches," Claire added. She wanted to take those blankets and packs off the rug in the dining room and get someone to help her bring them upstairs. Swamiji and Narayan could have the other third-floor room, across from Zinnie and Michaelaen. She left everyone, for the moment; she didn't really need any help. She took Swamiji's and Narayan's packs and lugged them up the stairs. She opened the window and let the air sweep through. They were going to love this room; no one had used it yet. It had, before Mrs. Kinkaid died, been her sewing room, and the dainty bouquets of violets through ribbon stripes on aged cream-colored wallpaper were very pretty, very quaint. There were also two big, low-to-the-floor windows that looked out onto the street and up to the park. From this part of the house more than anywhere else did you feel how attached you were to the dense woods, as you looked down into the tree boughs here. Claire went over to one of the windows and knelt down. What an absolutely wonderful house her husband had bought them. She held herself with her arms and felt emotional, sentimental tears start up when she suddenly caught sight of what it was that Andrew Dover was having delivered across the street. My God. She covered her mouth with one horrified hand. It was a huge and futuristic satellite dish. It could not be. It was. This was too obscene to be believed. She had to notify the others. Claire went swiftly, quietly down the stairs. She stopped at hers and Johnny's bedroom door and looked in to see the reassuring curve of his swarthy arm on the quilt, but it wasn't there. It wasn't anywhere. She stuck her body in and called his name. He wasn't there. Bewildered, she went the rest of the way downstairs.

"Anthony," Claire interrupted, "when did Daddy go out?"

"Early. He came in and gave me a kiss and told me to go back to sleep."

"All right."

"What's the matter, Claire?" Mary asked.

"Andrew Dover is having a satellite dish installed on his roof."

"Is he really?" Zinnie got up and had a look out the window.

"That'll cost him a pretty penny," said Stan.

"At least someone will have something interesting to watch at prime time," Freddy said to Stefan, and they both laughed.

"I can't believe this," said Claire.

"Not only that," Carmela, the Francophile, panted excitedly, "he can get television directly from Paris."

"What?" cried Claire. "This is too much!"

"Calm yourself, Claire," Swamiji leaned forward, concerned.

"You don't understand!" Claire cried. "This man's wife died two weeks ago!"

"Claire!" Mary grew angry. "Dharma is just outside!"

"Right. She's in front of our house watching her father install a multi-thousand-dollar monster on her roof across the street. Which I am absolutely sure she knew nothing about. Don't you think that's a little bit strange?"

"Well," Stan started to say, "people do all sorts of strange things when they lose a loved one. They—"

Claire interrupted him, "This just is not right, I tell you!"

"What is it exactly you object to?" Carmela wanted to know. "That he's getting on with his life or that he's ruining your view?"

119

Claire thought for a moment. "Both," she said. "And I thought Tree was your friend."

"She was the star of my play. I have more reason to be upset than you do. I mean, honestly, you hadn't laid eyes on her for years and years."

"What has that got to do with the fact that her husband is acting like this is the best thing that ever happened to him?"

"Claire!" Stan said.

"I hardly think—" Stefan said.

"You mean Tree never called you, Claire?" Zinnie frowned.

"Can't we change the subject?" Carmela moaned.

How, Claire wondered, could they all be so blind? Why were they making excuses for such abominable behavior? Because, she imagined, they hadn't been exposed to all the incriminating facts that she had.

"I saw you going into church this morning, Claire," Stefan said, appropriately enough.

"Oh, yes?"

"I thought you were out shooting houses this morning," Carmela accused.

"I was. I just like to start the day with a calm meditation." Freddy had come in while Claire was upstairs, and he and Stefan were acting with the same embarrassed delirium the little boys in Claire's fourth-grade class had done. Freddy had made a paper airplane of Mary's dollar-off detergent coupon. He shot it into Stefan's ear.

"Come on, you guys." Claire picked up the paper airplane and aimed it at Freddy.

Johnny stood silently outside the kitchen and beheld this scene. Last night, when he had gone to bed, his house had been at peace. There were sleeping children, a mother-in-law, and a sister or two, but this was almost a carnival.

Claire looked up, elbows deep into pouring bubbling chocolate pudding into the good stemware (the only set she had that matched, and that there would be enough of). "What?" she said, her eyes round in question.

Johnny turned his face. He couldn't bear to have them all see him so moved. It looked like a fucking movie in there. Relatives.

Meatballs frying. Chocolate pudding. Smells that would set you into a spin. Company. Johnny hadn't seen a house that full that wasn't a drug bust in fifteen years. He smelled like a horse. He went up the stairs before any of the others saw him, and hopped into the shower.

"Narayan," Claire said, "would you pass me that quart of milk there, please? Narayan? Narayan!"

"What?" said Narayan. "Oh. Sorry. What did you say?"

"Jet lag," Freddy laughed, indulgent towards flawless manhood.

"Never mind." Claire reached across the table herself and snatched it. Narayan could not take his eyes off Zinnie. Zinnie leaned, unperturbed, on her sister Carmela's blue coat. She combed her hair back with her fingers. Her lips were parted. Her knees were only just opened the slightest, finger breadth. Claire watched a moment longer than she should have and witnessed their eyes, heated siphons of what was up, meet.

Oh boy, thought Claire. She stirred her milk into a saucepan for the new batch, poured in My-T-Fine chocolate, and stirred and stirred until it came to a boil. Now, she decided. Now is the moment I would most love a cigarette. But she wouldn't; something inside her still pushed it off. She was remembering now that morning she had sneaked into an extremely early mass and walked up to the front. She floated, a ghostly Chagall figure, back to the tall, tall church, all of great archways and domes and oranges and greens, with stained-glass, extravagant, episodic windows in rich blues and beet-pink reds and whites that were silvery translucent like shaved abalone. They were magnificent. Jewels leaking rivers of prismed sunlight through the warm colors and cold corridors, through the vast spaces where tile and oak pews were the last thing to meet them. There then was Claire, dressed in drab colors to watch and not be watched. There was Claire, eyes leaking with the sheer terrifying beauty and drama of her own coming death and the passage of her soul to another dimension; one, her certainty, the other, her faith. She took a deep breath and filled her lungs with the here and now, wondering, finally, if there were no more small children waiting unknowingly inside her. "Yes," she answered her mother at the end of the few seconds it had taken these thoughts to fit in. "It was Johnny, all right."

"Daddy!" Anthony heard from the yard and ran in and up the stairs. They had heard every word, those kids.

"Well," Mary said, "I was waiting in the hopes of saying hello, but I hear from the pipes he's already in the shower."

"Aren't you staying for dinner?" Claire asked. She was peeved, now, at Johnny. He could have at least stuck his head in. Buying a racehorse was one thing. Deliberate bad manners quite another.

Mary stood and went in search of her hat.

"She's taking the bus up to Deauville," Zinnie said. "You know. To visit Mrs. Dixon."

"What, today? With everyone here?"

Mary, having found her hat, now went in search of her bag.

"Mrs. Dixon?" Swamiji inquired politely.

"Mrs. Dixon," Carmela informed him, "is a murderess who has been committed to a prison for the insane upstate in Deauville, New York. She was my mother's neighbor and my mother continues to visit her."

"By bus." Zinnie glared at her father.

"She shouldn't be visiting her at all." Stan shrugged. "I drive her to the bus station and that's all."

"Mom," Claire said, standing still, "I didn't know you still visit her."

Mary came busily back into the room, opened the cabinet with a mirror on the inside of its door, and applied her lipstick before them all. They watched her, aghast.

"Every fourth Sunday, she goes," Stan said.

"Not only she goes," Zinnie said as she threw her head back in disdain, "she brings her crumb cake from Gebhard's. And then the two of them walk around the asylum hallway just as cozy as you please."

"Really?" Stefan looked up, amazed. "They let her walk around outside?"

"That's this pansy Liberal Party stuff," Stan sniffed. "All prisoner's rights. What about the mothers of those kids she did in, eh? What about them? What about victim's rights?"

"It's not like that at all." Mary tightened her lips. Mrs. Dixon

122

was writing a book and she, Mary, was helping her do it. It was a terrible book. All about what had happened to her as a child.

It's so horrible children can't talk about the things that really hurt, thought Mary. And so they say nothing until sometimes, it all comes out in a horrifying reenactment. Mary blamed herself. This was her way of making recompense. She should have noticed sooner. If she hadn't been so preoccupied with her own problems, her own flesh and blood, she might have seen it, *should* have seen it, wouldn't she have? And so, yes, she was helping.

"I can't believe it," Claire said.

"Oh, sit down, Claire," Carmela said. "You can't believe anything today. Just sit down."

"Do you have the bus schedule, Stan?" Mary put powder on her nose.

"Got it." Stan stood reluctantly. Boy, did he love arugula salad, with that gorgonzola and the chopped egg, the way Claire did it up.

"Save a dinner for your father, Claire." Mary read his mind. "Put it in aluminum foil and he can just pop it into my microwave. He can pick it up after he comes back from the city."

"Mrs. Dixon," Carmela continued, enjoying Narayan and Swamiji's horrified fascination, "went on a rampage of murder in this very neighborhood."

"Yeah," Zinnie said, "and the people she killed were all children."

"Goodness!" Swamiji was appalled. Narayan made a face. He looked away. He didn't like to hear about such unpleasant things.

"She took their pictures and she killed them," Carmela continued, her eyes glowing.

"Do you mind?" Stefan said.

"Can't we find something else to discuss?" Stan agreed. He didn't like to see Zinnie upset.

"Zinnie's own son," Carmela informed Narayan and Swamiji, "Michaelaen, watched Mrs. Dixon photograph one of the children she intended to kill."

"Your father said that's enough." Mary narrowed her eyes.

And tried to kill me as well, thought Claire. Pulling a radio down and yanking it into my tub. Claire had escaped only by jumping out and answering the opportunely ringing phone. She remembered still the silent feeling in the house then, the palpable air of treachery. She had never told Mary about that part, worried that the poor woman had gone through enough. She doubted that if Mary knew that, she would still visit Mrs. Dixon. Frenzy was one thing, premeditation quite another. Claire shook her head sorrowfully. She held the little dog Floozie, who'd jumped up to her lap. "I just don't understand how you can go and visit that woman. After the things she did."

"She is sick," Mary said, robotlike. "There were things done to her, to make her that way."

"Yes," Claire said, "but to your own grandson!"

"She never did nothin' to Michaelaen," Mary whispered shrilly.

"Claire." Carmela nudged her. "Michaelaen's coming in."

They were all profoundly silent as Michaelaen came obliviously in, went to the sink, and washed his hands. The back of his neck told him they were all watching. He continued to lather his hands with soft-smelling oatmeal soap, but he turned his cheek slightly.

"How are they doing across the street?" Mary asked him.

"Hanging cables down the side of the house," Michaelaen said shyly.

Claire held her head. She saw the way they looked at her. They thought she was paranoid, reliving the excitement of that horrifying time, a time that inadvertently had brought her so much. She was a mother, now. She must think about that and not go making rash accusations. She put her hand around the letter in her pocket and went swiftly to talk to Johnny.

"What's with her?" Stan followed her out with his eyes.

"She just up and runs away," Freddy shook his head at Narayan, including him in his pert assessment of Claire's erratic behavior.

Narayan glared at him. "The best thing you can do is run away from evil, not fight it!"

"I'm afraid I don't agree with you there, old chap," Stefan said, his shoulders squared for German tanks and prison camps.

"The moment you begin to fight evil," Swamiji said swiftly, "you become part of evil yourself."

"Who is evil?" Mary cried, chip on shoulder well in place.

"More likely," mused Stefan, chewing his lip, concerned, "she's having a nervous breakdown."

"Claire?" Zinnie pooh-poohed the idea. "Breslinskys don't have nervous breakdowns."

"There's never been a nervous breakdown in the Breslinsky family," said Mary.

Stefan watched the empty doorway through which Claire had run. He put his slender hands into tweedy, well-turned pockets, and within a voice entirely Dr. Jackowitz he said, "Well." He puffed on his mean little pipe. "I suggest a few weeks at Cascade." And they (all but the Indians) couldn't help but let out with a mean-spirited little cavalcade of laughter.

Claire stood outside the shower door and looked at Johnny's puddle of clothes on the bed. This was the bed she had always wanted, with the man she had not even dared dream of. The windows faced the east and south. There was the still morning light to match the buttery walls. Even from here she could smell the clothes. What a smell! Women whose husbands are having affairs can smell the other woman on them. This is a well-known fact. So that was it. He was having an affair after all. She sat down on the bed by the clothes. Did people really die of broken hearts? She was lurched back to harsh reality and moved herself over some actual distance. Sheesh, what a smell. Johnny opened the shower-stall door and jumped when he saw her. Guilty conscience. More evidence. So: He was having an affair with a rancid gorilla.

He came shamelessly out, the great hulk of a man. She watched him. He used his towel like a dishtowel on that furry, humongous body: circling, stropping, shining. Then he turned on her hair dryer and aimed it consecutively, hum-ti-dum, at head and chest. He would never let her photograph him. He'd laugh out loud at the very idea. "What do you think I am?" he would say, holding his chest, horrified. "Some kind of porno nut?"

She rubbed her eye, exasperated.

They looked at each other. He came over, naked like that, and stood there in front of her. He sank to his knees and his head fell contritely into her lap. For one panic-stricken moment she knew that even if he was having an affair, she could not stop loving him. She understood quite clearly women through time immemorial who'd put up with all sorts of shameless behavior and for what? Not for the rent, surely. For the man. The great hell of a hunk of him, the bastard. "You bastard," she said.

He smiled up at her. His thick and blue-black hair was way too long. He would lose it one day, she noted with pleasure.

"I got something to show you," he said.

"I won't look."

"I'm starving," he said, giving up too easily, and she remembered how he'd walked through without even greeting her parents.

"How's Ben Kingsley doing?" he asked. "He sure knows how to eat, eh? No, I mean, for someone so skinny."

"So why didn't you come in and steal yourself a snack? Everybody else did." She picked up his clothes squeamishly and dropped them to the floor.

He looked into her eyes. One time when he was very young, when his mother was still alive back in Brooklyn—this was before she'd gotten sick—over in Bay Ridge, in the dead of the winter she'd taken him to the park on the edge of the water. It was a really sunny day and the air was stretched and tight. Everything glinted with refrozen snow. He must have been five. She'd gotten hold of a little second-hand two-wheeler with training wheels, and she'd taken him down there to try it out. She'd put him on it and held onto the back of the seat and run alongside it while he churned and pumped and balanced. He remembered her laughing, and that red scarf she always wore, whipping around her face. He remembered heading straight for the water, the crisp, heady air full of her carefree laughter, when all of a sudden the bike went without any wobble; it let go the trainers and went flat out on its own, on the wheels it was made to, it went. And for the first time, instead of being scared and falling, he kept right on pumping and felt the connection, the strength in his legs, to the pedals and the handlebars holding him up; and it was like he flew, like he was flying like some free bird from nobody's rooftop, straight into the unbroken brilliant bright blue of the water. And he looked into

Claire's still-there eyes. He closed up his own. She dug her short nails into the crux of his knees.

He was tired. He'd been through so much.

She said, "Look. I happen to know about the horse."

"I'm so glad," he said, "because I was scared shit to tell you."

She let go of him. "Very endearing. Big you scared of little me. But it's not going to make it any easier for you. I'm very upset. How do you think I felt, finding out like that from Freddy?"

"Fred? How the hell did he find out?"

"Johnny, what do you want? Me and you to sit here now and figure out how the hell Freddy would know my husband bought himself a racehorse?"

"Well, half. Half a racehorse. Wiggins bought the other half."

She pushed him hard with the heel of her hand. She growled.

"All right." He put his arms around her and she could feel his great heart pumping blood. "I only didn't tell you because I knew you would yell."

"Yell? I would have said 'no way.'"

"Claire, listen to me. A horse like this comes along once in a guy like me's life. I could never afford to keep her if Wiggins wasn't a trainer. She's got her own little stall nice and cozy right over here at Aqueduct."

"What a pity we moved. You could have rolled out of bed and dropped over to see her."

"Yeah, I thought of that, too."

"Johnny. I was being facetious."

"Oh. Well, we're still nice and close. Hop, skip, and a jump."

"And what about the bills?"

"Don't you worry about that. That's my business. I'll win big again any day now."

"Oh, I see."

"What? I never let you down yet, did I? Did I?"

"I'm not used to bill collectors. Credit companies. Somehow I don't think they'll get it that it's your business, not mine."

"That's not your job to worry about the bills. You let me worry about that. Your job is to feed me and keep me warm."

"What are you, a plant?"

Anthony threw open the door. "Aha!"

"Tch," Johnny said. "Two more minutes and you would have got an education."

"Go on! You know what. Get away from her!"

Limp with laughter at his rage, they let him yank them away from each other, till they were at opposite sides of the bed.

He raised his eyebrows. "And let that be a lesson to you both," he said, his pointer finger up in the air, hot tears in his eyes. He meant business, did Anthony. There would be no hanky-panky while he was about.

Dharma passed by the open door, on her way to who knew what. She didn't look in. Children all pretty much have an innate sense of discretion when it comes to adults. All except for Anthony.

"That reminds me," said Claire, taking the letter from her pocket and handing it to Johnny.

Anthony stayed sturdily on, guarding them from each other, but when he saw Johnny open the letter, he knew things had shifted from intimacy to, oh, some bill or something and so he left, choosing to go follow Dharma, who was following Floozie, who was on her way to investigate the goings-on across the street from Michaelaen's window. Downstairs was well and good, but up here you could step out onto the actual roof. It was on a low grade up here, panning out from Michaelaen's tiny balcony. From here you could peer out onto the entire block, up to the woods and down as far as Jamaica Avenue. Of course, you had to take care you didn't fall off.

While Johnny read Tree's timely (or untimely) letter, Claire plucked at the truant goose feathers that poked through the quilt. Imagine Mary not telling her how she went off on the bus to visit Mrs. Dixon. Oh, she'd known how she'd gone off to see her at that criminal asylum after the whole horrifying episode had taken place. She hadn't approved then (somehow Christian kindness seemed to stop at the wickedness of children murdered) but she had understood her mother's resigned loyalty. She was Irish, after all. Not raised in the shallow new age, but in a time and place that stood by its survivors, right or wrong, no matter how wrong, if they were of their own. Still and all, Claire shivered, Mrs. Dixon

128

had been so wrong, she had put her own darling Michaelaen in danger as well. Claire never would have met Johnny but for that terrible tragedy. He'd been assigned to the case and had suspected even her. "Expatriate," he'd called her. "Member of some weird Indian cult." If anyone had told her then that she'd be married to this man, she would have laughed out loud. But she was married to him, wasn't she? And Swamiji was downstairs eating crumb cake with her brothers-in-law. She looked sadly at Johnny. Brows knit, he was just getting through the one page. He was not the great reader, Johnny.

"Boy oh boy," he said.

"What do you think?" she asked.

"Hey. That's about as rough as it gets, you know?"

He smoothed the letter out on the coverlet and they looked at it together. It had gone to their old house first, back to the post office and on to here.

It was dated the day she had died. It read:

"Dear Claire,

"Seeing you the other day was just what I needed. You reminded me of all sorts of things I'd completely forgotten. Isn't it wonderful that we both have children? It would have been so sad if one of us had to feel sorry for the other one on that count. If that's the only thing I've done right in this life then at least I've done that."

Claire's eyes filled up with tears. Every time she read that part she cried.

"Will you come and visit me?" the letter continued, "sometime very soon, because I want to revisit the secret places of our childhood, all right? You are the only one who would understand. Your sister tells me how busy you are, but after seeing you, I just know you'll find the time for me. Some bonds are never broken. Not with time or space. You understand."

Yes—Claire smiled in spite of her tears—she would always understand. Tree had added,

"And Claire, remember how you always told me it didn't matter about finding the treasure? Well, now I think I understand what you meant. In fact, it's better not to."

She had signed the letter "your old friend, Tree." "P.S.," it read, "I tried to call but your phone's been shut off."

"Come on, Claire," Johnny hissed at her. "Stop blubberin' all over the place. Anthony will hear you and get all upset."

Claire snorted her emotions accommodatingly to a close. She knew what he really meant was that he couldn't stand to see or hear her cry, and if she didn't stop he would say some nasty bullying thing to upset her so she would. Her anger was one thing he was always prepared to deal with. She couldn't bear this predictable seesaw of her own charted course. She closed her eyes, lay down on her back, and consciously unclenched her fists. She took breath in through her nostrils and out slowly through her mouth. Oblivion, she called silently, come capture me.

"What is this, hah? What are you doin'? Posing for the imprimatur?"

She opened her eyes. "You mean the stigmata?"

"Yeah."

He climbed on top of her.

Once, he had told her that he had no courage. All those heroics he'd gotten medals for in the department were just a result of not caring if he lived or died. "Like, I could give a shit," was how he'd put it. "Every day was just one more have-to-get-up to the same do-it-all-the-hell-over." Only now, since they had Anthony, he said, now he was a total coward. If anything happened to him on the job, and Anthony was left alone, like if something would happen to her as well and Anthony would be left alone, the way he had been—"Aw jeez."

She knew just what he meant. She saw such a lonely spot there on his neck and she put her hand down on it.

Johnny got excited right away. One thing about his wife, she was always ready for him.

"Lock the door," she babbled as he locked the door.

He put his stubbled cheek down on her still wet one and they rolled back over Tree's crumpled letter. He pushed up her skirt and got hold of her silky damp panties. The last thing she thought of as he put his big hands 'round her madrigal thighs, was the swift glint of mischief from Swamiji's quick raisin eyes.

CHAPTER 6

White fog rolled up and over Richmond Hill. Not yet dispersed by daylight, it encompassed Claire and Floozie at her feet. "Don't wander away, now," Claire thought but didn't say. She didn't have to. With this animal, you only had to think something and she felt what you meant, telepathically. What with the kids in school all week, she and Floozie spent all sorts of time together now. Claire had taken pity on the always bedraggled little dog and trimmed her snarly coat with a cuticle scissors. Floozie had stood painstakingly still for the entire process.

Unfortunately, the early rays of actual sunshine weren't catching right for photography. It was only a vapor, pouring through, but it wasn't hitting the house quite the way she had hoped. She loved this high-speed black-and-white. You could do all sorts of things with it, and never have to bother with artificial light. She tapped her toe impatiently. This particular house had always interested her. It was one of those Italianate Victorians, all hooded windows and brackets under eaves, then broken suddenly by the generous, curvaceous sweep of a balcony, a tower, a terrace. She had pushed the film so it would develop grainy, still sharp but almost muted. That and the fog would be perfect.

There was talk of this area becoming protected by the Historical Association. It would be a terrible shame if they let these beautiful old homes be so radically destroyed by uncaring landlords interested in utilizing the great spaces; adding on illegal apartments, garish extensions, closing off majestic wraparound front porches and turning them into vast waiting rooms, extra bedrooms, windowless, Formica-paneled dens. This one was still intact architecturally, but simply white. She tried to imagine it in the traditional colors of Victoriana; God, there were so many combinations. The best renovation with color she had seen was in San Francisco, where they jazzed up the pediments with six and seven subtle tones at once.

It was awfully chilly up here on the hill. She shivered again and pulled her jacket tighter around her. It was Carmela's jacket, fashionable but last year's. Carmela had left it flung across a chair at her house when she'd borrowed Claire's old navy-blue pea jacket to go with some Marlene Dietrich thing she was affecting. Claire's jacket was so old it was right in step. And warm, she reflected sorrowfully. Not like this darn piece of floppy melodrama.

She searched the pockets, not expecting much, hoping without hope for a pair of gloves. There was a piece of paper in there, crumpled, which she opened up and read. "Because there was a peacock and a social rodent," it began in Carmela's tight script, "there were spider webs, but not where you could see them, touch them. They were in the arms of Ephesus, they jangled small change in their pockets. They were stale-bread eyes wide open. They were waiting for the thunder. Wash them down like silk kimono, chewed-up eye with spittle on it."

Uch. Yuch. That was Carmela, all right. All talent, no taste. Why did she write about horrible things like that?

Claire hadn't hesitated to read Carmela's note, never thought of herself as prying, even half believed it was written somehow for her. Why else had she left it there for her to find? Freud Schmoid, Johnny would say. Still . . .

"Tell you what," she told the dog, "how 'bout I buy you breakfast?" Terrific idea, agreed the dog, hopping in. On food they both agreed. It calmed and cured most any situation. Luckily, Floozie was so small she fit inconspicuously inside Claire's roomy film bag, she'd just stuff the film into the camera bag and off they'd go. "Just don't budge," Claire advised her. "Americans are not as permissive about dogs in restaurants as Europeans are, you know." No, Floozie hadn't known that, but it was useful information. You never knew where you found yourself in life. She jumped back out of the bag for a last sniff around.

Pancakes, that was what Floozie had in mind. Claire was thinking more along the lines of poached eggs on English muffins, juice, and good strong coffee. This school business wasn't such a bad idea. Zinnie was dropping the lot of them off this morning, so Claire could get her head start on the light. She didn't envy Zinnie, getting herself ready for work and the kids dressed as well. Especially Anthony. He was a real toughie when it came to getting ready, stalling and running and hiding under the table. But she also knew that kids tended not to behave as badly towards people who weren't their mother. Anyway, Zinnie would make it good and clear that she'd just leave him behind if he didn't get a move on. Claire wasn't going to worry about it. This was, if she wasn't mistaken, the first morning she'd actually had completely off since Anthony was born. Usually, she'd race back to make them all breakfast. Yes it was, it was true. She relished the very idea of going "out" to breakfast on her own. Let's see, she planned, I'll buy a newspaper and sit there and read it like an actual grown-up person, like a working girl, like a single. I will finish my entire meal without looking up once, without running to "Mommy, Mommy, Mommy, come quick" just to discover a shiny new toy advertised on the tube, without going to kiss someone's boo-boo, without running to break up a ninja battle under my dining room table, without jumping up to compose a Swamiji's tiffin, no matter how well loved the swami. She could go to Jahn's, the old turn-of-the-century ice cream parlor on Hillside and Myrtle, romantic and dark with real Tiffany lamps and Impressionist paintings by Papa Jahn himself. Good electric coffee there. Or Salerno's. Or she could hike across the Interboro to Freddy's place. Delicious cappuccino. Naw. They'd recognize her and not let her pay. She was really in the mood to chow down, and she didn't want anyone throwing it back in her face, mouthing off what a greedy horse she was, what an absolute pig. She also didn't feel like chitchatting with the help, which she would feel obliged to do. No, the hell with that. So where? Ah. She knew just the place.

"C'mon, Floozie, hop up in my bag—oh, never mind, you can use the exercise, I suppose. Just stay by my feet so you don't go into the street." Claire looked up suddenly and noticed the beautiful lines of the funeral parlor across the street. Funny, she'd never looked at it quite like this, architecturally. It was what? Free

Classic? Miraculously, it hadn't been destroyed in the renovation. For no other reason, probably, than it was big enough as it was. What the heck. She snapped it quickly and went on her way. Leaves fell in a shower with another gust of wind. So many fell at once it gave new, if redundant, meaning to the term "fall." It really did remind you why you loved this time of year. Everything covered with ivy had turned bright red, the same cheerful red of the maples, at least one on every street. They hiked along, she and Floozie did.

Floozie looked this way and that. She started to run into the street. "Wait!" Claire cried but it was too late; the car whizzing up Park Lane South seemed to come out of nowhere. Claire covered her eyes. It was her fault, her fault. Her heart came to an absolute and morose stop. It was over. The car just kept right on going. She went to retrieve the squashed body before someone else ran her over again, and the dog stood up. "Rap!" she barked angrily, "Rap! Rap!"

It wasn't possible. She was alive. Claire scooped her up and ran up the embankment like she had the dog on a plate. She didn't know where she was running, but she kept going. She only stopped running when she realized her camera was banging a hole in her side. Annoyed, the dog jumped down. Claire fell to the grass. She probed the dog's trembling body everywhere, jabbing and petting. "I can't believe it," she finally concluded. "They ran right over you and didn't touch you. Thank God."

"I'm all right," the dog thought. "Not a scratch."

"I'll never be so foolish again," Claire sobbed. "Don't ever think I don't love you. I do." She smothered her face in the dog's little belly.

"That's better." The dog stretched and yawned. They made their way to the Railroad Café without Claire much realizing where she was going, she was just headed in that direction, so that's where they found themselves. It was pretty much European enough not to make much of a lap dog, or at least nobody said anything, for Claire made no move to hide little Floozie, who had lived after all. They took a window seat and looked out over the old-fashioned Long Island Railroad station. It was only now starting to fill up with commuters, early risers on their harried way to the city, everybody in a hurry at this hour, shooting worried glances at the enormous, plain-faced clock. One from the old days, that one.

The sun had broken through. There was a chipped, white-painted fence along the yard and delicate vines grew up it, cockle-shells with purple morning glory. Claire was glad she'd chosen this spot after all. There were newspapers kept on wooden poles, like back in Munich. Outside, there was a pillared rain pagoda under which nobody stood. A blue-shadowed house in the crowded bright sunshine of the station. There were all sorts of people here. Israelis, Lebanese, Germans, Poles, Indians. Even a couple home-towners. Claire snuggled happily into her skin and Floozie into her. I'm done for now, Claire thought, but didn't care. Telemann was on the radio. And so they sat there, doing nothing. Silently, Claire prayed that the teacher in the pre-K, the woman to whom she had entrusted her only child, would love her little fellow, her curly-dark-haired, chubby-wristed, overheated, red-cheeked boy, and be kind to him when her patience would wear thin. And whose patience wouldn't wear thin with fourteen pre-schoolers all morning long?

Suddenly, Claire wanted to be home in her own kitchen. She could make herself pancakes, or even waffles. She remembered the old-fashioned waffle iron she'd found for three bucks at a yard sale. If she got home soon enough, she could make them all lunch. There was one heck of a raspberry bush still blooming in the yard. She laughed out loud, earning herself a couple of New York-style, world-weary but still wary looks from nearby tables. New Yorkers were so used to crazies they wouldn't get up, they just wouldn't make eye contact. Anyway, she laughed out loud, ignoring them. Who was she kidding, she was past the days of early-morning cafés with the workers. She had her own work to do. If she got home quickly enough, she could get some developing done in her make-shift lab down the cellar. She really would love to see how those houses turned out. She had an idea. Stefan and Carmela had given Anthony an expensive, beautiful set of watercolors last Christmas. She'd put it carefully away until he would appreciate it, and it had popped up when the family had moved. Something about coloring these houses in true combinations of subtle Victoriana intrigued her. If she gave herself some time, she might make some extra copies and give it a try. She'd originally given the paints to Dharma to distract her, and ever since, she'd had them on her mind. And she had four or five loads of laundry that ought to be done by now if she didn't want the laundry room to overflow. Oh well. She threw the money down onto the table for her coffee and a tip. She wasn't going to go and feel guilty; priorities had to be gotten straight here. Laundry could wait, couldn't it, but the beauty of autumn in Richmond Hill could not. It wouldn't have to, because she was here to screw it on straight, to record it as it was (or at least as she darn well saw it), wasn't she? Then she could still be there for the kids when they got out of school. Wearily, but getting used, now, to Claire's erratic mood swings, Floozie gave a philosophic hop into Claire's big sack. After you'd been through what she had, your devotion wasn't only grateful, it was ardent.

When they got back home, Johnny was just running out onto the street. "What are you doing up so early?" she greeted him. When he worked nights you seldom saw him before two. Never before noon.

He grabbed hold of her and whirled her around. "Oh, baby," he laughed, "she's running. We've got her running in the first race at Belmont!"

"Who? What?" Claire laughed along with him in bewilderment.

"Mail Call."

"The horse?"

"Darlin', it's just a claiming race, but this is it. This could be it! If she wins this, if nobody claims her, next time she'd go on to an allowance race!"

Claire tried not to feel annoyed. She smiled her broadest smile. She didn't like him to see that it hurt her, the fact that he had never found it exciting enough to lose a little sleep for herself or the baby. Fact was, she'd never seen him this excited about anything. She didn't want to be petty. She wasn't going to be. Cheerful camaraderie bubbled from her eyes.

"Good luck, darling," she sang. "Have fun!"

"Hey! Why don't you come? Anthony's in school. I'm only

staying for the first race anyway. I'd get you back right after lunch. Your mom will be here to get them lunch, won't she? And Zinnie's here after school."

"Oh, gee, Johnny, I just don't know. I was just going to call my mom and tell her not to bother to come. I thought I would stay home and work in the darkroom."

Johnny squinted at her, trying to understand.

"Honey, this is our big chance." He held onto her arms and his voice had something else to it. Pleading?

She was jealous. Jealous and resentful. She'd always thought if they had some big chance it would be something the two of them would have planned together. This was unfamiliar territory for her. She wanted to react the right way, the fair way, but she felt like it had been sprung on her. He read her face.

"What?" he said. "You don't do one thing for work in four years and all of a sudden just because I've got something going here that I really care about, that could really pull us out of the hole, you suddenly decide 'work' is so important it can't wait a couple of hours?"

"No, it's not like that," she said, but it was like that, she could hear the edge in her voice as well as he could. She was grudging and he was ready for her with the injured resentment that sprang readily up despite his surface of happiness. She never could just go easy into his trip. Spontaneously. It always had to be something they'd planned. She'd planned. For someone as wild and with as much action in her past as he had had, she was really predictable and sedentary. She knew it. But she also knew that although he'd used money he'd made on his own, gambling, it was still a lot of money they could have used for something sensible. The mortgage. New windows. A new roof. Anthony's school. It was his, but she couldn't help wishing he'd consulted her. He never knew when to stop. He always thought the next windfall would take them over the top. Over the hill to the poorhouse, more likely.

They looked unhappily at each other. The dog moved uncomfortably in her bag. Johnny turned to go. "I'll be back by three then," he said, polite. Truce. Not peace, but he had to get the hell away. They smiled at each other, but when their eyes met, both pairs were hurt.

Claire let herself in with her key, let the dog in, and watched her scamper into the kitchen for a drink. Swamiji and Narayan were out somewhere; their mats were folded and still in the dining room. The whole house was still. Empty and still. Claire looked at the table from where Tree's last letter had looked at her. It spoke to her like no reprimand she could make herself. She turned around and slammed the door shut. She ran down the path and caught Johnny in the street as he was turning the car around. He stopped short and rolled down the window.

"I was thinking," she said, shrugging. "Maybe I want to make a little bet."

"Get in here." He clenched his teeth at her and pulled her hook, line, and sinker through the window.

When they got to the track it was already buzzing with activity. Relinquishing their car to a respectful fellow, they walked in the shiny, tall glass doors and entered into a world of clean mirrored surfaces and hot cigar smoke. They went through the owner's turnstile and took the escalator up to the second floor. Johnny threw a penny clear across the room at the wishing well against the downstairs wall, and they raised eyebrows at each other when they saw it go right in. They even imagined they heard it hit the water with a sure plunk. There weren't too many women here, Claire realized as she looked around. Matter of fact, there weren't any. She had to walk double time to keep up with Johnny. He headed over to the big board suspended from the ceiling. This was quite a place, Belmont. There were boutiques up here, fast-food concessions, even an umbrella-shaded French café. The computerized board buzzed and changed, whizzed information on and then off again. A giant movie screen reran races from the previous wins of the horses running today. Johnny had forgotten her. She could see why. This was an entirely other world. Here men could come and be away from their reality. Claire knew their tarnished hearts held secret dreams, maybe-this-time feelings, a chance again at failing no one. This was all going to be okay. Johnny's horse would certainly lose, and that would be the end of this fiasco. They had no business owning a racehorse. No business at all.

"Okay." Johnny took her hand and she lurched after him. "Now we go downstairs to the owner's circle."

You could tell he said these words with tremendous satisfaction. Though he pretended this was all old hat, she could tell he was getting the greatest kick out of it. All sorts of guys were coming up to him to wish him good luck. He accepted their respect as his due, did Johnny. As he did her presence. He ignored her, but she knew that he knew she was there. She affected a stance she considered wifely, yet still in the running. Shoulders back, spine straight, then one saucy angle of her slender right knee. Were she alone she suspected she would still warrant a couple of motivated once-overs. To test this premise, she left Johnny standing and gazing at the board and headed across the great football field of a hall for the distant ladies' room. Yes, away from her husband, her child, her whole life, she could still pick up grungy wolf leers. Sadly, she admitted, this pleased her, and gave her some perverse intergalactic relevance. She returned to her husband revitalized, a new woman. It was so silly, but there it was. These men looked like a bunch of lowlifes to Claire, but then her standards had been honed and jaded by the plasticine world of advertising and the weariness of overseas. She hardly glanced. And so she missed the sharp, indulgent silhouette of Mr. Kinkaid beside the observation fence.

Outside, sumptuous trees and bushes surrounded the paddock. They walked through a turnstile where a fellow stamped their hands for identification and then they headed down the mucky horse path to the prestigious, picturesque owner's circle. Here were the fellows with the suits and ties, the big owners: they wore navy-blue jackets, maroon ties, and flannel trousers. Here were the broads. Two to a customer. Flashy, high-spirited women in makeup and big earrings, their hair pulled back in imitation of the wives of these guys they'd overseen at some luncheon, somewhere, once. Or in photographs on their sugar daddy's desk one day he was ravenous enough to let her up past his disapproving, respectable secretary. These owner fellows' wives didn't usually come to the weeklies. One demure young woman and her children went to sit genteelly under the tree on the white wrought-iron bench over the wide circle of grass. Her blond little girl ran in the shady periphery of the generous landmark, the hundred-and-sixty-year-old white pine tree. Her velvet sash streamed regally to and fro behind her.

The women stood and preened as the crowd took their places behind the fence on the observation stairs. Each owner went over to stand by his horse as the trainers brought them out. Then the jockeys arrived. Well. A shiver of anticipation fluttered through the crowd when out they came in their flippy colors, these miniature men in exactly the right place. They were magical, full of expertise and athlete's grace. There was something almost mystical about them, delicate and sure, riding their great, nervous steeds. They warranted respect, there was no denying that. Suddenly, Johnny's horse Mail Call was walked into the stall, and the trainer and the groom got her dressed. Her colors were powder blue and cream. She was number seven, this glorious beast. Claire's excited heart beat more quickly.

"Johnny! She's magnificent!"

The horse's ears perked forward to catch Claire's admiring words. Her flanks quivered with that fine-tuned nervousness that separates thoroughbred racehorses from any other living creature in the world.

"Ah, she likes you, lassie," Wiggins said to her. He was the horse's half owner as well as her trainer, and he rubbed the chestnut's beautiful hind soothingly. An awful lot of his dreams lay on this pound of luscious horseflesh here.

"You know how to talk to a lady, Mrs. Benedetto," he said. "She feels that, y'know."

"Claire. Please call me Claire."

"Fine, fine, here comes Michael, our jockey." He introduced Claire to the quick-eyed man who was to ride Mail Call. Claire liked him immediately.

"He just happens to be the best damn jockey in the country," Johnny boasted as they walked shyly into the owner's circle and the horses rode around to give everybody in the paddock a good look at them.

"How did you get him, then?" Claire asked.

Offended, Johnny made a face. "Hey. What do I look like?"

"No," Claire rushed to assure him, "I mean, how did we get so lucky? He's so, I don't know, magical."

Johnny smiled happily. "Yeah. Well, to tell you the truth," he admitted, "he kinda owed a favor."

"Gee. He's wonderful."

"Yeah. They don't come any better."

"And your horse, Johnny—"

"Our horse, toots."

They smiled at each other and walked the gracious owner's walk behind the rainbow-colored pack, down the tunnel to the track. This was really quite something. She was so glad she hadn't missed this, given it up for petty and small silly stuff. This here, as Johnny would say, was big time. He had already warned her that there are no cameras at the track. It was bad luck, they said. Plenty of cultures believed the soul of the subject was stolen a little every time he or she was photographed. Claire had worked with enough deeply emotionally wrought models to accept this as a possibility. She didn't mind not having her camera at all. As a matter of fact, she rather enjoyed not having it. This was indeed another world, and she could see how Johnny could get so wrapped up in it. A crisp wind blew them along and the sky was a cheerful cool blue.

They went upstairs to the windows to place their bets. Uniformed guards let them out the windowed walls to the owner's boxes.

"Hiya, Johnny." The guard smacked him on the back familiarly.

"Hey, Al, what's up?"

They made their way down through the rows of green boxes.

"Johnny." Claire pulled his sleeve and pointed out the wire suspended across the track. "Is this the finish line?"

"Yeah."

"Couldn't we go down there?"

"Hell. This here's the owner's box. Don't you want to see the race from up here? Feel the prestige?"

Claire looked out across the bleachers. Far away across the racetrack the horses were being lined up at the start. She looked longingly down at the wire so close to the track.

Johnny watched her face. "C'mon," he said. "You wanna smell the horses, right?"

Without her answering, they flew back out past the guard, down the chrome escalator, across the opened bridge to down in front. The steward climbed to his perch and signaled the race to begin.

Claire and Johnny stood right there at the wire. His knuckles were white against his program.

"It's just a race, Johnny." She leaned against him. "It doesn't indicate your destiny, you know."

If he heard her, he didn't let on. To a gambler, the moment is truth.

"And they're off!" came the cry.

"Where is she? Where is she?" Claire called out to no one. On the board, the numbers came up. In first place, four. Second place, two; third place, six; fourth place, five. Then it changed. First place, six; second place, four; third place, five; fourth place, one. Two was out. Where was Mail Call? "And it's Cherry Pie on the rail. Magdalaina in the front and they did the first quarter in twenty-three and four. They're in the back stretch, they're turning for home."

When Claire's heart had already given up and Johnny's face had frozen into congenial, resigned, heartbroken good sportedness, from way in the back came the words—the sweetest words to any hopeful's heart—"and it's Mail Call on the outside." Then, wonder of wonders, there she was on the board. She was fourth. Thank God. Claire caught her breath. It was one thing to lose. It was another to lose like a bum. At least they were on the board once, only wait a minute, she was over the hump and she was up now in line with the six and the four. She could hear Johnny screaming, loud. "Come on seven! Come on seven!" They were all in a row. It was the six, the four, and the seven. "Come on, seven!" That was her voice shouting, she realized. She could feel the surge of men pressing up around her to the wire. They were coming down the stretch. Everyone around her was shouting orders over this way and that. She could see the blue and cream of Mail Call and the blood pounded in her ears. She was screaming. Her arm was up in the air and she was on that horse's back. "Come on seven!" She was sure that horse could hear her. She was up on the fence. There was hollering everywhere. "They're at the eight pole," shouted the loudspeaker. The horses were up neck and neck. It was seven. She could feel the front legs of the horse flying over the track. "And it's seven," the loudspeaker cracked and rolled overhead. It was wild. She was hugging some fellow and Johnny was hugging some fellow. Then everything turned to a blur. It happened so fast. Johnny was dragging her over the fence to go stand in the winner's circle for a picture. Claire stood there between Johnny and Tony, dazed and bedraggled and laughing. Mail Call, ears up and sweating and snorting, basked in the glory and the jockey's caresses of praise. Johnny, upside-down with glee, put both palms to his head and gave thanks, holy Christ, to the ghost of his mother in heaven. Big Canadian geese flew in formation, like birds in a movie, right over their heads.

Johnny tooled the car into the drive with a generous sweep. One hand expertly maneuvered the wheel and the other rested on the leather behind Claire's head. Here they were. Owners of not just a home, but what would be, when they got finished with it, the veritable seat of charm. They were parents, and both of them simultaneously shook heads fondly at the thought of their own precious child. And now, wonder of wonders, they were owners of a racehorse. And this racehorse had won. The future stretched before them in one golden, assured ray of light. They sighed together. Butter would not melt in their mouths. For once and at long last, there wasn't a cloud in the sky. Perhaps they would buy more horses. Johnny obviously had the knack. One day they might buy some property out on the North Fork and, hell, breed and raise them. Johnny pulled the key out of the ignition and the car backfired. His brows knit imperceptibly together. One shutter, Claire noticed, hung embarrassingly shanty-like from their palace. They clicked their tongues in consecutive annoyance but smiled affectionately across at each other nonetheless. This was a day to remember. This, they both realized, was the day that their luck had changed. This was it. Their struggles were over.

"They're home!" came a whoop from inside. Floozie tore through the newly installed doggy door, a convenient flap Johnny had put right in the door for her. She headed for Claire, who couldn't help feeling singled out and special. And as teensy as Floozie was, she took such astonishing helicopter leaps that all you had to do was extend your elbow and there she was, perched in your crook. Anthony slammed out the back door barefoot. "Mommy, Daddy, guess what?"

"Where are your shoes?"

Anthony stopped, looked suddenly thoughtful, placed the tips of his fingers together and addressed his parents. "It is disrespectful to wear shoes in the home."

"Sheesh," Johnny said.

"Very true." Claire put Floozie down, picked Anthony up and held him to her. "What a clever big fellow you are to know that! Although, that theory usually works out better when the ceilings are not twelve feet high and there's something besides bare parquet on the floor." She put him down gently, then looked at Johnny. "Wouldn't it be great if we won enough money to buy a really excellent rug? Like a Hindu Kush. Or a Mazar-i-Sharif." Her eyes glowed, imagining. "Meanwhile," she looked around, "we've got bupkis."

"Not to worry." Anthony gave his head a rubbery wiggle, in exact imitation of Swamiji at his wisest. "It is in this way that an idea becomes a thought, a thought becomes a, becomes, uh—"

"A word," supplied Swamiji, padding to the door with a pile of folded towels in his arms. He put the tower of towels away one by one in the open linen closet across from the pantry, smoothing the neatly cornered top towel fondly. ". . . A word becomes an act."

"And," Anthony finished, "an act becomes a habit."

Claire and Johnny exchanged astonished looks. Neither of them had ever been able to convey the shortest memorized message to Anthony.

"How did you do that?" Johnny sat down at the kitchen table.

"Quite simple, really," Swamiji confided. "I imitated the colorful, hyperactive information-center methods of the television adverts." He held his breath for a moment and pulled the air into his face. Bright red, he now jutted his arms to and fro his little brown frame in a strobelike repetition. In a loud TV advertising voice, with a flat, nasal, Midwestern accent, Swamiji proceeded to campaign for a toy that not only demolished, destroyed, devastated, and dumped toxic waste upon its enemy, but exploded and put itself back together as well.

Everyone stared at him with glazed-over eyes.

"You must admit," Swamiji relinquished his beet color and returned to his more characteristic brown. "The sentiments which I've conveyed to him are admirable."

"Maybe I could get you down to the precinct in Brooklyn province." Johnny wiggled his head, too. "We could put you to work on the perps."

Misunderstanding Johnny's sarcasm, Swamiji basked in his words. "I would be honored." His head bobbed back, to and fro.

"And Ma," Anthony was out of breath with excitement, "you should see what he can do with his stomach!"

Claire remembered very well Swamiji's uncanny yogic practices.

"And you know what, Dad? Dad, listen!" He tugged on Johnny's sleeve. "He can disappear! Really!"

"He can? Boy, now, I'll really have to bring him down to meet the undercovers. They could always use a couple of pointers like that, eh?"

"A mere illusion caused by disillusion," Swamiji admitted humbly.

"Where's Zinnie?" Claire asked him.

"Ah. Narayan has taken her to the new-moon ceremony at the home of Ragu Panchyli. A goodly woman who works with a green card at the Key Food. She cash registers the money," he added, impressed, adding: "Sit down. I have prepared your supper."

Claire looked with trepidation at Johnny. He had set himself comfortably in and flicked the blue cloth napkin, which Swamiji had so nicely washed and ironed, onto his lap. Apparently, all this was less jarring for him than she had anticipated. And why not? He no doubt thought such service was his due: a chef de cuisine and manservant to go with his successful new career as bon vivant horseman.

"Where are Michaelaen and Dharma?" she asked.

"Oh, they're practicing full lotus," Anthony supplied.

"In front of the television," Swamiji said.

"Except the television's not on." Anthony watched his parents' reactions with dazzled eyes. "Mom," he said and sat down at his place without even being asked—"can I bring Swamiji to pre-K? Like to show my teacher?"

"We'll see, we'll see," Swamiji answered for her, and went humming to the stove. He returned with an iron wok full of simmering spicy vegetable biryani and a side dish of tandoori. He held this tantalizingly underneath Johnny's nose.

"Smells great." Johnny clapped his hands and rubbed them together. "So, who wants to hear our news? Anybody interested in whose horse came in first at Belmont this afternoon?"

Michaelaen and Dharma entered just then, both of them uncharacteristically subdued. They quietly took seats at the table and listened while Johnny told of his and Claire's adventure at the track. Swamiji interrupted him once to ask everyone to close their eyes for a moment and give thanks to the one true God. This, to Claire's astonishment, they did.

Look at this, Claire marveled, watching Vegetable Enemy Number One Johnny tear into the aromatic piazi, which was no more than glorified onion with chick peas. Her child, Mr. Don't-give-me-anything-but-macaroni-and-butter-or-Froot-Loops, sat contentedly munching nourishing kobi alu motor. Dharma ate. Michaelaen scarfed down everything in sight, even the spicy alu bengan, a mixture of eggplant and potatoes, two things he had always loudly proclaimed to detest.

Claire offered to fetch something, anything, but it was all done, thank you very much; she should relax. And so she did, a guest in her own kitchen, eating with relish and planning a luxurious afternoon developing film in the lab. The radio was on, and it was playing something delightfully Vivaldi. Floozie, contentedly kaput beside her curry dish, picked her head up and gave a slight growl. Claire looked out the window and noticed the top of Mr. Kinkaid's head skulking hurriedly away. He must have peeked in and seen Swamiji. She smiled to herself. Some days were indeed better than others.

She gave a great languid stretch and thought fleetingly of good Sister Rosaria from back in grammar school, who had warned, "When things are going too good, that's when I always know I'd better watch out." Claire shrugged and took a great mouthful of delectable piazi, then Claire looked into Dharma's drowsy eyes. The child looked back, and somewhere nearby the inelegant boip-boip-boip-boip of a new car alarm butted in.

"Ah, yes," Swamiji put down his spoon. "And your sister Carmela telephoned just before you came in."

"Oh?"

He rolled his eyeballs up inside his head to remember. "You must call her back at once. Mrs. um, Dixon has escaped from Deauville."

CHAPTER 7

"Okay, okay, okay, so who's the guy with all the arms and legs?" Zinnie groped her way down the coat-pocked hallway of the unfamiliar Panchyli house. Pairs of shoes lined the wall from the front door straight down the dimly lit hallway all the way to the back of the house, one of those mean, narrow buildings south of Jamaica Avenue. The homes to the left and right of this one had FOR SALE signs out front, symbolizing their occupants' indignation toward their new neighbors—never mind that this house sported newly installed windows and aluminum siding while theirs had peeling paint and rotting window sashes.

"Shiva, Zinnie. That's a statue representing Shiva."

"Brahma, Vishnu, and Shiva, right?"

Narayan's beautiful dark face lit up with delight. "You have been studying?"

"Hell, no. Their names are on the holy picture on the front door."

"Of course. Give me your shoes, please."

"What are you going to do with them?" She handed over her heels warily.

"I am going to eat them, what do you think? Here. I put them safely here behind the umbrella stand. You can remember?"

"Tch. I'll do my level best. What's that singing in there? They all sing? I thought this was a serious thing. Isn't Shiva the god of destruction? Are we sure we want to be here?"

"Destruction of evil is necessary, is it not? Destruction of war, destruction of fear?"

"Makes sense. Say. You really believe all this stuff? This reincarnation stuff?"

"This 'stuff' is my religion. And yes, I do believe in reincarnation."

"So what do you think you'll come back as? I mean, next time?"

"Be quiet. Or part of me shall come back as an octopus. And strangle you."

"Okay by me." She winked and turned and tiptoed carefully over the floorboards toward the back of the house. Narayan stood with open mouth and watched her delicate frame sway determinedly away from him. He cradled her shoes, in a swoon, to his heart. What was happening? He, the most desired of all the young men from abroad, went panting, open-mouthed, behind a half-pint, tough-lady American constable. It was inconceivable. Ludicrous, really. Where was his mind? In his pants, where his pocket was, that was where.

Oh, Narayan knew he was shallow. He had grown up with those brassy words in his pretty ears. His sisters, social-function martyrs all, had taunted him with it, his father, the magnanimous Solomon of the community, had sighed resignedly about it. His mother, goodly, indomitable charity-ball matriarch that she was, had thrown up her portly arms and collapsed, out of breath, onto her buttress of Salomé pillows. They were all in agreement about Narayan. When Swamiji had accepted him as a student and assistant, the family had practically hurled poor Narayan north towards Rishikesh. Good riddance and respectability all at once. What could be better? Who was to know he would wind up catapulting west to join the respectability-hungry, well-off Hindu families of Trinidad and Guyana in Queens? Ironically, it was Swamiji who had helped him come to terms with the inevitability of his shallowness, helped him recognize and acknowledge it until he was so comfortable that it no longer hurt him, cut him to the quick the way it once did.

So, he was shallow. He wasn't a thief. He wasn't a murderer. He simply liked shiny, pretty things. He indulged himself lavishly. So had Krishna. So had Buddha, for that matter, before his renouncement. Zinnie here was not simply shiny, she was gold, gold of the purest sort. He followed her down the hallway with foolish yearning. Foolish, because this attraction had the poignant impossibility they were both capable of acknowledging. Her family would see him as an interloper, an abomination, a black man. His family would see her only as a white woman. Where his family lived, the only white women they were unfortunate enough to have to tolerate were those repulsive blueish English women with red veiny noses and inclinations toward gin and tonic when it was still daylight. Or the other, still worse, sort, the missionary ilk, sprouting sturdy chin whiskers, their puny hair yanked back off their foreheads and their unadorned, unvarnished, uncared-for feet and toes—unconscious horrendous bulk kerplunked into delicate sandals as if to say, well, what of it? It was too monstrous. What, then, would his family think of Zinnie? A meat eater. Yes, she was delicately pink, they would reluctantly admit, but she would redden as she aged. And anyway—he could just see his sisters and his mother throw back their haughty heads and leave the room with a tinkle of their bells and bangles—it was unthinkable. They would never accept her. It didn't matter that she had completed university despite limited funds. They would never find that admirable. All they would see were those limited funds, a girl with a night job; they would shudder.

Zinnie, at the end of the hall, turned her head around to look for him, to wait for him. She would not enter that room without a backup. He saw her adjust her shoulder holster under her silk man-tailored jacket and rushed up to her, horrified.

"What is that? A gun? Zinnie, how could you?"

"What are you talking about? I always carry. I'm not allowed not to. I'm a cop, remember? Why do you think I always wear two shirts? Otherwise I look like the friggin' Frito Bandito. It's bad enough when I go for my lipstick, I pull out my rounds." She hoisted herself this way and that, adjusting her piece. "Most of the guys wear it on the waist with a pancake holster. I always take my off-duty. Personally, I like my service revolver 'cause it's big, intimidating when you see it." She stopped fiddling and looked up at him. "And it can't jam."

He watched her, stunned, his hands helpless at his sides. This whole thing was more absurd than even he had imagined. He would speak to Swamiji about cutting their visit still shorter. They must move along now and be on their way. Their business with herbs was only on the verge of an upswing as it was. If they waited too long to bypass the Tibetans from the monastery and do business with the laboratory in Berkeley, the lab might lose interest. Already timorous business people, they might decide to buy their herbs elsewhere. They might simply decide to produce their own. Contribute to the "made in America" movement. Oregon. He could just see it: They would pick his and Swamiji's brains and go from there. "Grown without pesticides in our own clean and mighty Northwest." Not a bad idea, he mulled. Perhaps he would one day integrate it into his own scheme. But for now, he and Swamiji had planned to head straightaway cross country and be home well before harvest. The postponement of that plan had never bothered him because he'd hoped for an opportunity to investigate his feelings for Zinnie. But really, he realized as she rearranged her weapon intimately near to her brassiere, there was no way these twain would ever meet. One hand upon his hip, one finger pressed between dry lips, he continued to watch her in the dim hallway there. Her eyes were bright with discomfort, her creamy throat blotchy with nerves. She took out a brush and brushed her hair. Such an impropriety. And on and on she brushed. She was used to men watching her, confined to close quarters with them for long periods of time on stakeouts, in and about locker rooms. He felt himself stiffen.

Zinnie yanked her hair up into a bun and twirled it around her head. She stuck a comb in to anchor it and turned to witness his approval. The curry from the kitchen and the incense from the ceremony mingled in her nostrils and for just a moment, pushed between him and the wall by two stout ladies in saris butting by, she thought she would pass out. The door at the end of the hall snapped back and forth and the chanting of the pandit carried loud and soft, loud and soft. Zinnie and Narayan felt each other's breath on their soft cheeks. She looked into his eyes and he, into hers. For one long moment they just stood there. They didn't kiss. They just stood against each other, holding up the green malfunctioning wall.

"Ah, there you are," the lady of the house barged through. "At last! We are all waiting for you!" Her eyes searched the hallway behind them.

Narayan went immediately up to her. "Swamiji could not come," was all he said, deciding correctly that the true whereabouts of Swamiji (babysitting three American children) might not go over well.

The lady tilted her head congenially, as if to say, who cares? What matter that I have organized my home for almost one hundred fifty souls of the community just so they might get a glimpse of him? To her credit, she never faltered, just threw her pink harney over one indignant, slightly elevated shoulder. "Oh," she beamed, "I just see you've honored us with a visitor as well." This was insult to injury, she thought. Inside waited no less than fourteen single Hindu girls, any one of them a respectable, prime candidate for Narayan, this enormous catch. All of them had taken off work for the occasion.

Mrs. Panchyli bustled them through. There was nothing to be done. Mrs. Panchyli had not come this far in the American community without accepting compromise. Going with the flow, as it were, as the security guard informed her often enough at the Key Food Store. And it wasn't as if this white girl wore his ring. She moved with authority, though, the girl. Perhaps she was a journalist? Was that one of those spy cameras she had hidden? It all just might turn around to my advantage, Mrs. Panchyli calculated. She must remember to make sure the girl sampled her luscious rice pudding. Who knew? They might all turn up on the front page of the color section of the Sunday *News*. Successful immigrants celebrating the holidays. She touched her perfect imitation Movado museum-piece watch for good luck.

Zinnie followed Narayan into the crowded room of chanting people. Besides the mob on the floor, there were plenty of them propped upright, sardine style, against the wall. The pandit sat on a series of clean white sheets on the floor. The amply endowed Mrs. Panchyli pushed her way past this multitude and bullied a prime space up front for Narayan and Zinnie. Incense fumed and smoked. On the sheets before the pandit, the family of the house sat solemnly; before them were paper plates laden and leaking with any number of Eastern fruits and cuisine, all offerings to Brahma. It was beautiful and impressive. The women were dressed and perfumed and garlanded with flowers. There was no furniture at all. If there was any, it had been removed, who knew to where. The grand Sony television remained, though, witness to prosperity. On the wall, brass-framed identical Kodak posters of long-haired white show cats posed imperiously on their valentine Cadillacs.

Zinnie found herself thinking of sodalities and ceremonies of First Holy Communion. The Indian people do not consider long-stemmed flowers of value, but rather vulgar and superfluous. Only the blossom will do, and they laugh out loud at Westerners who pay good money for "long-stemmed" flowers. Zinnie watched, astonished, as one old woman, the designated stem-disposer, sat in the doorway accumulating a great pile of stems to be thrown away before she passed the blossoms into the ceremonial room. It was all so pretty. Children ran up and down the stairs. Zinnie felt as though she'd stepped out of this world and into another, via coach-class flying carpet. As if she were, at least, off on vacation in a foreign country. Something fell from the ceiling onto her opened lap. She thought, alarmed, that she had been blessed, and this token was something, some small miracle, from heaven. Then she realized it was some small roach and she jumped up, barely stifling a shriek, then politely crouched back down again, this time more gingerly. The wizened old man beside her leaned over. She thought he was going to smack the bugger dead, but instead he flicked its derriere gently with a finger and mentioned to her in a singsong, slightly offhand way to, "just let the little fellow be off and on his way."

"Yeah, sure," Zinnie agreed, more interested now in the slender young man in shirtsleeves striding up to the offering sheet with a sharpened machete.

She moved her gun where her free hand could reach it and felt her heart quicken. Visions of Jim Jones and Guyanan suicidal maniacs flew through her imagination and she looked for the nearest way out. The pandit gazed at her and smiled sweetly. He began speaking, politely taking the time to pay special attention to the visitor and explain to her what they were doing. He was talking about goodness, but Zinnie found it hard to concentrate. She felt herself break into a sweat. The young fellow laid the knife down on the sheet. She looked around for Narayan, who had been

154

swept away to the kitchen and was being introduced around to what looked to Zinnie like a bevy of belly dancers. She found herself reassured by her own outrage. Narayan wouldn't be in the kitchen chatting up the girls if there were some plot afoot to capture her and hack off her digits.

Uncomfortable, she shifted her weight. Terror gave way to boredom and she thought of other things. Her ex, Freddy, and what he would say if he could see her now. He would pretend to be unimpressed, of course, but in reality—she grinned her lopsided grin to herself—he would be in the kitchen putting the make on Narayan with the rest of them. Oh, she'd always known what would please Freddy, all right. Or at least almost always. It was such a relief not to be married to him anymore, such a relief not to worry that he would come on to her partner, to the pizza man, even the mailman. She'd never forget the time she came home and found him giving the handsome utility inspector stale Lorna Doones and China tea in the good cups. There was nothing wrong with Freddy's libido.

Zinnie let the air out slowly, through her mouth. The pandit nodded approval. She at least knew rudimentary yoga, he conceded. Zinnie was just so glad not to have to worry about who she brought home for fear of Freddy embarrassing her. She loved him, her old pal Fred, father of her child, good sport and handsome devil, but it was only now that she was free enough of him to realize what terrible damage she'd let him do her. She'd always been so busy working around his preferences, that she hardly remembered what it was she herself liked.

Narayan came back into the room and slipped himself in next to her. He leaned over. "Zinnie," he whispered, "I've changed my mind. I shall return as a bird. And I shall sing to you."

"Okay. Only I hope next time you know enough to pick a better color." She whirled around. "Oh, God, I'm sorry. I didn't mean that. I meant—"

"It's all right, it's all right," he said, patting her hand. "So I shall come back as a red bird. So you will know what it is that I feel for you."

She smiled up at him. She felt her face turn noticeably scarlet and saw the shocked understanding of the perceptive pandit. Well, the hell with him, Zinnie snorted uncharacteristically. The hell with all of them. For once in her life she was going to let herself like what and whom she liked, consequences be damned. She had earned it. Around her, the ladies sang some Indian song so intense and catchingly rhythmic that she found herself swaying with them. This wasn't bad at all. She threw back her head, abandoned at last, and breathed in the exotic pulsating atmosphere. The song came to an end. They sang another. Mrs. Panchyli's thin voice stunned her in the sudden silence. The woman was talking—Zinnie's eyes opened, surprised—to her. Politely—perhaps malevolently—she inquired if she, Zinnie, had any song she would like to sing. To share with them.

"Oh, okay." Zinnie moved her shoulders irresistibly and went accommodatingly right into the first and only song she could think of. As she sang, the man of the house concluded the ceremony with a thwack of the machete on a brown coconut. White creamy milk splattered over the sheet and those nearest the pandit broke out in wide grins.

Out on the street an Italian mechanic, retired and under his Pontiac, bunked his head on the rusty end tailpipe when he heard, like a chorus of seraphim, the house full of Indians singing along to the second refrain of the song "Danny Boy."

Claire stood at Anthony's Fisher-Price easel and painted her photographs with soft watercolors. The children sat near her at the table, doing their homework. Anthony crayoned a Thanksgiving turkey orange and purple and black. Since Mrs. Dixon's escape, she would not let them out of her sight. She'd pick them up from school and they would remain in her view until bedtime. During the night she would wake up and walk through the hallway to check on them three and four times. It was a nightmare, but even this nightmare, day after day, took on a grim pattern of nonchalant routine. Anthony's birthday, usually a major event, was celebrated quietly within the family. After all, nobody knew where Mrs. Dixon had gone. Probably halfway to Peoria, the police concluded, after painstakingly searching the area. Still, they had plastered her face all over the news for three days. The publicity was sure to provide a lead somewhere.

Swamiji and Narayan had postponed their trip to Berkeley for a while. There seemed to be no great urgency for the moment, and their minds, Swamiji said, would anyway be back here in the province of Queens. Johnny had helped them lug the rest of their stuff up to Mrs. Kinkaid's old sewing room, and there they remained, nestled near the still unpruned branches of the backyard trees. Sometimes, when he fancied he smelled danger, Swamiji would bring his mat and blanket back downstairs and sleep like a guard dog behind the front door. No one minded, but he was difficult to wake up. When Johnny came in at all hours, he had the devil of a time moving Swamiji's body aside to peek in. Still, Johnny was grateful. His old local precinct, the 102, kept an eye on the place—but God knew they already had enough to do.

Breaking into Claire's thoughts, the back door jiggled and opened and Swamiji came in with Mary. They had been to the Key Food store. Swamiji and Mary got along like a house afire and shared the shopping. Oh, they would sit up together late at night, page after colorful page of coupons spread out before them. Armed with their scissors, they would attack the week's clipping. All well and good, but—Claire scratched her head when she opened the almost full fridge and freezer in the cellar—when would they eat all this stuff? Mary and Swamiji spent so much money saving money it was as if they were going for broke. What feverish dedication drove the two of them? And where would it end? Who was going to drink all those bottles of guava fruit drink? She supposed they could have a big party and certify it with rum. Or vodka. And what about those jars of apple sauce? Wouldn't apple sauce go bad? Not at these cool temperatures down here in the cellar, her mother and Swamiji had rushed to assure her, pleased with themselves and urgent to be gone on the next expedition. Well, one thing was for sure: she wouldn't have to buy any more Comet for the rest of her life. Or Scott toilet paper either.

Claire plodded through the harrowing towers of products in her mind as she watched them come in with their next contribution.

"Ma, what did you do?"

"Wait till you see." Swamiji was a-dither with excitement. He rubbed his hands, a sorcerer above a big brown bag. Oh, dear, worried Claire. America had finally gotten to him. Beaming, he and Mary unloaded five-pound tins of coffee onto the table. "Coffee?!" pooh-poohed the children, appalled at the waste of a perfectly good trip to the supermarket. "Where are the Chips Ahoy?"

"They weren't on sale," Swamiji explained and Michaelaen and Anthony, annoyed, returned to their own lives. What good were adults, after all, when they had every chance to buy good stuff and then didn't?

Dharma didn't say anything, but she was disgusted as well. She was tired of doing homework. She wanted to go out. She wanted to go back in the garage with Michaelaen and hide out.

"Tell you what," Mary said, taking in the whole scene, the fatigue on their faces, especially Claire's. "You go off, Claire, and do things you haven't had a chance to do, you know, dry cleaner's, library, cup of coffee with a friend, and Swamiji and I will stay here and look after the children."

Swamiji nodded amicably. They had the Sunday *Times* and the *Newsday* coupons they hadn't even had a chance to look through yet. And the crosswords. He and Mary argued like children over who got which crossword first.

Anthony put down his black crayon. He'd been heftily darkening that turkey's sky. He looked from Claire to the other children with long, weary lids. "Wanna watch Mr. Wodgers?" he asked them. He knew Mommy liked it when he watched Mr. Rogers. No guns, no perversions. It was his way of helping her out. He was uncanny, her son, bringing her back from the dead every time when she hadn't even known she'd been there. Well, he knew. Such a little fellow and here he was condescending to watch his baby show for her sake, just to please her. Allay her fatigue. Oh, sure. Most of the time she wanted to kill him. He was that kind of kid. Drove you to the edge. But when she really took off and her face took on that zombie glow, he understood, always knew. And he saved her. Anthony's compassion was a lot like someone who drove you off the edge of a cliff and then caught you with his handy net . . . but catch her he did. He did save her, every time.

Anyway, it wasn't because of Anthony that Claire went mad. Not anymore. Just a year had promoted him from baby to kid. And it wasn't Johnny either. It was herself. She was tired. And lately, the more she slept, the more she wanted to sleep. To escape the tedium of her own—what? What was it? Her faith? Yes, the truth was that she had finally got what she wanted, and she found herself clinging to it so hard that she couldn't stand back from it and look at it and love it. She couldn't detach, yes, that was the word, detach, because she was afraid nothing would come afterwards but death. The still everlasting embodied by the dead-as-a-doornail bird she and Anthony had seen that day last year in the yard, before any of this had begun. When they'd still been living over in South Ozone Park, where she'd hated every minute but had loved her dream of coming up here. Now here she was. She had everything she wanted, and now this monster had escaped.

It was as though her faith was only there when things were going her way, and now that they weren't, she was desolate. Sorrowfully, she looked around at the faces of her family looking, puzzled, back at hers, and she doubted there was any life after death after all. If one had anything to do with the other. But it did. Because without the one there was no sense to the other. Mrs. Dixon escaping from Deauville had loosened the screw that held her security so tentatively tight. There was no sense to life. To death. Everything probably stopped, simply stopped. You would see your last sight and the glass of your eyes would break and then that would be all; the sparkle of pain and of hope would just stop and relax to opaqueness. Claire shuddered. Who had ever been so cruel as to perpetrate dreams of a brassy eternal? A billowy cloud to hang onto. It was too disheartening. She would take Anthony out of Holy Child. There was no sense to handing over her false hopes to him as well. Here they were paying good money just to make him mentally ill. Yes, she thought and held her elbows and sat down carefully, that was it, she was mentally ill. She had stood vigilant too long.

"Claire!"

"What? I'm sorry. What?"

Mary clicked her tongue. "I'm talking to you. For heaven's sake!"

"Exactly," said Claire and she laughed. A wacky, gaudy laugh that stopped everyone's easy smiles and made them look at her, concerned.

Swamiji went over to Claire and stood behind her. He brushed the red-brown hair away from her face and stood with his cool palms pressed to her forehead. With his pinkies, one on top of the other, he made a firm impression where the third eye ought to be.

Frightened, Anthony ran to his mother. He crawled up onto her lap and sat there like a little baby. Claire came back. Mary put a cup of hot water in front of her and Dharma, a good girl really, bobbed a tea bag into it.

Claire laughed, self-deprecatingly this time, not crazily. They indeed talked her into going for a walk, as Mary had suggested, or at least leaving, getting out of the house for a while. When she eventually recognized that they meant it, she decided to take the opportunity to drop off the photo of the nursery school, the Italianate Victorian, with the owner. Anyone would be happy to have such a fine portrait of one's place. And she had colored it, too. It was the first she had done, as an experiment, because she really hadn't cared about how it would turn out. Yes, she would drop that off and have a walk besides. She wasn't doing any good to anyone in the state she was in. The next thing, she'd be yelling at the lot of them. They would all be better off with her gone. Her father had mentioned that there was a Second Empire Victorian over on 111th Street. She might pass by there with her camera.

"All right," she agreed and went to hunt for a new roll of black-and-white, 3200 ASA film. Mary had set the three kids to work at the stove, Claire noticed on her way out. They were making cherry Jell-O. The smell just filled the kitchen and delighted Swamiji, who'd never before had the pleasure. Claire approved the scene. There was nothing kids loved more than playing at the stove, the most forbidden of all places. They'd be safe under Mary's hawkeye tutelage, and happy to boot.

Outside, it was ugly weather, gray and blue, the slick streets mangled with drudgy bundles of wet yellow leaves. The tops of the trees were finally just about empty. Claire shivered cozily into her Lauren-Hutton-in-the-suburbs raincoat, yet another castoff, literally retrieved from the garbage behind Carmela's house. "What are you doing?" Carmela had shouted at her.

"What do you think I'm doing?" she'd shouted back.

"It's garbage," raged Carmela.

"It's Banana Republic." Claire'd folded the coat cheerfully into her satchel. Anything from last year was garbage to Carmela. The only things she kept were from Bendel's or Bergdorf's. Carmela bought and discarded clothes by what seemed to Claire the bucketful. BORN TO SHOP read the framed bumper sticker hung in her Imelda Marcos-type closet. Stan had given the sticker to her for her car, but she wouldn't kitsch up her fancy car. Still, there was enough of the girl from Richmond Hill in Carmela to appreciate her own decadence. All this consumeritis was all right with Claire as long as she got a chance to scrounge through it. Pride, Claire had long ago decided, had nothing to do with it. She petted the muted tan sleeve. It is worn and soft, she thought, like me, like me.

Above the woods, a white pearly streak came out over the bottom clouds. Swamiji, to her despair, would never join her in her jaunts through the forest. This was a terrible disappointment to Claire, who had always supposed they would picnic and stroll in and out of the woods together. It was, she tried to explain to him, her special place.

Yes, he'd agreed, it was a sacred place, but sacrilege had been done there and he wouldn't set foot in such a place.

"It's true that children were killed there," Claire admitted, "but your presence alone would—"

He had gone, he was already walking away ahead of her. She'd caught up with him. "This is a terrible place," he'd said, shivering, pulling his cashmere shawl about himself protectively. "Your Catholic priests should go there and remove the demons ceremoniously." She could just see herself showing up at the rectory door with this request. Somehow, she imagined it wouldn't go over big. Then again, it might. Now with Anthony connected to the school she didn't like to come across as the new neighborhood nut-job. ("Here she comes," the mothers on the corner waiting for their kids to come from the school would whisper, "Bats Benedetto.") At any rate, she would go herself, with holy water. Mary had a vast stash imported from Lourdes, kept in plastic bottles with blue (for Our Lady) caps.

I shall go, she decided finally, to the five-and-ten. A place where decisions could be made, where dreams could meander and youth be recalled. She was just enjoying the satisfaction of devastating a neatly packed curb full of leaves, when Andrew Dover fell into step alongside her. It was uncanny how all this man had to do was show up and already she was feeling foolish and defensive. Determined not to let him get at her, she flashed him one of her reasonable smiles. He could not see the jumble and confusion in her mind, could he? She had to keep reminding herself that she wasn't transparent. He had some shoes he wanted to drop off for Dharma, he explained, and didn't like to come when it was inconvenient for her.

She whirled on him. She couldn't help it. "Hey look, Andrew. I've been wanting to speak with you about Dharma for a while now. Let's just get one thing straight, all right? As far as her life is concerned, don't worry about propriety and whether or not you're disturbing Johnny or me. If you want to see your daughter, even if it's the middle of the night, don't hesitate. I mean, the poor kid could use a little parental warmth right now. As much as we care about the kid, she's still yours."

A group of laughing teenagers from the high school ran by in a tight boisterous ball. Black kids in a relatively white neighborhood, small wonder they stuck together. Andrew waited for them to pass before he answered her. He blew on his hands and rubbed them, not unhappily, together. "Yes, well, that's just it, you see." They were drawing closer to the el and she had to lean toward him to catch his words. "She's not my daughter, exactly."

"You're kidding! But I thought—"

"Look, when I married Theresa, she was already pregnant with Dharma. She just didn't know it."

"What?"

"Yes. It's true. I don't usually tell people this, but, well, in this case—I just didn't want you to think I was neglecting my own child."

"I see," Claire stopped and hoisted her great sack more comfortably on her back. "So you neglected someone else's."

"Sorry?" he cupped his ear, old-man style.

"I said," she shouted accusingly, "Dharma is still yours by marriage. By familiarity."

The blast of the train clacketted off in the direction of Woodhaven. A sudden furry whip of wind around Claire's legs gave her a fright. She was so startled, she grabbed Andrew's hand to steady

162

herself before she realized the wind was Floozie. She'd come all this way on her own. The little freshie had crossed three streets and run by who knew how many cars—maybe parked, maybe not. Floozie circled with admonishing yaps. She was right. Claire had had no reason to leave her behind. If anything, Floozie had proved time and time again that she was to be trusted, walking right beside her and a little bit behind with deferential devotion. Lying low in restaurants, unobtrusively still inside Claire's ever-present camera bag. so no overly conscientious waitress could come over to the table to snap "Outa-here." Claire cocked her elbow and, true to form and not to disappoint Claire (who sort of got a kick out of Andrew's astonishment—how many doggies had followed *him* through life?) Floozie helicoptered up and into her raincoat sleeve. Claire lowered Barnum eyes at Andrew. What a show-off she knew she was. Never mind.

Later, she would ask herself why she hadn't asked Andrew whose child, then, Dharma was? She already knew why. Some people have magnetic power over you—and you can't say just why. They have a way of never letting you get any further in processing your thoughts. They trick you, put you off, charm you with surprises. You can be standing there thinking, As soon as he finishes saying this, I'll ask him. But then he says something else and that distracts you and before you know it, you're walking off wondering what happened. Claire and Andrew walked together up Jamaica Avenue, a derelict place nowadays, but still blue and enclosed by the el tracks and memories of when it was all bustle. Shopkeepers lolled into work at eleven or noon these days, realistic, pessimistic. Only the bodegas left and right bustled with life.

They hurried by the hardware store. Stan, Claire's father, came out from behind an enormous speaker, and both Claire and Andrew waved but Stan didn't notice. He was utterly distracted. He laid the speaker in the gaping trunk of his car and went back in to get the other. A Korean boy stood guard so no one would walk off with the thing. All this was no surprise to Claire, who knew her father had found those speakers in a movie theater being demolished in Jamaica. He'd actually gone in and hauled them out while the demolition ball hovered (thanks to ten bucks in the operator's pocket) in the air above him. He wasn't going to let those Koreans keep those tweeters and woofers, by golly. No siree. No matter how much money was in that shopping bag of cash they'd paid for the hardware store with.

Inside, Mr. Lee was relieved. Was that guy kidding? Vivaldi at nine o'clock in the morning? Mr. Lee was too polite to correct his elders even if this was his store, but life would be an awful lot better with the portable Hitachi he'd replaced it with on the counter. If that one got too loud it went all tinny and they'd have to shut it off. Hee. Hee.

Neither Claire nor Andrew was anxious to talk to anyone else now. Andrew had committed a confidence to her and they couldn't just leave off like that, so they stood, self-conscious but determined to communicate, alongside the five-and-ten, like any casual pedestrians who'd bumped into each other just like that.

"Andrew," she began kindly. (The man *had* lost his wife, and whether Tree had cuckolded and trapped him once, they'd still stayed together for what, seven or eight years, right? That counted for something.) "What I don't understand is how you can stay away from Dharma now? I mean, excuse me for being so personal, but I don't know how to talk to you except directly."

"I'm so relieved." He shook his head. "I feel like I've been—hell, I *have* been avoiding you because I just didn't want you to know how I feel. I don't know why you should affect me in any way at all but, geez, this is so hard to say—"

Claire leaned toward him.

"The truth is, Claire, I feel no remorse. No remorse at all for Theresa's death. I don't know if she told you any of this before she died, I guess she did—" He searched her face.

"No, nothing. We never got to speak, never had the chance."

Claire saw something in those eyes. Was it relief? He tilted his head back and opened his mouth to the filthy, sorry sky between the track and the building. What now? Was he trying to control himself? He didn't seem to trust himself to speak. She looked politely away, into the window of the old yarn store, now an intergalactic tabernacle for the clairvoyant Mrs. Fatima. Been in the area fifteen years, the circular boasted. The storefront was all astrological murals, dream interpretations, and pink speckled light bulbs. She had it nice and comfy, did Mrs. Fatima, with sofas and bolster pillows and a fat recliner, everything done up in Gulden's yellow and indigo. And she had one of those little dogs, a chihua-hua—a male, from the attentive, mysterious disposition Floozie automatically assumed when she spied the dog in the window.

"I might as well tell you the truth," Andrew said. "Not because I particularly want you to know, but because you'll eventually find out anyhow. I drove her crazy. I wasn't very nice to her," he admitted. "Like she would get all dolled up and I would tell her she looked like she was ready to turn a trick. I did. She was so slutty. I used to insult her so she would leave me alone. I'd get her good and mad and then when I'd walk out she was glad to see me go. She would get all involved with that I Ching shit. You know—that book of changes where you throw down those Chinese coins and all. And all that Indian crap. Oh, she went for that big time. Her tastes were so bohemian. And the drugs that went with it. You know all about that."

She did? Claire almost laughed. It was so long since she'd herself done drugs that it felt like another lifetime.

Andrew went on, unencumbered by facts or acquiescence from her. She could see how he had charmed the neighborhood with his disarming frankness. He was getting into his theme now. And then, confession was so warming. He was a Catholic, after all. So was she, for that matter. They were all Catholics here. She felt a headache coming on. She wished he would stop talking about Tree this way, stop talking altogether. This was *her* walk, her little breakdown.

"I have to tell you, Andrew," she finally interrupted, "I can't stand hearing this. I don't want to hear the details of your life with my friend Tree. Really. I only am listening to you so you'll maybe, just maybe, give me a clue as to why you've abandoned your daughter. And please," she covered one eye with one hand, "I don't care that it wasn't your sperm from your loins that gave rise to her reality because, Buster, it was you there on Christmas, and birthdays, and through all the childhood diseases and that's what makes a father. So you still haven't told me why you've aban-doned your daughter to a neighbor you hardly—you don't even know."

He changed his tack. He dropped his head. "Dharma," he said, "never, ever liked me."

"Oh boo hoo."

"She didn't." He looked at Claire wildly. "Even when she was a baby she would push me away. Push me away!" he cried, tears, small and hot came out of his dignified man's eyes.

Claire looked around uncomfortably. The ladies from the Church Mini Second Hand House were passing by. It was sale day at the five-and-ten. To their credit, they never seemed to look at Andrew, just trotted by. They knew he'd lost a wife. Everyone knew. They wouldn't embarrass him for all the tea in China. A good man. Took all those kids last year on that trip to Valley Forge.

"All right," Andrew said. "I know you and John have been wonderful. Wonderful. I can't keep imposing upon your hospitality." He went to bite a cuticle in a nervous gesture. "Our problems are our problems." He bobbed up and down. "I only wish I knew someone who could stay with us, someone reliable. A woman. You know, who Dharma could relate to—like—"

"Portia McTavish?"

"Say! No. No, she's already done so much."

"I'll bet. Of course you know Dharma can't stomach Portia McTavish."

"Oh, right. But then, she doesn't like anyone. She hates my mother." He sighed. "Anyway, my mother is . . . sickly. She wouldn't be up to helping out much . . ."

"She likes me. Sort of. I think. She certainly likes Zinnie."

Andrew looked up at the Schenkers, a gray-haired couple walking arm in arm from the bakery. They'd had their colonial up for sale with Century 21 since Claire had moved in. The sign was still up and they were still here. Both they and Andrew knew they were ready to sign with another realtor and it might as well be him. He pulled himself together quickly enough, nodding at them handsomely. This was one slick canary. For a moment there she'd almost forgotten. She was tempted to ask him why a smooth operator like himself was content to live and work in Queens, but she could pretty much imagine what his reply would be. Better a big fish in a little pond, he would say. And of course he was right.

With everybody moving away, someone had to stay around to make the money on the ones just moving in. Someone had to close those deals, and it might as well be him. She could certainly see why people trusted him, what with his breezy, take-charge way about him, his light brown hair and oxblood shoes. And now he was a widower. What could be better? She bet he had healthy green plants in his office, plants that flourished and grew burgeoning shoots under his sensual magnetism and charm. She could just see it. And old-fashioned oak swivel chairs behind good, timeworn desks. Not too hard to find around here, if you waited till some three-generations-old business finally collapsed—and made sure you were the first fellow standing there nice enough to pick through the remains and offer handy, heartfelt green cash. Andrew had, she noticed, beneath the camouflage of his expensive tailoring, a fat rear end. She had to snap out of this. What was he saying?

". . . so I was looking through these advertisements for boarding schools someone gave me from the back of the *New York Times* color section. Good schools," he frowned, "not just farms for bad kids or anything like that. Let's face it, Dharma could use some discipline. It could be the best thing for her after all these years of Theresa's dumping her off with whoever would watch her after school so she could get dolled up and . . . well . . ." (He was going to be a gentleman here.) ". . . and go have fun." His tightened lips let loose and he looked, for once without his guard, betrayed.

Claire imagined the pretty room across from Anthony's suddenly free. No more depressed morbid presence, heavy with grief to occupy her sunny house. It would be such a relief. Her own family without intrusion, complication. If that room were empty, you never knew, maybe Carmela would move in. What, and leave her husband, her fancy life? It was just a thought, she defended herself to herself. Just because Carmela looked drawn and, well, haggard, didn't mean things were so bad for her. Still, she knew Carmela would never move back in with their parents again. Never. They'd all done that once already and Carmela would rather wallow in her misery than have to live with her parents' kind pity again. One divorce was bad enough. Two divorces?

They'd never be able to keep that look of martyred, baffled disenchantment from their eyes.

Of course, she could move to the city. SoHo. Yes, that was where Carmela probably would move if she ever left Stefan, though why she imagined Carmela leaving him was beyond her. Wishful thinking, probably. She wanted Carmela all to herself, the way it was when they were kids. Carmela might be a bitch, but she kept you guessing. She wasn't fun, though. Zinnie was fun, but Carmela was ambiguous, bitchy, affected, unrelenting, exhausting, theatrical, costly, ornamental, artsy, and tarty—and in Richmond Hill, there weren't that many around who were.

Another thing. If Dharma left, Anthony would have Michaelaen back. Claire had thought Zinnie and his staying would give the two boys a chance to grow as cousins, thought it would be magical for Anthony, but what had happened was that Dharma and Michaelaen had fallen into collusion. Of course—they were about the same age, whispering and secretive and closing Michaelaen's door against "babies," meaning Anthony. Her heart broke for her son, little waif alone again. At least Swamiji was there to insist the children be the best they could be. They would spend the rest of their lives benefitting from his holy influence. She stopped the ranting of her mind. Who was she kidding? She couldn't let Dharma be conveniently shipped off to some fancy, cold-hearted boarding school. Just the thought of Swamiji had reminded her of what she had to do.

"So how's this idea," she looked up at him with what she hoped were her still relatively persuasive Siberian-husky blue eyes. "You give me enough money to pay for Dharma's food and rent, a little extra for entertainment and clothes, and I'll take her in. Like a foster mother."

Mrs. Fatima, in her storefront, screwed up her eyes and her nostrils opened wide. She couldn't stop looking out at Claire. She tapped the end tip of her finger with a rat-tat-tat-tat on the shiny Formica tabletop. She just couldn't place her.

Andrew looked shocked. "I could never do that!"

"Why not? You're ready to ship her off to total strangers for what would surely be twenty times what I would ask you. At least with me she'd have a chance—" She revised her wording. "At

168

least if you knew she was with me, you could relax enough about her to go about your job, get the things done that a man has to do. I mean, I'm home anyway. I could help out and—" Here she remembered Johnny's new hobby, of which she would also remind him, in case he defied her idea. "—make a little extra money. Besides, I like Dharma."

Not love. Don't say love. Remember that little boy in the orphanage over in Brooklyn. Remember promises that left kids trying to understand. Standing hotly by while other kids went off to movies and libraries and they got to stay home, dribbling no-bounce basketballs around broken bottles by themselves because one thoughtless pretty white girl had promised she would be there. That they could count on her, not to worry. So, one thing at a time here.

She looked up and could see the wheels turning in Andrew's busy mind. No one in the parish could accuse him of neglect if he had his daughter with that nice policeman's family across the street. The wife a faint bit screwy, but probably harmless. Couldn't be too far off the mark if it was Mary Breslinsky's daughter. Of course, he would let it slip that he was paying her. Wouldn't want anyone to think he was using them. Not that Johnny would let him get away with that for much longer anyway.

"You are a saint," he bowed to Claire. "How can I ever thank you?"

"Don't thank me. Just let me figure out how much she costs me by the month and we can decide how much to add to it." He waited long enough for her to think he was turning it over in his reluctant, bereaved mind. "Done!" He looked at his watch. "Oh boy! Gotta run. I'm showing a house up on Park Lane South fifteen minutes ago."

Fleetingly, Claire thought to show him his wife's letter, in this new air of agreement between them, but she didn't. She put her left hand around its crumpled, folded form inside her pocket and she held it there. He shook her other hand and turned to go—then turned back. "Oh," he said, "let me give you the key and you can run over there and go through her clothes, get what she'll need."

"Okay." She pocketed the key.

"And then if you would just drop off the dry cleaning I left on the dining room table? I know it's a lot to ask but you can imagine what a madhouse it's been."

"Accommodating I am. Subservient I'm not."

Andrew blinked. His closed mouth drew back its corners. "Of course you're not. How stupid of me to have thought you might be."

"An oversight."

"Not to be forgotten."

"You bet." They eyed each other.

"Your appointment."

"Yuh. Till soon, then." He made his pointed finger and his thumb into a gun and shot her . . . a friendly gesture.

"Oh," she remembered. "You might also add on some money to supply her with paints. She really likes to paint."

He rushed away, eyebrows up, to indicate he'd heard.

"Now that, Floozie," she smiled after him and nuzzled the dog, "is what you call a real piece of *scheisse.*" The kind, noted Floozie, that doesn't stink. Claire went into the five-and-ten and gazed distracted at the never-changing shelves of loose dusting face powder and My Pinky lipstick and Cutex nail polish. She congratulated herself. She had accomplished what she'd set out to do, what was the "right" thing to do. She shivered in the sudden overheated gloom. She couldn't escape the nagging feeling that that was exactly the way Andrew Dover had intended her to feel.

Mrs. Fatima put on her wrap, turned the key in her store's lock, and went in one of the five-and-ten's doors just as Claire walked out the other.

Zinnie sat at the wheel of her battered silver Datsun on a side street of Forest Hills Gardens. This was not the first time she'd done this. Years ago, before she'd been on the job, when she'd been in college and night jobbing up on Austin Street, she used to come through here with Freddy and they'd dream about their future. Pretend that one day they'd be able to afford one of these places. Fairy tale castles. That's what they looked like. Come to think of it, she had the same car then that she had now.

Forest Hills Gardens is a neighborhood within all the other neighborhoods. It's set off limits on smooth, broad lawns, under old-fashioned street lamps that work. The cobblestoned roads have wrought-iron gates, big gates, the kind the artist uses to depict heaven's entrance, at each periphery. There's an abundance of red crawling ivy and lead-paned windows. Many of the houses have towers and turrets and it's all benignly nestled under eminent, lofty trees. Regular police don't have to bother in there, they've got their own intrepid security service. There are no cars. There is a reason for this. If you park in there, they boot your wheel and plaster your windows with some mucky glue that you can't get off for thirty-seven years. So nobody parks in Forest Hills Gardens without a permit. Even for twenty minutes. Already, Zinnie had had to lower her shield through the window at the diligent if mothballed guard weaving conspicuously in and out the silent streets. She watched his bumper round the bend and went back to her reverie. A last yellow leaf went floating to the just-blown curb. So this was bliss, eh? This was the spot she found herself thinking about when she was on a stakeout over in East New York, holed up in a truck with one eye on a door and one on the clock and neither of them going anywhere. There was a box bay bow window in a mansion across the road. She sipped her Styrofoam cup of black coffee. There were stuffed animals packed into that window. Some real child lived there, she realized, amazed it wasn't just a castle in Spain, the way it looked. She wondered what a kid from a place like that would be like. Like her own son who hung out in closets? All right, used to. Used to hang out in closets. She had to admit that this Swamiji had accomplished what four years of therapy had not for Michaelaen. Unbelievable. In three weeks he'd gained his trust and even introduced him to yoga. True, Michaelaen's interest there stemmed from some televised inclination toward the more glamorous and hostile ninja kung fu. But Swamiji had used that enthusiasm to goad Michaelaen into opening the door on his own darkness. This morning Michaelaen had confided to her that Swamiji said he had "met his dragon head on." "Yeah?" Zinnie had not turned, for fear of spooking him. The psychiatrist had told her she was stopping him from reaching deeper every time her eyes filled up with tears. Michaelaen didn't want to upset her and so he stopped his own self-investigations.

"What did he look like?" Zinnie had asked. He'd continued to cut out the cardboard figure of Uncle Scrooge from the back of the Corn Pops box with a scissors. "Like Mrs. Dixon," he'd said. Her heart had almost stopped beating and she had all she could do to not whirl around and take him in her arms. She had said nothing, hoping he would go further, and she was rewarded. "I mean like me watching Mrs. Dixon watching the children," he'd corrected his picture of his dragon.

"Okay," she'd said softly, biting her lip, and she didn't say any more, just looked at him and took a big breath. So he had done the same. That had been the end of it. And, she'd hoped somehow, the beginning.

Zinnie turned on the car radio. The Schubert serenade was playing. Right away she thought of Narayan. Those heartbreaking liquid eyes. She didn't know if this feeling was love or lust, because it sure as hell felt like both. She could kick herself. There was nothing possible about the situation, no way this could work out. And she couldn't let Michaelaen see her with this guy, let him see them in a romantic situation that would lead nowhere. The poor kid was confused enough by having a gay, if honorable, father. Although, Zinnie continued to believe, it was other people who were confused and not them. She, Freddy, and Michaelaen all seemed to deal perfectly well with Freddy's gayness. The only fly in the ointment was their mutually over-protective attitude towards each other when anyone would "put it to them."

She looked back at that lucky kid's dolls in that fairy tale house, and she thought of Michaelaen's quickly, politely put-away toys in Claire's own great, colorful house. Who was she kidding? She'd never even get to see the inside of a house like that, let alone live in one, own one. She would never have that life of handsome reserve. She would always live along somebody else's edge. Yes, she was proud and no one gave her what she wasn't already entitled to, but did it have to be so hard? Did it? These people. They had maids and roses and they didn't even look at them.

Zinnie appraised the villas left and right. She wondered what these people thought when they woke up under down comforters and the first thing they saw were lead-paned prisms of sunlight, like shimmering jewels on a Persian carpet. Narayan had grown up rich like that. Claire had told her. He was the first grandson of some maharaja, or something. And he'd gone to live with the ascetic Swamiji freely. No one had forced him. No wonder Carmela was always trying to get him to come to one of her shindigs. She was such a snob. Zinnie supposed if Narayan had had money once, he could probably get it again. If it was, after all, his inheritance, Zinnie wondered if this meant inheritance in India or an inheritance you could take out and buy a home with in a place like, say, this?

A yellow cab pulled up. A woman got out. You could tell she was rich. Not just had money. *Rich*. The color and cut of her short thick hair. Highlights you couldn't see. The drab subtlety of her loden coat. The woman lifted a garbage can and carried it into the driveway. Her driveway. There was something in that movement, in that simple act, that made it all seem suddenly achievable to Zinnie. She crossed the imaginary bridge. Rich, untouchable lady. Garbage can. Never the twain shall meet. But they did. It had, magically. Easy. And so, who knew, might she. That woman in this notoriously Irish Catholic paradise appeared to be some sort of Iranian. Or Western-educated Syrian. Something definitely not white bread. And here she was. At home, picking up her own garbage can and walking into her own palace backyard. True, it was one of the smaller palaces. Not even as grand as Carmela's. But it was stupendous nonetheless.

The whole neighborhood was a parody of English country estates set conveniently nose to nose so they could fit in one privileged area cut off from the poor people's world. Instead of forests stuffed with game for the hunt, they had their canyons of Wall Street and Madison Avenue to sport in. Zinnie wondered if that woman's husband was lighter or darker than she. Just a thought. So what, she wasn't allowed to think? She put her foot down on the gas and hightailed it out of there.

Claire knocked one more time on her mother's kitchen door, but she knew she wasn't there. The light would be on. The puppies snipped and whined. Stan had foresightedly boarded up the dog door for the time being, and they couldn't get out to do the world or themselves any harm.

Floozie watched them disdainfully from her perch on Claire's bag. These were the brothers and sisters who'd turned their backs on her when she'd been apprehended for the reprehensible behavior that had led her to death row. Never mind that they'd had nothing to do with her arrest. Had any of them come forward? Even to the door? Shed a tear? No. She sniffed and looked rather across the street at Iris von Lillienfeld's old pooch out on the porch. This then, she had heard, was her grandmother, and that then was where she'd look. The love of her grandfather's, the Mayor's life, or at least, she readjusted her reverie realistically, the last bitch with whom he'd shacked up.

Claire murmured and sputtered, linked up her hand luggage (where she went, she went loaded down as a pack mule on Ios) and smacked her boot soles against the flat, painted porch floor. It was cold. Claire followed Floozie's gaze across the street. Lord knew she didn't get over to see old Iris von Lillienfeld enough these days. They crossed the street. Floozie looked back to see if the other dogs were watching. They were. She sucked in her cheeks and lowered her eyes. Let them have a good look.

Here lived (some said still lived) Iris von Lillienfeld, brilliant if eccentric old foreign woman in a magnificent Queen Anne Victorian, a house young girls meandered by on their way home from school, their books clutched to their fanciful breasts; a house about which they would dream through high school, even on through college, marriages, and then walk past with their own children, still dreaming, a house that set you off, a boy-oh-boy-if-you-could-only-get-your-hands-on-it house. If that old woman would only die. But she wouldn't, would she?

And the house was filled with dolls, old dolls, bisque antique dolls that she had clothed in excellent, hand-pressed and mended antique togs, for whom she cleaned and which she petted and kept as in some silent orphanage of dreams. Here in her own world, Iris rose and dressed herself in champagne togs to do the job: fragile slips and dresses adorned with cameos on eighteen-carat chains and braids of emeralds woven through her vague coiffure. Iris came and went and walked about in a red silk coat with a gold embroidered dragon on its back.

Today Iris, ironing doily collars on a pint-sized ironing board set on top of a regular one, threw her hands up into the air when her wobbly squinting produced the face of Claire at her door.

"Ja, vot a surprise!" She flung the kitchen door open and took Claire into her bony embrace. Then she spied Floozie. "And who is this? My Natasha's *enkel*?! My Natasha's grandson?!"

"Granddaughter," Claire corrected, smiling, loosening Floozie's suddenly timid frame out onto the porcelain-topped table. Floozie looked skeptically about, slipped this way and that and looked pleadingly to Claire. Claire put her bag underneath the dog so she would be on more familiar ground, and the two women stood there inspecting the furry little gal.

"She favors my Natasha, I think," Iris appraised her critically.

"Yes, she's more poodle than, er, whatever it was that the Mayor was."

"Poodle? Natasha is not a poodle! Vot are you thinking? Natasha is a bichon frise."

"A what?"

"A bichon frise. I voodn't have a poodle."

"Oh."

"Vot's her name?"

"Floozie."

"Floozie? Vot kind of a name is dot? Why not just call her trollop? Or hussy?"

"Aw, no. Gee. It's an affectionate term. Endearing."

"What's endearing about an insult?" Iris put the kettle on. She might be old but she kept her kitchen fragrant and clean as a German bakery. Everything was white. The counter gleamed and the ceiling had one of those big ice-cube trays of fluorescent lights. This was all in direct contrast to the rest of the house, which was sort of dusty and dim with extravagance.

"Vot about calling her 'Duchess'?" Iris offered.

Claire looked at her dog. "She's got her name. Have you heard who's staying at my house?"

"Your mother told me. How's the little dollink doing?"

"Oh, Dharma, yes. All right, I guess. Do you know who else?"

Iris's eyebrows went up. "Kinkaid told me that. Got you coming and going." She rubbed her hands as though she were applying lotion.

Claire noticed an iron pan cooling on the sill. "Leeks?" she sniffed.

"Mmm," Iris looked away.

"What? What's the matter?"

Iris looked back shrewdly. Claire assessed vibrations well. She shrugged. "So? I cook a little something for an old man nobody cooks for anymore. So sue me."

"Who?" Her first thought, because of the guilty look she'd seen pass over Iris's face, was her own father, Stan. But of course that wasn't it—Mary cooked for Stan three times a day. She couldn't imagine. Then—"Not Mr. Kinkaid?"

"Come on," Iris swatted the dog off the table. *"Keine Tiere auf dem Tisch. Pfoof! Weg!"*

"Well, well, well." Claire grinned, then saw by Iris's tightening upper lip she'd been too familiar. There was something rigidly aristocratic about Iris, and it didn't take much to put her off, close her up to idle scrutiny. She decided to let it alone. "Heard any new poop on Mrs. Dixon?"

Iris snorted. "If anybody knows anything dot's your mother." Tit for tat was Iris.

"Yes. Well, my mother's feeling pretty bad about everything just about now."

"Pfoof. Wasn't her fault. Wrong place at the wrong time. Simple."

Claire and Iris looked doubtfully at each other. Everyone knew by now that Mrs. Dixon had escaped by bopping Mary Breslinsky on the head with a typewriter and climbing through an air-conditioning vent from a room she and Mary would sit in to discuss Mrs. Dixon's forthcoming book. A room not particularly heavily guarded owing to Mrs. Dixon's deteriorating health. Supposedly deteriorating health. Now, they figured, those arthritic hands and crippled back had all been an act. A trick. Mrs. Dixon was in the pink of health and had had no use for the wheelchair she'd been driven back and forth in, and which she had so slickly left behind.

"I'll bet she's in Boston," Iris said. "Didn't she have a sister-in-law?"

"Better tell the cops if you know anything about a relative." Iris looked stricken. "I heard dot on the news."

"Oh. Just so long as she doesn't come crawling around here anymore, that's all I worry about. It gets pretty tiresome doing graveyard shifts over at my house. I've got the three kids with me, you know. And it's not like you can let them out alone for a minute." She overheard the unpleasant whine in her own voice. She cleared her throat and lowered her pitch. "I just wish they'd catch her. Wherever she was headed—she's there by now. They should have thrown away the key when they had the chance."

Iris shook her head sadly. "Hard to believe anyone could molest and kill children like that. Let alone someone you know."

Claire couldn't bear the thought of Michaelaen watching Mrs. Dixon photographing one of those same children she later molested and killed.

Iris said, "Claire. Dear. I know it's very hard for you to understand. We can be very sophisticated in the ways of the world and still know nothing of evil. Real evil. It's not enough to say, vell, she was abused as a child as well. I mean, she was. Mrs. Dixon was. I know. So, see, evil doesn't start from thin air. But there are others who were abused and turned out to be normal, if sadder, adults. Where the evil takes over is the frightening element, *nicht Wahr?* Nobody knows about dot.

"Now, how about dot for a nice doggy?" Iris cooed, changing the subject. Her old Natasha had hobbled in to inspect Floozie and the two of them were making nicey-nice underneath the stepladder there.

"How does Anthony like having a dog?" Iris asked.

"Oh, just fine. She fits right in, this one."

At the sound of Anthony's name, Floozie bolted to the door and had a look out. Was he coming? Was he coming?

Claire moved uncomfortably in her chair. Usually, Iris couldn't do enough for her, pulling out cakes and rugalah. Perhaps she'd come at a bad time. Maybe Mr. Kinkaid was on his way? Kinkaid might be an obnoxious, belligerent, racist pain to her, but to Iris, who had spent so many years feeling, what? useless and alone, Kinkaid might have the quality of being, well, alive.

"So," Claire said and stretched, "just thought we'd stop over. See how you are. We'll be off, then."

Like that of so many flamboyant dressers, Iris's mind was comparatively no-nonsense. And she noticed that under Claire's blue eyes were circles she had never seen before. She tipped her chin. "Got troubles, girlie? What's dat Johnny up to?"

"Troubles with Johnny?" Claire smiled wryly. "Not really. I mean, he bought a horse without telling me, a racehorse. But no." She shook her head. "Not really troubles. Not when you have somebody like Dharma living with you. Now, she's got troubles."

Iris walked beside her to the door. "Her troubles are finally over, from wot I heard."

"Oh, yeah? What did you hear?"

"Pfff. Lots. Mrs. Dover was carrying on all over the place, from vot I understand. Small wonder she was pregnant when she died."

"She was? Who told you that?"

"Why, Jerry Mahegganey. From the funeral parlor. You didn't know?"

"No! How pregnant was she?"

Iris shrugged. "Not so much that it showed. But enough that she was."

"Yeah? No kidding?" She stopped short.

"What?"

"No nothing. I just wonder if she'd told Dharma. Confided in her."

"Huh. Vot I vonder is if she told the husband."

"Mm. Come on, Floozie. We'll come back soon. Okay?" She looked for a shot of warm confirmation from somewhere beneath Iris's pale blue cataracts, but Iris looked away. The cat, Lü, the Siamese, had come in, as old as anybody's hills and with eyes as blue as any of theirs. Claire remembered Lü. His name meant "the wanderer" in the I Ching. You never knew where he was till he was right there beside you, he was that quiet. She had the uncanny feeling he was there to see them out. Claire carried Floozie out with a make-believe good-bye grin on her face. Lü stood there intense as an Egyptian statue, watching them watching her, and something told her something was not right. She cast her eyes down on the wooden painted stoop cracks as she went carefully down the steps, looking up quickly at her loose and shimmering reflection in the window and was reminded of a feeling, not tingling, but some strange sensation on her right side.

Some sensitivity, like numbness, or stinging or more like both, all along her cheek and right shoulder and down her arm, until she suddenly remembered when she'd had that feeling before. Years ago, four or five years ago (a long time, but that was how peculiar and distinct the feeling was). And not just a feeling: she could almost see the effect on her skin, stung red on that side of her body, like a niacin flush and a bitterness in her mouth like some drug one would take in the old days. But she remembered the feeling and the moment as though it were yesterday. It was when she'd first come home from Europe and was living at her parents' house across the street. She had helped Iris move her giant foxglove from the shady side of the house to the sunnier side. Not having thought to protect herself, she'd wound up with this stinging numbness all over her hands, on her ear, the ear upon which the foxglove had leaned, her right ear, as though whispering its premonition, not itching exactly but irritating to the point of wonder. She realized what a strong and violent plant that flower was, for all its beauty, and marveled once again, standing there looking, looking at her own reverberating ear in peril's mirror.

CHAPTER 8

Claire took Floozie up to the woods and let her run around a little bit. It did Claire good as well. The air was fresher here, although the leaves had fallen. The bleak trees cut sharp and crooked lines against one another. Already the light was dim, and this only late afternoon. It was so still. She followed Floozie a little bit in off the road, but she didn't like to go too far. Danger didn't fascinate Claire. She was put off by those wild dogs. And, of course, the unlikely but persistent fear of Mrs. Dixon's presence. There were some horse-back riders coming through the path, so Claire let herself wander a wee bit farther in. Then a jogger flew past. An elderly Bavarian couple bummeled by. Those two were always in the woods; they walked in any weather, looking for pilzen or firewood or wild-flowers, according to the season. Claire saw them just about every time she came in here. They were reassuringly constant fixtures in this always-changing place. Claire waved and the couple nodded.

She was glad she had Floozie as an excuse to get away from it all, if only for fifteen minutes. Floozie glanced up from her reverie. She was happy to be here, too, she demonstrated with a wag of her tail. Claire wandered over towards "Make-out Rock," a mon-strous relic from no-one-knew-when and just about everyone's past. This forest was gaping with glacier holes. The rock probably came from the same era. Way taller than a child it was, and even she still had to reach up to hoist herself up onto it. She looked down at Floozie sniffing along the path, and her eyes stopped at the top of the stone stairway, just visible from her perch on this great rock that was hers and Tree's old meeting place. From here they had planned to run away, she remembered. She supposed she'd come here for that reason now. As children, they had

180

planned to meet here at midnight and take a Greyhound bus to—where was it? Florida? How they would have found their way to a bus station was beyond them, or at least her. Tree had probably had it all figured out, even back then. Claire had, of course, slept through that nocturnal appointment, never meaning to keep it anyway, just enjoying the thought of hurling such preadolescent defiance at her parents.

Claire wondered if Tree really had snuck out and waited for her, as she always claimed to have done. For Tree had always revelled in her enterprising truancy, had even stolen a gaudy tin biscuit box from her mother and filled it with treasure and buried it just here. So they would have something "to fall back on." She remembered there was a great deal of trouble from Tree's mother over that treasure. Tree had sworn her to secrecy or she would "really get killed." Tree's parents had both been old, even then, and sickly. Although knowing now what she hadn't then, Claire figured that they might have both been heavy drinkers. She could remember the smell of stale old people at Tree's house, that and no other children—a privileged, narrow smell that took her and Tree straight to Tree's bedroom, no stopping for cookies or popsicles from a nosy, nice mother. Mother-daughter communication amounted to just a call through on the way upstairs and a nod from behind a half-closed curtain amid the drone of muffled afternoon television. And there'd been nobody, Claire remembered distinctly, to bother their play.

She had a quick, fleeting memory of Carmela. Carmela? she asked herself. Yes, something with Carmela, angry and in tears, screaming at the both of them. It was . . . no, wait, it was because they had taken her paper dolls, or paper doll clothes. Oh, well. With Carmela it had always been something. Her list of atrocities was so long, Claire thought affectionately of her crazy sister.

She looked at her watch. If she went now, she could stop in at rehearsal. She could take a few shots for them as well. Maybe they could use them for the bulletin board outside the church. Or for the playbill. She marched from the woods with the eager enjoyment of someone who'd just gotten her good shot of oxygen, plopped Floozie into what was now "her" bag, and waited at the red light to cross Park Lane South. The traffic was a blur. Suddenly Claire had to go back. She turned and walked up the hill to where she'd stood before. It was just an absurd chance—a shot in the dark—but, she went over to the spot they'd just left, dropped to her knees, and started to dig. Floozie, thrust to the ground without sufficient reason, stood baffled with her feet still in the purse.

Claire huffed and heaved. The ground wasn't frozen yet and she made good headway. She put a hefty dent in the earth and then she sat back on her heels and inspected her work. Aside from some pine cones, fossilized Hershey's chocolate wrappers, and a beer bottle cap, there was nothing. But of course there was nothing. What had she expected, a perfectly intact tin box, unbothered by time and six neighborhoods full of enterprising children? She looked up at the black bony treetops, wood etchings against the purple sky. She loved a winter sky. So cold and clear and full of stars. The Bavarian couple passed by again, this time exchanging glances. Claire flogged herself mentally. It was just because of that letter, Tree's last living letter and what she had written about "revisiting the secret places of their childhood." And, "only she would know what she meant." Well, she didn't know what the hell Tree had meant, and she was getting a little darn tired of making a jackass out of herself. She stood up and brushed herself off. Her hands were filthy. "Let's get out of here," she told the dog out loud, as much to reassure herself as the puppy, and they marched down the pretty, now-dark hill, not daring to look over at the pine forest where the notorious Mrs. Dixon had not that long ago brutally murdered two children.

The auditorium at Holy Child converted magically into a gym and so Carmela and her cast seldom got to practice there. Rehearsals were held at the Union Congregational Church Community Room, a wonderful old place, one enormous space surrounded by wooden balconies from start to finish, its deep stage framed in walnut carvings. There were small milk-glass windows near the ceiling that let in shoots of street-lamp light.

"These are Protestants here, Floozie," Claire explained the importance of anonymity in this place to the dog. "They'll not take any bending of the rules." It wasn't like over at the Catholic

Church, where the decrees were so precise with dogmatic rigidity that they tended to skate majestically through with a kind-hearted, understanding look the other way. You didn't have to tell Floozie twice about the complexities of the human condition. When necessary, as now, she obligingly made herself scarce, burrowing cozily against her old friend the Olympus, and she went accommodatingly to sleep.

Carmela was striding importantly back and forth across the stage. One thing about Carmela, she had the posture and the presence of an aggrieved mother superior. And she had, Claire noted—uh oh, look out—one hand on her hip. Claire made herself invisible and sat down in one of the darkened back rows where she could watch the rehearsal unobserved. The Seven Dorks, Carmela's rock group, seemed to have been recruited from the hallways of Alcoholics Anonymous, where, indeed, they had been assembled. They milled about, happy house painters-turned-actors, smoking cigarettes and drinking lots and lots of coffee. They had their shiny, fifty-four-cup percolator on the card table there, red light reassuringly set to On. There were things to eat laid out as well. Lots of Boston eclairs and the more sensible carbuncle crullers. Carmela's scornful authoritativeness didn't much affect these guys. Oh, they did as they were told, shuffling back and forth into position the minute they were instructed, but they didn't take her rantings seriously, having faced their own tremendous burdens of self at one time or another in the recovery process. Each one of them had hit incontrovertible bottom and knew who he wasn't. So each was also, somehow, free. And—to Carmela—alarmingly unafraid. Although she badgered her cast members, Carmela also had a wary respect for them, an innate knowledge that you don't pick a real fight with someone who has nothing to lose.

She also didn't like the look of the things they read. Good things by important authors. *The Will to Happiness* by Hutschnecker. Marguerite Duras in French. In French? She'd picked the book up just to make sure. Yes. She'd dropped it like a hot potato. Let's see. What else? Oh. *The Snow Leopard* by Peter Mathiessen. Here were men, who, despite their obvious weaknesses, thought profound and wonderful thoughts. So, beneath their dissipated bodies in plain, plaid shirts and jeans from Sears, they might even be judging her. And what was this? She nudged the pile of books to get a look at the last. Harold Robbins? Carmela snorted, reassured, and clicked her gum.

She looked down at her dialogue and wondered what, if anything, she was doing. There wasn't enough action in her play, she knew that. But she didn't know about things like action. Claire did. Zinnie certainly did. She only knew about motivation. Different kinds of motivation in different kinds of people. Or the lack of it. So she would stay with that. If her womanliness was a failure—she looked down at her useless, flat belly—and her marriage was a failure—she looked mournfully across the stage to Stefan, his cool blue eyes pretending to read a magazine but riveted on that idiotic Portia McTavish . . . (Oh, she was an idiot all right: She carried an imitation Gucci bag for all the world to see.) Anyway—if all those things about herself were no good, then the least she could do for her long-ago vanished self-respect was to make this little play, out in the neverland of Queens, a good play. A play that would stand up to the scrutiny of, if no one else, herself.

At the same moment, Claire was also watching Stefan, sitting there in the second row behind a copy of *Vanity Fair*. *Vanity Fair?* thought Claire. Good grief. He was majestically sprawled out and dapper in his navy blue and camel, had just dropped benevolently by on his way out to Kennedy Airport, supporting his wife in her artistic endeavor, he was, while nonchalantly smoking a Davidoff cigarillo from Havana. They really were well suited, those two, she thought, then stopped herself. No need to be catty.

Zinnie wasn't here; she wouldn't be off duty until six, and then she always went straight back to Claire's house first to look in on Michaelaen. It didn't matter that she was starring in Carmela's play. At least not to her it didn't. She would yawn and laugh, unimpressed. "All right, all right, I'm coming," she would say. When on any given afternoon you're sending people off to prison for seven years, and then you're watching someone else get carried out in a body bag to boot, well, your priorities become simply and carefully organized. Zinnie also didn't much care for the rest of the cast. She'd locked up nicer whores plenty of times, she'd told

Claire out of the side of her mouth, as they'd stood there watching Portia recite her lines. The Dorks were all right, she'd decided although she had a funny feeling one of them was wanted for mail fraud. Anyway, Zinnie wasn't here now. And where was Narayan? Claire looked around uneasily. Wasn't he supposed to be here, too? She guessed not, then.

Ah. Portia McTavish was taking the stage. She had most of the lines. Zinnie had refused to memorize very much. "Look," she'd said, "if you want me in your friggin' play you can cut down my dialogue to the minimum or I won't be in it. It's as simple as that, so you can take it or leave it."

"We'll take it." Carmela had slammed the script down onto the table, shutting up the objecting Stefan. She believed her sister. One word from Stefan and she'd up and leave. Carmela needed Zinnie and she knew it. It wasn't a great play she had written. It was just a little story no better or worse than any other story out there, but it was brought to life by Zinnie's magical talent. Now all they had to do was pray she wouldn't be forced to go make an arrest the day of the performance or she'd be late and God knew what would happen. Stefan was inviting all his snooty friends, and although Carmela had been the one to insist he did, she was worried. What if the show fell on its face and she were made the laughingstock? There were moments she wished she'd never left her cushy magazine job and her nasty column. She sighed. At least then she was the critic and not the other way around. Oh well. Oh God. What were they doing to her dialogue?

"Script!" she cried, and the script girl came running, a girl from the high school Carmela had chosen for her docile nature and her uniform. She liked uniforms. They all did in her family, she remembered. Carmela stood center stage, tapping her head with a yellow number-two pencil. Portia McTavish puffed her sumptuous hair back from her face and perched seductively atop the green velvet settee that Stan had bolted to the floor there for her. It had had to be bolted because Carmela had contrived a scene where the Dorks toppled it over at the end of "Sixteen Tons," landing prettily in a propositional position at Portia/Snow White's feet. Carmela had finally decided upon a name for Snow White. It was Lola Schneewittchen.

"Lola Schneewittchen?!!" Portia had cried, horrified. "That's not a good name!"

"That's the idea." Carmela had filed her nails under Portia's nose. "It's what you call a spoof."

"What's that supposed to mean?" She'd whirled on Carmela, smelling a rat.

"It means," Zinnie'd told her, "you keep the new name or you go back to Snow White and you dye your hair black or wear a wig."

Portia instinctively, protectively grasped her cascade of honey-blond hair. "I'm an actress," she'd sniffed. "I can make the most out of any name."

"That's the spirit." Stefan had winked at Carmela. "A real trouper."

This was supposed to have been a dress rehearsal, Claire knew, but the only one who seemed to be in costume was Lola Schneewittchen. Low-cut, off-the-shoulder, and matching the sofa, Portia's dress made her look no more than a bust of ivory, posed there with her hubba-hubba shoulders going ever so slightly back and forth for all the world to see. It was disconcerting. At least it was annoying Carmela, Claire could tell, what with Stefan sitting there pretending to read.

Down the center aisle came Freddy. He was laden with costumes on hangers and in ripped-up dry-cleaner bags. He could barely see over the bundle as he tripped and grumbled his way down the dark and littered center aisle to the front of the hall. "Why the hell didn't you send one of your good-for-nothing actors to help me?" he snarled.

"Why didn't you get one of your useless waiters to go along with you?" Carmela yelled back. "You're an hour late!"

"The seamstress was late finishing! I stood around that godfor-saken dry cleaners on Jamaica Avenue just waiting and with nothing to do! Nothing! With not even a telephone. Christ!" he rasped, struggling up to the stage and dumping the costumes all over Portia.

"That seamstress was your idea," Carmela followed him with her pointer finger out.

"Watch out!" Portia opened her delicate hands to the air and wriggled free from the pile.

"Well, you see what I've got here," he shouted at her. "Why don't you try being a little bit accommodating? Who are you, all of a sudden, Her Majesty?"

Portia pulled herself up to her full haughty height and said, "No, dear, we all know the queen here is you."

"Well, if you know it"—Freddy whirled around and spat back without missing a beat—"then please act like it. 'Cause if you don't, I'll just hack off your eyelashes. And heaven knows they're skimpy enough as it is." Carmela clapped her hands, delighted.

"That's it. That's just the tone I want, Portia. Let's try it again and I want you to do the last scene just that way, can you do that?" You couldn't blame Portia; Freddy had walked right into that one. Knowing Freddy, he'd probably done it on purpose.

Portia shrugged and made a face. "Well, I can, of course I can, if you're sure that's what you're looking for."

"Just fine." Freddy stamped his foot. "And what about my costumes?"

"Help Freddy get them over to the dressing room," Carmela ordered Grumpy and Sneezy. She pushed them out of the way. "Kinkaid! Kinkaid, wake up and put that spotlight on Lola Schneewittchen. The purple one. Kinkaid!"

Kinkaid? Claire marveled at Carmela's aggressive powers of organization. Why indeed not Kinkaid? Retired electrical company employee. Who else? Free labor for Carmela. All workers got a piece of the door. And it would give him something to do, to be a part of this, and make him feel useful. He only had to set it up and show the high school kids what to do. His name would appear stoutly on the program. Claire remembered Iris von Lillienfeld mournfully. Iris would be at the window now, waiting for Kinkaid to come before the leek pie was cold. Was there no end to women's suffering, she wondered, enjoying herself despite herself. You had to hand it to Carmela, she smiled in the dark; she knew what would work and what wouldn't. An appreciative laugh rang out from the crew over something Lola Schneewittchen had just said.

Carmela nodded her head. "And wait one-two-three—" She

held one hand in the air."—for the laugh—not too long now—don't let the silence hit—just take it three counts into the laugh. Piano." She signalled to the piano player with the other hand, "Begin," and the song started up. Claire watched her admiringly. If Carmela were jealous of Portia, at least she used it to her own advantage.

The dog moved suddenly around with urgency. "Oh, all right," Claire whispered and they snuck out the side door to the garden. It was thick with grass and bushes and Claire made herself comfortable on a stone bench between a yew and a Sunday services announcement sign while Floozie gadded about. Claire raised her long brown skirt up to her knees and inspected her naked legs above their old Frye boots in the cold lamplight. She had just recently allowed herself the luxury of not shaving, and had accomplished soft and downy limbs, something she had never had before. All her adolescent and adult life she had thought it necessary to remove what was hers. But now she had defied the dictate. She was at last complete. She had—she used Andrew Dover's phrase—no remorse. Funny thing to say about your feelings towards a dead wife, that, she mulled, unless you'd killed her yourself. But then maybe not. She checked her suspicions, remembering the police had been quite happy with his alibi, remembering her mother's and Swamiji's exchanges of concerned looks. She would not allow suspicion to become paranoia. She breathed calmly in and out. What had been his alibi, after all? He'd been showing, no, he'd gone to look at an empty house with Portia McTavish, hadn't he? Claire made a face to herself. Those two could very easily be in cahoots. Of course, the cops weren't stupid. They could figure who was up to no good with whom as well as she could. But they didn't know any more than anyone else about what had happened that terrible night. There was no evidence of foul play, was there? And treachery isn't always planned. Lots of times it is a horrible, timely accident whose result benefits someone, as in a sin of omission. It was clear to her if to no one else that Andrew couldn't be happier over the death of his wife. He could hardly keep it jarred up, he was bubbling over with such enthusiasm. Claire sucked the evening air in greedily and grasped her healthy knees. She was alive. And Tree's young body lay confined to her grave just across Victory Field and the groaning uncaring traffic rushing up and down Woodhaven Boulevard.

The door she'd come out of opened up, revealing a sliver of yellow. She thought for a moment the large frame to be dealt with was Andrew's again, but it wasn't. It was Stefan's. When she saw him like that, away from Carmela, her first thought was that she ought to make some borscht. That was one thing Stefan swore nobody made like she did, and he was right. Nobody did. Fresh with dill and carrots and dahl, was her soup. She would slice up mushrooms and baby lima beans and barley, and add lots of onions, garlic, and black pepper. A lovely dollop of sour cream on top and croutons fried in butter were the finishing touch.

"What are you doing all alone out here?" Stefan smiled, delighted to see her.

"I just thought I must make you some borscht," she said. "You made me think of it."

He sat down beside her. "It's certainly cold enough."

"I like it." She breathed out to demonstrate she could blow tidy puffs of steam.

"So do I."

There was an undercurrent here. What kind, Claire wasn't sure, but she admitted grudgingly to herself that she did like to be alone with Stefan now and again. Not to flirt. It was just that Carmela was so consistently uptight whenever the two of them were together that usually they both chose not to talk nor even to look at each other in her presence lest they risk the inevitable squall of silence that would follow.

Rhythmic music filtered out from the hall.

"I hate that song," Stefan said.

"How can anybody hate 'Let Yourself Go'?" She looked at him, astonished.

"It's ridiculous," he said.

"I was just thinking how terrific it is." She put her arms out and did a little shimmy-shimmy à la Ginger Rogers with the top of her body. "Really, Stefan. I defy anyone, anyone but you, that is, to sit still during that song."

"It's not that," he bristled, "but you can't have a musical and have each song come from another era. It's outrageous. She's got the thirties, she's got the sixties, she's got the eighties. It's not done. She's got that song from the opera and the other one from the Temptations. She's even got that sentimental Disney thing! I mean for God's sake!"

"Well, maybe that's the fun of it. And it works. Everything fits. More or less."

"Era, yes. Category, no. You can't put a tap-dance number together with 'Stormy Weather.' "

"That's Zinnie's favorite song. She sings it great."

"You can't do that."

"Who says you can't?"

"Oh. That's what *she* says. Now you sound like her. You've all got that stubborn Irish streak, you girls."

"Well, I think it's a great idea," Claire retorted. "It's enjoyable. There's nothing wrong with enjoyable, is there, Stefan? Or does it interfere with your introspective Polish streak?"

Uh-oh. She knew that flinch. As in control as Stefan was, as able and ready as he always was to dish it out, he couldn't take much of it himself. His posture would become ramrod-straight, and you'd have to ply him with vodka if you wanted any more conversation. "Come on," she gave him a bossy, friendly whack, the kind of blow with which she'd seen an Australian photomodel girlfriend bop the male models when she wanted them to play along for a shot. The technique had always worked for her.

Strangely enough it seemed to work for Claire, too. She saw some glimmer of participation reenter Stefan's blue eyes. Then, across the yard, behind the trees, the other door opened and Andrew Dover came outside with Carmela. Oh, thought Claire, him. And she was just about to call out and wave to her sister when Andrew turned back and—what was he doing? Was he kissing her sister? For a moment she wasn't sure, and then Andrew's hands were gone and then they were holding Carmela's face. Claire almost slid to the ground on behalf of Stefan, who sat on, who didn't move an iota, though she could feel his heart like a stone in the courtyard. They both stayed frozen still.

"And she wonders why I won't let her get pregnant," Stefan snorted.

Claire groped for what to say. "I'm sure it didn't mean anything," she mumbled.

He turned his body to her. "Did you think they were kissing?"

"They weren't?"

"They were snorting coke."

"You're right," Claire realized, remembering the glint of what must have been a shiny box. "For a minute, I thought . . ." She had to laugh at herself. She was so out of the scene she thought all foul play had to do with procreation. Drugs had never occurred to her.

Andrew and Carmela slipped back inside the hall just as quickly as they'd come out.

"Tell me, Claire," Stefan said after some moments' pause. "Have you ever thought about divorce?"

Claire said nothing. There seemed nothing appropriate to say. They sat silently on, keeping each other's vigil. There were cats out, making their horrendous prowling address. Sometimes, she did, she thought about divorce. But really, only when Johnny'd hurt her again and she didn't know what to do. When he would want to go off and play cards or pool, and she would hole up on their bed with her books. He would be down there by the phone, weighing the nonchalance of her voice—"Not at all dear. Go ahead"—against the atmosphere that would rattle with bitterness behind each word.

For after all, she couldn't go anywhere, with a child fast asleep. And even if she could, it wasn't she Johnny wanted to be with just now. It didn't really bother her; once he was gone she was fine. But she couldn't bear his loud, sneaky precautions. "Can I get you anything, Claire?" She always knew it was cards or pool when he said that so nicely, "Can I get you anything, Claire?" But, no, she really didn't want a divorce, even at those times. She was just sulking about not getting all his attention. And cards or pool (or, nowadays, a horse) were anyway better than a woman.

"No," she lied to Stefan after a while. "I don't ever think about divorce." It wouldn't do to pretend she were emotionally free. She felt sorry for him, and she could probably even have an affair with him, if she were one for affairs. But she wasn't, and that was that. She wished she could cheer him up. But there was no cheering him now. He would have to stew in his own juice, would Stefan. The way she and everyone else did. Would. Must. Oh, the world was a sorry place.

"You know," he said, suddenly, relighting his stagnant cigarillo. "I was told when I married your sister that she was bad blood. I might have listened."

"Really? Who told you that, your filthy servants?"

"Pardon?"

"Not for nothing, Stefan, and I'm sure you are hurt and that's why you say something like that, but I don't see your family about, nor have I ever. And if it's a question of blood, perhaps yours is tainted as well."

He laughed, a hearty genuine laugh, and she felt better.

"Now about that borscht," she said.

He pulled back. "You are the most arbitrary person I've ever known," he said scornfully.

It hadn't bothered her what he'd said but how he'd said it. She wanted to know exactly what it was he meant, but he wouldn't go on, just left it at that. Claire said nothing. She was just beginning to enjoy the music again herself, tapping her foot and thinking how nice it was. Stefan always made you feel like a jerk, he was good for that. Mary had always told them that charm was the ability to make someone else feel clever, feel good-looking, feel exceptional. Well, Stefan had that power, but it wasn't really charm, because the minute he had you feeling that way, he'd pull your pants down with some other, more telling observation about you, some weakness he would weed out and call you on, and he would leave you there in the middle of the room like that. So it wasn't charm he had. It was the power to demean. Claire felt suddenly very sorry indeed for her sister, and she marveled once again at the innate strength and gumption she must have had to take a chance like this with a husband like that.

Stefan, with his uncanny sense for discerning insurrection, leaned calmly over and kissed Claire's downy cheek. Stung, she sat bolt upright and rattled the heel of her shoe. She wasn't going to let him think he had enough power to really upset her, but she wouldn't have disrespect toward her sister. She wouldn't have it. She wiped her cheek with disgusted fingers and made as if to fling

192

the kiss with her fingers to the grass. Stefan smiled, amused. Claire spat like a crosscountry trucker on top of the discarded kiss.

"You are wicked." His eyes sparkled.

She knew she wasn't, but she didn't mind anyone thinking she was. She just sat there, and he began to tell her a story about when he was a little boy, some kilometers outside Krakow. She didn't really listen. Stefan was always telling one heartwarming tales of his youth in the fields riding on the hay-laden horse carts, playing in the hallowed halls with inbred Tarnowian servants, visiting in the offices of friends of his father's. He had told her once of a grand duke who had given him marzipan and then asked him to carry a clandestine message to his mother. And he had. At least he said he had. If there had really been a grand duke. Knowing Stefan, there had been. Which was why, she supposed, you didn't just get up and walk off when he was speaking.

As he lit another match, she felt Stefan's eyes on her dirty hands. Submissively, she put them in her pockets. It wasn't that she didn't find Stefan attractive. When they had gone out on a date together, she'd found herself looking him up and down as husband material, even though they'd never been intimate. They had so many things in common. All the things she valued so, those Swedish films and recycling and V. S. Pritchett. She and Johnny didn't. Johnny made fun of all those things, whereas Stefan found them equally entrancing. So they were certainly more suited in that way.

Only, she remembered, the times when Stefan had come on to her more intently, with his opaque infusion of Parisian scent, she'd longed for the raw, rough smell of Johnny: all boy and tightened fists when he tried to make his way heroically through her outerwear, at the most splashed frugally with Old Spice, his one and only finishing touch. He made her laugh, did Johnny, because he was so pure, and he reminded her of herself before she'd run into and been run over by the big time. Her face softened even as she thought of him. Oh, yes, Johnny was tough and jaded. But only on the outside. Underneath, when you scraped away the callus there was a clear stream of integrity. Stefan, as diplomatic and smooth and polished and well-manicured as he was, Claire had the feeling if you took him apart, his callus would be wrapped and bitter inside, tight and careful as a walnut around his condescending heart.

Stefan's family ring glinted in the lamplight. Or was it the moon that already gleamed? Oh, it was. She looked up sentimentally and remembered very clearly how she'd coveted the sense of history that went with that family ring. She was glad now that she hadn't followed through. Oh, you were so much better off following your heart. Carmela said they had no contact whatsoever with his family and would never visit his family seat. There went the family jewels. Oh, well. Carmela had enough jewels. Although, Claire thought fleetingly, she hadn't chosen to wear them much lately. Claire wondered why. It couldn't be because of money. Claire remembered the weighty presence of wealth for which their home was so notorious. No, it couldn't be because of money.

She chuckled to herself. She had imagined a very different life for herself back then, seen herself quite another way. A more pronounced way, full of chocolate. With no swinging banging gate to run out and hitch shut in the middle of a blow. For then she had met Johnny. And then she knew you don't choose the one you love, love chooses you, and irrevocably. She looked over at Stefan, unkindly inspecting his spotless manicure, and she was sorry for him. She gathered her skirt to stand to go but Stefan, not to be left sitting there, stood first. Floozie, who had sensed Claire's movement as a sign of departure, ran toward her but stopped when Stefan stood. Stefan was so tall. Claire hated it when Floozie shivered like that. She looked so infernally unattractive. Claire went over to the little ragamuffin and stuffed the dog affectionately into her bag. Stefan held the door open for her and she headed to the back of the theater. She would leave by the front way, the way she'd come in.

"Claire," Stefan said from behind her, and she turned.

He held her tortoiseshell combs in his hand. "You dropped these," he said, and she took them back, returning them to her coiffure. Her fingers, passing close to her face, still held the fragrance of the earth she'd dug up just before, and now the newer, lingering cloy of patchouli remained from Stefan's milky kiss.

* * *

When Claire went home, she parked in the street to let Johnny in the driveway first. That way she'd get out in the morning when she wanted, without having to wake him. She walked into the back yard—her back yard, she thought possessively. She leaned against the wooden house and watched the yard in the cold starlit darkness. Floozie went over to the garage. It was a nice garage, with a loft in it from the days it had been a barn or carriage house. "Don't do anything over there," she warned the dog, but Floozie was sniffing at the door. Someone had left the light on in there. She clicked her tongue, then realized someone was inside and the door was ajar. Without moving from her spot, she craned her neck and saw a man—she thought it was a man—bent over a pile of something, going through a big old box.

She grabbed hold of the shovel propped against the clothesline pole and backed away. Her heart was pounding, and she could feel the blood pumping into her throat. Then she realized that it was Mr. Kinkaid.

"Mr. Kinkaid," she yelled, angry and relieved. "What the hell do you think you're doing?"

Kinkaid looked up, perplexed. "I'm looking for my Vernier caliper, that's what I'm doing."

"Your Vernier caliper?" She stalked over to him. "That's good. I thought we bought this place, to quote the former owner, 'hook, line, and sinker.' "

"That don't mean I can't come and get my stuff," he frowned, annoyed.

"Oh, really? Next time I come home the stained-glass window upstairs will be on its way to Florida, I suppose."

He looked up and held the hanging light-bulb towards her, squinting. "My wife gave me that Vernier caliper, fifty years ago. It measures to one thousandth of an inch. You want it?"

"Of course I don't want it. You just scared me. I didn't know who was there, that's all. I never thought it was you."

"Who'd ja think I was, Mrs. Dixon? Didja?" he grinned horribly. She was glad Swamiji and the warmth of her household were just inside the back door.

"Look. Find your thingamajig and scram, okay? And don't go

touching any of Johnny's stuff. He doesn't like anyone touching his stuff."

"Ohhhh no, we all none of us don't like nobody go touching our stuff," he mocked, with his tongue out like a nasty little kid. "Say!" he stopped. "Lookee here." He sat down on his haunches and picked up a pair of well-oiled, good rose clippers. The short, wrenchy kind, the only ones that are any good to anyone. "Why, these are Grace's," he said, struck. He petted them softly. His growly old face turned into some other man's. A fellow who loved his wife, must have lived for his wife, because Claire had never seen the old boy with a modicum of kindliness to him, and now here he was on her garage floor in the dirt and she thought he was a little bit all right. Or you could see how he must have been. Poor old coot.

"Grace," he said, "used to keep these in her basket. Hooboy, she loved that basket. She had the gloves, the hat, the trowel, the woiks. You see those flowers out there? The size of them? She's got them in two different series, so they come up every other year. Them foxglove only come up once every other year, see. So you have to time them. Grace? My wife? She had it all figured out. She had the yellow ones coming up the one year and the pink ones the other. Her hollyhocks were eight, ten feet high." He shook his head. "A lotta woik."

Claire nodded appreciatively. "I was just admiring her work," she said. "Just before I saw you."

"Really?" he whirled around like a dervish. "She must be here."

"Who?"

"Grace."

"Oh. Mr. Kinkaid, would you like to come inside for a cup of tea?"

"Now? No, not now. Too much to do."

Claire remembered Iris and her leek pie.

"Your sister Carmela's got me buildin' her a whole new setta row lights."

"Ah."

He laughed. A hollow cackle that filled the littered garage with strange and gone-forever memories.

"Well. I'll be going in the house now. Floozie, come on."

For the life of her, she didn't know why she backed out of there, but she did, leaving them to themselves, Grace and Mr. Kinkaid. And the rest of their things.

Claire stood for a moment at the back door and looked in before she turned the knob. Stan and Swamiji sat at the kitchen table. Dharma sat on Swamiji's lap. A long sloping row of dominoes went across the pinewood table. Mary stood, her calves in laddered stockings, at the old gas stove. All Claire wanted to do was take off her boots and climb up into an easy chair. The door opened to her touch but she was too delighted to be inside to bother carrying on that no one had locked up. Stan anyway always had a gun on him. Some tiny James Bond thing he was extremely fond of. Mary, God bless her, threw her arms up into the air as though she hadn't seen Claire for years. She plucked the coats up off Claire's chair. Her throne, Johnny called it, because no one else would have a big wing chair in the kitchen, but she loved it. He'd never brought the rocker downstairs for her, so she'd lugged this thing up from the cellar with Michaelaen and here it stayed, back from the table, right beside what would one day be the hearth. She'd found a pie-crust table at a yard sale to put beside it, and an old-fashioned tall reading lamp that was only ever on when she was at home. She climbed into the chair gratefully now. Stan stood with the coats Mary had dropped into his arms. He looked, puzzled, about him. There were coats in every room lately, whole lots of them. Nobody knew where to put them and no one wanted to bring the subject up. That would entail an enterprising solution, and no one wanted that job just now; hanging a pole from one end of a closet to the other. The measuring. The wedges that would first have to be nailed in.

"Stanley, put them in the dining room." Mary rattled her face imperiously at Stan, and he did as he was told. The room was full of the grand smell of sauerbraten and red cabbage. "Oh, it's nothing," Mary tut-tutted, noticing Claire's pleasure. "I've had it soaking since last week. Don't you go giving it another thought, now. If I didn't use it tonight, I'd have to put it in the freezer. Sure, no one's been coming over to eat by me since the kids are all here at your place," Mary admitted with a mixture of relief and regret.

"Looks like my own mother's place in here, now," she sniffed, admiring the warm rosy glow that came from the tobacco-stained lampshade from long ago.

"Oh, Mom," Claire said, pleased. She was a girl again, content to be curled up and taken care of. "Where's Anthony?"

"They're just doing the end of their Nintendo game and then they'll be down."

"Freddy fixed up the Nintendo?"

"He did." Mary beamed proudly. She would never get over the fact that she had the great fortune of having someone in her own family who could fix up computers and "all that."

"I thought Freddy spent the afternoon at the dry cleaners? Oooh, look at this. You've got the dog's dinner ready as well. Ma, you're the best."

"I am. I am that. One splendid mum."

"I just ran into Kinkaid in the garage. You remember Mr. Kinkaid, Daddy, he used to work for the electric company? We bought the house from the varmint."

"Oh, Kinkaid's not so bad," Stan said. "He's lived in Richmond Hill longer than I have."

"I haven't got the dumplings, now," Mary lamented. "I've only made the egg noodles." "Egg noodles." Swamiji's eyes glowed at Claire. "I can eat those."

"Yes." Claire looked at Dharma on his lap. "You can."

Swamiji, a vegetarian, was the picture of good health. He had hot Quaker Oats in a bowl every morning with fresh cream and honey and bananas. Then he would have a nice bowl of Brown Cow yogurt drizzled with honey and a topping glass of Tropicana. He was fine-boned as ever, but his belly had grown to a stretched-out, accessible, and cozy pot.

"Claire," Dharma said, addressing her directly for the first time in both their lives. "Do you know you were named for the song 'Au Claire de la Lune'?"

Mary said, "We were telling Dharma the sins of our past." She laughed.

"And," Dharma said, gripping Swamiji's teapot-handle ears dotingly, "do you know what the name 'Dharma' means?"

Mary looked at her, interested. "No."

"It means religion."

Swamiji nodded. "And moral duty."

"And," Dharma added, covering his mouth with her hand, "a way of life."

"Yes," Swamiji said.

"No kidding. I never gave it a second thought," Mary marveled. "I guess I thought it was Italian. Like Parma."

"My mother," Dharma said, "wanted to name me 'Dharana,' but she pointed to the wrong word on the page of holy words and the nurse copied 'Dharma.' Isn't that a scream?"

"Well, what does 'Dharana' mean?"

"It means rapture," Swamiji said.

"Also good," said Claire.

"Oh, 'Dharma' is far and away the better name," insisted Mary.

"You would think that." Claire laughed, knowing as she did, that if her mother weren't there she'd think it herself.

"Destiny did intervene," said Swamiji. "You see, *dharma* is a Buddhist and Hindu word, that on which the law of truth and virtue is based." He patted Dharma's head.

"Zinnie's name is Zenobia," Mary said. "It's Greek. 'Having life from Jupiter,' it means. Of course, all my girls' second names are Mary. After Our Lady."

Stan came back in. "I put the coats in the dining room," he said. "Claire, you know there are a lot of jackets and coats in there already?"

"I know, Dad. Kinkaid sold off those lion-clawed wardrobes that used to be all over the house. I wish he'd left me just a couple of them."

"The old fox," Mary said.

"Ma. Could you see Mr. Kinkaid and Iris von Lillienfeld together?"

"Lord, no." She threw the noodles into the sieve in the sink with a practiced dunk.

"Neither can I."

"What a thought! Now where is Zinnie? She said she'd be here for supper and the noodles are done."

"Calm yourself, calm yourself, calm yourself," Swamiji stood, deposing Dharma. "I am setting the table and lickety split."

Claire watched them all through dazed eyes. She knew she was there, but something had her looking at them through a feathery long lens. They were small and far away. She shivered and pulled her soft cardigan around her shoulders. She yawned. The telephone jangled.

"I'll get it," Anthony shouted from upstairs. Several moments passed while everyone craned their ears to hear who would be called. Finally: "Ma, pick up," and Claire picked up.

"Hullo," Claire said.

"Claire," Johnny said.

"All right?"

"Wait till you hear this."

"Where are you? It's such a racket."

"Oh. Don Peppe's. Hang on. Shut up!"

"Johnny?" There was a shuffle and some arguing and then Johnny was back on the phone.

"Honey? You know what happened?"

"Johnny, how come you're at Don Peppe's?" Don Peppe's was their restaurant. It was the place Johnny had officially proposed, or rather where she had officially accepted. He had, at one time, proposed several times a day. Only this time he'd taken her there with Zinnie and Mary and she'd said yes. Of course, by then, she was pretty pregnant. Sometimes she wondered if the pungent, homemade red wine they served had had anything to do with it. Don Peppe's was bright and loud and boisterous and if you didn't like garlic you'd just as soon not go. The china was cracked, and if you gave the fellow back a dirty knife, he'd just wipe it good on his white butcher's apron and smack it back down on the table. The restaurant was over by the track, and all the waiters had a sure-thing horse running tomorrow, or the next day. "Don't you think you been here long enough?" one of the waiters would chide as he chewed a fat cigar at you as you took your last mouthful of heavenly Italian cheesecake, the wet kind, the kind you only got there or at Angelo's over on Mulberry Street. So it wasn't some elegant and luxurious dining spot. It was a joint. But it was a spectacular joint. Claire thought it was romantic. She hated that he was there without her. Vexed, she waited for him to tell her to get in the car and drive down. She would say no, but she still wanted him to ask.

"Are you there, Claire?"

"Me, my mother, my father, Swamiji, and Dharma are here, Johnny."

"And me," Anthony said from the extension. "And Michael-aen," he added, always exact.

"Anthony, get off the phone," he shouted.

She closed her eyes.

They heard a click. "Claire, the horse broke down."

"What?"

"Yeah. She fell. She fell down. It was terrible. Claire?"

"Yes, Johnny, I'm here."

"She was hurt really bad. Her leg. It just broke. The bone was sticking out."

"Oh my God." She felt everyone stop in the kitchen around her. "It's the horse," she told them, more to relieve them than anything else.

"Johnny, what did they do?" She spoke back into the phone.

"It was bad. The ambulance came."

Claire watched the gravy on the stove boil up and over the top and down onto the gas jet. Mary jumped to attention and went for a towel. Claire's emotions did a loop-the-loop. If the horse was dead Johnny would be home again. It would be the end of the episode.

"They were going to put her down, you know. They had the injection all set. The vet had it up in the air. And I . . . I almost said okay. Only then the fucking horse starts to cry. With tears!" Claire blinked at the heartless nonchalance of fortune. Johnny talked on. He would have to go back to the animal hospital and then to the barn. Then he'd have to drive Pokey Ryan, his old partner, home.

"Yes, yes," she murmured. Because, that was it. There was nothing else to say. She could argue logic over a dead horse. Or a losing horse. Or even a winning horse. But no one, not even she, could argue over a crying horse. Claire almost felt sorry for him. Then she remembered the great stalagmite of bills that wobbled

201

the blotter on the desk. She heard the clatter and bustle of the waiters rushing by Johnny from the kitchen. She could imagine the overcrowded tables there and smell the oregano. The handsome Italian cooks clattering their copper pans in full view in the kitchen. The men and their wives at the tables, all dressed and made up. There was a pigeon house on top of the restaurant. Neat and painted, tidy with chicken wire. A squadron of the birds would take off suddenly, circling once over Aqueduct and heading dead north above the Queen of Martyrs belfry.

"They have to try and put a pin in the horse's leg," Claire told them, her voice under control when she hung up the phone. "Tomorrow. So the horse is sedated and they've taken her to the hospital."

Wordlessly, Mary took a plate away from the table. Claire knew she was saying a silent Hail Mary for the horse, and she wished she herself wasn't as coldhearted as she, at that moment, felt.

As they sat down to eat, the telephone rang once again. Johnny again, Claire figured, and stood and reached for the phone.

"Claire!"

Hungry and surly, Claire snarled, "Who is this?"

"Why it's Jupiter Dodd, darling. Anything wrong?"

"Hi!" she squeaked, shushing the table full of noise with the frantic, important, impoverished hope of green cash in her eyes. Mary buttoned their lips with her own, and they all giggled conspiratorially with her. Mary hadn't raised four kids for nothing.

"Did I catch you at a bad time?"

"No." She pulled the wire as taut as it would go into the other room.

"How's it coming?" Jupiter asked.

For a moment she had to think what he meant. The pictures. He meant the pictures. The houses he'd given her an advance to shoot and expected—when? Next week? Could it be already next week? "Terrific," she trilled. "Wait till you see them!" She looked around for the photos, saying this, and spotted them, far from complete, sticking out messily from underneath the lofty mountain range of coats across the table. There was a thud in her chest as if she'd been caught red-handed, just like the moment she got called on when she hadn't done her homework. But there was also the perverse, self-destructive admiration of another self inside her, standing off to the side and marvelling "now-here's-a-gal-who-has-more-important-things-to-do-than-make-a-living."

"What are you doing tonight?" asked Jupiter.

"Tonight?" she envisioned the hours before her: the washing up, the bathtubs—full of children and tears from shampoos—the search for wrinkled pajamas in the great pile of clean laundry in front of the dryer, the teeth to be monitored, the stories to be read, the lights to be put out and then on again for the very, I swear, very last drink of water tonight. "Thought I'd spin down to Monte Carlo for a few rounds of baccarat. Care to join me?"

"I know, I know, your life is a muddle. No sense complaining about it, though, is there?"

"Mmm. I guess not."

"Want to come into the city? I've got a thing, only black tie and cleavage. Everybody who's anyone will be there. Have you got a nice gown?"

"A gown?"

"Oh, and please not that hippie Nepali thing you had on at Carmela's."

"Excuse me! That's my best frock!"

"That's what it looks like. A frock. From a be-in."

"That shows you how old you are. That cycle has gone complete and the only place you see that sort of thing now is on the runway in Paris."

"More like the Khyber Pass."

"You bitch. You lied. You told me you loved my beautiful dress!"

"Claire, only you could love that dress."

"Liar, liar, pants on fire!"

"Oh, dear. You do need to get away."

"I can't. I wish I could, but I can't."

He didn't say anything.

"You could always come here," she said finally. "I do miss you. Now that I talk to you and hear how you throttle me so neatly."

"I'll come for the play. Not before. What are you having for dinner?"

"Sour meat, red cabbage, and noodles. Maybe chocolate pudding."

Jupiter made an obscene, shlurpy sound.

She looked frantically about at the dust and disorder. "If you hurry, I can keep it nice and warm for you."

"I'll pass."

"Thank God. I thought I'd have to run through the house with a mop."

"Not to worry."

"Okay."

"All my love."

"Me, too."

"Oh, and Claire?"

"Yes?"

"Deadline's next week."

"Right."

They hung up. She looked at the ceiling and covered one eye. The phone rang again. She picked it up. "Me again," said Jupiter. "I forgot. Remember that shot you had in your book? The black-and-white of that awful castle with the big gaudy stones like a sand castle? And the turrets out of cement? With the grotto to the one side?"

"Queens's classiest catering hall?"

"With the young couple groping each other on the steps. And her all made up like Maria Callas and him skinny and with the unrefined shirt and tie and the pimples?"

"Of course I remember it," she said defensively. If he wanted her to take it out of her book, she wouldn't.

"Well, we've decided to run it on the cover."

"You're kidding."

"I kid about life and death. Not covers."

"I can't believe it!"

"Fooph! They all love it. Diane Arbus stuff, they're all saying up here."

"Yes," she cried excitedly. "That's just how I meant it. Oh, to be understood!"

She could hear Jupiter smiling over there in Manhattan, underneath his Mary Poppins gold-and-silver stars. "Our Queens issue," he said. "Can't you see it?"

She had no doubt that he'd only just decided to use that shot for the cover when they'd hung up the phone. He was a kind-hearted sod, was Jupiter.

"Thank you, Jupiter Dodd."

"You're welcome, Claire Breslinsky."

They hung up again.

Meanwhile, on the south side of Jamaica Avenue over Mrs. Fatima's exclusive blue lagoon, up a couple of flights of stairs and in the deafening nearness of the el, Zinnie and Narayan, enraptured, removed each other's soggy, tender clothes. Their bodies glowed against each other and they melted together with an unavoidable, mysterious blank pull. On the corner was an always-open, red-and-yellow bodega that pumped out one torrid marenga on top of the other. He smelled at first of cumin. She of L'air du Temps. They mingled in a brackish, taut embrace. She felt the luster of his hairy body, and he watched her creamy arm clamp hopelessly against his massive self. "Oh boy," she said, "oh, God."

He silently moved, under the vertigo spell and the at-last and innermost height of dharana.

Dharma, always the first into pajamas, stood at the bottom of the stairs for the cleaning-of-the-teeth inspection. Claire thought she liked this part of the routine; children always liked to do what they did well, and Dharma was so good at hygiene. Her pink hippopot-amus buttons were done up demurely to the top of her soft-flannelled throat. Anthony whooped down the stairs and then came Michaelaen, a casual straggler intent on being viewed as a big boy.

"Let's see, now," Mary made a great fuss. Teeth, to the Irish, are of the utmost importance because they cost, if not treated as precious, such a lot. She opened their mouths like a no-nonsense browser at a horse fair.

"I'll be handling the stories tonight, if you please," Swamiji announced with a two-steps-back bow. He had a good one. He'd been clandestinely brushing up on his Hans Christian Andersen.

Claire had to go across the street and get Dharma's things, she remembered. Oh, she didn't feel like doing that at all. "Mom, will you come with me?" she asked.

"Swamiji and I will just finish up these dishes for you, Claire. We'd be most helpful that way, don't you think?"

"Sure," Claire agreed, unwilling to tell them she was afraid to go to that house in the dark. Swamiji had her ironing board set up in the kitchen. Mary would wash and wipe the dishes and Swamiji would iron. He was, he said happily, her dhoby. He did have, she noted, a plastic atomizer filled with sachet and water for the collars and cuffs. Not once since they'd moved in had any of them had an ironed shirt or blouse actually on a hanger in a closet. This was always a last-moment thing, done in a hurry on a floor cushion of folded towels. So she was afraid to go to the house alone but, weighing that against the prospect of returning to a lavender-scented wardrobe, decided she would give it a go. She remembered her father was still here.

"Dad?" she called down to the cellar.

"What?" he turned down the radio. He had on the trickling Chopin.

She went down the stairs and sidled up to the workbench where he was re-gluing her chopping block.

"Do you think you could come with me? Daddy," she said, "I'm afraid to go into Dharma's house alone."

"Well, then don't go, knucklehead."

"Daddy, please. I have to get Dharma's clothes for school and—"

"All right," he stopped her. He'd spent what felt like most of his life interrupting whatever it was he was doing for his kids, to do something else for one of his kids.

They went out the back way and walked around the house. Floozie zoomed out the doggie door and ran up to them. Claire let her walk along beside her. It was good for her. She looked a little pudgy, their Floozie. Claire took out the keys. Stan whistled the good parts of the Chopin. "Smells like snow, don't it?"

Claire pushed in the Dovers' door. She looked down on the floor. A tumble of mail cluttered the spot where they stood. She picked it all up and Stan went around turning on lights. Claire paged nosily through the bills and the letters. There was something from a child-services agency. Claire slipped this easily into her pocket.

"Okay," Stan said. "There you go. No ghosts can get you now."

"Daddy! You can't just leave me here."

He threw his head back and laughed. "Honey, you sound like you're ten years old. Is this the daughter who singlehandedly spent ten years circumnavigating the globe?"

"This is different," she frowned. "I knew her."

"All right, I'll stand right here and wait for you."

Satisfied, she bolted through to Dharma's room, noting that the clothes for the dry cleaner Andrew had told her he'd left on the table were actually on the floor. Perhaps he'd come back. Astonishing, she clicked her tongue, how neatly that little girl kept her own things. Claire wasn't going to be discriminating. She was going to take as much as she could carry. Why not? She wasn't going to let any child-welfare agency get its hands on her. That was for sure. She had every intention of keeping this child, it dawned on her, amazed at her own determination to accept the responsibility.

"Dad," she called through. "What do you think about Johnny and me keeping Dharma?"

"She's got her own home, Claire. No matter what it seems like now. Don't go getting excited about something that can't be. And her father might not have time for her now, but get past the tragedy of the moment, he'll be wanting her back."

"Sure he will," Claire muttered sarcastically under her breath.

"What's that?" he called.

"Nothing."

"Hurry up, will you?" he complained. "I've got to walk the puppies for your mother before they go messing up her kitchen."

"Right there!" She plunked everything neatly into a laundry basket and started to go, then spotted Dharma's jewelry box. Imagining Andrew might take offense if she just walked off with the whole thing, she opened it up, meaning to rummage through and just take what Dharma might especially like. An enormous green stone glittered at her. She picked it up. It was an emerald! Claire sat down on her haunches and held the stone between herself and the hourglass lamp. No, it wasn't an emerald. There was something more dense, more alluring about it. Claire had spent time in Pagan and Mandalay in the north of Myanmar and more time still in Kandy, Sri Lanka. She knew which stones were good and which weren't. This one, she suspected, was quite magical. It was certainly worth a lot of money. A sapphire, it came to her. Of course! Rare, this color in a sapphire. Although sapphires and emeralds are basically the same stone. And the size! Wherever did she get it? It must have been Tree's. Claire wrapped it carefully in her handkerchief and put it into her pocket. She didn't tell her father. She knew why, too. He'd tell her she was overstepping boundaries. It was none of her business. Knowing he was right, she put the box away and they locked up and went back across the street.

Mary was in the kitchen. "They're all tucked in," she said. "So all you have to do is lock up."

Was there a note of disgust in her voice? She was all done in, poor thing. She probably just wanted to be in her own house with her old bones in a nice hot bath.

"You've done too much, Mom. Go. Go home."

Mary touched her head. "Ever since old Mrs. Dixon whacked me with the typewriter I'm feeling a little creaky."

"Claire's talking about keeping the Dover girl," Stan said.

"What rubbish," Mary said. "She has a grandmother. Although—"

"It's not rubbish. I even spoke to Andrew about it."

"Oh, Andrew. That's a good one. What does he know about what it takes to raise a child?"

"Exactly my point," Claire said.

Mary turned and scrutinized her daughter. "And then the minute you've got her settled in and you're used to her and she to you, he'll up and marry someone new and he'll want her back."

"And what?" Claire sputtered. "Suddenly set up housekeeping and be a proper daddy? You can't be serious. He doesn't even look at Dharma when he speaks to her!"

Mary's jaw set with disapproval. "You're so critical of everything about Andrew, Claire. It makes one wonder why. I mean why, so much? He hasn't had an easy lot, you know. Not by a long shot. Why, the way you speak! As though Theresa had been a decent wife to him. As though her shameless behavior was somehow commendable because she flaunted it at him and called it bohemianism. As though that somehow made it virtuous! I don't know, but I get the feeling you've condemned Andrew Dover on the very grounds that you've consecrated your old friend on. Just because he conscientiously went out to work each day, committed the contemptible crime of being steady and conservative and behaving with dignity when his wife was out and hard at it to make him a laughingstock. I'm not one to be speaking ill of the dead, mind, but you mustn't go allowing yourself to write it off as dullness and tedium that killed Theresa Dover. And it certainly wasn't Andrew himself. If anything, it was he who stood by her while she behaved abominably! There. I've said it. I'm sorry if that upsets you, but there it is."

Grudgingly, Claire admitted to herself that this was so. But it was also so that treachery often lurked under the guise of respectability.

"And what if," Mary pounded the table with her pointer finger, "the grandmother turns around and joins AA and cleans up her act?"

"Can you see Andrew, or his mother, wanting Dharma around ever, for any reason?"

Mary shrugged agreement. "Isn't it sad? You'd think it just the opposite, wouldn't you? She being such a bonny lass and all. God love 'er."

"She is that," Stan said, washing his hands in the sink.

"Is she?" Claire asked. "I mean I know she has beautiful hair and eyes. Is she a beauty?"

"That one?" Stan wiped his hands on the dish towel. "She'll be having them all coming and going, you watch."

"You think?"

"Hadn't you noticed, Claire?" Mary laughed.

Claire shook her head. "No. All I ever see is her mother in her, or her sadness."

"Well," Mary sighed, "that takes a sort of an eye as well." She paused. "Look at all the years I lived next door to Mrs. Dixon. I still can't believe she would hurt those children."

"She did, though." Claire narrowed her eyes. "And by the way, something I never told you: One day she tried to electrocute me. In the bathtub. She pulled on the extension wire from the hall and dropped the live portable radio into the tub with me. She came into our house. So remember that next time you start feeling sorry for her."

They looked at her, astonished. "You saw her?" Stan asked.

"Well, no, but I know now that it was her. I never told you because I had no proof. But I know it was her."

"What are you saying?" Mary said. "Now you're telling us that because time has gone by you don't need to have proof?"

"She did. It was one day you and Dad had taken Michaelaen bowling. I remember because I stole Carmela's car afterwards, and she was fit to be tied. Remember? I went to visit Johnny. I wanted to see where he lived."

"Of course I don't remember. That was four years ago."

"Almost five. And I remember everything. Oh, this you'll remember. You got your hair cut off that day. You must remember that."

She shook her head, bewildered.

The doorbell rang.

"Get that, Dad," Claire said, "before it wakes up the kids."

Carmela came in, kaput.

Claire's heart sank. Whatever it was Carmela wanted, Claire doubted she had it in her to give.

"Sure you look," Mary clucked, "like you've died and gone to Hades."

"Still looking," Stan shuffled in, "better than most folks in Falak al aflak."

"Except women"—Carmela stared, glaze-eyed, at him—"don't get in to Falak al aflak. Only men and their horses, but thanks all the same, old faithful."

"Well nirvana, then," he said, "apropos Swamiji. Where is the old boy anyway?"

"He's upstairs," Claire said.

"What's wrong with plain old paradise?" Mary wanted to know.

"Mary, you started it," Stanley yelled at her.

"Let's go," Mary said. "All this heathen influence," she muttered.

"Mary!" Stan yanked her arm. "If it weren't for him, you'd still be wheezing with your hay fever!"

"I know. You're right." She straightened her braids. "I'm ashamed of myself and well I should be. That dried nettle Swamiji got me takin' cleared me up like a charm." She smacked her own face. "Take that!" she said.

" 'Bye," they all said at once, and Mary and Stan went down the porch steps. Claire shut the door. "What's up?"

"Where's Zinnie?"

"Beats me. Why?"

"Claire! She didn't come to dress rehearsal!"

"Oh."

They both looked at the phone. "Nobody called," Claire assured her. "If they had, somebody would have been here."

"Are you sure?"

"Yes."

"Well, if she's not dead, I'm going to kill her."

"Calm down," Claire said. They both sat down. "It isn't like her to not call and say goodnight to Michaelaen." Undercover cops had all sorts of ex-cons out there who might want them dead. So you never knew.

Carmela took out a cigarette and fished around her Gucci bag for a light.

"Please don't smoke in here," Claire begged.

Carmela snapped her Dunhill torch into effect, ignoring her sister. She scanned the room. "That hassock is new," she accused.

"Yes," she admitted.

"I just saw one like that at Roche Bobois," Carmela said, suspicious.

"You know how I haunt the material shops on Liberty Avenue. It's all crap, which is why nobody bothers over there, but if you're relentless, you occasionally run into a piece of something breathtaking. As they think you have no money or you wouldn't be there, they only charge you a pittance."

Carmela, her bag, cigarette, and ashtray clutched to her lap, crouched across the room to inspect the fabric with her fingers. "I mean, if you think it's worth risking your life going over there, just to save money," she said, "be my guest."

Claire stayed where she was and wouldn't answer. Carmela would argue about anything right now. Claire had had to go back to the shop five or six times until she'd gotten the merchants to agree to a good price. It was prerequisite to bargaining. If you didn't, they considered you a fool. But Claire knew very well she wasn't going to get killed exploring Liberty Avenue, east of Lefferts, despite the fact that she was the only "white" person far and wide. They were used to her. They thought she was quite mad, scooting from store to store. Whenever she was there, she was in a hurry, wearing her warm Tibetan hat—they probably thought she was a Russian woman, which would explain it all.

The marketplace reminded one of Istanbul and Cayenne, Port-au-Prince and Herat all at once. There were strong smells of turmeric and nutmeg, red chile peppers and syrupy coffee. She held her shoulder bag across her chest and tightly in front of her. Where poor people lived and worked and shopped, pickpockets and addicts did too. But there was also honor there, faces not numbed by years of television and white bread. There were sparkling eyes, and children climbing the merchandise while granny was sick because childcare by strangers was unheard of. Claire loved this side of Liberty. Music from Paramaribo bumped into music from Delhi and Montego Bay. So her visits weren't just a shopping spree, they were travel. When you returned home, you felt that you had *been* somewhere. Claire regarded the hassock triumphantly. She always valued things that much more when Carmela coveted them.

"I found a poem of yours," she said, an offering.

"Oh? Which one?"

"That one about Ephesus."

"Ephesus?"

"And something, 'spittle in it'?"

"Oh. I hope you threw it away."

"I never throw anything away."

"Right. Recycling Claire. But my poems you may dispose of. You have my permission." She stopped. "I have another." She looked hopefully at Claire.

"Oh, good."

Carmela shuffled through her agenda, ripped out a page, and presented it to her. "Read it out loud," she instructed, pursing her lips in pleased expectation. She wiggled into her seat.

Claire cleared her throat.

> Today aboard two subway trains
> a rice sprout song to pale the rain
> A shiny licorice-looking ant
> with pincer wriggling, threadlike gams
> came in behind his shadow
> called me out, 'Ondine,' he said.
> And on and on I tasted fruit
> that ripened mold and rounded mute
> all ready as a nightshade bed
> woke up and found my child instead.

The clock ticked on the mantel, the only sound. Claire folded the paper in half.

Carmela grinned. "It was a dream. I mean I really dreamed it. Good, eh?"

"Certainly frightening."

"Tch. If I thought you were going to qualify it, I wouldn't have shown you."

"Well, then, don't show them to me anymore. You always write your dreams in poems, and then I wind up dreaming about them. So quit it. Or start dreaming nicer stuff. And by the way, how come you never told Tree Dover my telephone number? How come you never even told me she was trying to get in touch with me?"

Carmela's face fell. "What do you mean?" was all she could think of to say.

"I mean, why is it that Tree Dover asked about me and getting in touch with me on a number of occasions and you never gave

213

her my number, never even mentioned to me that she was starring in your play?"

"I did tell you."

"You did not."

Carmela raised open palms in a quick, casual movement. "I thought I had done. It must have slipped my mind."

"How could it slip your mind? You knew how I felt about Tree, how I adored her while we were growing up."

"And how she always dumped you when she found someone more interesting to play with?"

"Oh. Now you're going to tell me that you were protecting me from her hurtful influence? All of a sudden you're worried about my feelings? Carmela, do you mind? You just had a cigarette."

"If you must know, I didn't want you to have Tree back."

"Have her back? You make it sound like—"

"Well, maybe that's how it seemed to me. You always doubled off with her. And she was my friend. I found her first. I brought her home first."

"You did?"

"Yes. Tree was my age, not yours."

"She was not."

"She was, too."

"God, this is ridiculous. Now we're fighting over the dead."

Carmela smashed her cigarette out in Claire's pink seashell. She loosened her thick mane of black hair from its clip, and shook it free, a sign of surrender and reason. She could accept default if it was accompanied by the compensation she took in her own beauty.

Claire wondered, should she confide in Carmela about Tree's stone? Carmela knew a bit about stones from Stefan. She decided not to. She would ask Iris von Lillienfeld, instead, ensuring it got no further. Iris was tight-lipped as a clam.

"Do you have your car?" she asked Carmela.

"I thought you'd drive me home. Stefan took my car to the airport."

Resigned, Claire said, "I'll walk you. I've got to take Floozie out anyway."

Oh, she didn't like that idea. "What about the kids?"

"Swamiji's here. I'll just tell him."

"He's always here. When's he leaving?"

"Mom?" Anthony came down the stairs. His cheek on one side was all crumpled and imprinted with the folds of his pillow. She went up to him and held him around his small, chubby waist. "Mom," he said, "what do you call these again?" He pointed down his leg.

"Ankles."

"Ah, ankles!" He turned, glad, and went back up the stairs, ignoring Carmela.

Swamiji stood at the landing, arms out for him. He signalled Claire to go with a couple of waves of his hand, indicating he had heard her plans. Carmela already stood waiting in her cherry-red Susan Slade scarf, and the dog was at the door with her "let's get this show on the road" attitude. So Claire put on her coat and they left, catching their breath at the snap in the air. They hurried up the block.

"You don't have to look so smug and satisfied with your life," Carmela said when they got up by the woods.

"Carmela." Claire held up her hand like a traffic cop in fair warning. "I don't want to do this. Whatever it is, just stop. I understand you need a good fight, but I don't have a shred of spunk left in me right now, so save it for the morning, all right? Just save it, or wait till your husband gets home and give it to him."

They continued along, Carmela on the sidewalk and Claire in the stiff, grassy dirt. How easy life is when you put your foot down, Claire congratulated herself, enjoying the silence. Here and there dog walkers stopped and went and stopped again, reassured by each other's presence, people in pajamas and overcoats hoping the dogs would be quick about it. Claire looked sideways at Carmela, knowing she'd be steamed, and saw instead tears rolling down the side of her distorted, silent, wet, red face.

"Melly!" Claire took her in her arms, reverting instantly to childhood and its deeper endearments.

Carmela sagged into the embrace, no defenses. She sobbed and sobbed, not caring who heard, or who saw.

Claire let her cry, then led her to the bench where usually just

215

the gay fellows got acquainted. This was their territory here, and one or two of them, affronted, gave them peremptory looks. Claire scowled back at them. It seemed Carmela would never stop crying. Finally, she sniffed to a teeth-chattering end and wiped her face with a motion that reminded Claire of their mother, a motion that said: Lord oh Lord, the whole world is a-weary. Claire just hoped they wouldn't get mugged sitting out there like that, unprotected. Who knew?

"You don't understand," Carmela finally steadied herself enough to say.

Me, again, Claire thought but didn't say.

"You have a normal life. A kid. Everything going along nicely. You own a nice house. Your husband loves you." She went down the list. On and on she went. Claire blew compassionately on her poor hands. Floozie, pleased as Tuesday's punch, roamed the mangy curb. They looked up Park Lane South toward the fairy-tale castle Carmela called home. "And don't hand me that 'I ought to be grateful' shit," she snapped.

"Listen," Claire whispered, "I understand you're exhausted. You've been doing so much. Why don't you just go home and get some sleep? I'll come and pick you up in the morning and we'll"— She raced silently through an unlikely range of possibilities— "we'll drive somewhere together. Out to the beach! Just you and me. How about that?"

"I can't. I have to do the dress rehearsal over. It's Zinnie's day off. At least it better be."

Claire lowered her head so Carmela wouldn't recognize her relief. "Carmela," she said kindly, from a loving place, from where you were supposed to be able to say all sorts of otherwise forbidden things. "Maybe you and Stefan ought to think about starting a family. You could stop getting high, you know. And stop taking the pill."

Carmela stood up with a jerk and sat back down again. She looked up through the webwork of branches above them to the sky. Squirrels and raccoons and rats made last-minute adjustments just beside them in the woods. Carmela snorted. "I haven't been on the pill for ages."

"But you said—"

216

"I know what I said. I didn't want you to feel sorry for me. I didn't want you to know, okay?" she sniffed into her ironed linen handkerchief. She spoke so softly that Claire had to lean over to hear her. "Last week I was feeling, you know, randy, and maybe thinking like just what you said. I knew he was home because the light was on in his room." She laughed. "We've always had separate bedrooms. Anyway, I went down the hallway and Piece, his man, gives me this look, like this movement like, blocking me from going down the hall. I mean, I looked at him like he was wacky, but I know how strange Stefan's servants all are. He moved back, of course, and I kept on going, but I didn't like him acting like that. I guess I was feeling defensive, this-is-my-house and all that, so I just barged into Stefan's room without knocking and there he was, down on his knees, in front of page after page of opened-up magazines, and he's, he was—"

"It's all right," Claire stopped her. "I understand."

Carmela kept on. "That wasn't the worst thing. The worst thing was that he looked up at me, just as cool as you please, he didn't miss a beat," she laughed. "And you know what he said? He looks at me and he goes, 'Well, get out.' Like, he lifts up his chin, dismissing me, and he goes, just like this, 'Get out.' " She shook her head. "The stupid thing was that when I saw him like that, I wasn't really upset yet. Just shocked. I would have gone over to him and, I mean, I didn't even care that he was turned on . . . by *pictures*. . . . I would have just . . ." Here she hesitated. ". . . just been his wife. Only he said, 'Well, get out,' like that."

Claire's heart went out to her. "Oh, Carmela," she said. But what else could you say? It was so brutal.

"Don't tell Mommy."

"Tch. Of course not. I wouldn't tell anyone. Not even Johnny. I swear."

"All right." She blew her nose. "I feel better."

Claire knew she didn't. But at least the secret wasn't beating her up, nuts to get out.

"Clairy," Carmela sobbed, wretched again with a new burst of passion, "I'm out on the birch tree behind the blockade!"

"I know, I know." Claire held her carefully and they went up the lane together, stepping gingerly so they didn't see that someone stood behind them and watched them, mouth agape and wondering just what to do here.

So Claire, after she'd seen to it that Carmela was safely in the door of her home, went back down Richmond Hill, distracted with concern and unaware that she was being followed. Floozie, terrified, kept running, and Claire had all she could do to keep up with her. Finally, she did, and gave her a good whack on the tail to boot for running off, then stashed the dog inside her coat as they drew near her house. There was a light on in Iris's kitchen. Good, Claire thought, and climbed the back steps, her fingers closing around the glamorous stone in her pocket. She knocked on the door. Lü, the cat, a sphinx on the porcelain breadbox, regarded her through the window.

"Iris?" Claire rapped on the glass. She hated to ring the bell. Maybe Iris had gone to sleep and left the light on. Maybe, jeepers creepers, she was in there with Mr. Kinkaid. Of course she wasn't, Claire checked herself. She leaned on the door to reach over to ring the bell, and the door swung open. "Iris?" she called again. How could she leave the door open like that, she thought angrily. Anyone could just walk in. Maybe Iris was finally losing it, she worried. But no, Iris was far from losing it. She'd been through wars and exile and the equally humbling phenomenon of years of long-unalleviated boredom, and she wasn't going to lose it over one more uneventful autumn. Or wasn't that just what one lost it over? On the other hand, she could have hit her head and fallen, or simply fallen and broken her hip.

"Iris?" Claire called again. There was a funny smell. She didn't like to just barge in. What if Iris was in the tub? She might scare her to death. "Iris?" She walked into the kitchen. The cat didn't move. She felt Floozie stiffen and shiver. Where was Iris's dog, Natasha? "Natasha?" she called. "Iris?" She walked across the kitchen. She wasn't going to go looking all over the house, just through to the dining room. She switched on the light. If there was one thing that terrified Claire, it was a lonely house in the dark. She switched the whole row of lights on at once, peered through to the dining room, didn't see the woman standing there in the pantry backed up against the shelves of labeled jars, turned back around into the kitchen, noticed a game of double solitaire spread out on the kitchen table, deliberated for a moment, moved a black card onto a red one, then thought, That's where she is; walking Natasha. I probably would have bumped into her if I'd kept on walking. She smiled in expectation, turned, and looked into the pale open eyes of Mrs. Dixon, dead.

The sound of screams reverberated through the white tile kitchen till Claire realized they were her own. "Now, now," a voice behind her said, "she's dead. Stop screaming now, she's dead."

It was Iris, behind her, patting her head with loose, old-lady hands. "Shh," she kept saying from behind Claire, "Sshhh. *Ist ja Alles in Ordnung. Ist ja Alles wieder Gut.* It's all right now. Everything's all right."

You could hear the rattle of the wind outside and the insistent banging of the door against the can. It was so cold inside the kitchen. So cold and so dreary and white.

A squad car from far away came closer and closer and then, instead of going on, it stopped. Claire could hear its whoop-whoop out on the corner. Red lights spun around the room from its reflection.

"I'll go," Iris said. "I've got to go. I called nine-one-one."

In horror, Claire watched her go.

"Don't leave me here, alone," she called out in a whimper, but Iris was gone and she looked again into the eyes of Mrs. Dixon. She covered her own face with her hands. She'd hanged herself. Claire just couldn't look at her.

Iris came back in with a pair of moustachioed policemen. They took one look at Mrs. Dixon and one of them whistled. Things started to happen quickly then. The other one went back outside, and before Claire knew it the room was filled up with cops, both uniforms and undercovers.

"I just went to bring a dish a few blocks away. I was only gone for fifteen minutes!" Iris insisted over and over. "She was fine when I left her. She was just staying here for safekeeping. She wouldn't have hurt nobody else. Dot was over. All dot was over."

Mary and Stan came from across the street. Mary put a blanket over Claire and then Johnny was there. He picked her up like she was one of the kids and carried her down the stairs and into the

219

car. Claire looked around for Floozie, and the little dog jumped into her still-trembling arms before he slammed the door. She wanted to go home. "Just get me home," was all she thought, "and let me hold my little boy and go to sleep."

Johnny was very tender with Claire when they got home. He picked her up and carried her across the threshold like a newly-wed. Then he put her down on the couch and went in to make her a cup of tea. "Claire, there is no more of your oolong," he called in. "Do you want plain Lipton?"

"Yes. Yes, fine, anything," she said, astonished that life went on, that normal things like drinking tea and putting on your slippers kept on. What she wanted was a good stiff bourbon, not tea, but even with this ordeal, she knew she'd better not ask for it. Just the smell could start him off on a binge. She got up and went up the stairs to check on Anthony. He was in his bed, so little, so young. She walked over and pulled his blanket up an inch. His fist flew by his lips in some warrior dream episode. She smiled down at him kindly, full of love. He was safe now. No matter what happened, as long as he was all right, she would be, too. She pulled herself together standing there and went down the hallway to check on the others. Swamiji, at the nursery doorway, was sitting upright in lotus position and sound asleep. She knew if she were someone else, his spirit would return and he would jump up with a frightening jolt. She stepped carefully over him. Michael-aen was not in bed. Neither, she realized fearfully, was Dharma. How could they have gotten past Swamiji, she wondered, how? He was worse than a guard dog, and the only thing that would disturb him was what he'd programmed himself for: a threat to the children's safety. In the closet. She walked over stealthily and opened the door a crack.

"Shh!" Michaelaen said.

"What are you doing?" she hissed. "Where's Dharma?"

"She's in here, Aunt Claire. She's asleep."

"Well, come out."

Michaelaen sighed the sigh of the weary. "Aunt Claire," he explained patiently, "if I make her come out, she'll get scared again. And I just got her to sleep. She just cries and cries. Please don't tell, Aunt Claire."

Claire went into the giant closet with her nephew. Sure enough, Dharma lay, asleep and peaceful, on a pile of coats and quilts and pillows. Claire's parents were right, she realized. Dharma was a precious child and very, very beautiful there in the flickering waver of flashlight.

"Where is my mother?" Michaelaen demanded suddenly.

"Shh," Claire signalled him out of the closet. "Your mother is fine. They're held up in overtime," she lied, worried now again about Zinnie. "I'm supposed to kiss you once for her and tuck you in good."

Michaelaen scratched his neck. "Aunt Claire?"

"Yes. Come. Hop into bed." She went and got the bottle of holy water she kept on the nightstand and sprinkled it onto his and Dharma's heads. They were always half annoyed at the cold shock before sleep, but they were pleased by the love in the gesture. She screwed the cap back on and blessed herself as well.

"Aunt Claire, please can't I stay here with Dharma? If she wakes up she'll be real scared if I'm not here."

"Of course you can. Your mother will be proud of you," she added, "taking such good care of someone in need."

"Well, don't go tellin' nobody." Michaelaen narrowed his eyes nastily at her.

"I won't. You don't have to worry about that," she lied again easily. She brought the sleeping bag over from the bed and placed it on top of their great cozy pile. "Just in case it gets colder," she said.

Michaelaen nodded, important and world-weary now.

"Michaelaen? May I ask you something?"

"What? Just whisper. What?"

"What is it that Dharma is afraid of?"

Michaelaen shrugged.

"Because," Claire said gently, "if nobody helps her find a way outside, you know, out of her dreams, well, maybe she'll always have to have them. I mean, if someone could help her work them out, maybe she could be free of them. Like you, when you went and talked about things to the therapist. See what I mean?"

Michaelaen shrugged again. He knew what she meant. It used to be himself inside the closet for safety, never wanting to come out. Claire sighed and patted his head and got up to go. By tomorrow the news about Mrs. Dixon would be all over school. What he needed most right now was a good night's sleep. She wondered if she ought to tell him herself. No, she guessed, it was Zinnie's business. On the other hand, she realized, if Zinnie wasn't about when he woke up tomorrow morning—and she most probably wouldn't be—he would hear that she herself had come across Mrs. Dixon hanged, and he'd know Claire hadn't told him. What would he think about then?

"Michaelaen?"

"What?"

"I've got to tell you something. Something terrible. No, don't worry, not about your mommy. It's this. Tonight, Mrs. Dixon was found dead. She was here in Queens all along. She was staying in Iris von Lillienfeld's house. She hanged herself to death. I guess the guilt just finally got to her and she couldn't live with it anymore."

Michaelaen, eyes round with this news, came over and stood beside her. She had changed all of their lives for the worse, that terrible woman. Uneasily, Claire realized that she was relieved that Mrs. Dixon was dead. Delighted, even.

"So you never have to be afraid of her. Not ever again."

"Oh, I was never really afraid of her," Michaelaen said, scratching Floozie affectionately.

"Well, I was. Michaelaen, there's no shame to admitting that someone as monstrous as she was frightened you. You don't have to be macho here. She really was evil."

"She never hurt me or nuthin'. I mean, she just took our pitchas."

"Michaelaen, she murdered those children."

"I know she did, Aunt Claire."

"And she locked you in her refrigerator."

"No, she didn't."

"All right," Claire sighed. She didn't want to make things worse. Michaelaen was doing so well now.

Michaelaen shut his lips tight. He knew he'd gone into that

222

refrigerator on his own. To hide. They kept trying to make him say he hadn't. Boy.

"Did you brush your teeth?"

"Yeah."

"You want me to sit here a while?"

"Aunt Claire? Did she kill Miss von Lillienfeld?"

"No, honey, she's fine. Just sad and sorry she hadn't told somebody that she was hiding her." She remembered the day she had gone over there. Iris's unease. Now she knew why. And she had thought it was because she was waiting for Mr. Kinkaid.

"Maybe she was blackmailing her," Michaelaen suggested with all the knowledgable sophistication of the seasoned television viewer.

"I don't think so. They were friends for so many years, you know. I don't think she was afraid of Mrs. Dixon. Miss von Lillienfeld doesn't scare that easily. When the police were questioning her, she let them have it pretty good. She's a pretty tough old cookie."

"Are they gonna put her in jail?"

"I don't know. She's very old. I hope not. Grandma was with her when I left. They were drinking vodka."

"That's good."

"Yes."

He yawned.

"I'll let you be. Give me Floozie, now. Give me a kiss . . . Good night."

"Good night. Aunt Claire?"

"Yes?"

"That dream. The one Dharma always has again and again?"

"Uh huh?"

"It's about that big flower in front of the house. When it's summer."

"I don't understand."

"Yes, you know. That flower so pretty, like gorgeous. With the dots and all. That's what Dharma's afraid of. She always dreams she cuts it down."

"The foxglove?"

"That's it. Foxglove. She told me if she told you it would hurt you."

"No, it doesn't hurt me." She smiled, stunned with pleasure that Dharma should care what she felt. "Thank you for telling me."

"You're welcome. And she said she dreamed you put little silverbells on all the more beautiful flowers, so no one will miss them."

"What?" said Claire.

"Like in *The Nightingale*. In the garden of the Emperor's palace. So everyone would see them."

"Did they do that?"

"Yes. Swamiji read it to us."

"Michaelaen," she said, "what else?"

Michaelaen rocked from side to side. Claire interpreted this to mean this session is over, so she turned to go.

"Cause she's scared if you get scared, then you'll die, too."

"Oh, poor thing," she said.

"Yes," Michaelaen said.

"You make sure she understands I'm not going to die for a long, long time. Not for as long as the lot of you need me, at least."

"Okay. Good night."

"Good night. Oh. One more thing. Did Dharma ever tell you where she got her stones? The pretty stones?"

"Oh, those," he yawned again. "Her father gave them to her."

"You're sure?"

"That's what she told me."

"All right. Sleep now. Say your prayers."

She stepped carefully around Swamiji and left the door open just a crack. The light in the hall was on. However big they acted, Claire knew light was a tangible strength for children. She stood in the hallway at the top of the stairs and looked out the high, stained-glass window at the Dover house across the street. Tree would turn in her grave if she could see that satellite dish atop her good Queen Anne Victorian. Claire pushed open the vent. She turned and heard someone scream. She shut off the light by pulling the plug behind her out of the wall socket, and crept back to the window. The scream again. Up and down the block she saw nothing, only parts of things torn loose from the wind and bumping into crumpled other things. She fine-tuned her ears and eyes. No one was up. Someone was screaming, really screaming. A woman, losing it. It was someone's TV on the next block. "Oh, God," she said out loud, remembering the eyes of Mrs. Dixon. She would have to look into them now for lots of long and lonely moments when no Johnny waited down the stairs to comfort her. She'd have to look, because that was the only way to forget it. If you tried not to see it, it would always be there, wouldn't it?

Imagine Dharma worried that she would perish, too. A natural fear in someone who'd just lost her mother, she supposed. But as she stood there, hesitating at the top of the step, she remembered her own dream just the night before. There were people, officials on the pier at Brighton, explaining to her that she was losing her hearing, they were going to give her a course in communication. She had to go to the restroom and so she did, walking along the vast planks until she got there, and opened the door onto a poisonous, fast-spreading cloudy gas. Quickly thinking, she ran and raced away—gasping for air, coughing already.

Claire shook her head. Funny she should remember that now. Dharma's dream must have jarred her own. And Carmela's too. All these dreams at once. What was she, the dream lady? Oh, it made you tired. It made you just want to quit. She rubbed her neck and heard it crack. Suddenly, she had a yen to be wedged up tight against the hard, familiar calm of her husband's own mysterious body. Down the ever-steepening hardwood stairs she went, strangely unconsoled by the gray and horrifying dragon's end.

CHAPTER 9

Alone in the dawn among the withering lettuce, Narayan looked at the house.
He could hear his bewildered incentive, Zinnie's bewitching and
vaporous song. Was it possible that no one else could hear her?
Was he the only one up? The only one who lived at this moment?
It was a nice old song Lenny Welch used to sing, "Since I Fell For
You." A sad song, but Zinnie sang it with such joy that it tran-
scended its own meaning. "Hello," he called. "Hello, Zinnie?" He
cupped his mouth and called up to her window. A crow, black and
enormous, sat between them up there on the sleek birch branches,
listening too. Zinnie was drying her hair while she sang. She
supposed she went on unobserved. Narayan hesitated. I would flee
and I would stay, he thought, experiencing dread. In the end, he
decided he'd better get going and buy the bread. Tonight would
be the play and there was much to be done. Fetching the bread
was his job. Every day he went. He'd walk down to the Jamaica
Avenue bakery and buy a loaf from the back door just after it
came from the oven. This was his offering to the family.

At first he'd thought that when he left for Berkeley, then they
would miss him, not tasting that superb freshness every morning;
they would be reminded that he was no longer there. Now, it had
come to mean something else. Now it was he who would miss the
hauling of the bread, the face of the baker, the kindly passage of
the silvery change. The pale, even faces of this family who rose
each day to muesli when they could have any sugared cereal from
the shelves of any luxury supermarket. It was he who would miss
them. Terribly.

The empty streets grew light and he walked, reconsidering. It
wasn't as though there were no Indian families here in Queens.

226

Wasn't it true that there were families moving in left and right of Lefferts Boulevard? All the grand old houses were going to Punjabis. He had never seen an Indian and American couple, though. Not with children. But surely there must be such a thing. He'd seen couples like that down in Calangute, in Goa. White and black, with some inevitably dwindling magnetism between them, people who'd run away from both societies, only that never seemed to be very successful together. Somehow, you always got the feeling they had no friends who weren't there for the precise reason that the couple was interracial. They were sorry, gloomy misfits in their pretty, rented homes along the beach, with their canopy beds from the Portuguese settlers and dirt floors and rats in the kitchen.

This, however, was America. Who, as the albino Jews from Matancherie shrugged and said, knew?

The empty street began to fill with the darting forms of sleepy people, each attached to a dog by a chain. He smiled benignly at each one of them. They clutched their coats around themselves and hurried their dogs along. Narayan might see himself as a harmless, well-educated chap strolling down Venus's own street, but they saw him as a big black man without a dog up here in their neighborhood, so what was he up to?

Narayan, without incident, obtained his bread and headed back to Claire's house. He deliberated about his future. He told himself he was arguing the pros and cons of a relationship, but the truth was, Narayan was already hooked. The real question was where, then, would they live? This was charming enough, he mused as he looked around, but there was something shabby about it. He much preferred up east of the woods, the Kew Gardens part where Stefan and Carmela lived. It was more to his class. They could never live in India. Never. Zinnie would never put up with his sisters' arrogant superiority. Let alone his mother, a woman not unlike the matriarchal Mrs. Panchyli. He broke into a sweat at the thought.

Just then, Narayan spotted billowing smoke from a basement window. Without hesitation, he raced to the corner and pulled down the fire alarm. He raced back to the house, a big gray one, and pounded on the door. It was treacherously silent.

227

"Hallo!" he shouted. "Fire! Make haste! Come out of the house! Fire!"

Somewhere a shutter flew open and he heard the sound of running feet up someone's stairway. He banged on the door again. He looked frantically about. A boy, Michaelaen's age, watched him, wide-eyed, from the corner. "Fire!" Narayan alerted him. The door before him opened. A portly woman, fiftyish, neatly set for the day in a dotted print house dress protected by an apron, stepped back with alarm. She held one arm across the door, barring him.

"Fire!" he gasped and pointed to the side of her house.

"What?" she squinted, no fool she. He probably wanted to get in so he could rob her. Well, she wasn't born yesterday. She shut the door. "Malcolm!" she cried. Down the steps came Malcolm, shaving cream over half of his face, suspenders down around his pants. He grabbed hold of a golf club and threw open the door. "Fire!" Narayan blinked at both of them, stepping back and pointing to the side of their house. Something in his rebuking demeanor let them know he wasn't there to do them harm, and they followed him out to the porch where they stood, the three of them, watching the innocent puffy blue air from the dryer escape in a billow of sachet from the vent.

"I've rung the alarm," he assured them. "Is anyone left in the house? Any children or animals?" He was fully prepared for grand valiance.

"What are you, some kinda nut?" Malcolm kept a good grip on his club. "That's just the dryer! The regular dryer!"

His wife stood, beginning to shiver with cold, right behind him.

Not only that, but the fire brigade would arrive at any moment. Narayan, sensing dilemma, ran charivari away up the block, leaving his bread and his lofty intentions behind.

Nervous excitement rattled the bristling cold branches around Mary's house. This was the day her one daughter's play was to open with the other daughter to sing the brilliant lead. A chill went right through her. There wasn't a leaf left on any a tree. A sickle moon ventured out, loud as the day, and the sun stood one-eighty degrees there against it. Must mean something, Mary thought,

228

she, a great one for symbolics but always too busy to bother. It wasn't good to see the new moon through the glass, though, she knew well enough. It didn't bode well. What rubbish, she scoffed at herself, but she lowered the heat on the iron. She was spray-starching and ironing her best green silk dress; she wouldn't chance scorching it. Freddy was having them all back to his place right after the show. A little spray starch never hurt, she consoled herself, keeping it hidden just the same from the likes of ecologically conscientious Claire. Ridiculous notions! All these experts! They should have lived as she had, down south of Cork on the ledge of the land out of fair Skibbereen, yank your laundry through a wringer and blue-rinse it again and again. These young girls didn't know what progress was. She held the can at an adequate angle and let go a frothy white mist. Like a shower·of ease, this stuff was. Like a bloody fine advert they'd show on the telly. Oop. She heard someone coming. Mary put the can out of sight behind the cannisters and peered through the curtains. "Bugger," she said.

It was Iris von Lillienfeld. She considered pretending not to be home, but that wouldn't do any good; Iris'd only come back and she'd do it when the rest of them were about or Stan would be wanting his tea. She might as well face her. Mary patted her hair and flung open the door. "Sure, look who's come to grace this house," she beamed and held out her strong arms with a delighted, bright counterfeit welcome.

Over at Claire's, mayhem reigned. For some reason, Carmela felt her home was off-limits to the cast and she'd directed them to Claire's. When Claire got a good look at the dwarfs (in this case "dorks"), she understood why. They were a salty lot.

Johnny put every quart of classic Coke under the onions in the pantry. "The hell with them," he said, "let them buy their own damn Coke." Swamiji agreed. He'd got the sodas each for ninety-eight cents at the big coupon sale, and he and Mary had transported them home against a stiff, frosty wind. Swamiji, lips busily pursed, now trundled ginger ales, one by one, down to the cellar. These were Anthony's, he sniffed. "Children thrive on effervescence."

"Oh." Claire, astonished, folded her arms across her chest. "And what am I supposed to serve them, water?"

"Yes. Or just plain tea is good enough. And, by the way, it's not your job to serve them anything. That is what they have 'take-out' for. This is the twentieth century, New York, U.S.A."

"Wait a minute." She recognized Zinnie's favorite argument. "Aren't you the fellow who renounced the world?"

"That means," Swamiji spoke with his head down at the bottom of the refrigerator, "that I own nothing and everything." He emerged, agitated, with Michaelaen's most-favorite chocolate puddings in miniature Rubbermaids. He and Mary had made them the night before with the extra half-gallon of milk. No way these ne'er-do-wells, these vultures, were going to make off with the children's own yummies, as far as he was concerned. And where were Dharma's lemon yogurts? He dove back in.

"I suppose you're right," Claire agreed distractedly and went into the dining room in search of Carmela. Freddy, on his knees, looked up with a mouthful of pins. He was hemming Portia's costume. Portia stood on Claire's newly upholstered hassock.

"Portia, would you mind taking off your shoes, please?" she asked her, more nicely than she felt.

"If she takes off her shoes," Freddy protested without opening his teeth, "she won't hem right."

"Well, then put her on some telephone books."

"All right, all right, you don't have to be so testy," he said, and he winked at Portia.

Claire was about to say she would let that one pass when she noticed Andrew sprawled comfortably across her love seat. Just his being here, languidly ogling Portia's creamy big jugs—half in and half out of quivering blue crepe de chine—burned her up. He was supposed to be visiting with Dharma. That was the reason he'd come.

The telephone rang on the table beside her and she picked it up angrily. Through the living room flew the dorks. They were rehearsing the bit where they stood on the top of the couch and tipped it over slowly, nicely balanced, the way Cary Grant and Katharine Hepburn would do.

"What!" sputtered Claire.

Carmela raced up and patted her hand. "Now, Claire," she pacified her. "Don't be cross. It works so much better on your couch than on the one we've got over on the stage. Daddy said he'd be very, very careful when they move it. You know how fastidious he is."

"I never said—"

"Oh, I know you didn't, darling, but just look how well it works. Just watch! All their hard work is finally paying off. They're not real dancers, you know. They could use any break they can get."

"What about using your couch, then, if it's so important!"

"My couch?! Stefan's Louis quinzième? You must be joking. He'd never let it out of the house."

"Well, I'm not sure Johnny would want our"—They looked together at the clumsy, club-footed atrocity before them—"Our whatever-it-is, out of the house, either."

"Oh, yes, he would. He said we could. He did. He said if it never came back it would be all too soon."

Claire bit her lip. "Carmela, if anything happens to that couch, I'm holding you personally responsible. I don't care what Johnny said, got it?"

Carmela arched one pencilled brow. "You're starting to sound more and more like him every day, do you know it?"

"Carmela—"

"Is that for me?" Carmela looked at the receiver in Claire's trembling hand.

"Hello?" said Claire.

"Claire? It's Mommy. Got the whole shebang at your place, I hear. You all right?"

"Tch. Yeah. I guess so."

"Claire, don't worry, dear. Nothing lasts forever. Tomorrow this will all be over, won't it?"

"I guess so." She watched Carmela sashay off to go bully a dork.

"And Daddy's there, isn't he?"

"He's here, all right, Mom. He's carting off my couch for props."

"Oh, well. He'll bring it back. Mind he watches the legs. That was your Great-Aunt Greta from Pomerania's good stuff."

"There are moments I wonder why I just didn't stay in South Ozone Park," Claire heard herself whine.

Mary laughed. "You wanted a houseful of people."

"I did."

"Next time, careful what you wish for. You'll get it."

"I know."

"And dear, it means so much to Carmela." She said this with the same worried, tragic tone in which she'd taken to referring to Carmela all the time lately. Poor Carmela. On the verge of her very own play being produced and she didn't even get her house messed up.

"Oh. Claire. The reason I called. Remember what you told me that time, about Mrs. Dixon coming into the house back then and yanking the hall wire of the radio so it would fall into your tub and electrocute you?"

"Of course I remember." Claire was losing patience. Someone had ordered pizza and the delivery boy was here and now everyone was waiting for everyone else to go pay. Well, she wasn't going to.

"That was the day I got my hair cut, remember? You told me that was the same day. Is that right?"

"Yes."

"Well, I didn't quite know what to make of it and I couldn't for the life of me remember back that far. You know how I forget. And it was so long ago. Anyway, Iris von Lillienfeld was here a little while ago and we had a nice cup of rosy together and we got to talking, Claire and . . . Claire? It couldn't have been Mrs. Dixon tried to do that to you, because Mrs. Dixon was with me. All day. See, that was the day she drove me to the cemetery to go visit Michael's grave. We never did mention that to you because, well, no one wanted to upset you, like. Are you listening, Claire?"

"Yes," Claire whispered.

"Because, first we went to the cemetery and then she took me to her salon where she always went, on Myrtle Avenue, there, in Glendale, oh, what's it called? Laraine's. Or Elaine's or something. But the point is, she and I were together all the live-long day. See, after I had my braids cut off, I was feeling a mite low and she took me to Jahn's for a double-fudge marshmallow ice cream sundae. Isn't it odd? I remember every detail just as though it were yesterday. And all because Iris remembered that Mrs. Dixon and I went to the cemetery. Iris had given me such a nice potted plant for the grave. A pale peach rose." She waited, shyly. "It's still there. It took. Anyway, that was the same day I had my hair cut. She says she remembered thinking it was symbolic, that I'd made the decision to move on, like. To come back to the living. And I was annoyed—I hate that psychoanalysis stuff—because I'd come back to the living way long before that, see, and I told her so, good. So Iris and I were talking over old times, the good things about Mrs. Dixon, you know, the way you will be wanting to speak well of the dead and all, she was a good neighbor after all, and I was telling Iris how kind she'd been to me that day, she'd even paid for those sundaes, you know, and all of a sudden I remembered how you said how she'd tried to do that to you on the day I'd got my hair cut and so help me, Claire, it all came back to me in a rush. And I remembered the whole episode, like. So you see, Claire, it couldn't have been Mrs. Dixon who tried to do that to you. Because, see, she was with me."

At the Harvard Club, where Jupiter Dodd used to like to take Claire to lunch, in the room set aside for ladies with their well-behaved children, or simply guests unwilling to wait with the rest, there is a painting on the wall by John Singer Sargent. It's called *Chess Game* and in it, on the edge of a shimmering lily pond, in oasis-dappled light, recline two players, a pantalooned young man and a veiled and slender woman. They are engrossed. He knows what he's about. She is dark, self-possessed, and serious. The chess board, however, is suspended above ground. Such a mystic thing for such solid sport. He might not really be there, one considers, and neither, perhaps, is she, just an inspiration to his imagination. But then again, they're always there, those two, up on the dark red, time-honored wall, playing.

Claire often thought about that painting. And talked about it. Such an ideal spot to be. "You can't live in a painting," Zinnie would remind her. "No," she would say. She was thinking of that painting now in her own house, and not mentioning it to Zinnie, who sat with her on the stairs, because she knew what she would say. And Zinnie, who had enjoyed psychology in college, always insisted that the painting reminded Claire of Michael. There was truth in everything, Claire supposed, but she knew Zinnie worried about her. Zinnie looked so happy lately. She glowed with an inner light. Everyone dismissed it as a by-product of show biz, but Claire knew there was something going on with Narayan. She could hear them whispering downstairs late into the night. The two of them were so dazed, they were banging into walls. Also, she had watched from her bedroom window as Narayan pulled Zinnie into the garage and kissed her. Not only had Zinnie let him, Claire remembered, she had watched Zinnie's black-stockinged leg travel up and around Narayan's waist like a lasso.

She and Zinnie played Go Fish. The cast had all gone home, or, as Carmela said, to their respective hovels. They had started off playing cards with the kids, Claire and Zinnie, but the kids had gotten bored and petered off, Anthony first, who now played distractedly with the Jacob's Ladder Narayan had made him from ribbons and glue and old cardboard. Johnny lay, half dozing, on the loveseat. Anthony caught Claire's eye and led her gaze to the spot under Johnny's arm, where his robe was washed thin. Anthony was always full of tricks and games and festivities lately. Conspiratorially, mother and son locked eyes. He pussyfooted silently across the room, grazed a finger along Johnny's breast till he reached the pit of his arm and then wiggled the digit. Johnny's arm flew down protectively and he lurched. Anthony howled with laughter. "Let's do it again!" he cried and so they did. Johnny closed his eyes and Anthony went back to where he'd been originally sitting and they repeated the entire charade. Anthony enjoyed himself just as much each time as the first and he laughed with abandon.

Swamiji, sewing up the wash-worn seams of Claire's embroidered Chinese pillowcases, smiled dotingly.

It was very still outside the house.

Dharma pulled Claire's great lot of hair behind her head and wound it into a French braid. Michaelaen and Narayan were captivated with their game of Nintendo. Stan had insisted upon his radio station and no one had bothered to change it. Even though their own lives tended them towards more current music, the Breslinsky girls all felt most at home and contented within the strains of the classical music on which Stan had raised them. These pieces were so lovely; Barber's adagio for strings and then Haydn's concerto for flute and oboe. No one wanted to move. It was like being under a spell. The weather wasn't sunny, but quick, silver clouds were gathering and a woolpack of pearly light shone through Swamiji's now spotless windows, lifting everyone's spirits up and keeping them aloft.

The dog slept in a rectangle of light on Freddy's old Dhera Gaz in the middle of the room. Floozie had always liked that rug. It might have gotten her into trouble back when she lived with Fred, but it had, in the end, led her here, hadn't it? There would be hamburgers and macaroni and cheese for supper. She sighed happily, yawned, stretched, turned over, and went back to sleep.

"The thing is," Claire said suddenly, "if Mrs. Dixon wasn't the one who pulled the wire on the radio—and it wasn't, it's perfectly clear now that it wasn't—then who did do it?"

Everyone groaned. "Go fish," said Zinnie.

"I mean," she continued nonetheless, "that changes everything, doesn't it?" She looked from one face to another. No one would meet her eyes. They knew what she was getting at. She had this tic in her head that Andrew Dover had killed his wife and she couldn't, or wouldn't, shake it.

As far as Johnny was concerned, the case was closed. He had never wanted to hear Mrs. Dixon's name again; *that* case was long closed. And Andrew Dover had been with Portia McTavish the day Theresa Dover had died. They'd been seen by sources left and right. Christ, they'd even stopped at Freddy's. So the guy was guilty of adultery, so what? So was half the world. What were you gonna do, hang him for cheating? Anyway, the coroner had said it was open and shut; she'd died of a stroke, brought on by drugs and alcohol. Both her parents had died that way, hadn't they? Far as he could tell, Theresa Dover was just one more slut junkie out of the way. You couldn't say that to Claire, though. His wife was a slight bit pixillated in her brain. He looked at her over there across the room, with the little girl brushing her hair and putting it back in a fancy rope like that, all reddish and fluffy and dark. That same old ache he always got from the sudden sight of her came back with impatience. He rolled the toothpick around in his mouth. You get a house, you pay a mortgage, and you can't even screw your wife, he grumbled to himself, standing up to get rid of the hardness.

Claire felt his itchy look, mistook it for annoyance and she figured she'd better change the subject. This was turning into a sore topic. If only she could get Johnny alone for a couple of minutes, she knew she could blow in his ear and loosen him up enough to hear her out. He stood up and started for the door. Now where was he off to? "Now where are you off to?" She tried not to wear her interrogator's face.

"The barn," he said.

"Aw, Johnny, today? You promised you'd be here all day. The minute you have any time off lately, you're off to the track."

"Yeah, Dad," Anthony piped up, backing her up.

"I'm just going over to the barn," Johnny stretched, filling the room with his big hulking self. "We're getting the horse a goat, while she heals."

"A goat?" they all cried.

"Yeah, why? Keep her company. They like goats." He looked at all of them looking at him with open mouths. "Whatsa matter? You got something against goats?"

"I wanna go!" Anthony cried.

"Me too," Michaelaen pleaded.

"All right, all right," Claire gave in, watching, spellbound, as Johnny loaded the bullets into his Colt Detective Special. Usually, she looked away, pretending to herself that life would never be that bad again. Still, she was glad he wore it. He was alive. And protected. She might feel safe enough inside her white light, but she liked her husband in a gun. "Just be back way before supper," she warned. "I want you all in and out of here and the place cleaned up before I have to get dressed for the play."

"We'll be back, don't you worry," they all promised. Sure. They all promised the moon when it took them to the track. She would not be annoyed, she vowed. She couldn't stand women who were always annoyed. She would relax, smile, and enjoy their happiness. There was anyway no sense to being upset when it would get her nowhere. Somehow, the bills would get paid and the mortgage dealt with. And if they didn't, she would deal with that, too. Isn't that what mommies and housewives the world over did? Well, she would do it, too.

"Dharma?" she turned around and looked into the uncanny, curious eyes, so like those of her schoolmate. "Did you want to go with them?"

"Good Lord, no," Dharma assured her. She wasn't one for horses. They were so big. They smelled of, well, horse.

Johnny came back in. He whacked the chair beside Swamiji's head with a bing.

"Didn't you tell me you had a number you wanted me to play for you?"

"I have a number I appreciate that you might use, if you like."

Johnny rocked back and forth expectantly.

"One sixty-five," said Swamiji. "Leviticus."

"Whatever," Johnny grinned at Claire.

She shook her head. "You're too much. Now, where's Anthony?"

"He's with Michaelaen."

They both peered suspiciously out the window, the most precious thing in their lives out there walking around in a pair of rickety sneakers.

"You'll be careful." She tried not to sound worried.

Anthony, out on the lawn, sneezed twice. Johnny and Claire glanced, concerned, at each other.

"I didn't hear any 'God bless you's' in there," his grown-up, curmudgeony voice came reprimandingly through the shut window.

"Go on," she said. "Get out of here."

"Remind me to call Red when I get back," he said. "He's not feelin' too hot."

Johnny went out the door and whisked Anthony into the air, depositing him beside Michaelaen in the back seat of the car.

"Move over, fart breath," Anthony said.

"Get a grip, rhinoceros nostrils," Michaelaen said.

Claire watched Johnny strap him in. She whispered, "God bless you," and she went back to her place. She was nervous. There was so much still to do.

"You are veddy, veddy wise," Swamiji bobbed his head whimsically at Claire. Floozie got up, looked around for a cozier spot, jumped up and squished herself in the space between him and the side of his chair.

"Got no choice." Claire shrugged, anyway pleased that he'd noticed.

"Yes, but you're letting him follow his bliss."

"He'd do it anyway," she snorted, "whether I let him or not."

"Ah, people always do what they want to do," he agreed, "but if you don't permit him with grace, it would not be his bliss."

"That's one way of looking at it."

"There is so much power in one's attitude," Swamiji squinted one eye and threaded the needle he held in the air. "If only people knew."

"Knew what?" Dharma stopped pulling the hairs from the brush and looked up.

"How much power they have."

"Oh," they both said.

In the garlicky, Jell-O-boxed pantry, where the mirror hung amid the cans of bright yellow creamed corn and wheat-germ jars filled with pasta and grains, Mary stood before her in her shimmering green dress. The dress was all right, Claire supposed, but the hat had to go. It had a veil, a sort of stiff go-to-meeting netting thing that stuck up into the air.

"Something wrong?" Mary painted green eyeshadow across her crepey lids with a shaky, unpracticed hand.

"No, nothing." She didn't like to tell her she looked like she was off to a wedding in Woodhaven. It didn't matter. Mary would take it as a compliment anyhow. "You look terrific, Ma." Now where was Johnny? He'd just come in and he'd gone off again. If she wasn't mistaken, it was O.T.B. before they were closed.

"I'm as nervous as a girl. My own daughter singing lead in an off-Broadway play. And another one wrote the whole thing . . . it's too brilliant."

"Off-Broadway?"

"All right, Off-off-Broadway."

"How about, 'Only forty-five minutes from Broadway'?" Claire suggested.

"Oh, you're just jealous," Mary threw her gloves at her. "I can't get this bloody hat on!"

"You might take that as a sign, Mother. Maybe it's just not meant to be."

"Oh, you and your signs!"

"Come on, let me help. Hmm. Hold still, will you? No, you're right. It needs a bobby pin."

"Bobby pin, my foot! You'll ruin my hat."

"Don't you have a hat pin?"

"Bugger. Why would I carry about a loose hat pin?"

"Better than a loose hat. Oh, stop! Ma! What, are you going to cry over a silly old hat? Mom! Tch. Here, take this Kleenex. Now stop it or you'll ruin your pretty eye makeup."

"Serve me right." Mary sniffed, "trussied up like a bleedin' harlot."

"Oh, you're not. You look beautiful. Just beautiful."

"D'you think so?" She turned to face her and the hat slipped down to the bridge of her nose. They both laughed long and hard. Nerves. They were both nerved up with excitement.

"Hang on." Claire dried her own eyes. "I know where I saw some hat pins." She grabbed her keys and threw on her coat.

"Ah, now, don't be goin' out for it," Mary moaned.

"Be still. I'll be right back. I have to run over Dharma's anyway, to get her winter boots. Suppose it snows?"

"Oh, now, don't go there, using her things. I don't want any dead woman's things."

"You make it sound so sinister." She pushed her out of the way with her shoulder and regarded herself in the mirror. She didn't look so bad. "It won't snow. It's too early for snow."

"By the way," Mary tried to sound casual, "what's Swamiji goin' to wear?"

"Same old Swami winter wear. You know him." Mary didn't say anything. "What? What's the matter? You're worried what someone will say about Swamiji, aren't you? Mom," her voice rose shrilly, "how can you go to church every day and be a Christian when you read the papers, clicking your tongue at the devil on the very streets of Queens county, and then you turn around and question what the other parishioners will think of someone . . . someone . . ." she sputtered, ". . . better than all of them, just because if he's black you think he ought to wear a suit and tie like a Pakistani urologist and not the homespun of the holy man he is."

"What do you think of this polish?" Mary extended her nails for inspection. Claire's righteous heart melted. Plenty of Clorox and Spic and Span and ammonia had gone into those knuckly mitts. "Boy. Gorgeous. Where'd you find that one?"

"Right down here in Woolworth's. Would you believe it? Oop! Who's that?" She flipped her eye shadow case into the air in an acrobatic frenzy. It landed somewhere in the colander full of bleeding eggplant for tomorrow's parmigian.

"I'll never find it now," she cried.

"It's in the pot of water pressing the eggplant down," Claire reassured her. "I'll get the door while you fish it out. It's Zinnie. She just had to go to the bank."

"What's this?" Zinnie stood there accusingly, having let herself in the back door, a Parcel Post package in her hand. "And there's a letter for Swamiji."

"You look beautiful, dear!" Mary whispered.

"Well, who's it addressed to?" Claire grabbed the package from her. "Dharma? She'll like that. I wonder who's sending her something? It isn't her birthday, is it? Christ, I don't even know when her birthday is, do you believe it?"

"Can you do up my buttons?" Zinnie turned and led them out of the pantry. She was corseted up in a black, low-cut dress. All the ladies in the cast were dressed low-cut. Carmela thought they might as well keep the men in their seats once the parish wives had gotten them there. Otherwise it would look so bad, she said, all the fellows out in the lunch room smoking and guffawing. Carmela didn't much like men, anymore, or give them much credit, Claire noticed, for all her manufactured girlie magnets to attract their attention.

Zinnie wriggled happily across the kitchen. She loved playing the bitchy witch, she said. She'd always felt sorry for her, could never relate to those good fairy people, with their namby-pamby

240

pinks and blues and their magic wands and their powdered wigs. "These here," she hoisted her chest up with no-nonsense fingers, unringed and untaloned, "are the goods." Later they would paint her face downward to age her, but for now she looked the dandy enchantress she was.

"Holy Jesus," Stan exclaimed as he came up from the cellar. "Look at you!"

"If I don't eat something now," Zinnie beseeched Claire, "I won't have anything till after the play. I can't wait."

"I'll run in and get that hatpin later, Mom," Claire said. "Don't worry."

"Tea and toast," suggested Mary. She screwed in her best Cladagh earrings.

"Anything! English muffins!" Zinnie drew Anthony's Peter Pan sword from its sheath and broke lance around the kitchen. "Food!" she cried out. "My bounty, me pretty, my just deserts before the party begins! This will be my wish! Hand over, or next you'll walk the plank!"

"Ow. Watch it, will you? That hurts. And get off the table before Anthony sees you and thinks that's a great idea," said Claire.

"I won't!"

"You jolly well will." Mary smacked her on the feet.

"Where are the children?" Claire asked.

"I can see them from here," Zinnie said, "they're all three of them out in the yard."

"What are they up to?"

"Doing the pony, from the look of it. Wait. Oh. They're playing potsy."

"Quiet, everyone!" Stanley held up his hand. "It's Debussy!"

"Give me the butter, Mom," Claire instructed.

"It's 'Reflections in the Water,' " Stan insisted, not believing, still, after all these years of his inspired instruction, they wouldn't be more delighted.

Swamiji cleared his throat from the doorway. Only the rippling sound of music was between them but Claire knew, right then, that that was it, he'd be gone from them soon. There was an open space, like weight, in a circle between them.

"What's up?" Zinnie slid from the table.

"It's this letter that's come for me finally," Swamiji said, "from the people at Berkeley." So the five of them sat down to listen and completely forgot Dharma's package sitting there in full view on the cool pantry shelf.

Mrs. Fatima put down her spoon, snapped her purse shut, and pushed the table away from her great lap with a scrape. She looked herself over in the silver papered wall. This dress was clean enough. Her daughters had already left for the play. She herself had never been to an American play. She wondered if she should wear something else. No, she would have her coat on the whole time anyway. It was cold in those auditoriums and she was sure it would snow. She'd been watching channel seven. She would wear the Totes her oldest daughter had given her for her birthday. She opened her purse up again and looked inside. Her pudgy face lit up with greedy delight. Andrew Dover paid her handsomely. And all she had to do was put off any dark-skinned people from buying north of Jamaica Avenue. So many came in for a reading when they wanted to buy a new house, white and black. They were all superstitious. Such an enormous purchase required much deliberation and why not a consultation with an astrologer as well as a real estate agent? Who better than the local fortuneteller? It didn't matter that she wasn't a real astrologer. They thought she was. And Andrew Dover had always just finished dropping some amazing story of how he had gone to her for a reading, just on a lark, and had gotten such great advice about not buying that old building on Eighty-sixth Street that nobody could move and which was now condemned. Crazy, he would shake his head, wonderingly, but true!

Mrs. Fatima knew enough of the lingo to give them a good scare. Ill winds to the north. Sunlight and much happiness to the south. And all the while acting as though she didn't know what it was they were asking about. It was so simple it was absurd. All she had to do was keep her eyes open and see who went in and out of Dover Estates. Didn't hurt anybody. She was a woman who wouldn't hurt a soul. But this was America. Gotta make a buck, right? She tottered across the dirty floor with her tub of rum raisin ice cream and closed it safely away in her portable freezer. She shut it tight and let loose a satisfied and well-fed belch, then went to pull down the gate and lock up. You had to lock up. This neighborhood was going to the dogs.

Dharma took hold of her package and climbed the stairs. She went into the closet and unwrapped the paper and the string and pushed them under Michaelaen's Ninja Turtles toy sewers. Carefully, she opened the glossy white box. There was pretty tissue paper. She plucked it off, and underneath found a pair of earrings on black velvet, glittering tourmaline. "Unlucky," she could just hear her mother say. Still, they were hers. She held them up to her ears, got up and ran with them like that to the mirror. She stood up on the neatly filled suitcase. In the last slanting rays of afternoon light they were shimmering and irresistible. She smiled unhappily into the blazing yellow mirror.

Claire went through Tree's front hallway with the same trepidation she always felt in there. Only this time she was all alone. Well— she looked at loyal Floozie at her feet—not *all* alone. She'd just get what she needed and be out before she went and got spooked. She was always much more of a coward at night and soon it would be dark. One of the cats from down the block was outside in the yard yowling unpleasantly. Was that Lü? Miss von Lillienfeld's cat? She peeked out the window at the scattered yard. What was he doing over here? Oh. The moon.

She scanned the room quickly. Andrew shouldn't leave his valuables out like that, on his desk. His passport, his money, and checks and things. Although, she realized, the only snoop here was she.

In Dharma's room, she found the rest of the things she needed quickly. She was a little taken aback at the disarray. Probably Andrew had been in there looking for another school uniform to give her. She went back inside to inspect the hats along the wall. Those hats were valuable, she realized. They ought to be wrapped up and put into boxes for Dharma one day when she could appreciate them. Tonight, she would discuss it with Andrew, after the play. Or before. Andrew, elusive as silk when there was anything time-consuming to be dealt with, had to be tackled and tied down in front of Johnny. He didn't brush Johnny off lightly, she noticed. He was even, if she wasn't mistaken, a little bit afraid of him. No one would mind, surely, if she just borrowed the one hatpin for her mom. She slid the most beautiful one, a cluster of dangling pink foxglove petals, from a crispy red straw bonnet. "My God," she said to Floozie. It was a good ten inches long. "I don't think we need anything that, um, phallic." She stuck it back in and went for another, a glass-blown daisy poking modestly out of a white linen cloche.

Gorgeous stuff, she thought, wrapping the shorter, more suitable pin in a hanky and putting it carefully into her pocket. There was one really stunning, glass-blown one, she noticed, depicting the borage flower. It was stuck into a brown sunbonnet. There must be a set. Yes, it was borage, all right. You couldn't mistake that flower, the color too blue, the five-petal star unique. That was the flower of happiness, she remembered, having photographed all Swamiji's herbs and labelled them to boot. *Borago officinalis:* The Latin name clicked into her consciousness. She cheerfully congratulated herself for a memory, which, though reduced in efficiency from years of abuse, still, apparently, occasionally functioned. The hell, she said, and she switched the pins. Her mother deserved all the happiness she could get.

She looked thoughtfully around the hallway of hats and drifted, no longer intimidated by the emptiness of the house, into Tree's kitchen. Here, then, was where the two of them would have sat chatting over steaming cups of coffee, or tea, from the look of Tree's exotic row of cannisters. There were brightly colored Chinese tins: rectangles, exquisite oblongs, and unusual hexagons. All of them were from the notorious Kennedy Town in Hong Kong. They were just too delightfully beautiful, she marveled, sitting down to look more closely, and open, and sniff. The Great Wall of China was pictured wrapped in pale greens and blues around a six-sided Woo Long tea tin. There was a clove spice tea in a black cannister oblong dotted with gold, pinks, reds, and greens. She pulled off the lid, all red and yellow circles, and swooned. Such a sweet, far-off fragrance! It transported her to the high hills of clean, melting snow.

244

Floozie, set to get going since a while, nipped at her feet. Claire ignored her. There was nothing in fact she enjoyed more than this sort of reverie. But the prettiest picture, on the jasmine tea tin, and certainly the gaudiest, was a six-sided scene on green grass and blue sky of a throng of twenty-four brightly clothed children carrying a phoenix lantern and playing cymbals and drums and bright golden horns.

Claire slid out of her coat. The lid, as she held it, popped off, and as she wedged it back on carefully she noticed, stuck behind the others, Tree's mother's paisley tin from years ago.

"The treasure tin!" she cried out loud. She almost could not believe her eyes. Then she realized. But of course, where else would you keep your tin but with the others? You see, she congratulated her adult self, you lose your fear, you'll be rewarded! The jasmine tea lid popped off again and fell, clattering, to the floor. She almost jumped through the roof. Floozie sprang onto her lap, soothing them both. Claire jimmied open the lid of the old paisley tin with a dime from her pocket.

It was like looking into a fairy box. She didn't know what she had expected, but it wasn't what she saw, for there, in front of her, were enough emeralds and opals and rubies and heaven-knew-what other glittering gems to finance a first-class overland expedition for eleven to North Dharam Sala and back to Graubunden.

She hadn't a clue what to think. She didn't know—should she take this home and hand it over to Johnny? But then, why? Who, in this business, was he? She could just hear the disgust in his voice when she tried to talk to him about it. Oh, she should have taken that other stone she'd found straight to Iris when things had calmed down. She shouldn't have hid it in her underwear drawer. She would bring it tonight and show Iris. Should she take all this and hide it for Dharma? Because certainly Andrew had no idea of the worth in this tin on his high kitchen shelf.

Or did he? Was that why he suddenly seemed to have money? No more cares in the world? A cold chill went through her. Suppose he came home as she was leaving the house with this hoard? He'd have her arrested. Or, worse, he'd accuse her and then let it go, making it look like he'd dropped charges out of the goodness of his heart. In Richmond Hill, there weren't many who would give her the benefit of the doubt. The half of them looked at her as though she were loony as it was, what with the Buddha in the backyard and the swami in the hammock in the upstairs window and she herself, lurching deliberately about with her long-lens Olympus and her ugly, runt-legged dog.

She put the lid back on. "Come on, Floozie," she said, suddenly not feeling so well. She'd better get back, before they all started accusing her of making them miss the first act and plotting to bamboozle Carmela's play. They would say she was jealous of Carmela. They might be, she conceded at this point, quite right.

The whole house was lit up as they crossed the street. Stefan was sitting out on the front steps. He was wearing a tux and he'd taken the doormat to sit on. "You'd better hurry," he glowered, accusingly. "They're all waiting for you. Where, in the name of God, have you been?"

"Stefan!" she gasped. "In Tree's house. In Dharma's house, you won't believe what I found!"

Michaelaen flung open the door. "Here she is!" he cried out. Anthony flew from inside. "Mommy!" he shouted, and threw himself into her arms.

"Don't you know what's happened?" Stefan yelled at her.

"Claire!" Mary came out the door.

"What's wrong?"

Freddy came out, too. He didn't look happy. "You won't believe it," he said, "they've forecast a storm."

"Tonight," Mary sobbed, peering furiously up to the sky.

"Don't you see?" Freddy took hold of her elbows. "Now, none of the good ones will come."

"Good ones?"

"Critics! Newspaper people! You think it's easy to get them out here?"

Claire shook her head at the sky. "That can't be." But it could.

"Come inside," Mary said. They were standing out there on the porch in a huddle. Mary shepherded them in. Stan stood there holding Mary's coat. He was dressed in his well-brushed, if shiny, nice navy-blue suit and the cranberry tie Carmela had given him last Christmas. He looked tired, Stan did, but still handsome. He held Dharma's hand. She'd been ready to go since this morning, their Dharma, only now she was complete with her muff.

"You'd better get dressed," Mary told Claire.

"Oh, I can go as I am," she said.

They all looked, she was almost amused to note, aghast. "All right, all right. Maybe I'll just run up and jump into the tub. I can be ready in ten minutes. Where's Zinnie?" she asked.

"She's already there, Aunt Claire. We didn't know where you was!"

"Where you were," Mary corrected automatically. "Claire," she called as Claire went flying up the stairs, "put on that nice beige sheath. We'll wait for you."

"Beige sheath?" she wrapped her hair in a towel and jumped into the tub. Was her mother finally losing her marbles? She hadn't had a beige sheath since high school. Quickly she slathered her body top to toe in Mysore government sandalwood soap and rinsed off with the handy hose she'd insisted Johnny put in for shampooing the kids. You see, she told him silently, now, doesn't that save time? She was getting a little bit giddy with excitement for her sisters. And wait till she told them about the treasure!

There was not, as she'd hoped, some magically installed appropriate outfit hanging in the closet. There was some sort of commotion going on downstairs. Her mother would take care of it. Johnny was dressed and gone, she saw. How could she miss it, his old clothes strewn dramatically across the room. Those socks, she sighed, would never get clean.

Let me see. She stood back. Come on, come on. What would look great? All right then, what was clean and pressed? Why on Earth had she waited this long to get dressed? She would simply wear black. There was one lot of clothes Claire would keep for her more bloated intervals throughout the year. Now if she could come up with an opaque pair of tights with no run. But where were they? There you go! She went down on her knees and shimmied through to the back of the closet floor and came up with a still-good pair of sort-of riding boots. They were a little bit scuffed. She dumped open her purse and blackened the toes and heels with her mascara, then rubbed them briskly with a tissue and threw the mascara into the bin. She needed a new mascara, anyhow. She peered into the mirror. There were eyebrows there she hadn't seen since she was a girl, and then for only as short a time as it took her to run for a tweezer and pluck them out. Claire didn't know what sensual female warrior instinct drove her to proclaim herself entitled to her own antennae, despite the perpetual signals of self-loathing from all the major networks, but there it was.

She flew down the stairway, still brushing her hair, and knew by the relieved looks on her family's worried faces that she hadn't made a mistake. She would do for her sisters, her family. She wouldn't embarrass them with her eccentric foreign clothing. This, after all, was their night.

Swamiji stood at the front door, swaddled in cashmere, all set to go. He had bought a corsage for Mary and she wore it, reverently, upon a rubber band atop her gloves. Freddy, very dapper, swept them into the double-parked little parade of cars. Johnny had gone on ahead and had been instructed to stay put at the door. Guard the take. Just in case. You never knew what might happen. This wasn't the old days, Mary's eyes shone feverishly as she told Swamiji, when you could walk the streets without the slightest regard.

Yes, yes, they all agreed and slammed the door as Mary pulled her phosphorescent skirts in and out of the way. Anthony sat on Claire's lap. For one night, just this special occasion, they would drive the few blocks without seat belts. She nuzzled his hair, just like his father's own, with her nose. This, then, was a moment to cherish. Here they were on their way to what would always be looked back upon as a milestone in every one of their lives. They would not all be here together next year, she knew, counting heads in the old car as it went bumping along the great potholes. Swamiji was in the lead car with her parents but in hers, commandeered by Fred, were an astonishingly dressed Iris von Lillienfeld (Iris had really dug out the glad rags for this one) and Mr. Kinkaid, who was pressed in there beside her. He'd done them all the honor of reviving his retired brown suit. Narayan had the other two kids riding with him in Stefan's fancy car.

"Get a load of this," Claire opened her hand underneath Iris's aristocratic, freely running nose. Iris couldn't see what it was at first, and Claire had to be patient while she took aim and focused her eyes. The stinging smell of mothballs and the green-olive tilt of martinis lit up the rear of the car. It would take more than that under Iris's belt to slow her down, though. She didn't miss a beat. "I'll give you five thousand for it," she said, gazing back out the window. "Tonight."

"Yeah? Well, it's not mine to sell, but thanks anyway. I should have shown you this when I found it." She would have gone on but they were already there. Andrew Dover stood behind a poster-festooned card table at the front door. He wore, if Claire wasn't mistaken, a paisley ascot. Johnny stood self-consciously beside him.

"Just as I predicted," Fred complained. "Nowhere to park."

"We should have walked." Iris rapped her ring against the window pane.

Mr. Kinkaid, genuinely concerned for the hammertoes squashed inside his brand-new shoes, resolved to take himself home early. *Victory at Sea* would be on at eleven.

Claire watched Johnny as they drove past. He wore his beloved black silk shirt, black jeans, and a black gangster jacket. He smoothed his lapels and rocked back and forth, always comfortable in his chase-the-perp Reeboks. His Felony Flyers, he called them. She knew he was self-conscious. He chewed his gum quickly, that determined upper-lip never moving. A no-frills kind of guy. You'd never catch him with a beeper, he would be too worried about what his friends would think. But he had one tonight, just in case. She knew just in case what. Just in case the horse took a turn for the worse. Oh, well, at least they fit together, she and him, dressed in black, the uniform of Bay Ridge. When she looked at him like that, she couldn't help remembering Anthony's christening.

Johnny had insisted upon having the party at one of those enormous, gaudy halls where even the restrooms are Capodimonte ornate but the food is the essence of good taste, so she'd agreed. Actually, she hadn't agreed, but she'd been so happy, she'd said yes. It had cost a fortune. That didn't matter, Johnny said, this was his son. At the very beginning, when everyone was finally seated and Claire appropriately throned in a white wicker giant's chair, they'd lowered the lights and Johnny carried the four-month-old Anthony in above his head and across the entire football field of a floor under a spotlight while the band thundered out the theme from *Rocky*.

Claire had thought she would die. But she hadn't died. The funny thing was, there was so much raw pride and joy on Johnny's face that she'd found herself tearing up with the same heartfelt sentiment as the rest of those cops' wives. They all knew that this was what made life worth living. Not the stars all lit up in the last Broadway show, or the paintings, magnificent paintings that hung on a gallery wall. These were the moments. They downed their diluted screwdrivers with gusto. Lord knew, come tomorrow, they'd be back folding laundry at the dryer.

Jupiter Dodd, in a floor-length ranch mink, gingerly stepped from a yellow city cab. It was like, "Yuch. Queens sidewalk." He kept hold of the side of his hem and looked helplessly about.

Freddy leapt from the car.

"Now look vot he's doing!" Iris screeched. That wasn't all. The hubbub of horns from behind them got louder and meaner. Freddy could have cared less. He shook Jupiter's hand pleasantly and invited him to come along with them. Delighted, Jupiter joined them in the back seat.

Finally, they were in the auditorium. The lights dimmed once, sending the last of them, hushed and hurried, to their seats. Carmela peeked out at them, scrutinizing the faces of these, her unworthy judges. She watched through a slit in the heavy purple curtains. Terror was what she felt. All the smugness disappeared. This had been a terrible mistake. If she could call it off, she would. There were so many things she should have rewritten. What was the matter with her?

She watched her parents take their seats in the third row, center. They were too dressed, too working class. What was her mother wearing? Was that a cape? How could these bumpkins be her parents? Then she saw her father take her mother's lopsided hand and kiss it tenderly. Their eyes met for a moment, Stan's and

Mary's, and she saw something there that she had missed, that she hadn't thought to write about and that she knew, right then, was what was failing: very simply, faith.

She prayed frantically, suddenly, for that gallivanting predicted snowstorm that would send them all straightaway home. Once, as a child, unprepared for a math test, this had worked. Of course, she'd failed the make-up test as well, but by then the great terror had passed.

The audience fidgeted excitedly, noisily. They stretched and craned their necks, took off their coats, folded them into their laps, stood up and sat on top of them instead. Some jerk was selling candy before the intermission. What a moron. Where was Claire? She was supposed to be photographing everyone. She should be shooting the group of Manhattanites who'd just clattered disdainfully, rambunctiously in. She lit a cigarette. Where was Freddy? He was supposed to make sure the right people got the good seats. And where was Stefan?

"No smoking back here, Mrs. Stefanovitch," the elderly custodian reminded her.

"Drop dead," she said.

Backstage, in the star-determined cubby set aside for her, Narayan was filling Zinnie up with Prana.

"Prana," he explained, "is the vital force of the body and the universe, which makes everything move."

"Big boy," she wiggled her eyebrows at him, "you can fill me up with anything you like."

"Oh, Zinnie," he said, crooking his head, "you are so very beautiful. If you go out on the stage and sing, the world will take you away from me."

"No, it won't." She went and stood next to him. "It never could. Or did you forget last night already?"

"Forget?" He rushed to take her in his arms.

Whatever had they done to deserve such happiness? They stood and held each other, frightened by good fortune.

Claire was in the men's room, photographing dorks. They lined themselves up against the white tile wall good-naturedly. They were enjoying themselves. They loved this sort of thing. Born cavorters. You had to give them credit, they did look their parts: all jazzed up and rock-and-rolly.

Over the loudspeaker crackled the last of the seventy-eights, the program's preliminary diversion. Billie Holiday warbled "Blue Moon."

Freddy and Jupiter Dodd were in the school kitchen, clandestinely having a solitary coffee klatch. What was astonishing was that they had always seen each other from afar and never gotten the chance to really talk.

"I mean," Fred pulled a linen napkin accommodatingly across Jupiter's gabardined knees. ". . . Of course I always knew who you *were*. I could hardly help that. I mean, who doesn't know who you are? Last time I was on Mykonos—"

"You don't go to Mykonos? Oh, not really. So do I."

"Well, that's what I'm saying. Last time I was there, eating fish with my feet in the water at Spiro's, I heard you'd just left the island. I have to tell you, I was, well, upset that I'd missed you."

Jupiter Dodd grabbed his bottom lip softly with his magnificent row of revitalized top caps.

Freddy watched him from between the blunt white cup at his lips and his heavy, lashy lids.

They were neither of them fools. Or naive. This, they both knew right away, could be it.

The lights went off and on for the last time and there was the commotion of coughing and laughs that are a prelude to any show. An extra flutter of noisy excitement rose as the news spread that it was indeed snowing outside. The late stragglers wore the proof on the shoulders of their topcoats. There were the expected groans and a smattering of enthusiastic hands rubbing together in anticipation of an early ski season, for once. Men and women cleared their throats.

A piano played from offstage and the curtain pitched, then glided open on a woman standing by a window overlooking darkest night above a lake. The lake shimmered with myriad reflections. A sickle moon and stars glittered.

Really, a mirror had been placed low on a black velvet drop cloth with appropriate holes and attached to a spotlight, but the scene looked, for all the world, like a Renaissance princess behold-ing her doubts in an August Lake Como.

She began to sing, very slowly, "Autumn Leaves." A hush of unfolding magic suspended the audience. Then a man, off to the side, began to weep inconsolably.

It had an odd and disconcerting effect, and it seemed to be part of the scene, but it was only Stan.

Zinnie, singing louder and louder, appeared to grow stronger and stronger.

Carmela, sick in the ladies' room, missed the entire opening number and only made it back for the laughs in Scene Two, where by now Portia, as Lola Schneewittchen, the Queen's young fan, had snuck in with the professional backup singers to try out for the remainder of the Central States Tour. One singer was missing, eloped with a yogurt bacteria inspector from Madison, Wisconsin.

Because the dorks were so crude to the young girl, really com-ing on strong and giving her "what she was looking for, after all," the rock star, named Alte Königen, took pity on her. Well, she liked her. She was flattered. The kid knew all her songs by heart. She decided to stick it to her band and make them eat their filthy words. She would champion the girl. She made a bet with Doc, the lead guitar player, best-looking and smart aleck of the group, that she could have this, this Lola Schneewittchen, Pygmalionized in no time at all. She would have her singing as well as any one of the other pros.

That it would backfire against her was clear to everyone but Alte Königen, but the audience loved it, especially loved Alte Königen, who they believed to be doing a great job being furious at the dorks but who, in truth, was no great actress but very angry with her father for his sobs.

Claire, back from her shoot in the men's room, slipped into a spot in the rear. There were no more seats. She smiled with relief more than with laughter. Carmela needed success more than anyone she knew. The wish to light a cigarette materialized, then evaporated, and Claire watched, fascinated, as Oral Gratifier Number One became the conquerer. The conquerette.

Swamiji was up in front beside her parents. Look at this, she told herself, this was wonderful. Only .... only what? For the first time now, she should be able to relax. Mrs. Dixon was dead. Dead, she told herself again. And the kids were safe. Did Dharma know that she was an heiress? Would the jewels go to her or would Andrew get to keep the lot? At any rate, that was a pleasant problem. At least old Dixon was dead.

Yes, a nagging voice agreed, but if it hadn't been Dixon, that day in her home trying to kill her, who had? The fact that no one else believed her was not exactly a consolation, but perhaps they were right, no one had. Yes, that must be it. The radio had fallen of its own accord into the tub. She'd probably knocked it in herself as she'd bolted to get the ringing phone. Yes, that was it.

Claire sat and laughed with the rest of the audience as the dorks sang and danced to "Let Yourself Go." Claire gasped along with the rest as the dorks achieved a splendid, flawless couch catapult on Great Aunt Greta's couch. She remembered very well that the radio had been tucked safely away on the back of the shelf, though. Her own father had secured it there. There was no way out for it but with a good strong yank.

Well, so then, she must have yanked it with her body. No. No, that didn't gel. She couldn't push away the persistent feeling of something else, something palpable in the house that she'd recognized only after it had almost taken her with it. Still, tonight was tonight and the children *were* safe. That was the main thing. She looked for Narayan's tall frame, for they would be sitting with him. No, there were Anthony and Michaelaen up front with her parents. Narayan must have generously given them his seat. And where was Dharma? Claire looked around. She was startled to see her in the last row, beside Andrew Dover in the aisle seat.

"Claire," Johnny whispered urgently in her ear, "I gotta go!"

"Oh, Johnny, no, not now! You can't!"

"It's Red. Red Torneo. He had a heart attack. Claire, I gotta go."

"Oh, honey, I'm sorry! Go. Go ahead. Don't worry. Wait! I'll come."

"No, stay. Bad enough, I have to leave. He's at the vet's hospital down in Brooklyn there, on the Belt Parkway. I'll call you as soon as I know anything. I'll call you at Freddy's, all right?"

"All right." She turned around and he was gone.

She hated that, when he would take off without that special look between them. It was her own fault. She should have been more sensitive to Johnny's old friend. She should have found the time, made the time to have him over, fuss over him a little bit. God. She'd never forgive herself if he didn't make it. He was all her husband had on his own side, and she'd neglected him. She'd even suspected Johnny of having the beeper because of the horse. He'd known something was up. He'd told her he was worried about Red, and she hadn't listened.

A cold misery crept through her. She felt the green stone in her pocket. She walked hurriedly out to the vestibule to see if she might catch Johnny. He was gone. She pushed the heavy school door open and beheld the swirling and profound silence of night-time snow. Narayan stood on the corner. He looked left and right.

"Narayan!" she called.

"Ho! Claire!" He put his arms up in the air and twirled around in a circle.

She laughed. "What are you doing?"

"I'm going to find Zinnie tea. She wants tea. Hot tea."

"What about the lunch room?"

"They have only coffee. And no lemon."

"There's nothing open, now."

"I daresay there is. This is America."

"Try the bodega," she called and pointed towards Jamaica Avenue. "That way."

"I am gone," he whooped, and ran and slid down past the convent towards the el train.

Claire watched him go with fond reluctance. Something in her wanted to chase after him and rev up a snowball fight.

"Narayan!" she called out.

He turned and jogged in place. "What is it, Maharani Claire?"

He got a snowball right between the eyes.

She got another back. But his heart wasn't in it. He laughed and waved and turned and zigzagged away.

Claire turned back smiling and spotted Andrew, headed home with Dharma by the hand. She called out but they didn't turn; they kept on walking. Andrew carried a small suitcase.

For a moment, Claire didn't know what to think. She felt

255

betrayed. She remembered a story her mother had told her to keep her from getting her hopes up about keeping Dharma. It was about Mrs. Cashin, years ago, who'd taken a newborn from the Foundling Home. Then, when the child was two, they'd taken it back. They took it away. Every time Claire's mother told the story, her eyes would fill up, remembering Mrs. Cashin and her empty house, her empty baby buggy and the pain, conveyed over years and years and mother to mother. Claire stood there watching the two of them walk away into the teeming snow, and she felt so sorry for Mrs. Cashin. She raised her face and opened her mouth to the snow. Then she went back inside. Knowing they wouldn't return, she sat down in Andrew's seat. Portia was singing "Smoke Gets in Your Eyes," rather nasally, she thought. She'd never found it a silly song until she heard *her* sing it. Still. Perhaps that was the point. She couldn't see Andrew leaving just now. It was, for one thing, very rude. She wondered, guiltily, if Dharma had needed her and they hadn't been able to find her.

"You're Claire Breslinsky, aren't you?" the woman beside her leaned over.

"Benedetto, yes. Née Breslinsky. I'm sorry. Do I know you?"

"I'm Dharma's teacher," she whispered.

"Ah. Hello." She pointed to her chair. "She was just here."

"Yes. What a shame she had to leave just now."

"She wasn't sick?"

"Sick? No, I don't think so. Her father told her it was time to go. She seemed excited."

"Sshhhhh!" The man in front of them turned and hissed.

They sat behaved and quiet, the two women. Then the teacher said, "I was so glad when Dharma moved in with you."

"You were?"

"Phh. Suddenly she was coming to school in neat clothes. What a difference. Homework done."

"She didn't used to?"

"Lord, no."

"Sshhh!" someone else hushed them.

Claire and the teacher half-stood simultaneously and headed, crouched, for the back where no one was. They went into the vestibule.

256

"I left my cigarettes inside," the teacher said.

"Don't smoke," Claire said, meaning she herself didn't and so couldn't offer her one, then realized the woman took it as advice. What difference did it make?

The teacher hugged herself for warmth. "I hate to sound like I know what I'm talking about here," she said, "but some kids have an orderly home life and some come from chaos. Dharma was one of those poor, unattended kids who kind of fended for herself. No parental supervision on projects, no one who took an interest in what was going on."

She would have, though, Claire thought. Tree would have, had she lived. After she and I hung out together for a while, I would have influenced her to take more of an interest. It would have rubbed off. No one could tell her that that child was better off without her mother.

"Why, the very day that child's mother died, there was a problem." The teacher's eyes glowed, warming to her gripe. Claire wondered if she'd made a mistake coming out here. "That was the first day Dharma was supposed to go home for lunch. I'd had a letter the day before, giving permission to have her released. But no one had come." She squinched up her face. "It was one of those rare days when our school crossing guard was sick, or she would have noticed something was wrong. I didn't even have lunch duty that day, but I just happened to look out from the teacher's room and saw the kid standing on the corner by the school, floating up and down on her own, not knowing if she was coming or going." She shook her head.

Claire shook hers, too. Then she said, "Miss . . . uh—"

"Wingertner. Mrs. Meta Wingertner. Please call me Meta."

"Meta, that was that day? That day Theresa Dover died?"

"That very day. To tell you the truth, I felt awful. Here's the mother at home dead. No wonder she didn't pick Dharma up! And here I was thinking, you know, what an inconsiderate parent she was. I was burned up at her and she was dead. Tch."

"But didn't Dharma walk home on her own, usually?"

"Well, I guess she did. But this was lunch. I guess her mother told her to wait. And no one ever came. Isn't it sad?"

257

"I have to go back in," Claire said, suddenly cold. Then, "How do you like the play?"

"Isn't it grand? Don't know how we'll get home in all this snow, though." She gave an excited, girlish shrug. "Nice to have met you."

"For me too," Claire said. "Oh. Mrs. uh . . . Meta? Would you remember . . . When you saw Dharma outside school, was it just as all the other children were let out?"

"Well, that was just it. She'd been waiting there for fifteen minutes, easily. I know, because I'd gone to the ladies' for a smoke before I headed up to the teachers' room and that's when I spotted her. Boy. Poor kid."

"Yes."

They went back to their seats.

Alte Königen, the rock star, was beginning to feel jarred by her new backup singer's successful solos. Doc the dork was shaking his head and telling her again and again how right she had been to insist upon keeping her. He strode back and forth, raving, marvelling, admitting how wrong he'd been. This new gal was just what they'd needed: new blood!

Alte Königen laughed, delightedly, and kissed both his rosy cheeks as he marched out the papier-mâché hotel-room door. His midterm break would be over and he would soon be heading back to school himself. Alte Königen stood center stage and the light changed suddenly and she looked, heartbroken, towards the empty doorway and she sang, very softly, "For Your Love."

Claire sat, transfixed. Before the song had come to an end, Claire stood up and was out the door. She looked at her watch. She made it to her house, walking normally, in a minute and a half. She trod the easy snow across the street and banged on Andrew Dover's door.

On Jamaica Avenue, Narayan found the bodega easily enough. He stood, shivering but happy, by the door while the chap packed him up three cups of Tetley tea. He'd found her a ripe avocado as well. A young fellow came in, oh my, he looked ill, poor fellow. And cold. Narayan was just about to ask him had he heard the latest weather report when the boy, for he wasn't more than a boy,

258

pulled out a .380 semiautomatic and told the man beside the cash register, "Put it in the bag. Put the cash in the bag. All of it."

"Don't shoot! Don't shoot!" the frightened little man called out.

"Put the fuckin' money in the bag," the boy insisted. He kept moving towards the door and then back. He knocked the metal tower of potato chips on clips onto the floor.

The man behind the counter put the money in the first bag at hand. The one with Narayan's tea. He put all the money in and then he picked up the change tray and put the money from underneath in as well. It all happened so fast. The boy grabbed the bag, ran into Narayan, ran out the door. A shot rang out. The man behind the counter was on the floor, crouched down. His brother stood in the cereal aisle. He held his Smith and Wesson .38 in front of his heaving chest. "I got him," he said.

"Not him!" the man behind the counter raised his head and wailed. "The white boy!"

Narayan stood, still holding his ripe avocado. He staggered out the door. The old van skidded in a circle and drove away. The snow twirled round and round. It all looked clean. There was no sound now. He fell to his knees. "What?" Narayan whispered and dropped into the splendid white. His shimmering eyes became opaque and saw nothing else. A river of red trickled out of his mouth, burned a hole in the snow, and then stopped.

Claire pounded on the door. Still no one came. "Andrew!" she called. "Open the door! I know what you're up to," she shouted, not caring who heard. Let them come. Let them call the cops. "Andrew!" she pounded harder. Then she remembered. She walked swiftly down the driveway and climbed up on the garbage pail to the bathroom window. She pushed it up but it wouldn't budge. She leaned against the window and thought for a moment, regrouping her strength, then pushed again. This time it came unstuck and went right up. She projected herself in, landing with her arms, thwack, onto the tub. Her elbows ached immediately. She pulled her legs down under herself in the tub and straightened up. "Andrew!" she yelled. She'd find him, by God. "Andrew! Give it up!" She threw on the light.

The house was in darkness; she didn't know which way to go.

She decided, as she always did when given the choice, to go left. As she went, she groped the walls for light switches. Her rage and fear for Dharma kept any fear she might have for herself at bay, but as she went along, finding no one, fear grew inside her like a nightmare. Suppose he was crouched somewhere, hiding, waiting for her? She moved, rigid with tension, toward the front door. In the overhead light, the hats cast eerie shadows down the hall. The house was utterly still. As fast as her legs would carry her, she ran for the door. Instead of its giving way when she got there, it stayed shut, waiting for her to unlatch chains and unbolt locks while she watched, terrified, behind her. When the door opened, her anxiety landed her headlong onto the porch and into the snow. She ran, tripping, across the street. Her key, oh, blessed key, was in the geranium pot right where she'd left it. She got herself in the door. She shut it, heard it lock, and shivered with relief. She snapped the hall light on. Safe. But something was wrong. Where was Floozie? Then she realized, in all the excitement, she'd forgotten to lock shut the doggy door. Floozie was probably skulking around the school, where she'd followed her scent. Omigosh! She remembered her folder of photographs for Jupiter Dodd. She'd left them on her chair, back in the auditorium. Anyway, that didn't matter. The first thing she would do was call the precinct. Wait a minute. She would call from upstairs so she could watch Andrew's house in case he tried to leave. She took the stairs two at a time. Her bedroom felt different with only her inside the house. So cool and big. She cracked the window, tilted the wooden blinds enough to look out, and picked up the phone, kneeling on her overstuffed blue chair. Only what, exactly, would she tell them? That a father was kidnapping his daughter? No, wait. She put the phone back down. She had to think this out. The doorbell rang. She hadn't seen anyone come up the walk. She ran downstairs. "Who is it?" she called.

"Claire? Claire, are you all right?" It was Stefan.

"Thank God." She opened the door.

He hurried in and grabbed hold of her shoulders. "Are you all right?"

"Yes, I'm fine. I'm worried about Dharma. It's Andrew. He's taking her away."

"But what's the matter?"

"Oh, Stefan, I should have known what he was up to when I saw the passport on the front desk. I should have known. I know, it sounds confusing, but you see, Andrew is . . . he's demented." She sat down, exhausted. She got up and raced back up the stairs. "I have to watch his house," she gasped. He followed her up the stairs. She went back to her place by the window and looked out. "I know he's taking her away," she murmured, "because I saw her suitcase open over there before, but I didn't put it together."

Stefan turned and walked around the room.

"He killed her, Stefan. I know he did. I always suspected him but now I'm sure."

"Sure?" He lowered his eyes and gazed at her. "But how? How, Claire? You have no proof."

"I know I don't. But I'm sure." She looked up at him pacing. "What are you doing here?"

He laughed. "I was worried. You left so . . . suddenly."

"Is the play all right?"

"Yes, yes. The play is barrelling along. Which is, actually, why I'm here now. You see, I'm leaving Carmela."

"Excuse me?"

"I am. There's no reason to stay anymore. I've got her on her way."

Claire couldn't help thinking he'd done nothing but hold her back, for all the fancy show of it. If anything, Carmela had been an asset to him.

"She'll do all right," he was saying. "She always has done." He looked at Claire, sitting there prettily on her silly chair. He was doing what he thought was a considerate job of explaining why he could not love her sister, how he had, all this time, loved her instead, and as he went on, he just happened to look in her eyes at the same moment something happened, something clicked, and she remembered something that now fit. Her look passed, in that split second, as her eyeballs moved sideways across the parquet floor, from one of puzzlement to decisiveness to denial to fear.

"Oh, what a shame," he said. "Now, you will tell me exactly what it is you are thinking and I will spare you my romantic tale of how you are the one I love. Okay?"

"I was, oh Stefan, I was thinking what a beautiful cologne you use," for she had just remembered where she'd smelled it so intensely once before. The night she had gone to Iris von Lillienfeld's house and had discovered Mrs. Dixon. Only now she knew it wasn't only the elusive odor of patchouli she'd recognized, but the smell of patchouli mingled with fear. Or death.

"Where have Dharma and Andrew gone, I wonder?" she asked, too casually.

"Why would I know that?" He looked at her blankly.

"Gee. I don't know." She looked to her feet. None of them would be back for hours. All the adults would go to Freddy's, and the children would go with Stan to her mother's house. The only hope she had would be if Johnny were to come back. But he wouldn't. He would stay all night at the hospital. The only thing she could do would be to keep Stefan talking. Now she knew. It wasn't Andrew who had killed Theresa Dover. It was Stefan.

Stefan grinned from ear to ear. "Tell me how you knew," he said, as though they'd been playing some board game and she'd caught him out.

She stared at him, frozen, and she saw his expression change and become completely cold and separate. She prayed with all her heart that Swamiji would not decide to return here with Anthony. The only thing she could not bear was something happening to Anthony.

"Stefan!" she jumped up. "We have to go alert the others. He'll be getting away!"

He stayed where he was and pushed her back with splayed fingers on her chest. "Come-come-come-come-come-come-come-come-come." He shook his head pleasantly. "Let's not patronize each other, shall we?"

"All right." She smiled and held his gaze. She would fight him for her son. She straightened her spine and tried crazily to think of something, any tale that would captivate him, a thousand and one Arabian nights, anything, the truth, even, anything at all that would keep him away from her. "It all began," she said, "with a little girl's dream that would not go away." She kept her voice husky and low, in a singsong. "Dharma is so terrified of the beautiful flowers, the foxglove, that used to grow out in my garden, out her bedroom window in fact, all summer long. But I never knew why. And now I do. I think I do. I just figured it out." She took a step backwards. If she jumped out the window, she might break an arm but she probably wouldn't break her neck. The porch was underneath them. She watched his eyes open with interest.

"Sit down," he smiled. He was too close. She sat back down.

"It was a day in early September," she carried on in the tone she used to tell the children stories. She felt him relax, ease up. "The children had just started school. Theresa Dover had planned to take her daughter somewhere in the afternoon. I was sure it was Andrew, or had to do with Andrew, but I see now, it was you. She was going to bring her to you. Or meet you. Across the street, at her house. You went there. You walked. You went in."

"I always went to see her in my man Piece's clothes," Stefan continued for her in some new voice she had never heard. It was the voice of a little boy. It sent a chill right down her spine. "He has this English working-class cap. Nobody dreamed it was me. Never. They would look right through me and they wouldn't know." He laughed. "This time, Theresa was drunk." His tone was easy, confidential. "She was always drunk or stoned. At first it was funny, you know, she was a blast, always 'on'." He shrugged. "But she started to get so sloppy. Really. I didn't mind. It wasn't she I wanted anyhow. It was the girl. The little girl." He looked at Claire. "Do you know that she is mine? I mean really, actually mine?"

"You mean—"

"She is my daughter, yes."

"That's why you sent her gifts. Stones."

"Oh, she loved stones. I used to leave them for her, signed, 'your true father,' and 'your mystery father.' Tonight she knows for sure that I am he. She always wondered, I know. She yearned for me. Her mother told her, confidentially, her father was some-one special, a sort of prince. So she always waited. She knew, one day, her prince would come." Stefan beamed with the telling. Then his face dropped and his voice changed again. "But then her mother found them. Found the stones. And that I could not have.

Uh. All sorts of complications. She said she wouldn't let me see the little girl." Stefan began to roll up his sleeves. "Up until then, I used to sleep with the mother. On and off. That's a beautiful thing, to sleep with the mother while you're thinking of the daughter. Just after you've played a little bit with the daughter." He nodded his head and rubbed his eyes. "She told me she was pregnant. It was mine, she said. Well. Who knew? The woman would sleep with anyone. Can you imagine? She wanted money for an abortion." Stefan cleared the loose phlegm from his throat. "She wanted to keep the stones and she wanted cash as well!" He sighed. "I'm taking Dharma with me to Zurich. Tonight."

Claire didn't know what she was going to do. Her mind raced frantically. "I thought it must have been Andrew," she said again. "I was sure it was Andrew."

Stefan made a disgusted, belittling sound. "Him," he said. "He would do anything for money. So you know what he is. Do you know how I got him here? I told him if he delivered Dharma here to me, with her passport, I would give him twenty thousand dollars. Ffff. And he did." Stefan looked worriedly out the door. Claire wondered if he had killed Andrew. His face looked so dissipated, so haggard. She wondered how she hadn't known before. His exhaustion was so evident, if she could keep him off guard, throw him off balance and take a chance for the stairs . . . She started to talk again about the day of the murder; she knew it interested him, she'd seen him come alive when he talked about it. It soothed him, threw him off the track. She watched him visibly relax. "So Dharma," she said, "was afraid of her nightmare of the foxglove. Horrified. But why, I kept asking myself, why? *Digitalis purpurea,* the foxglove, kills all right, but it's immediately recognizable in the simple autopsy lab test they do. And so I knew she hadn't died that way. I tried to remember the mythological legends, how the bad fairies gave the blossoms to the fox so he could soften his tread by wearing them on his toes when he prowled the roosts. But I knew it wasn't a legend. I knew something very real had happened. And despite all logic, I kept coming back to the poisonous foxglove, over and over, and knew, just knew from Dharma's horror, that it was all somehow connected. And it is connected, Stefan, isn't it? She saw something, didn't she?" As she talked and as she kept on going, she did see. It all fit together, nicely, deadly.

"You waited until she passed out, didn't you?" Claire said, the venom in her loathing this time there for him to hear. Oh, and he heard her. He took his chin in one hand, his elbow in the other. He watched her, fascinated.

It was strangely like the old days, Claire and Stefan, talking, talking. She would jump out the frigging window. She didn't care anymore. She was even looking forward to it.

"You took one of Tree's hat pins down from the wall and you stuck it, firmly, into her brain. Didn't you?"

He had his tongue out of his mouth a bit and he was biting it. He was all excited.

"Only then, you heard someone. It was Dharma, home from school. She'd managed it that Dharma would come home for lunch that day because she thought she would confront you, she would put it to you that they needed money, right in front of Dharma, whom she knew you loved. Only Tree got drunk. Real drunk. And you helped her along until she finally passed out. It all was so easy. Only Dharma didn't get picked up, as her mother surely said she would. But she was a resilient kid. She'd been stranded before. She came home on her own. And when she didn't get an answer at the door, instead of ringing and ringing, she just came around to the side of the house and climbed in the bathroom window the way she always had done when her mother was passed out, drunk or stoned. And she saw her mother on the floor again, didn't she? Only this time, she was dead. It was the hatpin Tree had of a flower. It was foxglove, wasn't it? Foxglove, blown from glass. The morbid, lovely digitalis."

Stefan sat up. "Yes," his voice squeaked with delight.

Claire unclenched her fists with conscious determination. "I remember your story of the bowman who would boast that he could kill an elephant. You were telling me then, weren't you? I remember wondering, even then, why you were telling that story."

Stefan opened his hands and looked into them. She could hear the quick, excited intake of his breath. She kept on talking. "After Dharma left, you took the hatpin and returned it to the hat. You knew Dharma hadn't seen you. She couldn't have seen you or she would have told someone. She ran back to school. She pretended she had never left. It was easy, in the crowded confusion of lunchtime comings and goings. She knew she was in trouble for accepting the stones. She knew this all had something to do with the stones. For hiding them. She thought it was somehow her fault."

"It was her fault." Stefan stopped laughing. "Oh, it was."

Claire hated him, then. That innocent little girl had been guilty of nothing. She hated him almost as much as she was frightened.

"You got away with it, too, didn't you?" She pretended to admire him with her tone.

He rubbed his forehead wearily. "It was not so easy. She moved. And she opened her eyes and saw me coming. But she misunderstood. She thought I was going to kiss her. She closed up her eyes to be kissed and moved the hair away from behind her ear so I would kiss her where she liked it. Even as I did it, as I rammed it in, I heard the bell. I jumped behind the chifforobe. I thought Theresa would get up. I took a big vase down in my hands to hit her with. Fortunately, she stayed where she was. And when I thought to come out, I heard the window open in the bathroom. I froze. But no one came. Only now you say she had come in, then run away. Funny, that she would see her mother there like that with the beautiful flower growing out of her ear. It is poetic, somehow, don't you think?"

Claire stayed still.

"When I was sure I could," he went on casually, "I came out and bent over her body. She was quite dead. I pulled the hatpin from her ear. It was so minute a hole. Exquisite. I had to look again to be sure. I knew right then, no one would ever notice it. I would be safe. She had such beautiful ears. One little drop of blood," he marveled, "lost in the ear canal." He shivered. "Oh, yes, I knew they'd think she died from a stroke. The brain just stopped functioning, stopped sending messages. The heart just stopped." He laughed. "Not to mention that she was so coked up. She had coke all over her fingertips, under her fingernails, from smearing it onto her gums. She liked to have it on her senses, for sex. And, what was it? Oh, yuh, gin. She loved her gin. She reeked of it. I can't imagine what her liver looked like. Really. She would have died soon anyway, no doubt. What I really did was save little Dharma the agony of watching her mother suffer. Quite true. She was a mess. They would have seen that as soon as they opened her up." He swept his pale aristocratic fingers through his white-blond hair. "Poor Dharma, having to live with such a common slob . . . Dharma." He looked back at Claire, remembering her suddenly. "Is like a delicate jewel herself." He made a soft, angelic face.

"Did you touch her, Stefan?"

"Dharma?" he whirled around. "No!" He trembled, thinking of it. "It's all too much. I must tell you, I am so very tired. I wish we didn't have to fly tonight. What time is it? I can't seem to— Sometimes, I wish it would be over. I just wish—"

"What happened to Mrs. Dixon, Stefan?" Claire tried to prop herself casually on one elbow so when she straightened up, she would be that much farther away from him.

"Oh, that was strange. She wasn't supposed to die, you know. Not at first. It wasn't as though she'd ever hurt anyone. I thought I would just take her away from von Lillienfield's house and . . . All I did was suggest . . . Well, no, that's not true. I tied her hands in a silk kerchief. But she didn't even fight. I just slipped the noose around her neck. She made it so absurdly easy. I told her what to do and she just did it. It was wild. Really. It was almost comical." He stroked his left breast thoughtfully. "Shame, really. She had been so useful. Setting herself up. She used to have access to so many little children." When he said, "little children," his lips pursed into a tight, happy bow. He snorted. "Or she used to. Do you know, she really thought she deserved to die. So what can you do? She kept saying it was all for the best."

In a moment, he would be distracted enough so that she could make it out the window. He stood up and walked behind her. She was frightened he would grab her hands. She leaned on one arm and asked him, "How did you set her up?" She smiled. "You set her up, right?"

"Oh. Her. I'll tell you how. Some years ago, I caught her out. I saw her at a chicken-meat film. You know, kiddies. I couldn't believe it. I knew I could use it against her. I knew it even then.

It was so easy. I only had to watch her. Follow her lead. It was so easy when I pursued you. Always being right next door. I knew she would take the children's pictures. I used to watch her watching them. Then, when you fell in love with your detective," his expression changed, "I was very angry at you, Claire."

She remembered the searing landing of the radio behind her in the bathtub. Yes, she knew now that he had been angry. "But," his voice went back to its nonchalant meander, "I only had to choose another sister."

He put the tips of his fingers in his mouth and touched them with his tongue. "It had to be Carmela, though. Zinnie—" He rubbed his fingertips back and forth across his fleshy bottom lip. "—never wanted me. Zinnie knew something was wrong."

"She didn't," Claire shook her head.

"Oh, she did. She told me once to stay away from Michaelaen. Did you know that?"

"No."

Stefan wrinkled up his nose. "I don't know why. It wasn't as though I'd come on to him."

"But Mrs. Dixon—"

"Then she started this bloody book with Mary," he interrupted. He looked at Claire with endearing eyes. "I mean, I couldn't have that." He yawned.

"But how did you find her?" Claire wondered out loud. "When even the police couldn't?"

"Find her?" he laughed. "What do you think—she just walked off the grounds and grabbed a bus? Uh!" He tut-tutted her naïveté. "That was all arranged. I was waiting with a car." He banged his chest. "Me! I drove her back and put her in her own house before they knew she was missing!" His voice changed again. "She was very good, staying put in the attic. But then she got frightened. She went to see her friend. I had to kill her. It was all becoming," he shrugged, "so tiresome."

There was a noise from down the block. Claire's heart stopped and listened. Could it be them, coming home first? She strained to hear. Stefan threw his head back. She watched his upraised chin. She watched his eyes watch, sideways, listening, too, and then come back to her. They locked eyes. She felt herself shrink. She was the hunted bird, locked safe inside his paws. "You hear?" The corners of his mouth turned up. "They've gone."

She bolted. She was going to throw herself through the window but he threw himself in front of her, they fell to the floor, and he covered her completely with his body. He drew her hair back into a bundle with his delicate hands. "If it could only always be like this." He quivered, catching her face in his hands.

Her arms were pinned behind her. He lifted her onto the bed. His breath was sour on her face. A smart pain ripped her left side. She was dazed for a moment by the stinging of it, the tangible feeling in the midst of her fear and then she realized what it was. It was the hatpin she'd wrapped in her hanky and taken for her mother. She had forgotten. It was on the floor. If only she could get her hands on it. . . .

Stefan's hands ran down her shoulders. He cupped her breasts and reached behind her, grabbing hold of her wrists. He was excited, breathing heavily. What was he going to do? What did he want? Oh, please, she prayed, let him try to rape me before he kills me, just give me time to stab him, please.

A noise at the front door shocked them both momentarily. They were like lovers, caught at love. Claire started to scream but Stefan was faster. He covered her mouth with his hands and shoved the end of a knitted blanket into it. He bound her wrists with the measuring tape from her sewing box. She flung herself, a netted mackerel, around the bed. She would fall off and some-one would hear her. Stefan fell on top of her and pinned her down. Her tongue was pressed down with the fuzzy pressure of the blanket. It was terrible. Terrible. Surely they would hear her moans. Then she saw what Stefan had in his hand. He was going to hit her with the iron fruitman's hammer she kept by the bed to be safe from prowlers. She froze. He tied her knees with some-thing. She did not want to die like this. Stefan smiled without teeth; a patronizing, malevolent smile. Tears of despair welled up and out of her and streamed down her face. She did not want to die.

* * *

At the front door down the stairs, Freddy turned and faced Jupiter Dodd. "If I let you in for a cup of coffee," he said flirtatiously, "it really only means a cup of coffee."

"Heh, heh, heh," said Jupiter.

Upstairs, Stefan removed Claire's boots and bound her feet carefully, lovingly, with the venetian blind cord. His hands were mottled black from the mascara she'd rubbed on the boots. He pulled the cord tight and knotted it good.

"Porco!" Freddy said. "She took the key out! I swear, it's always here."

"Come on," Jupiter said, "I'm freezing. Let's just go to the restaurant."

"It must be here someplace," Fred insisted, grappling through the snow. "What I didn't understand," he muttered, "was why Lola Schneewittchen refused to marry Doc? I mean after she knew he was going back to medical school."

"Yes. One can't help thinking staying on in Wisconsin with the bashful one was a dumb move."

"To open a nail salon," Freddy shuddered.

"My shoes are ruined," Jupiter remarked.

Sirens wailed again on Jamaica Avenue. "Something must be going on," Fred said.

Claire and Stefan lay together upstairs on the bed. They strained their ears, marking off the two men's progress. They listened as the two of them trod off, happy, involved. They heard two car doors slam. The car drove away up the block.

Stefan rolled her over. His eyes met hers again. She thought, I won't even know now if I'm pregnant. I'll never even know. The tears ran from her eyes and she could hear herself, far far away, whimpering. I wanted to tell Anthony he would have a new brother or sister, she thought. I wanted to hold him once more and just smell his sweet skin.

Stefan devoured her face with his eyes. He hugged her to him with an intimate, cherishing embrace. They understood each other now. She had often wondered how those poor children had felt before he killed them. Now she knew.

Stefan was dreaming: something long ago, it was back in Poland. They were on holiday. They were running in a field of tall

270

grain. She wanted something. His mother caught him and they laughed, rolling, over and over and over. . . .

"Claire?" a small voice came from the doorway. They looked together at Dharma standing there in silhouette. "Claire?" she said again.

"No!" Stefan sat up and swiped his hair back guiltily. "No, Dharma, go back downstairs. Go wait for me where I told you."

"My father," Dharma said, "I mean Andrew . . ." She stopped, confused.

"What about Andrew?" Stefan said, alert, sitting straight up in the half light, the room as though moonlit from all the snow.

"He's groaning. I think he's hurt. I think we have to call Doctor Finneran."

"Be a good girl, now, Dharma," Stefan said with no edge to his voice. "Go stay with him while I help Claire. And then I'll come and help Andrew."

Dharma wasn't sure what to do. This was her father. Her real father. But Claire—what was going on? Maybe they were having sex. That was it. She turned and went back down the stairs. Claire saw, as Dharma passed under the hall light, that the child was wearing lipstick. With all the terrible force of her life, with no arms to project herself and no voice with which to scream, Claire shoved Stefan off of her. She saw him in passing as if in slow motion, rocking on one leg, as the other leg whipped into the air ungracefully, off balance, while she ploughed into the window. The window broke, but Claire remained on the one side of it, hampered by the sill and the odd, bent broken pieces of the blinds. A siren screamed nearby, came nearer still, then passed them, going somewhere else. Surprised—they both had thought it was for them—they turned and faced each other. Only Dharma stood once more now at the door, summoned by the bright commotion. The hat pin glittered, broken in the other glass, the flower, coddled in the dusky splinters, this blue ember in its ashes. "My mother," Dharma said. She took one look at Claire. She picked up the hat pin. Stefan held out his hand. He knew that she would give it to him. Dharma stuck it, without hesitation, through his open palm.

Stunned, thrust forward by the pain, he staggered past them.

Then, ridiculously, like some lofty, mythological white horse, he rose up solemnly and passed, affronted, from their sight.

Dharma ran to Claire. She tried to free her hands but her own now trembled so, she couldn't. She pulled the blanket tenderly from Claire's mouth and they heard him going down the stairs and outside into the cold. They heard him running, fast and coatless, up Richmond Hill towards his darker sacrilegious grounds, the woods. His shortcut home.

Mr. Kinkaid, out on the sidewalk, the only one of them not to go with Narayan's dead body to the hospital, watched Stefan Stefanovitch run up into the woods. His body looked all red against the whiteness, and there were dogs, a lot of dogs he had, running nipping at him in the quiet snow.

EPILOGUE

On the second Sunday of Advent, with the fireplace at long last opened and a fire lit, Claire prepared macaroni puttanesca while Red Torneo sat, propped up with dandy pillows, and ate unsalted popcorn in Claire's noisy rocker.

"What I don't understand," he said, smacking the dog (Red hated all dogs), "is where was that guy Andrew while all of this was going on?"

Claire stood still for a moment, remembering. It seemed such a long time ago. "Andrew"—she licked her fingers to test the ratio of capers to garlic to Gaeta olives—"was knocked out on the kitchen floor. Stefan met him here because he figured Dharma had her jewelry here. He'd searched Andrew's house and hadn't found it. Then Stefan had given Andrew a mickey. Right there, as a matter of fact." She pointed to the spot on the floor where Floozie had taken refuge. Far enough away from Red Torneo's range. Remembering, the dog got up and moved herself over again. The little chicken. That whole night of chaos she'd hidden from everything in Michaelaen's big closet. Stefan had kicked her first, and good. So she'd hid. No Lassie she, they all acknowledged.

No, thought the dog, but still here to think about it.

"Where the hell is Johnny?" Red growled.

"Don't get so excited. He'll be back before the pasta's in the pot. He always is."

Red nodded approval. Johnny wasn't hanging at the track anymore, at least. He was selling his share of the horse on Tuesday. At least Wiggins could breed her. Get something out of her. Effing horse almost lost them the house. Johnny was always gettin' mixed up in these schemes. Too much energy. Red looked around the great big kitchen. Woulda been a shame if they'd lost this place. "You know, your husband, he ain't too bright."

"Oh, yes?"

"I mean, he goes out and leaves a broad like you all alone with a handsome lookin' fella like me."

"Shut up, Red."

"Mommy?"

"Wash your hands. Dinner in fifteen."

On that night, when everything had happened, Red Torneo's heart had stopped in a craps game down in Brooklyn. The guy next to him had stopped playing, taken a good long look at Red, leaned right over, and threw the dice back in for a seven.

Well, the ambulance had come. The paramedics had jolted him back to life, but when Johnny had heard that one from the other men, it gave him something to think about.

So now, Claire figured, not only were they an AA and Al Anon family, but a Gambler's Anonymous one as well.

"I'm not dependent on nuthin' but my family, now," Johnny would boast, his eye on the clock.

Red shuffled the cards he always carried in his pocket. "So, what happened to all them jewels? In that tin box?"

Claire emerged from the pantry carrying a nice head of Boston lettuce. "They're being sold. Iris is handling it. The money will go to a fund for sexually abused children. It was Dharma's idea and Andrew and Carmela agreed." She looked up and smiled. "Though I believe Andrew agreed under protest."

Red shook his head sadly. "I can't get over how Stefanovitch jumped off that bridge there up in the woods. I mean, hey, what a way to go. I don't care what you did, being driven off a bridge by a snarlin' pack of bloodthirsty dogs—" He held his cheek.

"Yes," Claire said.

"And then bleedin' to death. Christ."

"Yes."

"Sad about the other fella, though. That there Pakistani fella."

Claire clattered the dirtied bowls into the sink and filled it with warm suds. She still couldn't talk about that, about Narayan.

There would be another letter in a day or two from Swamiji.

He hadn't gone to Berkeley after all. He hadn't had the heart without dear Narayan. Perhaps next year. It had been difficult for him, the trip to Benares with the body. Standing with Narayan's distraught family at the Ganges. He wasn't going to say it hadn't been difficult. And yes, beautiful. There had been a splendid grace as well. Having Zinnie along with him had—well, he didn't know how he would have gotten through it without Zenobia. He wanted Claire to know that he was doing all right, though. Coming along. He didn't want her overwrought and worried about him now. Now that she had other things on her mind.

"Anthony!" she shouted, "call your Aunt Zinnie and Michaelaen and see if they've left their apartment yet. If they're still home, tell them I've already put the macaroni in."

"Awright, Ma," he said.

Claire put an English muffin on a small plate, spread cream cheese across it, and put some of that nice plum preserve with the slivovitz on, too. She pulled the teabag out of the good teacup, the Aynsley Pembroke, she'd like that, and wound it and squashed it around a spoon.

Dharma came in and headed straight for the refrigerator. "Wait a minute," Claire said to her. "Take this up to Carmela and tell her if she doesn't eat it, she's got to go live with Mommy and Daddy and the dogs. Oh. Take a napkin."

Dharma made a face at Anthony and minced, in charge and show-offy, out of the room with the tray.

Johnny's car honked and came sweeping up the driveway.

"He's here!" Anthony whooped, not bothering to turn off the tap, and he flew out the back door.

"You let him get away with that?" Red crooked his thumb at the door and glowered at the water left running.

"Ma! Daddy got a big load of wood in the trunk!"

Claire clicked her tongue. She'd wanted to go with him to get it. She shook her head, resigned. Johnny always did things as he pleased. Red made as if to get up. "Don't you move," she boxed him in. "That's all I need. Another heart attack."

Johnny appeared at the doorway. His eyes were steeped with anxiety at the solemnity of his very own wood for the fire.

She laughed. "Wait, I'll help."

"Oh, no, you won't." He looked her up and down. "Kinkaid's out here." He lined his forehead at her. "We got enough for supper?"

Red rolled his tongue around his cheek. He couldn't stand Kinkaid. As soon as the two of them got together, though, they rigged up a game of gin rummy.

Mary and Stan barged, red-faced, through the double Dutch doors. Mary wore her inevitable small tower of white bakery boxes. Johnny, Kinkaid, and Stan each carted their great manly piles of wood.

"Looks like birch," Mary admired. "Nothing burns prettier than birch."

"Burns too quick," Kinkaid said.

Johnny tore apart a loaf of semolina bread from the counter and stuffed a bite into his mouth.

"Wash your hands," Claire said.

"Wash your hands. Wash your hands," Anthony mimicked. "Wash your hands."

Johnny smacked him on the head. "Don't make fun of your mother!"

"Don't hit him!" she yelled.

"What can I do?" Mary rolled up her sleeves.

"You can put those spoons around the table, would you, Mom?"

"Hang on! Make that louder!" Stan rushed to the radio. "That's Tchaikovsky!"

Johnny sat down and started right in scarfing big black salty olives.

"Save some for the rest, will you?" Claire scolded, passing him the hot cherry peppers anyhow.

"Wait till you hear this," he told them all. "Soon, we won't be having any more of these petty, contemptible money worries."

Petty? Claire's antenna went right up. Contemptible? Pretty hoity-toity terms for Johnny. Right away she knew something was up. "What's up?" She stood at his elbow with a dish of sliced tomatoes.

"Now, don't go sayin' nuthin' until I'm through, all right?" He

276

stopped, his eyes going from face to face, waiting for their undivided attention. "I got this honey of a deal. You all know that old pipe-cleaner factory? They made it into condos and none of them sold? Well, say hello to the new owner. Of the whole thing! Well, I mean, not yet. But soon. Real soon."

"What?"

"Yeah," he grinned. "Well. Me and Andrew. See, we got it all figured out—"

"Anthony! Shut that television off and come to the table."

Carmela, the poet from her tower, deigned to come down and have a look in on what was going on. Claire pushed her into a seat before she could think about how it would look. She had to be hungry, up there rewriting her play since days and days, insisting still that art be more important than people. Claire had thought she would give up writing altogether, what with the offhand, sidestepping reviews of her play as the mere backdrop to real tragedy it had been. And then no one had understood why the lead singer had taken off, not to return, more than halfway through the performance. By the time the whole story came out it was anyway the next day and, in New York, who cared anymore?

Carmela, however, was made of sterner stuff. She plodded on. She wept, very late, when she thought no one could hear her. Claire knew she did because she would hear her as she made her own insomniac rounds around the quiet house, headed always towards the broad front window and the tree, that elderly peach tree that stood there still under the broken street lamp, grizzled and too old, waiting with life all the same in the dark. She would catch her breath. Claire laid a calming hand across her softening middle. Winter would pass and spring would come. There would be peaches on her peach tree. On her and Johnny's peach tree.

Dharma sat down carefully now beside Carmela and took her hand in her own small one and held it. Carmela sniffed but Claire noticed that she didn't pull away.

One good thing: Claire wouldn't have to deal with Portia McTavish for a while. She'd up and decided "an actor's life for me," enrolled herself at the American Academy of Dramatic Arts, and moved in with her older sister Juliet, who had a two-bedroom apartment in Greenwich Village.

"Zinnie and Michaelaen are late," Claire complained.

"As usual," said Mary.

Claire wanted to get them all out of here and the dishes done early, so she could take a ride down to that old synagogue by the beach. There would never be enough light, now. The days were so short. Never mind. She would drive down tomorrow. Grillo, the sculptor, had turned it into some sort of gallery and she wanted to go have a look. Maybe she would shoot it for her book.

A car door slammed. "Must be them." Anthony ran to the door. Suddenly Floozie got up and charged the door, yapping and snarling.

"Must be Fred," Stan said.

"Yup," said Johnny.

"Mr. Dodd is with him, Mom," Anthony warned. He knew better than to ruin the surprise and let on they'd brought Mr. Dodd's old upright piano. And in an orange trolley.

"What else is new?" Mary made nonchalant eyes at Red Torneo and nudged her Stan with a hearty elbow.

Chairs scraped into place, Anthony ran down the stairs to go, quick, to get the ginger ale, and Tchaikovsky stopped the minute they all sat down and the Seaman's Furniture ad began.

Up the block and over the woods, a lone red cardinal flew.